BEYOND THE SENTINEL STARS

Sherry D. Ramsey

The Nearspace Trilogy:

One's Aspect to the Sun
Dark Beneath the Moon
Beyond the Sentinel Stars

BEYOND THE SENTINEL STARS

Sherry D. Ramsey

TYCHE BOOKS LTD.

Published by Tyche Books Ltd.
Calgary, Alberta, Canada
www.TycheBooks.com

Cover Art by Ashley Walters
Cover Layout by Lucia Starkey
Interior Layout by Ryah Deines
Editorial by M. L. D. Curelas

First Tyche Books Ltd Edition 2017
Print ISBN: 978-1-928025-78-8
Ebook ISBN: 978-1-928025-79-5

Author photograph: John Ratchford

This book was funded in part by a grant from the Alberta Media Fund.

For Julie and Nancy: friends, partners, story doctors, and red-pen-wielders extraordinaire.

"OUR bugles sang truce, for the night-cloud had lower'd, and the sentinel stars set their watch in the sky . . ."
-The Soldier's Dream *by Thomas Campbell (1774–1844)*

"The Chron incursion heralded the bloodiest, scariest, most bewildering chapter in the history of humankind. They attacked without preamble, without parley, without provocation. They were not interested in taking prisoners, negotiating terms, seizing assets or ransoming us to their will. They were simply here to kill us.

And a century and a half later, we're still left to wonder why."
- Dr. Simon Parsengill,
Legacy of the Chron War: Humankind's Greatest Unsolved Mystery
March, 2278

Chapter 1 — Lanar
Dangerous Times

THE CAFF WAS bitter, the company grim, and the cinnamon *pano* not even half as good as Commander Yuskeya Blue's. In the Nearspace Protectorate's administrative boardroom on FarView Station, the stale scents of long-past meetings, recycled air, and lingering recriminations commingled unpleasantly. The chairs in the boardroom grew increasingly uncomfortable, in direct proportion to the number of times the same discussion points had circled the table. And considering the topic under discussion, the Protectorate motto, *In Astra Pax,* seemed out of place on its engraved plaque at the far end of the room. *Peace Among the Stars*, indeed. We couldn't even get peace in this room. I rubbed my knuckles over the worn fabric on my chair's arm rest, gauging whether the time was right to speak yet.

"I still say we take the fight to them." Admiral Antar Mauronet drummed his blunt fingers on the polished surface of the table. The short-bitten nails betrayed an anxiety he took pains not to display to his fellow officers. "The Chron are bogeymen left over from a century and a half ago. We can't allow those old fears—"

"Completely irresponsible," Fleet Admiral Chanda Botek interrupted with a thoroughly insulting snort. I hid a half smile behind my hand. One of the highest-ranking Vilisians in the

Protectorate, Botek had a reputation—well-earned, in my experience—for speaking her mind. Her long black braid swung behind her chair as she shook her head in disapproval, prismatic rank insignia glinting at the throat of her dark blue uniform. "We know little to nothing about the Chron's activities during that time. The reports we have indicate that they're every bit as dangerous now as they were the last time we had the misfortune to encounter them."

"Reports that are completely unverified," Mauronet snapped.

Silence descended, prefaced by a sudden intake of breath by all present. Not quite a gasp, but something closely related. Everyone managed not to look directly at me.

Mauronet visibly checked himself. I caught the hint of a flush creeping up his neck as he turned to me. "With all due respect to your sister, Admiral Mahane," he said gruffly. "I'm not suggesting she's unreliable."

"No, no, only her *reports*," I said with a nod. He bristled, but I ignored him and continued, "And those have been fully corroborated by our own Commander Blue. Who is, as I'm sure you'll agree, *quite* reliable. To say nothing of Lieutenant Gerazan Soto, another Protectorate officer with a stellar record and a recent encounter with the Chron. Who, you might recall, demonstrated their threat level rather obviously by destroying the ship to which he was assigned. The *Protectorate* ship."

I didn't particularly like Admiral Mauronet. I'd watched with some surprise as he rose from a brash cadet through the Protectorate ranks to Admiral. His often-unguarded temper and a certain deficiency of tact would have hampered his promotions had I been the one signing the papers. But I'd declined that level of responsibility several times over, and I had to live with the decisions I'd opted to let someone else make.

I did take a certain amount of pleasure in knowing that although Mauronet considered me a brash youngster myself, I had a good twenty years on him. Since I'd joined the Protectorate at the ripe old age of forty-five, though, I'd been a member of its ranks for only a few years longer than he had.

At any rate, it made me quietly happy to see the flush continue its slow crawl up his neck and face, finally reddening even the patch of pale skin poking through a fringe of salt-and-pepper hair on top of his head.

"Of course," he agreed, since he wasn't foolish enough to cast aspersions on the credibility of other Protectorate officers. Not in this company. "I'm just saying that their situation—caught off guard in an uncharted system, stranded, encountering a new species of aliens—well, the threat might have appeared worse than it was."

"I hardly think you can blame rattled nerves in this situation, Mauronet. As Admiral Mahane points out, they blew up the *Domtaw*." That was Mare Ker, the Vice-Admiral in charge of the Lambda Saggitae system and the Protectorate Admin-governed world there, Anar. Ker and I had once taken down a data-running ring operating between Anar and its sister planet Damir, and I knew she respected those who served under her command. Mauronet's arrogance obviously rankled the diminutive Vilisian, and she glared at him as she spoke.

Around the table, others shifted uncomfortably in their seats. I suspected more than the well-worn chairs were bothering them. Only Mauronet had declared himself willing to rush headlong into full conflict with the Chron, although I felt confident we all knew it was coming.

"We simply need more data," Harle Southwind said from the seat next to mine. "We need to understand the extent of the threat. And we'll have to accept whatever help the Corvids—if that's what we're still calling them—are willing to offer."

Southwind's Lobor features held the quiet imperturbability so characteristic of the wolf-like aliens, and he spoke with calm and practicality. That nature made him perfectly suited to his position in the Protectorate Authority's top investigative division. Only his left ear, flicking back and forth, betrayed his agitation. With our chairs clustered close in the cramped boardroom, I could almost feel the fervid heat radiating from his body.

"The Council wants to send a full diplomatic mission to the Corvids," Chanda Botek said. She sighed and pulled her braid forward, running long amber fingers down the intricate weave. Even Fleet Admirals could have a tell for emotions, and coupled with the faint metallic scent in the air, I knew she was battling frustration. "But they're currently in a full-blown tizzy over how best to get there and what gifts to bring, if you can believe it." She let the braid fall away again.

"How to get there? Won't they take one of the diplomatic launches with a Protectorate escort?" asked Harle Southwind.

Botek shook her head with a sharp jerk. "They want to keep it low-profile and quiet since most of this is still not general knowledge. They think it will be too obvious if they go with a Protectorate escort, and indicate to the Corvids that we don't think they're capable of protecting our people. But it's too dangerous to send them without one—we know the Chron have made incursions into that system very recently. So, we're at a standstill." She rubbed a hand over her face. "It's still a polite argument, but we're not getting anywhere."

"And meanwhile, we lack the information the Corvids could give us about the Chron, and leave ourselves open to attack. It's ridiculous," Mauronet snapped. He sat back in his chair sharply and the servos whirred in protest. "We don't have time for this."

"I thought the Corvids sent us all their data?" Mare Ker asked. She turned to me. "Your sister delivered it, didn't she?"

I spread my hands. "Unfortunately, not all the data was intact, so there are considerable gaps. We don't know how much is missing in the corrupted files."

Mauronet looked ready for another outburst, but I cut him off. "We didn't get the original datachip—only a copy. So, it's in everyone's best interest to get the diplomats to the Corvids as soon as possible." This seemed like the right time to float my unorthodox idea. I leaned back in my own chair and pursed my lips.

"I could ask the *Tane Ikai* to go back."

Mauronet shot me a look of pure dislike. "Your sister's a merchant trader, who apparently couldn't even take care of a simple data chip when the Corvids entrusted it to her. What good will it do to send her? As if the Council would ever approve it anyway."

I clenched my hands in my lap to quell a sudden urge to punch Mauronet. "I think if you read the full report filed by my sister and *the Protectorate officers who were with her*, you'll understand how the data ended up corrupted. But you've all read the documents the Corvids sent. They specifically invited Luta and the crew of her ship back into Corvid space anytime they wish to travel there. There's already a connection, the aliens trust her and her crew, and the ship is armed as well or better than one of our Pixiu-class escorts."

"The Council would never agree," Mauronet reiterated.

"Why not? There's no contact protocol or diplomatic dance that overrides that direct invitation. The envoys will have protection, but nothing ostentatious or outwardly aggressive," I said. "It's the perfect solution. Commander Blue's still on special assignment on the *Tane Ikai* anyway, and we could place a couple of other officers on board as well, so we'll have a presence."

I stopped talking then, so they could think it through.

As they pondered, I glanced around the faces at the table. Most of them looked frustrated, annoyed, or thoughtful—or some combination thereof. Except for one person who hadn't said anything for a while. She regarded me with brown eyes sparking with contained amusement, a hint of a smile quirking one side of her generous mouth. No one else in the room knew that I'd taken the idea to her first through an encoded message, and received her blessing to suggest it.

Although she was now in her seventies, Fleet Commander Regina Holles had aged gracefully and carried her years with dignity—and had likely benefited from a Vigor-Us® treatment or two. She looked and carried herself as if she were no more than fifty. She wore her dark chocolate hair in an intricate coiled design close to her head, a shock of white running back from one temple. She was still, in my estimation, quite beautiful. When I looked at her, I still saw the woman I'd known and loved at the academy, and remained friends with since then.

Regina had a habit of saying little until others at the table had finished talking. When she did speak, people listened. Now she cleared her throat, a delicate noise that nonetheless made every head turn in her direction. Regina wasn't the only Fleet Commander in the Protectorate, but she was the only one in the room.

"*Admiralo* Mahane has a propensity for skirting around difficult issues," she drawled, "and there have been times when I've taken him to task for that. But this time, I think his idea has merit. We're entrusted with protecting the safety of Nearspace and all its inhabitants, and if there's a clear risk to that safety— which I think has been sufficiently demonstrated—we must take whatever measures we deem necessary, even unorthodox ones, to counter that risk."

"With all due respect, Fleet Commander, isn't that what I've been saying?" Mauronet protested. "Go after the Chron, take them out before they even enter Nearspace, and the threat is neutralized."

"If a positive outcome were assured, or even probable," Chanda Botek said. "Which it is not. We need whatever intelligence the envoys can get before we can make any plans."

Regina held up a finely-manicured hand before the bickering could start again. "I agree with Fleet Admiral Botek. We don't have enough data on which to construct a solid attack plan." She looked pointedly at Mauronet, then let her gaze drift around the others at the table. "What no-one has seen fit to mention so far today—the proverbial elephant in the room—is that the Protectorate is stretched too thinly around Nearspace to even consider massing enough ships to go hunting Chron."

Mauronet and several other humans in the room flushed, and the pink undertones of Chanda Botek's amber skin deepened. I caught the distinct scent of wet wool that signalled embarrassment in the Vilisian scent language. Harle Southwind didn't look any different, but who could tell under all that fur? His left ear flicked a little faster.

"Even considering the planets that are self-policing?" the Lobor asked. "We must have some patrols that could be downloaded to other forces, even temporarily."

Regina Holles tapped her fingernails on the desk. "Not without leaving them open to elevated risk. Anyone can do the math. The Protectorate fleet patrols eleven inhabited systems and GI 892. We protect eighteen inhabited planets, for two of which we provide the entirety of policing and security. We can't be everywhere at once. And we aren't. We've grown complacent in a century without any real threat from outside Nearspace, I'm afraid. If we pulled even a quarter of those ships and personnel to go off chasing war—"

She let the sentence hang without ending it for a moment. "Add to that the possibility the Chron could drop in via some wormhole we don't even know about—"

Mauronet snorted. "Unlikely."

Regina glared at him. "Did *you* know about the wormhole into Tau Ceti before Luta Paixon brought us that information?"

"But it's in a perfect hiding place, in the debris ring!" he protested. "It was simply lucky for them we didn't find it."

The Fleet Commander stared so long at him, face expressionless except for a single raised eyebrow, that I almost began to feel sorry for Mauronet. When she spoke, she merely said evenly, "So you're suggesting we stake the safety of Nearspace on the chances of the Chron not getting *lucky* a second time?"

Mauronet swallowed and was the first to look away, the skin around his eyes tightening.

Regina Holles sat forward, resting her elbows on the scuffed surface of the table and lacing her fingers together. "Admiral Mahane, please contact your sister for me, and see if you can enlist her help. If she has any trepidation, however, I won't ask her to do this. If she's willing to go back to Corvid space, put three more of our people on board—your choice—and I'll contact the Administrative Council with our idea. I'll suggest the diplomatic mission last no more than a week. I won't impose on your sister any further than that. Then the envoys can return with a full report, and we'll know where we stand."

I nodded once. "I'll get her to estimate her lead time."

Fleet Commander Regina Holles raised her eyebrows at me. "But you're going to *ask* her first, correct, Admiral?"

I grinned. "I'll ask. But I'm confident I can predict her answer."

The meeting wrapped up shortly after that. I lingered, chatting with Harle Southwind, since our paths hadn't crossed for several months. After we'd exchanged small talk, he glanced around casually and said in a low voice, "Lanar, could we meet tomorrow? There's something I want to discuss with you."

"Sure. When and where?"

He considered. "Your ship, or mine. Either one will do."

Not a social meeting, then. The last time we'd talked, Harle had hinted about an investigation involving PrimeCorp, so maybe there was more to report on that. "Come on over to the *Cheswick*, then. Have lunch with me in my quarters?"

A half-smile stretched over his muzzle. "Do you have any *jarlees* wine to go with it?"

I returned the smile. "Absolutely. See you then."

When I left the Lobor, I found Antar Mauronet waiting alone

in the corridor outside the boardroom. I would have walked past without pausing, but he stepped in front of me with a sneer. "Must be nice to always get your way," he said.

"You heard the Fleet Commander," I said, keeping my voice mild. "We can't hare off and leave Nearspace unprotected. This is just a little insurance."

"Might be a good idea if that was true," he snarled. "The Fleet Commander's just scared to stick her neck out."

I chuckled. "I can't say I've ever known Regina Holles to be scared of anything much. Aside from recklessly endangering Nearspace, that is."

He leaned in to hiss in my face, face congested an ugly red and angry eyes bulging unpleasantly. "Guess you'd know. You're the one who used to sleep with her, I hear. Which is pretty disgusting, considering how much older she—"

Mauronet didn't get any further with that sentence. Without thinking, I hauled back, let fly, and clocked him squarely on the jaw. Since it surprised even me, he didn't see it coming. He hit the carpeted corridor like a bag of wet laundry.

I squatted beside him as he swore and reached to cradle his jaw in one hand. "Word of advice, Mauronet," I said in as friendly a voice as I could manage. My hand had started to throb, but I wouldn't let him see that. "Consider yourself lucky you said that to me, and not to the Fleet Commander herself. Because she would have hit you where no-one would see the bruises."

Not waiting for him to answer, I stood, turned, and headed to the docking bays and my ship.

THE NEARSPACE PROTECTORATE Vessel *S. Cheswick* was quiet when I returned. The night crew, skeletal since we were docked at FarView Station, had started their shift, and I poked my head in at the bridge to let them know I was back on board. The overhead lights burned low, most of the illumination coming from the glow of unattended consoles.

"All quiet, Admiral. You should get some sleep." Commander Linna Drake glanced up as I entered the bridge, then back down to her datapad. I couldn't tell if she was reading a report or a novel of questionable quality. With Drake, it could be either. Now in her sixties, the wiry commander was a lifelong officer and showed no sign of slowing down, either mentally or physically. Her dark blue eyes could look through a person's defences as if they were glass. I slept well with Linna Drake on night duty.

"*Okej*, just thought I'd check in. Who's on communications tonight? I want to contact my sister, but I'm not sure where she is currently."

"Medenez," she said without looking up. "I can ask him to start a tracer. He should have a best guess by the time you get to your quarters and you can ping him from there."

"Thanks, do that." I turned to go but something tipped her off.

"What happened to your hand, sir?" Drake's voice sharpened on the question, all trace of her relaxed nonchalance vanishing. Originally, I'd tried to avoid her attempts to "mother" me, but she never got the message. Eventually I stopped trying and resigned myself to giving in with good grace.

I held up my hand ruefully. The knuckles had begun to darken and looked puffy and swollen. "I had a bit of a disagreement with Mauronet over a diplomatic matter."

"You thought he was being undiplomatic?"

"I thought he was being damned rude. But to be honest, I didn't really think about it at all. I punched him before I knew I was going to do it."

She'd left the command chair and crossed to me, examining the hand with professional interest. "Caught him on the jaw, I'd guess. Did he go down?"

"Very satisfactorily."

Drake nodded and released my hand. She put her fists on her hips and cocked her head at me, looking up from her diminutive height. "Ice it while you're talking to your sister. Are you in trouble for this?"

I shrugged. "No one was around. I doubt he'll make waves." I'd begun to feel badly about the whole thing before I'd even made it back to the *Cheswick*, and I thought Drake knew me well enough to figure that part out. I shouldn't have let Mauronet's bullying get to me. He'd been perfectly correct about my one-time relationship with Regina Holles, after all. He just didn't realize how long in the past it was, or that we were, contrary to outward appearances, the same age. In fact, if I remembered correctly, I was five years older than Regina.

Drake did her best to smother a smile. "See you in the morning, sir."

"Goodnight, Commander."

She had her head bent over the glow of her datapad again by the time I'd reached the doorway. Without looking up, she said, "I'll try to give you five minute's warning if FarView security comes with an arrest warrant. Maybe you can escape justice and stow away on a scruffy trader bound out-system."

I threw her a grin and a salute. "You read too many adventure novels, but I appreciate the thought," I said. "See you in the morning."

WHEN I PINGED Medenez, he had good news and bad.

"I have a location on the *Tane Ikai, Admiralo*," he said, his voice clipped and efficient. "They're in FTL WaVe range, and I messaged the comm. Unfortunately, Captain Paixon has retired for the night, and she'll speak with you tomorrow. Is it an emergency, sir?"

I shook my head. I knew Medenez was tenacious, and if I'd said it was urgent he'd have called down every regulation in the book until Luta's comm officer agreed to get her in front of the screen. But it wasn't necessary. She might react better to my suggestion on a good night's sleep, anyway. I told Medenez to leave it until morning, took Linna Drake's advice, and stuck a coldpack from the med cabinet on my hand.

My personal comm rang and I answered it, audio only. "Mahane."

"Fisticuffs outside my boardroom? Whatever got into you, Lanar?" Fleet Commander Regina Holles' voice was low, smooth, and highly amused. "Let me see that you're not in need of medical attention. Put your video on."

I sighed and sat in front of the screen, deliberately keeping my coldpack-encased hand below her field of vision. "I'm perfectly fine, Regina, and it was only one little punch, not a barroom brawl. How did you even find out? I wouldn't expect Mauronet to go crying to you—or anyone, for that matter."

Regina had taken her chocolate-brown hair down from the severe coils she'd worn it in for the meeting, and it fell around her face in soft waves. She tilted her head at me pityingly.

"Security cameras, Lanar dear. They have those on civilian stations, you know? Fortunately, the techs know that anything involving Protectorate personnel comes to me and me alone before any other eyes get on it." She smiled. "And take credit where it's due. It was a beautiful punch that put that unpleasant man flat on his *azeno*. I watched it three times and I was sorry to tell them to erase it. How's your hand?"

I sighed and lifted the coldpack so she could see it. "It's fine. And Mauronet probably didn't deserve it. If you're going to call me on the carpet, go ahead. I over-reacted."

Regina snorted. "He absolutely deserved it, if for nothing more than what he said about your sister in the meeting. The audio didn't pick up all of what he said to you in the corridor, but I suspect there was more to it than that—" she held up a hand when I tried to interrupt. "I'm not going to ask about it. I *did* hear what you said to him, and I think it's better for my professional relationship with him that I don't know."

I nodded gravely. "You could be right about that, Fleet Commander."

Her smile faded, and I saw worry gather like a cloud overshadowing her face. Suddenly she looked all of her years. "You'll get in touch with Luta soon, Lanar? I wouldn't say it in that room, but I'm worried. I read the depositions of every one of Luta's crew, and all the data we could extract from the Corvid chip. Even with much of it corrupted, there was enough to scare anyone with a particle of sense."

I nodded again. "I'll be talking to her in the morning. Already set up."

"And you think she'll go? We can't keep bickering with the Council on this."

"I think she will. She'll complain about it—and with good reason, because she hasn't had much time to recover from the last 'favour' I asked her to do—but I think she'll go."

She seemed satisfied. "Keep Commander Blue on board with her and add those other names. I trust you to pick them."

"I'm going to make a list before I go to sleep. It will depend on where Luta is and who's close enough, but I'll do what I can. We want to move as quickly as possible."

"And what about PrimeCorp?" she demanded. "Did you read the files your sister brought back? Damning as hell, and completely inadmissible in court. What have they been playing at all these years?"

I shook my head, the old burn of anger at PrimeCorp simmering in my gut. They'd taken so much from my family, and had apparently taken even more from Nearspace. "Their ambassadors on the Council are denying everything, dismissing the files as illegally obtained, or probably manufactured, and setting up scapegoats, as far as I can see. By the time we get them to hand over files, there'll be none left to find." I leaned back in my chair, drumming the fingers of my uninjured hand on the armrest. "I shouldn't have been so quick to give those files to the Council. Should have moved quietly and come up behind them. I just thought we *had* them this time."

"Don't blame yourself. You did what you thought was right, just like you always do. And even over the screen, I could see your face tighten when I mentioned PrimeCorp. Let it go for now. We're not going to solve the PrimeCorp problem tonight." Regina smiled and leaned back from her screen, curling a long strand of dark hair around her finger. Bands of white threaded through it, striping it like a candy cane. "You look good, Lanar. As always."

"So do you, Regina."

"Not the same, and you know it," she said with a laugh. "Don't worry, I'm sworn to secrecy about your nano-whatever-they-are. I just sometimes wonder what might have happened if we'd stayed together. Where would we be now?"

I grinned. "You'd have worn me out long ago. I'd be divorced or dead from fatigue."

She quirked a half-smile. "Or I'd be the envy of every woman in Nearspace, and they'd be whispering about what I'd done to land such a handsome younger husband. Ah well." She straightened in her chair. "It's good to see you, Lanar, even under the circumstances. You'll keep me informed about your sister?"

I inclined my head. "Right away."

Regina leaned close to the screen and blew me a kiss. "Try to stay out of trouble, dear." She cut the connection before I had a chance to agree or protest.

The coldpack beeped, signalling it had been in place long enough, and I pulled the adhesive free and tossed the whole thing in the recycler. I'd been tired before, but now agitation spurred me around my quarters, pacing evenly from the kitchenette to the view wall and back again. I traversed the small space three more times, trying to relax into the movement of my body, before stopping in front of the view wall. Beyond it, ships moved with slow grace, approaching or leaving the station, and further out a sprinkling of stars flickered in the deep black of space. I let my forehead lean into the cool, smooth solidity of the wall. The transparent barrier seemed little enough to separate me from the vacuum beyond.

I just sometimes wonder what might have happened if we'd stayed together.

Regina's words, but they conjured another name—Soranna. Her face flashed in my memory, wide dark eyes and sunflower hair, mouth parted in the beginning of a laugh. We'd been married only ten years, not long enough for the issues of her aging and my non-aging to affect us. When she'd died, the problem, if it would ever have existed, had died with her. That was the image I still kept on a shelf in my living quarters, and had done so for forty-five years now. It horrified me to think that if I lived long enough, I might forget what she looked like.

Maybe that was the reason I'd never remarried. Although Luta and Hirin had managed all right. Not perfectly, and it had caused problems, but—they were still together.

I pushed back from the view wall with a sigh, turned down the lights, and picked up my datapad. I needed names for Luta in the morning, if she agreed to my plan. I had no time to spend on the past tonight. The future was enough to worry about.

"YOU'RE SERIOUS?"

Luta's glare was almost strong enough for me to feel it through the comm screen. My sister was a sweetheart, but when she wasn't happy with you, you knew it. Those eyes could cut through you when she was angry as easily as they poured compassion on you when you hurt. Her auburn hair was caught back in a clip, and since it was still early, I suspected she hadn't been awake long.

"Let me explain," I said meekly. "I wouldn't ask if it wasn't really important."

Her eyes softened for a moment, but then she leaned back in

her chair and crossed her arms, head cocked at a belligerent angle. "All right, so talk. But remember, the last time I did you and the Protectorate a favour, it didn't turn out so well for me."

I couldn't argue with her there. A few short weeks ago I'd asked her, on behalf of the Protectorate, to deliver a Lobor historian to a newly-discovered system. As a result, she and her crew had been stranded, kidnapped, shot at, chased, made first contact with an alien race, and Luta herself had almost died when her nanobioscavengers had malfunctioned. I wouldn't have been too pleased with me, either.

"This will be different," I assured her, holding up a placatory hand. Too late, I realized it was the one with the bruised knuckles and dropped it back down, but her eyes narrowed and I knew she'd seen. Before she could comment, I hurried on. "The Corvids invited you back to their system. All I'm asking you to do is take them up on their invitation. Stay for a few days, and come home."

"Why?"

The holo of a forest on the wall behind her told me that Luta was in her quarters, not on the bridge. For a moment, my brother-in-law Hirin's head appeared in my line of vision, leaning over Luta's shoulder. My mother's infusion of nanobioscavengers had taken his apparent age from ninety to something more like sixty, and he was enjoying his rejuvenation. His close-cropped hair had darkened from pure white to peppery grey, and his blue eyes were bright. He was also now free of the virus PrimeCorp had inflicted on him years ago. He smiled and waved a silent hello, then pointed at Luta and pulled a face. She must have noticed me trying not to laugh because she shooed him away.

"That datapacket you brought us from the Corvids—well, some of it was corrupted. We couldn't retrieve everything."

Luta's lips thinned out to a pale white line. "Jahelia Sord took the original and left us a copy. Could it have been deliberate tampering?"

I shrugged. "We'd have to find her and ask. I don't know why she'd leave a partially corrupted copy, though. Why leave it at all if she didn't want us to have the information?"

"Jahelia Sord has interesting ideas about what's amusing," Luta said wryly. "But I guess the original could have had problems. Although Cerevare didn't mention that, and we can't ask her about it, since she's still with the Chron—the good Chron." She grimaced. I knew she hadn't liked leaving the Lobor historian behind with the aliens, but it had been Cerevare Brindlepaw's decision. "We need a way to differentiate between the ones that want to kill us and the ones that want to help us."

"I'll get right to work on that," I told her, "but in the meantime, here's all we want you to do. Take a few Protectorate people on the *Tane Ikai* and escort a diplomatic envoy to the Corvid station. You don't have to do anything official; the Council envoys will handle everything. Just keep them safe, and keep an eye on things while you're there. Let the diplomats do their thing and gather whatever information the Corvids will share, and then escort them back. That's it. A week, at most. No forays into Chron space. No uncharted systems. A quick visit and back home."

She leaned forward, green eyes narrowing. "Wait a second. The damaged wormhole into the connecting system isn't expected to right itself for five years or so. How are we getting to the Corvids at all?"

I smiled. If Luta didn't know the answer to this, it meant the secret was still safe. "Remember what the Corvids told you about a 'replacement' wormhole spontaneously generating when one was damaged?"

She nodded, pursing her lips. "So it happened just the way Fha said it would, and the Protectorate knows where it is?"

"You got it, and we got lucky. It's only about fifty thousand klicks from the damaged one, and under constant Protectorate surveillance."

"And the Protectorate can't do this—why?"

I rubbed a hand along the back of my neck, feeling the knot of tension there. "The Council wants this to look like an extremely peaceable visit. No Protectorate military ships involved. But we think it's unwise to send them off on their own. And you—"

Luta closed her eyes and finished for me. "—have a standing invitation to return any time I want, which the Council wouldn't stop me from exercising for fear of insulting the Corvids."

"Lucky for you, that part of the datapacket wasn't corrupted at all."

Her eyes flew open, and she cocked her head to one side, regarding me. "And you have no problem sending your little sister back into harm's way?"

"Hey, it's *big* sister, as you're so fond of reminding me," I said. I rolled my shoulders. "I do have a problem with it, Luta. It worries the hell out of me. But honestly, I think the risk is minimal, and the *Tane Ikai* is well-outfitted. And you'll have Yuskeya and other officers in case anything happens. The thing is, we need this visit to happen. We don't know enough about an enemy that could show up any day and start hammering away at us the way they did a century and a half ago. We're stretched too thin across too much space."

"And there's the little matter of PrimeCorp's involvement with the Chron," Luta added. "Is the Council going to address that? Or the Protectorate? Anyone? Or does PrimeCorp just continue on its merry way, doing whatever the hell it wants as usual?"

I blew out a long sigh. "Would you believe, we didn't even *get* to that part in the meeting? The investigation is supposedly started. Higher-ups in the Protectorate know about the evidence you brought back, but they're trying to keep a lid on it for now." I hadn't told her, yet, that there were some of those high-level officers who simply didn't believe the claims that she and her crew had encountered PrimeCorp ships in the uncharted Chron systems. They knew something about our family's long-time conflict with PrimeCorp, and had decided that she'd been mistaken—or was willingly misinterpreting something. I'm not sure how they could explain away the evidence of the PrimeCorp files Jahelia Sord had obtained, but I was going to make it my job to find out. Luta would have to know about the skepticism eventually, but she was quite annoyed enough at me for one conversation. My implicit belief in her wouldn't be enough to soothe her indignation.

"You're keeping it very quiet. I haven't heard even a whisper about it in the open yet." She leaned forward and picked up a steaming mug that Hirin must have just set down on the desk for her. He moved behind her again and winked at me. A double caff would surely improve her mood. "We need the information on the Chron from the Corvids, but we also need the information on PrimeCorp's involvement from Cerevare. Will we be able to talk to the Corvids about establishing a communications link with the peaceful Chron?"

"Well, one thing at a time. But if you happen to discuss that with your Corvid friend—Fha?—while you're there, I'm sure no-one would mind."

She was obviously determined to make me sweat for this. "I'm on the way to Eri with a cargo hold full of ore. You're lucky you caught me before I made the skip to Eridani."

"I'll arrange a subcontract for the ore if you leave it on Jertenda instead, and head back to FarView. I'll get my people here, ready for pickup, and we'll escort you out to the new wormhole." I met her eyes. "It's not just a favour for me, or for the Protectorate. It's for all of Nearspace."

She must have caught something in my voice, because she looked past the screen and said, "Hirin, you've heard the discussion. What do you think?"

My brother-in-law's smiling face appeared again over Luta's shoulder. They still made a May-December couple, but the nanobioscavengers had closed the gap considerably. They couldn't do for him what they'd done for Luta and me for seventy years, but he was evidently delighted with the changes.

"I've made a few more upgrades to various ship systems since the last time we went through that wormhole," Hirin said. "I think we'll be better prepared for anything we find out there. And this mission sounds simple enough." He winked at me before Luta could turn and look at him.

"Oh, they always *sound* simple. You don't think the crew will have something to say about this?" Luta asked. "I promised them some vacation time on Eri when we arrive with this load of ore."

Hirin shrugged. "This crew will go where you ask them to," he said with assurance. "They might grumble, but they won't mean it."

Luta turned back to face me through the screen. "Well, there you have it," she said. "The old man thinks we're going, so I guess we're going." Now, though, a smile hid behind her words, and I knew she wasn't really annoyed anymore.

"One more thing," I said, before she could say goodbye.

She raised an eyebrow.

"Don't tell Mother, all right?"

Luta laughed, her green eyes crinkling at the corners. She still looked no more than thirty, despite her eighty-five years, thanks again to our mother's nanotechnology. "Afraid you'll get in trouble for sending me outside of Nearspace?"

I shook my head. "Just security. Mother has connections on the Council, and we want to keep things under the radar for now. The crew should keep it quiet, too. *Okej?*"

"I don't know why I let you talk me into these things," she said in mock annoyance, "but *okej*. I'll go to Jertenda and then come to FarView. We should be there in three days."

I nodded. "*Gis la revido,* Luta. Take care."

"Talk to you soon, little brother," she echoed with a smile, and broke the connection.

I sat back from the screen and hoped we were doing the right thing.

Chapter 2 — Luta
Blast From The Past

"I GUESS I'D better let them know," I said to Hirin, after ending the conversation with my brother the *Admiralo*. I knew that having Lanar in the Nearspace Protectorate was a net benefit to all of us, but some days it didn't feel that way. I stood from behind my desk and stretched, feeling the muscles pull and release. I hadn't really gotten back into my routine of *tae-ga-chi* since I'd been sick, and my body was beginning to feel it.

Hirin slid an arm around my waist and pulled me into a warm hug. "You didn't have to say yes, you know. You could have turned him down. Lanar wouldn't have minded."

I gave him a mock glare. "I thought *you* wanted to go." Then I quickly kissed him on the cheek and added, "I'm just teasing. But I think this time, he *would* have minded. Lanar's worried."

"The notion of another Chron war has everybody on edge," Hirin agreed.

"Oh *damne!*"

"What?"

I pulled out of Hirin's arms and put my fists on my hips. "Did you see his knuckles? They were all bruised and swollen. Like he punched someone—or something. I meant to ask him about it, but then he distracted me with this whole mission thing."

Hirin looked skeptical. "Lanar's never been much of a

brawler, has he?"

"No, he's more used to charming his way out of sticky situations. But I saw his hand—and the way he tried to hide it from me. That tells me he was fighting."

Hirin laughed. "Thanks for reminding me why I never try to lie to you. It's a pointless exercise."

I pretended to swat him, took my datapad from the desk, and headed for the bridge of my ship. At least there, I might get some respect.

Only Baden and Maja were on the bridge when I arrived. Seated next to each other at the communications console, his dark head and her blonde one leaned close together as they studied something on a datapad. Without looking up, Baden said, "Good morning, Captain."

"Good morning," I said brightly. "How are you both? Sleep well?"

Maja turned and looked at me, a suspicious tilt to her head. "Mother? What's up?"

I sat in the command chair and tried to look innocent. "Why does something have to be up for me to wish you a good morning?"

"Haha, right," Maja said, turning her skimchair completely around to face me. My daughter had undergone her own transformation recently, and she looked relaxed and comfortable, the hard lines that used to bracket her eyes and mouth softened away. This morning she'd pulled her blonde hair into a knot at the nape of her neck and wore a blue sweater that matched her eyes. Her change had nothing to do with nanotechnology, though. It was mostly her relationship with my comm officer. And partly, I hoped, her healed relationship with me. "If I've learned one new thing about you in the past few weeks, it's that you are never this cheery first thing in the morning. Something's definitely up."

So much for respect.

"*Okej*, you got me. But how about we get everyone up here so I don't have to explain this multiple times?" I asked. "Baden, you can leave Viss out because he was on watch duty last night and he might be asleep, but get Rei and Yuskeya, would you?"

"This sounds serious," Maja observed with a smile. "I think I'd better make a galley run and grab us both a double caff."

Baden nodded agreement as he commed my pilot and navigator, and Maja hurried down the corridor away from the bridge. When they'd both answered, he swivelled his skimchair to face me.

"Is it?" he asked. "Serious, I mean?"

I sighed. "Not really. At least, not immediately. But it's the Protectorate, and the situation is—worrisome."

"So there's no rest for the weary?" His teasing tone couldn't mask the undercurrent of concern.

"How about a delayed rest?" I asked. "And why am I talking to you about this when I just said I'd explain to everyone at the same time?"

Baden laughed and ran a hand through his cocoa-coloured hair. "Guess you caught me, Captain." He turned back to the comm board and gave me a minute to gather my thoughts.

It took less than five minutes for Maja to return and Rei and Yuskeya to gain the bridge as well. Viss was with them after all, and it didn't take a genius to figure out that he'd probably been in Yuskeya's quarters when Baden commed her. Despite some rocky weeks when they'd each found out the other had been keeping secrets, they'd repaired their relationship, which made me happy. I didn't know what would happen for them when Yuskeya was inevitably recalled to a post on a Protectorate ship, but I hoped they'd find a way to work it out.

Maja had gone one better than she'd said, and brought hot drinks for all.

"Bless you," Rei said with a grin as she accepted the double caff Maja handed her. "It won't make up for the extra half hour of beauty sleep I'm losing thanks to your mother, but it will help." With her long chestnut hair pulled up in a messy knot and her *pridattii* facial markings tracing the contours of her face like swirling runnels of spilled ink, Rei was unlikely to suffer any ill effects from a lack of "beauty" sleep. Rei was an exceptional pilot and my best friend of five years, and I already knew I'd trust her to pilot me anywhere.

"*Dankon,*" Yuskeya told Maja, inclining her head as she took the proffered mug. Steam curled from the top and I knew it held sweet, milky chai. Maja had taken on the unofficial role of stores officer, and made sure she knew everyone's favourites in the food and drinks department.

Holding the mug with both hands, Commander Yuskeya Blue carefully lowered herself into her seat at the navigation console, her long dark braid twined into an intricate coil this morning. She was one of my brother's most trusted officers, on "loan" to the *Tane Ikai* for over a year now—although for most of that time I hadn't known about her Protectorate affiliation. I'd been more than a little angry with Lanar when I found out he'd put a Protectorate officer on my ship without my knowledge—but I couldn't be angry with Yuskeya. Dignified, competent, and brilliant, I couldn't have asked for a better navigator and medic. Why was I worrying about how Viss would take it when the Protectorate wanted her back? What would *I* do?

Somehow Maja had known or guessed that Viss would turn up on the bridge too, because she'd brought a caff for him as well. He took it gravely and toasted the rest of us before taking a sip. "Here's to whatever bad news the Captain has in store for us," he said. "It's bound to be interesting, if nothing else."

"Hey," I protested, "it's not always bad news when I call everybody together on the bridge, is it?"

They looked around at each other, silently considering—or pretending to.

"Well, maybe not always," Rei conceded. "Nine times out of ten?"

"Maybe eight times out of ten," Baden said. "And only about seven of those involve someone else shooting at us."

"Har har, very funny," I said. "Do you want to know what's up, or not?"

"Go ahead, Luta," Hirin said. "I'll make sure they behave."

They did quiet down then, and I put Lanar's request to them, conveying the explanation for why the Protectorate had to do an end run around the Council. As I'd expected, they were accepting.

"Admiral Mahane wouldn't ask unless it was important," Yuskeya said, hands cupped around her steaming mug. "I consider it my duty to agree with his suggestion."

Viss nodded. "He's a good guy. If he says it's important to Nearspace that we go, I don't have a problem with it. Although I would have liked to break down the intakes—"

I held up a hand. "If we go, it's as soon as possible. Any major overhauls will have to wait until we get back—or, hey, you could do it while we're there. The Corvids will be happy to help if you need it."

The engineer grimaced. "They're friendly and helpful enough. But a little odd to have around. I think I'll handle the maintenance on my own, if it's all the same to you."

The Corvids had helped us install a special drive when we'd been at their station last, and while it had ultimately saved our lives, both Viss and Baden had found the crow-like aliens' presence discomfiting. In order to co-exist in the same physical space with us, they wore all-encompassing black enviro-suits, which responded to the Corvids' movements by constantly shifting and reconfiguring the small, flat hexagon-shaped discs of which they were constructed. The suits moved and flowed around the Corvids' seven-foot-tall bodies, hinting at arms, hands, and legs without completely revealing them. At least their helmets were completely transparent, oblong-shaped to accommodate the aliens' beak-like mouths, with some sort of holographic displays on the inside faceplate. The Corvids communicated via speakers on the lower rim of the helmet, and fortunately for us could speak fluent Esper.

"The diplomats will travel on their own ship, and we'll have some other Protectorate observers on board with us. For now, let's get prepped for at least a month of self-sufficiency if needed. The last time we did Lanar a favour it didn't go as planned, so let's not get caught off-guard this time. And we'll have a few extra mouths to feed."

Maja stood. "I'll review ship's stores. We'll have to replenish some stock."

As the others dispersed to make their own preparations, she stopped next to my chair and put a hand on my arm. "Are you okay with this? You haven't been back on your feet all that long, and it was a trip to the Corvid system that started everything." Her blue eyes shone with a concern that wouldn't have existed a few short months ago, when our relationship was about as bad as it had ever been. If what we'd been through lately had any redeeming aspect, it was that the bond between my daughter and I had been restored.

I nodded and smiled. "I'm okay. What happened had nothing to do with the Corvids, after all. They were nothing but helpful. And if they can offer any keys to preparing us for the Chron, we have to do it."

She leaned in to kiss my cheek. "All right, then. I'll be sure to lay in lots of that pastina you like so much."

"And hope we don't need it all," I said.

THE NEXT FEW days went according to plan. Lanar made good on his promise, and by the time we touched down on Jertenda, the subcontract for the ore delivery was arranged. We restocked there, and a little over two days got us back to FarView. Now we were waiting for one more Protectorate officer to arrive. The Council launch conveying the diplomats would rendezvous with us out near the new wormhole and we'd go through together.

Our Protectorate guests were installed in the passenger suites. One was Lieutenant Gerazan Soto, whom we'd rescued from an abortive mission at the start of our last misadventure. He and Rei had formed a quick and close bond, and they were both delighted to be back on the same ship for our jaunt to Corvid space. I expected they'd be pretty much inseparable during the travel times to and from the Corvid station, which made me smile.

The second was a pale-furred, dark-eyed Lobor Lieutenant-Commander named Emar Summergale. She shook my hand firmly when I met her at the docking station, her skin exuding the feverish heat I had now come to expect from Lobors. Her dark Protectorate uniform was spotless, and the highly-polished starburst insignia on her collar sparkled under the overheads. As I walked her down the corridor to her quarters, she politely bombarded me with questions about Cerevare Brindlepaw.

"She is something of a hero in my eyes," Summergale explained, her partially-furred hands clasped behind her back as we walked.

"She's a lovely person," I said. "I very much enjoyed having her on board the *Tane Ikai*."

The Lobor's ears twitched. "I am rather in awe of Brindlepaw's decision to remain with the peaceful Chron. It must not have been an easy decision."

I smiled. "I think, for Cerevare, it was incredibly easy," I said. "She viewed it as the chance of a lifetime—a lifetime spent studying the Chron without any real hope of ever understanding them, let alone meeting and conversing with them. Finding a segment of the population who want peace, not war, made the opportunity irresistible."

"But certainly a dangerous decision to make, especially for a civilian," she observed. "I heard that she remained on the Chron station even though it was still under attack!"

"She did. I tried to talk her out of it. I thought it was too dangerous to stay. But she practically laughed at the notion that she should leave."

"My, my," Summergale said. "Quite a personality."

"And quite a hand at *quozit*," I said. "If you ever meet, you should challenge her to a game."

The Lieutenant-Commander looked slightly scandalized at the notion, but merely smiled in that canine way the Lobors have. I suspected that if we could arrange communications with Cerevare, the Lieutenant-Commander would be first in line to speak with her.

The third officer arrived just before we were scheduled to leave to meet the Council launch. He was a tall, thin human with close-cropped black hair, dusky skin, and a peppering of darker freckles across his nose and cheeks. He arrived at the airlock and introduced himself in a rich, deep voice as Lieutenant-Commander Jolah Didkovsky. As I shook his hand and introduced myself, he asked immediately after Yuskeya, saying that they'd been classmates at the Protectorate *akademio* and he'd heard a rumour she was aboard. I led him to the galley to find her.

She turned from pouring a mug of hot chai when we entered, and her face positively lit with pleased amazement. "Jolah! What are you doing here?"

He set his duffel bag on the floor and crossed the room with arms spread wide to catch her in a hug. "You didn't see my name on the passenger list?"

I watched with a hint of bemusement as they hugged warmly. Yuskeya was generally so reserved that such effusiveness was out of character. The only other man I'd ever seen her hug was Viss. "The Captain didn't share it with me," she said with a laugh.

"Well, I would have, if you'd asked me!" I protested. "I wasn't trying to keep it secret!"

"You're forgiven," she said. "Jolah, still drinking triple caff?

Would you like one?"

"I'd love it," he said, and turned to me. "Captain, do you mind if I just stop off here? I'll settle in later if that's all right."

"Not at all. Yuskeya can show you the way when you're done here. Yuskeya, I can put Maja on the nav board for the first part of the run if you'd like. She has enough hours in now to handle it, and she'll love the opportunity." When Maja decided to stay aboard the *Tane Ikai* for a while, following the end of her marriage and our reconciliation, she'd started learning navigation to, as she said, "make herself useful." Although she hadn't quite graduated to deep space navigation yet, she could easily take us away from the planet and start us on a set course.

Yuskeya smiled her gratitude. "That would be wonderful, Captain, thank you. We have a lot of catching-up to do."

"Then I'll leave you to it."

I'll admit my ship was beginning to feel a little cramped. I was secretly glad that none of our Protectorate passengers out-ranked Yuskeya, and wondered if Lanar had done that on purpose. If anything catastrophic came up and I had to let the Protectorate contingent commandeer my ship, it wouldn't be so bad if Yuskeya was at the helm. I wondered idly what sort of relationship she'd had with Jolah Didkovsky. I sensed that it could have been more than simple friendship and wondered what Viss would think of the admittedly handsome Lieutenant-Commander.

I shook off those thoughts and let my feet carry me all the way forward to the bridge to find Maja and install her at the nav board. With all of our new passengers aboard, it was time to head into the Delta Pavonis system to find the new wormhole coordinates Lanar had given me. I took a deep breath. We were leaving the safe boundaries of Nearspace proper again. I hoped it would all go better than the last time.

Silly me.

WE'D BEEN GUESTS at the Corvid *uruglat*, or space station, for just about the full week, and I was growing weary of all that unrelieved black. They were obviously an intelligent and sophisticated species, but their taste in decorating left a lot to be desired.

Don't get me wrong, I liked the Corvids. Once I'd gotten past my initial surprise at their crow-like beaks and sleek black feathers, I *expected* them to be different, expected everything about them to be alien. It was just that their station was black on the outside and black on the inside and everything else about it was black, and it got old after a while.

I said as much to Hirin as we lay in bed that night. "Night" by our internal clocks, anyway; the rhythm of the Corvid station operated on a different cycle, but we'd all managed to make accommodations. Folks came and went at all hours in making those accommodations, and at the moment, the *Tane Ikai* was unnaturally quiet. No throb of engines, only the soft hiss of the life support system cycling air throughout the ship and the occasional gurgle from an internal pipe. And for once, no voices or footsteps in the corridors. The Corvids had offered to outfit quarters on the station for us and for the diplomats, but that would have meant creating and constantly maintaining an atmosphere for us, in a much larger space. So, we compromised. Most of the interactions between the envoys and the Corvids happened via hologrammatic projections in the launch's cargo space, which had been hastily outfitted as a makeshift boardroom. The diplomats had comfortable chairs and a big table, and the Corvids "beamed" themselves in. It was working. The Corvids had provided opportunities for us and for the diplomats to explore other areas of their station for limited time periods, or wearing EVA suits, but for the most part, it was easier for us to stay aboard our own ships where they were docked.

If you can call sticking partway through the gelatinous wall of a space station "docked." That's what the Corvids called it. The rest of us were still a little unsure. The *Tane Ikai* sat on one side of an entirely black docking bay, and the diplomats' launch, the *Airavata*, took up the other side. The Corvids had assured us that the bay would be pressurized and atmospherically safe for us at all times, so that we could come and go between the ships as we pleased. At the diplomats' invitation, the three Protectorate observers had been present on the *Airavata* for most of the sessions with the Corvids.

"I still don't get the all-black decor," I said to Hirin. "Fha says they can distinguish other colours, but they all seem to have a propensity for black. It's soothing, or something. But you'd think it would get boring. It would drive me insane." We'd had tours of many parts of the station: recreation areas, engineering and physical plants, eating and command stations. All various tones of black, interspersed with grey.

Hirin, curled at my back, chuckled. "We don't know when they're listening to us, remember. Fha said anytime we called out her name, she'd hear and know that we were looking for her."

I did my best to shrug. "I've concluded that they don't much care one way or the other what we say or think about them as a species. They're the most well-adjusted beings I've ever come across."

"They don't seem to be holding back anything about the Chron, anyway," Hirin said. "Gerazan says they've filled in all the missing pieces from the data packet they gave us before."

I sighed. "Good. I know this is all for the good of Nearspace, but to tell you the truth, I'm getting kind of—"

"Bored?" Hirin finished for me.

I chuckled. "Exactly. You too?"

I felt him nod. "We're not the diplomats, and although I know we were planning a vacation, this isn't quite what I envisioned. It was interesting for the first few days, but now—"

"You're tired of sleeping on a ship that's not going anywhere."

He squeezed my hand, where our fingers had interlaced. "You know me too well."

I rolled to kiss him. "I ought to, after sixty years."

"I was in that nursing home Earthside for too long, I guess," he mused. "Now that I have the chance again, I just want to be on the move."

I snuggled closer to him. "I feel the same way, and I've never really stopped moving."

The ship trembled violently, and something fell over on the desk across the room.

Hirin's grip tightened around me, and I glanced up instinctively at the port above my head. Nothing to see through it except the unrelieved black of the docking bay's interior.

"What the hell—" Hirin started.

A hologram of one of our hosts appeared without warning in the room. "I apologize for the interruption," the crow-like

Corvid said politely, "but we are under attack." As usual, only its head was visible, the rest of its body covered in a sand-coloured, rough-hewn robe with a rolled collar. The most remarkable thing about the Corvids' robes, I'd realized, was that they were not black.

"By whom?" I asked as I rolled out of bed. Hirin was right behind me.

The comm buzzed just then, and Rei's voice asked, "Captain, what's happening?"

"Don't know," I said shortly. "Better get our crew to the bridge. And find out where all the envoys are. I want everyone aboard this ship or the launch immediately. Comm the bridge of the *Airavata* and tell them we'll keep them informed." I realized belatedly that that might not be necessary; they might have their own Corvid hologram on the launch, imparting the same information.

"Aye," Rei said, and was gone. I pulled on a pair of jeans, not caring if the hologram could "see" me. I expected the Corvids were too preoccupied to spy on us. The ship shuddered again. The station must have taken another hit.

The Corvid hadn't answered me but the hologram remained. "Is it the Chron?"

"Several Chron ships have entered the system," the Corvid said finally, as if reluctant to give up the information. It was the first time I'd known one to be reticent. After a week on the station, I'd learned how to distinguish some of the Corvids from the others by striations in their "beaks." This one I knew as Jarama.

"How'd they get past the asteroid field?" Hirin asked as I opened the door of the cabin.

"Unknown," Jarama replied. "We believe we can keep you safe, Captain, but it would be wise to prepare your ships in case it becomes necessary to release you from the *uruglat*."

I didn't like the idea of being "released" into a system with Chron fighters flitting around, probably just itching to turn their energy weapons on anything human, but I kept it to myself. I was too busy sprinting down the corridor to the bridge, and wondering why I was always in the vicinity whenever all hell decided to break loose.

I EXPECTED A barrage of questions as soon as my feet hit the bridge decking, but only Rei and Viss had made it there ahead of me. Rei was already at the pilot's console, her agile fingers calibrating the boards. She flashed a question at me, her eyes serious behind the beautiful dark *pridattii* tattoos, but I could only shrug. Viss sat at the secondary engineering board, cursing and muttering under his breath. The primary engineering station is one deck down, but in times of crisis Viss likes to be on the bridge with the rest of us. I don't blame him one bit.

"Anything wrong?" I asked him.

He didn't look up. "The drives aren't meant to cold-start like this after days of being shut down," he scolded, although his remarks weren't addressed to me, or anyone else. He continued in the same vein. "Look at that—three seconds for a response from the field actuator? That's way below acceptable—"

I tuned him out. The drives—the ship, really—were Viss's babies, and he could always find something to complain about if everyone didn't treat them that way. If there was something seriously wrong, he'd tell me. The rest of the griping, well, that was just Viss.

Baden, Maja, and Yuskeya arrived on the bridge in a flurry, just as everything shook again from another impact. Whatever they were hitting the station with, it was pretty serious. I'd seen the gelatinous outer skin of the *uruglat* absorb a Chron torp as if it were nothing more than an errant fly. Anything that could shake this place was something new.

Baden Methyr slid into the communications chair, although at the moment there didn't seem to be anyone apart from the *Airavata* to communicate with. The Chron had a reputation for not answering when anyone called, and also for not calling, themselves. Maja pulled a spare skimchair over beside him, after flashing me a worried smile. I winked at her. *Not to worry.*

Right.

Yuskeya took her place at the navigation board and looked at me expectantly.

"Here's all I know," I said, sitting in the command chair while Hirin fetched up at the weapons board. "The station is under attack by Chron. The Corvids will try to protect us, but may have to release us—probably without much warning. I want everything ready to go in a heartbeat if we need it. Everything,"

I repeated, glancing over at Hirin. He nodded. He took his job as *de facto* weapons officer seriously, even if he'd only invented the position to give himself something to do.

"No chatter on the comm," Baden said, his fingers working the board methodically.

"*Okej*, where is everyone else?" I asked. "Keeping everyone safe is what we're here to do, so let's do it."

Baden had his head cocked to one side, listening to something only he could hear over the comm panel. "*Airavata* reports one of the diplomats is not on board. The other five are accounted for. The representative from Vele—her name is Andresson—was off the ship when the attack started."

Damne. I swore silently. "What about Summergale and Jolah?"

Rei answered. "They were both over at the *Airavata*, last I knew."

"Scan for their ID chips and comm them."

After a tense moment, Rei shook her head. "Neither is aboard, and no answers on the comm."

"Baden, comm the *Airavata* and ask if Lieutenant-Commanders Summergale and Didkovsky are aboard over there. If they are, tell them to stay put. We can sort out who's on what ship later if we have to leave."

We waited for an answer. Finally, Baden shook his head. "Neither are aboard the *Airavata*. Someone said they went with Andresson for a tour of the Corvid waste reclamation centre."

I swore aloud this time, not caring who heard me. "Fha!" I called. "Fha, are you there?"

The next hit, when it came a long few minutes later, must have knocked something loose. The *Tane Ikai* lurched, tilting crazily to starwise, and I had to grab the arms of my chair to keep from being thrown to the floor. The viewscreen still showed nothing but black.

"Are we free of the station?" I demanded.

"Still through the wall, as far as I can tell," Rei said in a tone of disgust. She didn't much care for the whole Corvid docking system. She said it made her claustrophobic. I was starting to know what she meant.

The hologram of Fha appeared near my chair, although it was flickering and less substantial than usual. Her wheat-coloured robe skewed awkwardly across her shoulders. "Captain," she said, slightly breathless, "this is really not a good—"

"Three of our people are missing," I broke in. "They apparently went on a tour of your reclamation centre, but they're not answering their communication devices."

Fha's hologram didn't seem to move, and I thought it had frozen. Finally, she said, "Yes, they were observed in that area of the *uruglat*. Unfortunately, we have lost communications with that sector."

A trickle of fear sped like icy water down my spine. "Is it badly damaged? Do you think they're safe?"

Yuskeya was at my side. "Captain, I could suit up and go find them."

"What?" Viss looked up from the engineering board. As engrossed in the drive details as he was, he'd still heard that.

Fha flickered out, then surged back stronger. "The station has not been breached. Some systems are experiencing interference, however. Communications is one of them."

"Captain?" As she pressed, I remembered Yuskeya's beaming face when she caught sight of Jolah Didkovsky in the galley. She didn't turn to look at Viss.

"Fha, are there obstacles to moving around inside the *uruglat*? I need to know if it's possible or prudent to send a search team for my missing people. They would have their own life-support suits."

Static. Then, "—would not recommend it at this time. There is interior debris in some areas."

"We can't leave them here, Luta," Yuskeya said, and I knew she must be desperate, to break with her own code of always calling me "Captain" when we were on the bridge.

"I can't risk anyone else," I said. "We'll sit tight. They might turn up any minute."

"The Captain's right, Yuskeya. Give it a minute." Viss couldn't leave the engineering board, but most of his attention was on our little by-play. She still didn't answer him.

I felt Yuskeya's hand on my arm and turned to meet her eyes. I thought I knew what I'd find in them, though. Even after Yuskeya's true affiliation as a Protectorate officer had been revealed, she'd always acted as if she were under my command.

When we'd been stranded in Corvid space weeks earlier, I'd asked her if she thought I should turn over command of the ship to her. She'd refused then, saying that only in dire circumstances, if she thought the Protectorate wouldn't approve of my choices, would she ever consider suggesting that she take command. As I met her steady, brown-eyed gaze, I was afraid that perhaps that moment had arrived. And I knew I couldn't actually stop her if she insisted on going to look for the others. Her face said plainly that she was about to do just that.

"All right, go," I said. "Full EVA suit. Comm open at all times. Report every minute!" I was practically shouting the last instructions because she'd run to the EVA storage next to the airlock, wrenched down one of the silvery suits, and started struggling into it the moment I'd told her to go.

"Captain!" Viss' voice bloomed with disappointment, but he didn't say more.

"Fha? Is there clear passage from our docking bay to your waste reclamation centre?"

"Test," Yuskeya said over her helmet mic. "Captain, can you hear me?"

I gave Yuskeya a thumbs-up as Fha finally answered. "—do not have reports—all areas. Passable with caution, perhaps."

That was good enough for Yuskeya. She crossed to Viss and put a hand on his arm, then leaned in to touch the faceplate of her helmet briefly to his forehead. "It'll be fine," she murmured, and I knew that even though her helmet mic fed to the entire bridge, the words were for him. Then she turned and passed through the airlock door without another word.

"*Christos.* Does she even know where the reclamation centre is?" Baden asked.

"We were down there the other day," Viss said, his voice harsh. "She knows the goddamned way."

"I know the way." Yuskeya's voice sounded tinny and small. "This corridor is clear. Moving ahead."

"Captain Paixon." The hologram of Jarama was back suddenly, materializing half-in and half-out of one of the spare consoles. Things must be going badly for the Corvids. I'd never seen them make a mistake like that.

"What's happening?"

"The Chron have improved at bypassing our asteroid

defences," the Corvid said, and his hologram and Fha's both wavered as the station took another hit.

"No kidding," I muttered. "Does this happen a lot?"

Neither of the Corvids answered for a long moment. Then Jarama said, "The frequency is gradually increasing. Although we continually change our algorithms, it does not seem to—"

His voice cut off, but the hologram remained visible, its beak-like mouth moving silently.

"Afraid I'm no good at beak-reading," Baden said, but there was little humour in his voice.

"Lift mechanism is not working, I'm taking the central stairwell down." Yuskeya's voice sounded thin and noisy with static. The Corvids used circular stairwells to physically connect upper and lower levels. No doubt there was some feature of their mysterious anatomy that made ladders inconvenient.

"Tell the *Airavata* we're doing what we can to locate the others," I told Baden. "They should prepare to leave the station at a moment's notice, with or without them. We have to be ready, whatever happens."

The next minute stretched as if we clung to the rim of a black hole, elongating into nothingness punctuated only by the dull reverberations of strikes and launches. Yuskeya didn't report in again.

"Yuskeya?" I said over the comm. "Where are you now?"

With a loud buzz of static, Jarama's voice reasserted itself in sync with his hologram.

"Captain, we believe we should release your ships now, so that you have a chance to make it back to your Nearspace and alert the others. Also, we cannot continue to guarantee your safety docked here."

A chance?

I found myself out of my chair, although I didn't remember standing up. "I sent one of my crew to search for the three missing people. They're still somewhere on the *uruglat*."

And now it's four.

"We . . . care for them," Fha said, the audio breaking up. "Must strengthen . . . *at* . . . releas . . . ships." Her hologram winked out.

"What about the Chron? If they come after us?"

Maja left her seat and came to stand on the other side of my chair, face pale but determined. "I can take the navigation board."

"We will try to keep them engaged, or destroy them," Jarama said. His hologram had stabilized as Fha's disappeared. "Remember that your activator drive can be used to shut down ships following you too closely."

Hirin nodded. He'd probably thought of that already. "Unfortunately, the drive can't disable torps or other weapons they might fire at us."

"Is your ship ready to release, Captain?"

"No!" Viss protested, but I glanced at Rei and Hirin, who both nodded.

"We don't want to abandon our people, but we can safely leave," I said, trying to keep my voice steady. "Good luck, Jarama. Someone will return as soon as possible. Someone better able to help you." *The whole damned Protectorate fleet, if necessary.*

"And to you, Captain," he said gravely, and disappeared.

The ship lurched again, and Maja clutched at my arm to keep her balance.

"This is a mistake," Viss said with an unaccustomed timbre of despair in his voice. "We shouldn't leave them."

"We don't have a choice," I said, my voice sharper than I intended. "If the Corvids have to release us to save their station, we can't stop them. They'll look after Yuskeya and the others."

"If they can," Viss rasped. "*Christos*, what a mess."

The ship canted slowly to one side, and Maja and I both clutched at the command chair to stay upright. A loud sucking noise surrounded us, and then the station retracted from the *Tane Ikai*, leaving no trace of itself on the ports or viewscreens. Someday I really wanted to know what kind of material that thing was made of. Right now, though, I had more pressing things to think about.

WE EMERGED ON a side of the station that was, for the moment, free of any ships but ourselves and the Council launch.

"*Airavata* is asking for instructions," Baden said.

"Tell them to make for the wormhole back to Nearspace with all speed," I said. "We'll follow and protect them. I'm assuming the Corvids weren't too busy to send us both the nav coordinates to get through the asteroid field."

"Got them," Rei confirmed, her fingers skating over the piloting board.

"*Airavata* confirms that they do as well," Baden said.

"Let them know the Corvids will take care of our people," I instructed, silently hoping I was right about that.

"Four Chron ships in the system," Hirin reported. He'd slid into the secondary navigation console until Maja could get her feet under her enough to cross to Yuskeya's board. "Debris that would account for a fifth. They're on the other side of the station. A number of the small Corvid vessels are harrying them."

"Then let's get out of here while they're busy," I said. "Rei, make for the wormhole. Keep us just behind the *Airavata*. Hirin, let's have torps loaded into the rear firing tubes just in case."

I reached across the chair and gripped Maja's arm. "You can do this."

She nodded once, her eyes very blue and dark with worry. She pulled free of my hand and crossed quickly to the nav board, letting Hirin move to his usual place. Her fingers moved into the unfamiliar routine on the board without hesitation, and she kept her eyes on her screen.

"Viss."

"Captain?" He didn't look around at me.

"*Viss.*"

That time his eyes met mine. Dark and angry.

"We'll come back for them. Or the Protectorate will. I promise."

He pressed his lips together in a straight, flat line, but nodded once before he turned back to the board.

The *Tane Ikai* pushed away from the station under the maneuvering drives, following the Council launch. I checked the rear viewscreen to assess damage to the station, my heart pounding out a Morse code that said *this is wrong, this is wrong, go back*. It felt cowardly, disgraceful, running away when the Corvids could be in trouble, when four of our complement were still back there. Realistically, though, I didn't know what we could do to help. We were armed, but the *Airavata* was not, and our mission was to protect them. The *uruglat* looked the same as it had when we arrived, but considering its nature, that didn't necessarily mean anything.

"*Airavata* has engaged their burst drive," Rei announced. "Kicking ours over now too." The two ships shot forward, covering the yawn of dark space that separated us from the relative safety of the wormhole.

We were only halfway there when Maja said in a clipped voice, "One of the Chron ships has broken away to follow us. Corvid runners are in pursuit."

"On it," Hirin said, before I could even give him an order. Since we were technically "sharing" the captainship of the *Tane Ikai* now, I couldn't complain.

"Try the activator drive?"

Hirin nodded. "It's worked before." We'd managed to stop a Chron ship that way a few weeks ago, when it was determined to stop us from returning to Nearspace. I hoped that hadn't been a fluke.

"You'll only get one shot." I knew I didn't have to remind him. The device needed time to recharge after every use. It wasn't intended as a weapon, only as an activator for the mechanism that allowed wormholes to be temporarily duplicated and their endpoints manipulated. Corvid technology that the Chron had appropriated from them a long time ago. But the Corvids had told us that firing the drive at another ship had the happy side effect of shutting down just about any kind of drive system and disrupting internal electronics. If your main objective was to stop your enemy from increasing speed or making any evasive maneuvers, you just had to get your aim right and try for a direct hit. On the one chance you had.

Like I said, not intended as a weapon.

They fired on us, but the torpedo faded right and went wide. Rei did her best to keep us moving at a good speed while maneuvering enough that we didn't make an easy target, either.

"Firing," Hirin said. "I hope I don't catch any of the Corvids with it."

"Take the chance. They know we have the device and that we're likely to use it."

There was no flash, no visual indication that we'd fired anything at all. The only other time we'd used it, I'd been so close to unconscious that I wouldn't have noticed if it had shot flaming balls of gas at the enemy. But I saw what I needed to see. The Chron ship behind us didn't stop, since all we'd done was shut down the drives. The effect couldn't apply any brakes or counter-force. But suddenly they weren't gaining on us anymore, and they were simply hurtling along in a straight trajectory, no maneuvering. Their drives had to be down.

Rei whooped once and Baden pushed a fist into the air. Ahead of us, the *Airavata* neared the asteroid field guarding the mouth of the wormhole.

"Stay as close as you can, but give us enough room to maneuver here," I told Rei.

"*Airavata* says they're switching to autopilot so the computer can follow the safe navigation coordinates," Baden reported.

"Doing the same," Rei said. The field of rolling, tumbling asteroids loomed large ahead, and I stifled an involuntary gasp as the *Airavata* disappeared into the chaos, seemingly avoiding one of the grey stone behemoths by inches.

A flash on the rear viewscreen drew my attention.

The Corvid runners must have taken advantage of the Chron ship's sudden vulnerability. The flash was a Corvid energy weapon, blowing the Chron ship to bits.

The bridge went unusually silent. I felt a thick knot of guilt twist in my stomach. I knew the Chron in that ship would have done the same thing to us if they'd had a chance. It didn't make me feel better. We'd slowed them down, and the Corvids had taken them out. Far in the distance, Chron and Corvid ships buzzed around the Corvid station like angry insects. I wondered how long the battle would go on, and when it would be safe to return.

As we reached the wormhole, Maja said quietly, "If the Chron have gotten better at bypassing those asteroid fields, how long is it going to take them to get to Nearspace?"

I shook my head. "Not long, I'm afraid. Not long at all. And we have to get the others back before they do."

Chapter 3 — Lanar
Wheels Within Wheels

I MUST HAVE been feeling guilty after I sent Luta off on her mission for the Protectorate, because I decided that my next task, after meeting with Harle Southwind at lunchtime, would be to see what I could do to shake up the PrimeCorp investigation. I also knew I wouldn't be able to simply sit around FarView Station while Luta and her crew were away. Although I had utter faith in her abilities, she worried me. She often took chances without thinking enough about the consequences, but I rarely mentioned it. It only led to arguments I seldom won. So most of the time I kept my worries to myself and my mind otherwise engaged.

Although Luta had brought back considerable evidence of PrimeCorp's transgressions, both past and present, the reports had met with a good deal of skepticism. Even some factions within the Protectorate found it difficult to credit, and PrimeCorp's Council ambassadors issued flat out denials. As soon as the investigation had officially launched, a flock of PrimeCorp lawyers had filed motions and set up legal obstacles to try and block it. So far they'd refused to comply with demands for access to their internal files and had denied any knowledge of the men and women Luta had seen in the Chron system wearing PrimeCorp uniforms. And despite having their pictures and ID implant data, we'd failed to tie them to PrimeCorp through the Nearspace database. Either they weren't connected, which I found unlikely, or PrimeCorp had managed to keep the connections secret. PrimeCorp claimed they were being set up—by a rival corporation, or perhaps even by the Protectorate itself. The PrimeCorp drive signatures Luta had recorded could be explained away as stolen parts, or refurbished PrimeCorp ships that had been decommissioned and sold to private buyers.

There were plenty of damning things in the files Jahelia Sord had stolen from the PrimeCorp Main computers, and we'd let them know we had some of them. The PrimeCorp lawyers were kicking up a huge fuss about the provenance of those files, but we'd declined to comment, letting them stew. They didn't know we had the Chron-Esper dictionary dating back to the time of the first Chron war, or where it had come from. I'd advised that we hold that back even from the Council for now, and Regina Holles and the other Fleet Commanders had agreed. It was one thing to accuse PrimeCorp of not reporting exploration results and interacting with alien species outside Nearspace, but to accuse them of starting the Chron War? We needed more information before we showed our hand on that.

Harle showed up right on time and I welcomed him into my quarters. He'd worn his usual impeccable uniform—Lobor officers tended to consider themselves "on duty" unless they were on official leave, and rarely dressed in casual clothes outside their own quarters. He'd brought a warm loaf of *gada*, a dark, seeded Lobor bread, and we settled in to a lunch of albondigas, a meatball soup I knew Harle particularly liked. As Harle had requested, I'd set out a bottle of deep purple *jarlees* wine. With my mother now living on Kiando with the Chairman of the planet's governing corporation, I was always likely to have a supply of the local delicacy on hand. We broke the *gada* into chunks, Lobor-style, and ate for a few minutes, talking about inconsequentials. Then Harle got to the point of the meeting.

"Remember a few months back, I told you we were looking at something possibly big happening with PrimeCorp?" he asked, setting down his soup spoon with a satisfied sigh.

"I remember," I said. "I've wondered about it even more

since Luta brought back her revelations."

He nodded. "I don't know yet if they're related, but I wouldn't be surprised. We've been watching some interesting movements in former PrimeCorp executives over the past five years or so."

"What do you mean?" I put my wineglass down and leaned forward with my elbows straddling my empty bowl.

He considered, seeming to choose his words carefully. "It's nothing overt," he said, "but a pattern that made us take notice. Executives, some fairly high up on the corporate ladder, would leave PrimeCorp and almost immediately take up positions with another, rival corporation."

I frowned. "That's a little odd. When an exec leaves, aren't they usually bound by a non-compete clause? I thought that was pretty standard."

"Exactly," he said, nodding. "No-one wants former employees taking secrets to a rival. But these exec movements are out of the ordinary," he continued. "When they take a new position, it's at a rival corporation, but always at a division that just manages to squeak around some very particular language in the PrimeCorp non-competition agreement."

"What kind of language?"

"It comes down to an exclusion that extends to business interests that correlate closely to the position they're leaving, but leave the field open for interests that deal with a different business sector."

I nodded slowly. "So someone leaving, say, a mining division, couldn't go to work for a rival mining division, but they could go to work for a pharmaceutical division? But most corporations wouldn't forbid that, would they? Whatever mining operation knowledge someone might leave here with is not really going to benefit a pharmaceutical operation."

"No, but according to the standards that most Nearspace corps apply, they'd usually be precluded from taking a related position—like our mining operation post, for example—for a minimum of five years, if not more, right?"

I sipped wine and nodded. "Five years seems reasonable. But I think it's possible to get a court to overturn that if it's deemed too restrictive on a person's ability to make a living."

"Right. So, what if I told you the PrimeCorp clause says six months," Harle said, leaning forward and putting his lightly furred hands on the table, "and what if I told you further that all of these execs, within a year or two of moving to the new corporation, somehow manage to transfer to divisions where they *do* have knowledge and experience, and also end up in a more powerful position than the one they started out in?"

"Hmm. Six months is short, and that does seem sort of coincidental. How many people are we talking about, here?"

"Over the past five years, across all divisions, twenty-seven."

"Twenty-seven? That's too many coincidences!" I said.

Harle leaned back and tapped the leathery pads of his fingers together. "I know. It's suspicious. For PrimeCorp to lose that many high-level execs should be pretty devastating. But they've obviously taken it in stride."

"We are talking very upper level?"

He nodded.

"But for them all to end up that quickly in powerful positions where they have experience . . . why would PrimeCorp make the non-compete period so short? That seems counterintuitive to their interests."

"The Protectorate has a theory," he said. He pushed his chair back from the table and stood, then slowly paced the width of the room. As he walked with his slightly bouncing gait, he also bounced an index finger off his lips.

"If you plan to go to war with someone, what's one of the first things you might want to do?" he mused, then answered his own question. "Put spies where they can find out the enemy's weaknesses and vulnerabilities. *To know your Enemy, you must become your Enemy.* So, imagine if those twenty-seven execs weren't fired, and didn't quit. PrimeCorp has a pretty good record of holding on to its upper-level folks. Imagine if they left for some other reason."

I tapped my fingertips together, then joined him at the viewwall, where he'd stopped pacing. "You're saying the terminations could be in the interests of a greater good—that is, putting people loyal to PrimeCorp inside its rivals." From here, we could look down along the hub of FarView Station, windows winking on every level, launches and ships gliding slowly to and from the docking arms. "But—PrimeCorp spying on its rivals? Sorry to break it to you, Harle, but there's nothing *terribly* unusual in that."

"The numbers are unusual," he observed mildly. "But here's the other wrinkle. In the time since each of those executives has made the internal move, a couple of other things have also happened. Each one has had direct influence on subsequent hirings and firings in their divisions. And key positions on the Boards of Directors have also changed in each of those companies, and in all cases—*all* of them—the new Directors have some connection to the moved executive. Sometimes you have to dig pretty deep to find that connection," he said, "but in every case, it's there."

"Hmm," I said. "*Okej.* That takes us outside the boundaries of coincidence."

The Lobor nodded. "That looks like someone is plotting internal corporate takeovers. And that's just the stuff we *know* about." He turned away from the view wall to face me, ears pricked forward. His rounded, canine eyes, dark brown and luminous in the small space, were very, very serious. "And although this may sound very conspiracy-theory-ish, imagine how much easier it would be to effect those takeovers if everyone was distracted because Nearspace was embroiled in a war with the Chron?"

I felt something stir in my gut. "*Merde.* Harle, are you serious? What could they hope to gain?"

"You're right. A war shouldn't benefit them," he said, "because PrimeCorp depends on a stable business environment across all of Nearspace, just like any other corporation. So, we still don't understand how that all fits together."

It was my turn to pace, connections lighting up inside my brain. "But the fighting with the Chron acts as a distraction, while PrimeCorp quietly takes control of all these other corporations or divisions of corporations. If they can get planetary control, they can replace that world's ambassador with one of their own choosing—"

"—and once they have enough ambassadors in the Council, they essentially control Nearspace," Harle Southwind finished in a tight voice. "The few corporations that might be left, and the autonomous and Authority-governed worlds, wouldn't be enough to outvote them on anything."

I stopped pacing. "But to collaborate with the Chron and

bring war to Nearspace? That's—that's treason."

"Agreed," Harle said, his ears flattening. His lips drew away from his teeth in a snarl. "But if they control the Council, who's going to prosecute them?"

I took a deep breath and blew it out, contemplating the very different Nearspace Harle had just conjured into the realm of possibility. "So, what do we do? You heard Regina. We can't go after the Chron militarily—unless you have enough evidence to move against PrimeCorp?"

"Not yet. Much of this is supposition, coming up with a theory that makes sense of all the pieces. But this is why I wanted to talk to you. Fleet Commander Holles suggested it."

"What can I do?"

The Lobor shrugged in a very human gesture, spreading his hands wide, leathery palms facing up. "I don't know, exactly. But Regina says you and your family—you've got history with PrimeCorp. She thought you might be able to help. We need more details. We've tried to get someone on the inside, but apart from people they move out themselves, PrimeCorp is locked up tighter than a Protectorate brig." He sighed and let his hands drop. "I don't know. I'm just asking for ideas."

Mother, I thought. That's who might be able to help, and that's why Regina had made the suggestion.

Harle handed me a datachip. "That's the list of corporations who have hired on ex-PrimeCorp execs, and the names of the execs themselves. I thought it might be useful to you."

I looked out the view wall again, tucking the datachip absently into my pocket. The station looked so peaceful, so quiet against the backdrop of space, even though I knew that within its reinforced walls, thousands of people went busily and unsuspectingly about their business. People the Protectorate had a duty to look after.

"Leave it with me, Harle," I said finally. "I'll have to think about it a bit."

"Or course. And Lanar—keep this entirely between us, all right. We're still suspicious that information is leaking somewhere."

"A mole? In the Protectorate?"

Harle shrugged. "I'm not saying that for sure. But . . . we can't let PrimeCorp know how much we suspect. We have to play this close to the chest."

I nodded. "Whatever you say, Harle. And I'm sure we'll come up with something."

He turned to survey the station as well. "We have to, Lanar. And soon."

AFTER MY DISCUSSION with Harle Southwind, the best place to start was to pay Mother a visit. She might not have called in all her inside sources at PrimeCorp when she decided to stop hiding her research data, so it was possible she'd still have a contact there who might have knowledge of use to us. But it wasn't the kind of question you ask over FTL WaVe, no matter how good your encryption is.

Unfortunately, I couldn't head straight out to talk to Mother in person. I sent an inter-system message to make certain she was at home and found out that she wasn't. She'd finally gone to Damyadi Station, to consult with representatives of the Schulyer Group about their new anti-aging technology. She was expected back in five days.

So, I had almost a week to fill. I didn't want to spend it worrying about Luta, so I filed a routine patrol route that would keep us actively watching for signs of Chron trouble, gave my crew six hours' notice that we were leaving, and got underway. I took along copies of all the datachips of information we had concerning PrimeCorp and their activities, as well as the one Harle had given me. No matter how much time I spent poring over them, though, nothing new leaped out at me.

Our route brought the *Cheswick* finally around to Mu Cassiopeia and the planet Kiando. Although the main colonies on Kiando were built around heavy metal mining operations for the Duntmindi Corporation, much of the planet was still untouched wilderness. The other major industry was wine-making with the native *jarlee* fruit, but neither of those had brought my mother to the planet. It was the anti-aging research sponsored by Gusain Buig, head of Duntmindi's operations on the planet and elsewhere. And after she'd met the Chairman, her relationship with the man himself. I was glad to see her happy again after all her sacrificed years spent evading PrimeCorp.

As soon as we skipped through into Mu Cassiopeia, I put the

call through to Mother. I had to leave a message, but she pinged back within half an hour from her office in Gusain Buig's house. "Lanar! I heard a rumour you were looking for me. What brings you?" she asked, green hazel eyes shining as she leaned close to the screen with a smile. She held up an admonishing finger. "I hope it's not all business. Sometimes a son should just come and visit his mother because he loves her, you know."

I grinned. "If I tell you how much I love you, can I sneak in just a little bit of business, too?"

She sat back from the screen and crossed her arms in mock annoyance. "I suppose, if you must. Will you join us for dinner?"

"That would be great. We should arrive just in time and I'll come down in the launch."

"I'll tell Gusain. He'll be pleased to see you too." She closed the connection with a little finger wave and a smile.

I still find the resemblance between Mother and Luta disconcerting. The nanobioscavengers have held them at nearly the same physical age, and although the similarity is not that of identical twins, they could be sisters. I hadn't counted on my worries about Luta being triggered by seeing Mother, so I changed my clothes and went down to the workout room for a bit of physical distraction to fill some of the four hours until we reached the planet.

Gusain Buig's home sits on the outskirts of Ando City, the planetary capital, more a mansion than a mere house. Among its many accoutrements is a personal landing pad plenty big enough to accommodate the ship's boat from the *S. Cheswick*. The pilot brought us in low over the mining fields studded like giant footprints across the continent's arid deserts. Occasionally a splash of bright, verdant green signaled an oasis, or rippling blue announced one of the many small seas. On the outskirts of the city, terraced hills hosted row upon row of pale, burgundy-veined leaves of *jarlee* vines trailing over arched trellises. The city itself boasted few very tall buildings, since the first settlers had opted to build downward as much as up. The Ando City region tended to extremes of temperature, so the inhabitants wanted cool havens in the summer heat and warm sanctuaries from winter's bite. For a community of miners, going underground made perfect sense. I gave the sergeant who piloted me down leave to head into town for his own supper, an offer he gladly accepted. The food on the *Cheswick* is good, but it's not exactly restaurant fare.

Mother greeted me at the door. Her auburn hair, a little lighter than Luta's, was braided and coiled on top of her head, and she wore a long green sweater, jeans, and soft knee-high boots. Long earrings, tiny jade stones dangling from fine silver chains, hung almost to her shoulders. To the casual observer she wouldn't look much older than I did, but when I leaned in to kiss her cheek the lines around her eyes and mouth were more visible. Worry, rather than age, was responsible for most of them.

As I kissed her cheek she hugged me tightly. "So good to see you," she said, almost a whisper. She'd never be able to make up for the seventy years she'd spent separated from us, running from PrimeCorp and hoping we'd have normal lives without her, but at least the unique circumstances of our longevity meant she had a chance to try.

She released me from the hug, tucking her arm through mine to lead me into the house. "Dinner's ready," she said. "Can the business part of the visit wait until after that?"

"Absolutely," I told her.

"How's Luta? Have you talked to her lately?"

"She seems to be fully recovered." The truth, if not the whole truth. Guilt gave me a nudge in the gut. I'd asked Luta to keep her mission quiet, and then gone to see Mother without thinking that I'd have to lie about it myself.

"And you? No problems with your bioscavs?" She craned her head sideways, studying me as we walked, as if she could tell by looking if the tiny machines in my body were causing any problems. Who knew, maybe she could.

I chuckled. "Not that I can tell. I still run on the treadmill when the vastness of space gets boring, and I don't seem to suffer any ill effects."

"Good." She nodded in satisfaction.

"So, you went to see Schulyer Group? Did you visit their labs? Examine their research?"

After many years and ongoing research by more than one corporation and lab, it seemed that another anti-aging breakthrough might be on the horizon. Mother's research, carried out by her team at PrimeCorp three-quarters of a century ago, was to date the only successful method for halting the aging process—and because of ethical concerns, she'd fought to keep the technology out of the hands of anyone at all in that time. It lived in a handful of us, and that was all. Thirty years ago, Nicadico Corporation had released a treatment they called Longate, but it had been an unmitigated disaster. After several courses of treatment, patients invariably succumbed to cascading organ failure, and the subsequent investigation unearthed any number of bribes, deceptions, and deficiencies in the testing protocols. No one had tried again until PrimeCorp launched its Vigor-Us treatment ten years after that, but that wasn't true anti-aging, just a rejuvenation process that could effect some health and appearance benefits.

Then Schulyer Group had approached Mother, with the revelation that they had arrived at a new treatment—one that built on and improved Longate, fixing its myriad flaws. They wanted her to vet their research and make sure it was sound before they proceeded to human trials.

And so poor Mother found herself faced with the same ethical dilemma she'd battled for decades now. Could one corporation be trusted to fairly administer the secret of immortality for all, and were we, as a species, even ready for that knowledge? She'd known PrimeCorp couldn't be trusted and had sacrificed a normal life and family to keep the research out of their hands. But somehow Luta had convinced her that she no longer needed to be the guardian of the fate of humankind; that by keeping the research to herself, she'd effectively placed herself in the same position she didn't want PrimeCorp to occupy. And so she'd decided to release her own research data to the public and let PrimeCorp come after her through the legal system if they wished. As far as I knew, they hadn't made a move to do so yet.

Luckily for her, PrimeCorp was going to be a little busy in the next while. She might not have anything to worry about.

She pulled a deep breath and let it out. "It's . . . promising," she said, bringing me back to the present. "I think I can offer some suggestions, but their data looks good. I brought back a bag full of encrypted datachips to read and study, and then we'll schedule another meeting."

We turned a corner and the dining room came into view.

Chairman Gusain Buig stood near a fireplace, head bent to read something on the datapad he held. He turned when we entered the room and flashed a warm smile, then set the datapad on the mantel. He clasped his hands together and set them over his heart, then bent forward in two quick bows, the standard Kiandon greeting. Buig stood an easy six feet tall, and had dressed as casually as Mother had this evening, in a cozy-looking pullover the same icy-blue as his eyes, and black denim jeans. His greying hair betrayed him as no longer exactly young, but his face was warm and his smile genuine as he extended a hand toward a tray waiting on the sideboard. I wondered for the first time if Mother had dosed him with nanobioscavengers yet, and immediately assumed she had.

"You'll have some *jarlees* wine before supper?" he asked, although it wasn't really a question. Few humans or Lobors turned down an offer of the delicacy, although it had never really taken off with Vilisians.

"And with supper as well, if I'm lucky," I said with a smile. I was glad I'd opted to change out of my Protectorate uniform and into something more casual before leaving the *Cheswick*.

Although I'd been here only a few weeks ago, we managed to fill the time before dinner and over the meal with catching up on personal news and discussing the latest developments in Nearspace. It turned out that Gusain and Mother knew more than I'd expected about the information Luta had brought back with her from what we'd all started informally calling "Otherspace." It made sense; Gusain was, after all, the top executive of Duntmindi, and Duntmindi had three ambassadors on the Nearspace Worlds Administrative Council, one for each of the planets the corporation controlled. It just hadn't occurred to me that the ambassadors would report so fully to the corporation's Chairman.

"I can't say I feel any sympathy for PrimeCorp, or for Alin Sedmamin," Buig said as we sipped spicy chai over rich, whipped-cream topped apple-*jarlees* pastries. "I find it hard to believe even they would consort with Chron, but the evidence seems irrefutable."

"PrimeCorp isn't ready to admit to that."

He nodded. "I've heard they're denying all involvement. Explaining away the ships as no longer associated with them, the logos on the attackers being an attempt at a set-up . . .”

I tilted my head at him and shrugged. He was right; that was exactly what they were saying. “Do *you* believe any of that?”

He flashed a humourless grin. “Not for a second. But I wish I could. I don’t like the alternative. That they could be collaborating with known enemies of Nearspace.”

“They’re slowing the investigation,” I said. “If there’s a possibility that those Chron are heading for Nearspace, we need to know everything we can about them as soon as possible.”

Mother tapped her fork absently on the rim of her plate, gazing into the distance. “What I don’t understand,” she said pensively, “is, if the Chron really are planning a renewed assault on Nearspace, why would PrimeCorp be involved? The corporation’s interests are tied to a healthy and prosperous business environment all through Nearspace. Wouldn’t war adversely affect that?”

Buig sipped coffee. “Maybe. But if you read Earth history, there were times when a war actually boosted an economy. Not that the cost in lives could provide justification for starting or prolonging a war, but economies often came out improved overall.”

“I can’t believe even PrimeCorp could sink that low,” Mother said, shaking her head. “And I could believe almost anything about them.”

I ate the last bite of the delicious pastry and chased it with a sip of chai. Possibly the best I’d ever had. I’d ask Gusain later where he got it. Yuskeya Blue loved chai, and I’d pass the name along to her. “Well, that’s one of the reasons I’m here,” I said. “See if you can believe this.” As briefly as I could—although it wasn’t a simple situation—I relayed what Harle Southwind had told me about the movements of PrimeCorp executives and the possibility that PrimeCorp was eyeing a Nearspace political coup.

By the time I’d finished, both Gusain and Mother had leaned forward in their chairs. Gusain frowned. “I wonder if we’ve hired anyone ex-PrimeCorp lately,” he said speculatively. “I don’t think so, but I wouldn’t necessarily know about every hire.”

I shrugged. “You might want to check into that, but you didn’t hear any of this from me.”

"This sounds like exactly the kind of thing PrimeCorp would do," Mother said, "but I'm not sure how it ties into working with the Chron." She rested her chin on her hands, eyes fixed on the remains of our dinner but not, I expected, really seeing it. Her lips compressed into a thin line, relaxed, compressed again. "Collaborating with the Chron to attack Nearspace, in an elaborate scheme to usurp the political power here? That's monstrous. Even for PrimeCorp, that's monstrous."

I spread my hands. "We don't know that's what's happening. And I don't know how PrimeCorp could extricate itself from a Chron alliance later—or why they think they could trust the aliens. But we see it as a possibility."

Mother stood and moved to stand behind Gusain's chair, settling her hands lightly on his shoulders as if seeking comfort from the contact. "All right. What can we do about it?"

That "we" made me chuckle. "I'm not sure 'we' are going to do much, but *I* came here to ask you a question," I said. "We need information more than anything else. I wondered if you might still have any contacts, anyone at all, inside the workings anywhere at PrimeCorp. I know you got your research connections out when we took PrimeCorp to court on Vele, but is there anyone else?"

She raised her eyebrows and tilted her head to one side, considering. "Someone who could act as a spy?"

I grimaced. "I hesitate to use that particular word, even in this most confidential company," I said. "But someone who might have the ability and the willingness to collect information PrimeCorp is trying to block us from, yes."

She clasped her hands behind her back and paced away from us. The dining table would seat twenty guests easily, but we'd clustered at one end of the gleaming expanse of polished dark wood. She walked the length of it, then turned and came back. When she reached her chair, she stopped. "I still have a few contacts," she said cautiously. "But I'm not sure any of them would be willing or able to do this. I'd have to know more about the kind of access you'd need. Even then, I might not know them well enough to ask them to take the risk."

I rubbed the back of my neck and nodded. "It is a lot to ask, and not worth it if you weren't sure they could get access." I reached into my pocket for a datachip case and selected the one

Harle had given me. "Go over this when you have time," I said. "There are more details about the executives and divisions involved."

Mother held out her hand and I dropped the chip into it. I felt my shoulders start to droop and pulled them back with an effort. I didn't want Mother to feel bad about this. "It's all right if you can't help. You were just one of the names on my list. We'll find another way."

She smiled and pocketed the chip. "I'll take a look and get back to you about it as soon as I can."

"I hear rumblings that Alin Sedmamin might be out of a job soon," Gusain Buig said with a wry smile. "Maybe he'll be willing to go rogue and help you out."

"Really? I figured he'd be throwing some other poor sucker to the wolves. That seems to be his style."

Gusain shrugged. "Maybe the Board has finally decided he's more of a liability than an asset. Or maybe he wouldn't get on board with the plan you've suggested."

"I'd be surprised if anything was too dark for his scruples," I said, draining what was left of my chai. It had gone dead cold, but it wasn't unpleasant even that way. "And even if it were an issue for him, I'd expect to see him wind up dead, not simply fired. If that's what they're really up to, it's far too big to risk him spilling everything at this point."

"Well, the rumour mills grind exceedingly hard where PrimeCorp is concerned lately," he said. "There might be nothing to it at all."

Gusain's datapad chimed and he retrieved it from the mantel, a frown pulling his brows together when he read the screen.

"Priority communication for you, Lanar," he said, passing the datapad to me. "Must be pretty serious for your ship to use the inter-gov channel to reach you."

"I let the pilot leave the ship's boat and go into town," I said, taking the device. "He probably shut down the onboard orbital relay."

I keyed in my passcode and the message appeared on the screen.

Received: from [205485.62.08] Nearspace Protectorate Authority FarView Stn Admin
STATIC ELECTRONIC MESSAGE: 26.2

Encryption:
securetext/novis/noaud/npalock/CONFIDENTIAL
Receipt notification: enabled
CONFIRMATION REQUIRED
*From: "Fleet Admiral Regina Holles" <rholles.npaFA*web>*
To: "Admiral Lanar Mahane" <ID 54298654213npa>
Date: Wed, 20 Feb 2285 12:30:01 -0400

Lanar
Corvid station attacked while Luta and envoys docked. Ambassador Andresson, LC Jolah Didkovsky, LC Emar Summergale, and Cmdr Yuskeya Blue stranded. Others returned okay. Return to FarView stat.
Regina

I felt a hot, prickling feeling creep up the backs of my arms, and my stomach went suddenly leaden—nothing to do with the dinner we'd eaten.

"Lanar? What's wrong?"

My shock must have shown on my face. "Trouble, naturally," I said, quickly closing the message and handing the datapad back to Gusain. I stood too quickly, tipping my chair, and had to catch the back of it to keep it from falling. "Occupational hazard, I'm afraid. Recalled in the middle of fun."

"What kind of trouble?" Mother was not buying my attempts to keep it light. She came around the table and put a hand on my arm. In the mirror set into the wall above the fireplace, I could see both mine and Mother's reflections, and we looked more like siblings than mother and son. *But she wasn't my sister; Luta was. And I'd sent her into danger.*

"I'm not entirely sure yet," I told her, and squeezed her hand. "They'll fill me in when I get there."

I thumbed my implant and called the sergeant. "Hope you're finished your supper," I said. "We have to return to the ship immediately. Tell me where you are and I'll come to you."

I heard his muffled voice talking to someone in the

background, and then he rattled off a street address.

"There aren't many places downtown where you'll fit that vessel," Gusain said. "Let me send a driver for him, and you wait here."

That made more sense, but I knew I couldn't stay with Mother to wait. She'd badger me until I'd told her every detail, and I'd end up revealing how I'd unwittingly sent Luta into danger.

"Thanks, Gusain. I'll head to the landing pad and get all the prelims out of the way so we can take off as soon as he gets here." He nodded and hurried out of the room.

Without waiting for her to argue with me, I pulled Mother into a quick hug. "Thanks for dinner," I said, planting a quick kiss on her cheek. "I'll be in touch soon."

She grasped my arms firmly as I tried to disengage. "You're not telling me everything, but *okej*," she said. Her eyes were darkly serious. "I'll think about what you asked, and go over the data. Maybe there's someone who could help . . . I'll just have to give it some thought."

I nodded. "We'll talk soon, I promise."

"And I'll find out what you're trying to hide," she said, one side of her mouth twisting into a half-smile. "*I* promise."

"Love you," I said, and fled to my ship.

THE TRAVEL TIME between Kiando and FarView was a full twenty-three hours at normal speeds. I had Linna Drake run the burst drive at full capacity, and that shaved a few hours off the time. When we arrived at FarView, Regina met me herself at the airlock when the *Cheswick* docked. "Luta and the others are fine," she reiterated as soon as she saw me. Maybe something in my face made her think she had to remind me.

"What happened?" I asked, as we strode toward her office. "Luta wouldn't willingly leave anyone behind, especially not Yuskeya. I sometimes wonder if I'll be able to convince her to let Yuskeya leave the *Tane Ikai* at all."

Regina puffed, almost jogging to keep up with me. I hadn't realized how I was barrelling along the corridor and slowed my steps for her. Not only were her legs shorter, but she was effectively a lot older than I was. Not that she'd ever, in a million years, ask me to slow down for her.

"She didn't have a choice. The Corvids had to release the ships from the station in order to protect themselves, and Yuskeya had gone into the station to find Andresson and the others. Then the Chron ships went after them, too, and they barely managed to get through the wormhole. The *Tane Ikai* took some damage—not much, nothing too serious—but enough that it wasn't safe for them to stay in the system. They're back here now and yes, we'll foot the bill for all repairs."

"But Yuskeya and the others were fine when Luta had to leave?"

She didn't answer right away, and I stopped walking. "Regina?"

She sighed. "I don't know. They don't know. The Corvids said they'd take care of them, but there was no actual word from them direct to Luta." She put a hand on my arm. "Lanar, I'm sending you to get them. I know you'd probably insist on it, so let's just skip that step, *okej*?"

Regina smiled tentatively at me and I blew out a deep breath. I was angry, but not at her, and I had to remind myself of that. "*Okej*. So Luta's here?"

"Yes. Go find her, get her to tell you what happened. The envoys are putting their reports together—what they can, although they're distraught—so you'll have all that information to take with you. I know you haven't met the Corvids before, but I trust you in that department. You're the best one to go." She smiled. "And I know you want to."

"Regina, you're the best." I stooped impulsively and kissed her cheek.

She flushed and pretended to brush dust off her jacket. "That is the most disrespectful behaviour—" she blustered. "What if Antar Mauronet had seen *that*, now? Really, Lanar, sometimes I don't know what to do with you." But a smile lurked at the corners of her lips. A little out of sync with the hint of wistfulness in her eyes, and it was my turn to flush.

"You ship out the day after tomorrow," she said, her voice all business again.

"We should probably go—"

She cut me off with a raised palm. "Not until weapons and engineering have a full maintenance cycle. I'm not sending you out unprepared. And you need time to talk to Luta."

I might have argued further, but a look at her face told me there'd be no point and I bit down my reply.

We continued down the corridor in silence and rounded the corner to enter the Protectorate's administrative space. Antar Mauronet waited in the hallway outside Regina's office. His jaw still bore the mottled blue and yellow bruise I'd left there, but he made no attempt to cover it up. He stood half-blocking the door, as if determined to speak with Regina whether she wanted to or not. He almost smirked when he saw us together, obviously thought better of it, and addressed himself to Regina.

"Fleet Commander, I hope recent developments have persuaded you to change your mind," he said, only stepping back at the last moment as Regina didn't pause but kept walking toward the doorway, silently daring him to stop her.

She opened it and stepped inside. Mauronet followed without being invited and I brought up the rear.

"About what, Admiral?" she asked him, continuing through to her office.

"About going after the Chron," he said firmly. "Their aggressive actions show that we can't wait around—"

"Precisely what has changed since our last discussion about this, Admiral?" Regina inquired, lowering herself into her chair. She folded her hands and settled them on the desk in front of her. Her voice was a dangerous calm I knew well, but Mauronet continued, oblivious.

"What—why—the attack on the Corvids!" he blustered in response. "It's clear that Nearspace is next!"

"That may or may not be the case, although—" she held up a hand to stop his next outburst, "—I believe that you're probably right. However, unless you've magically found more ships for the fleet, the problem hasn't changed. We're already spread more thinly than we should be. If we take ships out of Nearspace in an aggressive mission, we leave ourselves open to a flank attack."

"Place ships to cover the operant artifact in Tau Ceti and the Delta Pavonis wormholes leading out of Nearspace," Mauronet said, in a pinched voice that obviously cost him an effort to control. "If we create a bottleneck at the entry points—"

Regina Holles suddenly slammed both palms down on the surface of her desk with a resounding slap. Mauronet jumped as if the slap had hit him in the face. "*If* those are the only two entry points," she hissed. "*But what if they're not?*"

"Maybe the Authority diplomats have better information about that now," I said, hoping to be a calming force in the face of this rising storm. "If the Corvids have broader intelligence about the Chron movements—they did know about the Tau Ceti wormhole, after all—they might be able to shed more light on what we're facing."

I suppose I should have known better than to put myself in between those two. They both resented my interference, for different reasons. Regina glanced at me coldly, Mauronet with heat. I held up my hands and started to back toward the door.

"Just trying to be helpful. I'll excuse myself if you two want to duke it out. I have to get my ship ready, anyway."

"Ready for what?" Mauronet asked with suspicion.

"Ready to carry out the orders I've given him," Regina snapped, "which are not your concern. Admiral Mahane, you are dismissed. Thank you for your input, and check in with me before you leave the station."

"Of course, Fleet Commander," I said, suitably chastised for making light of the situation happening between them. I closed the door very, very softly as I left the Fleet Commander's office. I didn't start to chuckle until I was sure neither of them would hear me.

Chapter 4 — Luta
Don't Shoot the Messenger

THE DAY AFTER our ignominious escape from the Corvid system, the *Tane Ikai* was in a repair dock at FarView Station, and I was hurrying to meet Lanar. We'd had a chance to tell our stories about what had happened at the Corvid station, and been assured that a rescue mission would be launched soon. I didn't know why it wasn't immediate, but I hoped Lanar might be able to tell me that.

His ship, the Nearspace Protectorate Vessel *S. Cheswick*, was a Pegasus-class cruiser with a crew of fifty, the real workhorse ships of the Protectorate patrol network. They could run surveillance, scout trouble zones, deploy Protectorate troops planetside via its onboard shuttles, or actively participate in battle. Lanar had been in command of this one for ten years now. He could have had a Fleet Commander promotion anytime he wanted, but he'd told me once that he felt more needed and useful on the bridge of the *Cheswick* than he expected to feel anywhere else. Honestly, I was happy to have him stay an *Admiralo*. It meant he could turn up anywhere in Nearspace, sometimes even right where and when I needed him.

FarView was a typical station, catering to both the military and the tourist market, which meant an interesting mix of shops and services. I hadn't had a chance to visit any of those yet, with everything else we had to do, but I wasn't in Lanar's office on his ship very long before I started to think I'd rather be shopping.

"You could have been killed!"

Lanar paced the breadth of his office, just behind the bridge of the *Cheswick*. We both tend to pace when we're agitated or need to think. Must be a genetic thing. I must remember to ask Mother someday whether she does, or Dad did.

I held up a palm. "Hey, you were the one who sent us there, don't forget. I wasn't just randomly joyriding around in the Corvid system for fun."

"I thought it would be safe! You told us the Chron incursions into Corvid space were rare." He obviously wasn't done ranting yet. I just didn't know why I was on the receiving end.

"Well, that's what they said. I guess the Corvids underestimated," I snapped. "Do you think I'm not upset about what happened?"

Lanar looked like he'd snap back, but then something flickered in his eyes. He crossed to where I sat on the smartly-upholstered sofa next to the view wall and took my hands, pulling me to my feet and enveloping me in a hug. "Luta, I'm sorry. I'm mad at myself, not you. I would never have knowingly sent you into danger."

I hugged him back, and said into his shoulder, "What a mess."

"If it's any consolation, the envoys came back with a lot more information about the Chron, from the Corvids. All those gaps in the data are filling in now, thanks to your help." He let me go and moved to the tiny drinks dispenser on a cabinet in the corner. "Double caff?" When I nodded, he pulled a steaming drink for each of us.

I took mine hesitantly, as if I didn't really deserve it, and sat back down. "Some help we were. We came back without four of our people, and we didn't even fire a torp at a Chron ship."

"You weren't there to fight. You did the right thing. You got everyone else back. How's the *Tane Ikai*?"

"She'll be better in two days, they tell me. What happens now?"

He quirked a half-smile. "The *S. Cheswick* ships out the day after tomorrow for the Corvid system."

"Just you? And why the delay?"

Despite the smile, there was no humour in his grey eyes. "They won't send us out without making sure the ship is at one hundred percent. We can't spare any other ships—not when we don't know what the Chron are planning. The Corvids will know we're coming—we'll send a message through the wormhole before we skip through, and with luck they'll send us the coordinates to navigate the asteroids. We go in, collect Yuskeya and the others, and come home. Offering assistance to the Corvids if they need it."

I was squeezing my mug so hard I was afraid I might crumple it. "Is it my fault they're sending you? I mean, because it was your idea to send me?"

Lanar shook his head, looking at me somewhat fiercely. "Absolutely not. I would have volunteered even if Regina hadn't asked me."

"Because it was your idea to send me!"

"Because it's what I *do*," he said. "Stop worrying about it. We'll be back in a few days."

"That sounds like famous last words," I said, but I went on before he could come up with a retort. "But honestly, I had a hunch you might be leading the rescue team, and so did someone else. Viss wants to go with you. I know it's not within Protectorate protocol—"

He held up a hand, stopping me gently. "It's actually not a bad idea. Viss has been there; he knows the system and the aliens."

I frowned. "I told him I doubted you'd go for the idea, because I wouldn't expect Protectorate regulations to let a civilian tag along on a mission like this."

Lanar absently ran a finger over the double row of nine colourful starburst pins on the collar of his uniform, lingering on the ninth purple star, the one that marked him as an Admiral. "Luta, Viss isn't *exactly* like any other civilian."

"You told me before that he wasn't another undercover Protect—"

"He isn't! I was straight with you on that." He stood and crossed to the view wall, staring out toward the main part of the station. The *Cheswick* hung at the dock end of one of the station arms, and from here we could see into the brightly-lit centre hub of the station. A small sea of people moved inside. Women shopping. Parents and kids roaming around wide-eyed. Lobors and Vilisians scattered through the mix. Protectorate officers looking for a fancier meal than they were used to getting in the mess. And maybe some fancier company than they'd had in a while.

"Viss's history with the Protectorate goes a long way back," he said, shoving his free hand deep into the pocket of his pants. "You must have known there was something there, when I had him . . . transporting that illegal PrimeCorp tech for us."

"Smuggling, you mean? On my ship?"

He turned sharply to look at me, but I grinned.

"Don't worry, I already forgave you for that, remember? And yes, I suppose I must have known you wouldn't just pick him randomly. You knew something I didn't."

He nodded. "And I still don't think it's my place to tell you Viss's life history. How many times have you told me how much your crew respects each other's secrets, when I was worried one of them might tell PrimeCorp more about you than you wanted them to know?"

I shrugged. "You're right. I don't need to know."

"But I will tell you that Viss has history with the Protectorate, the kind of history that makes him a welcome addition on board any Protectorate ship. If he wants to come with me to collect Yuskeya, no one is going to have a problem with that."

"I like your use of the word 'collect'. Makes the job sound like a casual jaunt in a rented flitter."

His eyes were serious now. "I wasn't being flippant."

I stood and crossed to him, and he put a comforting arm around my shoulders. "I know. I just want it to go smoothly. And the last foray into that system sure didn't."

We stood for a moment, and then he held me at arm's length. "If Viss comes with me, who's going to run engineering on the *Tane Ikai*? Even if, as I hope, we're only gone for a few days?"

I put my hands on my hips. "Hirin and I ran that ship alone for a long time, if you'll remember. I think we can limp along for a few days, especially since I've got no plans other than a couple of cargo drops. I might go as far as Kiando to visit Mother."

He laughed. "No offense intended! I'm sure you and Hirin

can manage just fine. In fact, you'll probably get along better than I will. Viss will be as cranky as an Erian snowcat, being away from both Yuskeya and your ship."

I didn't want to think too much about the *Tane Ikai* with neither Viss nor Yuskeya aboard.

Lanar continued, "I was just at Mother's, asking her for a favour. She'd be happy to see you."

"What kind of favour? Are you all right?"

He smiled. "Of course, I'm all right. I just wondered if she might still have a contact at PrimeCorp who could help us. We need someone on the inside to look into some things for us."

"But you're not going to tell me exactly what those things are."

"Well . . ."

"Never mind. I'm not going to pump you for classified information. But I will ask if you're going to tell me what happened to your hand?"

"What do you mean?" But his hand twitched inside his pocket, and it was the one I'd seen bruised.

"You were in a fight."

He slid it out and displayed it for me. No sign of the bruises that had spread yellow and purple smudges over his knuckles.

"Big deal. I know about your nanobioscavs, remember?" I said with sarcasm. "Now, tell."

"*Okej*, you win. I . . . had to teach someone a lesson. No, hang on," he said quickly, waving the hand. "That's not really true. I didn't have to do it, and I didn't even plan to do it. I just reacted without thinking."

I crossed my arms and stared at him in my best disapproving-big-sister mode. "That impulsiveness gets you in trouble sometimes."

He chuckled. "Oh yes, and you're the soul of sober second thought."

I chose to take the high ground and ignore that. "So tell me, what did you get impulsive over, and who met the business end of your knuckles?"

Lanar went back to his chair and sat down casually. "That worm, Antar Mauronet. Remember him? He tried to impound the *Tane Ikai* that time you and Hirin helped Sektan Ouvieron catch the smugglers?"

"I'm not likely to forget Mauronet, even if it was something like thirty years ago," I said dryly, returning to my chair, too. "But it does make me think that he probably deserved it. Not bad-mouthing me, was he? I don't think our paths have crossed since then."

"He doesn't seem to like you any better than he did then, but no, it wasn't about you. He made some insinuations about Regina Holles that were uncalled-for. I let him know my thoughts."

My heart twisted a little. For a while I'd thought Lanar and Regina—they seemed so well-suited, I really thought they might make a permanent couple. And it had been the first time I'd seen Lanar truly happy with a woman since Soranna had died. But the Protectorate life doesn't make the best planting ground for long-term relationships to grow. I suspected Lanar still had a soft spot for her, though.

"She came to see me when we docked," I said. "I forgive you for your rash actions if you were defending her. I always liked her."

Lanar pursed his lips. "You know she's a Fleet Commander, don't you? I don't see her much, but she was here on FarView for the meeting where I suggested you go to the Chron system with the diplomats, and she's still here. She and I—well, we'd discussed it beforehand and she was all for it." He smiled. "She always liked you, too, and still does. I know she'd love to see you wearing a Protectorate uniform, though."

I held up a hand. "*Dios* forfend," I said. "I have enough Protectorate trouble as it is."

Lanar's door pinged and he called, "Come in!" When it slid aside, Viss stood in the opening, a duffel bag slung over one shoulder. He'd changed out of his scruffy blue shipsuit and wore wheat-coloured casual pants, military-style boots, and a short, chocolate-toned leather jacket that I didn't think I'd ever seen before. With his salt-and-pepper buzz cut, he could have been an off-duty Protectorate officer.

He grinned at us. "Am I too early?"

I shook my head. "No, the question has been put and answered. You're welcome to go along on the mission. But they're not leaving until the day after tomorrow."

Disappointment flashed across his face, but he came into the room and offered a hand for Lanar to shake. "Admiral, good to see you. Thanks for including me in this. But why the delay?"

"Maintenance cycle. Fleet Commander's orders," Lanar explained briefly. "Good to see you, too, Viss, although I wish the circumstances were different."

Viss shrugged, but his brown eyes were very intense. "We'll get them back." I knew his casual attitude hid a very real concern.

Lanar crossed to the chairs and sat down again, motioning us over to join him. "So, tell me exactly what happened out there this time," he said, adding with a grin, "I promise not to freak out again."

"If you do, I'm walking out and going shopping," I warned him. I looked at Viss, but he nodded, content to let me tell it. "Honestly, I don't know. The Corvids didn't have time—or the inclination—to tell us much about what was happening, just that the Chron were attacking. The Corvids didn't seem prepared for it. It shook up the station, I can tell you that. Jarama—one of the Corvids—said the Chron had breached the asteroid navigation barrier to get into the system, and that they'd figured out a way to bypass it. I guess, although they hadn't said anything to us previously, that this is getting to be a more common occurrence."

Viss chimed in. "The Chron had heavy torps—maybe even something like a ship's cannon. The Corvids said the station wasn't breached, but the Captain's right—it sure was getting shaken up. The Corvids were holding their own, but the battle was still raging around the station when we entered the asteroid field."

"Lanar?"

He looked away from Viss and over at me.

"What's going to happen now?"

He flashed me a smile. "Viss and I are going to go collect our lost sheep from the Corvids, and you're going to get back to business. Or a rest. Whatever works for you."

"I mean, big-picture. Nearspace. Chron."

He stood again and went to the view-wall on the other side of the room. This one wasn't an actual window but a screen, currently showing a feed from the external cameras, stars winking quietly against the dark expanse. "I don't know. I have a bad feeling about the Chron, and about how unprepared we seem to be. And I'm not the only one. You didn't hear this from me, but the Protectorate might be spread too thin to offer an effective resistance if they do come."

"The planets—well, some of them—have security forces. They'll come to the fight, right?"

"We can't count on the five PrimeCorp worlds—we don't know which way they're preparing to jump. And we don't know what other alliances they might have formed. You saw them in Chron space. Something's brewing, and it's killing me that I don't know what it is."

I looked at him closely. "But . . . you have a theory? Intel?"

"Not really. But if the Corvids can't keep the Chron contained, and they've been holding them off all this time—"

He didn't have to finish the thought. And it might be even worse than Lanar was admitting; he might be downplaying the dangers for my sake.

"What's driving them?" I asked, although we hadn't had an answer to that in over a century. "Why can they possibly hate us so much?"

He sighed and ran a hand through his hair. "We still don't know. Too bad you didn't have a chance to ask your Chron friend. If we knew that—"

"Maybe we'd know how to stop them." I stood to cross the office and joined him at the view wall. Space was so damned big. How could it possibly not have enough room for all of us to coexist? "Maybe Cerevare can get some answers for us. We need to set up a comm relay to her. And maybe the data from the Corvids will help."

Lanar shrugged. "It's definitely useful. But even they don't have the big answers, the reasons that drive the Chron. They told you that themselves, didn't they? You're right about Professor Brindlepaw, though. I'm going to work on getting a message to her as soon as possible."

Viss asked, "Do you think the Chron will get through? To Nearspace?"

"Yes." Lanar's usually cheery face was pale, his grey eyes shadowed. "If they're determined enough—and the evidence points to that—they'll be here, probably before we're ready for them."

"But we're getting ready."

"There are a few in the Protectorate who think we should take the fight to them, but that's not practical. Regina Holles is pushing for us to mobilize without causing panic throughout Nearspace, even though she's very candid about our shortfall of firepower and resources. Some of the corporations don't believe any of it, so they're not even putting their planetary security forces on notice. The Council wants to be cautious, not cause 'undue alarm'."

"In other words, they're going to wait until it's too late."

Lanar sighed again. "That's how it seems to me."

It was exactly what I didn't want to hear.

WHEN I ARRIVED back at the *Tane Ikai*, there was more news I didn't want to hear. Rei met me near the airlock.

"Maja got a message," she said in a quiet voice. "I don't know what it was, but it upset her, I think. She stayed in her cabin, even though we were supposed to do *nicardi* together." The Erian martial art is a more intense workout than I care for, but Rei had been teaching Maja, and my daughter loved it. No doubt she still had plenty of pent-up frustration from our years of bickering, and the screaming likely helped with that.

I suppressed a sigh. "I'll talk to her." Maja and I had managed to get past those years of near-estrangement over the past few months, so it wasn't our relationship that made me hesitate. It was just that I felt mentally exhausted after my talk with Lanar and what I really wanted was a nap. I went to see Maja anyway.

She was pale but composed when she let me into her cabin. What had been plain and sparse passenger quarters when Maja came on board had been transformed into a cozy living space that now looked larger than it was. Someday I should ask my daughter to redecorate my captain's quarters. Somehow, even during long stretches of in-system space travel, it was one thing I never managed.

"Rei thought you might be upset about something," I explained. "Want to talk?"

She sat on the bed, which she'd covered with a colourful handmade coverlet from a little market on Kiando, and wriggled back until she leaned against the wall. She pulled her knees up and locked her hands around them with a sigh. "It was a message from Taso," she said. Taso was her ex-husband, who'd left her for a younger woman some months before she'd joined us on the *Tane Ikai* to help deal with Hirin's—at that time—failing health.

"What did he want?"

Maja shook her head, the hint of a frown creasing her forehead. "I don't really know. He sounded—odd. Rambled for a bit, just small talk, even though we haven't spoken in months." The message was naturally a one-way affair, since Taso was still back in Sol system—on Earth, I assumed.

I leaned against the edge of the desk and slipped my hands into my pockets. "That does seem strange. Why call if he had nothing of consequence to say?"

"It gets stranger. He said he was thinking about coming out to see me, wanted me to send a message and let him know where I was planning to be in the next little while."

I raised my eyebrows. "Did he mention the divorce?"

She shook her head again, impatiently this time. "He didn't mention anything important at all, other than coming to visit. I was just so surprised to hear from him at all—it sort of threw me. I can't think straight."

I crossed the room and sat on the bed beside her, scooting back until I fetched up against the wall, too. With one arm I gave her a quick hug, still slightly amazed that we were both comfortable with that after so long when I wouldn't even have contemplated it. "Are you going to reply?"

She leaned into the hug and I felt her sigh. "I suppose I should try to find out what this is really about."

"If you want. But you have no obligation to try and make him feel better. *He* left *you*, remember?"

"I know. It's just—so weird. I've hardly even thought about him in weeks."

I pulled back and grinned. "Not surprising. Baden hasn't been giving you much time to think about other men."

She grinned back. "No, he hasn't. And I haven't wanted to."

"So, send Taso a message and then put him out of your mind for now."

She nodded. "We probably have more important things to worry about anyway, don't we?"

"You mean Yuskeya and the others? Your Uncle Lanar is heading out first thing in the morning to retrieve them. Viss is going along, too. And Lanar feels sure they'll be back in a few days. The Corvids will be expecting a retrieval mission, so I'm sure it'll be fine."

She crossed her arms and tilted her head at me, her blue eyes considering. "You're not all that sure. And we don't know what happened after we left the system."

I sighed. "No, we don't. But we'll hope for the best, and take some comfort that it's Lanar going. There's no-one I'd trust more on that mission."

"Did he say anything about the Chron? What's the Protectorate plan?"

There was no point in trying to hide it, I supposed. They were going to figure things out for themselves anyway; they'd all been there. Still, I hated to be the one to tell my daughter that another Chron war could be imminent. "The Protectorate thinks we may be in for some trouble," I said carefully.

Mercifully, Hirin called me on the comm circuit just then and I was spared any further discussion.

"Luta, could you come down to the galley for a minute? I've got some inquiries about cargo to Cengare, should fit into our schedule for when the repairs are finished."

I thumbed my forearm implant. "If you promise to have a double caff waiting for me when I get there."

His grin made his voice warm and smooth. "Already poured."

Maja grinned at me. "He's one in a million."

"Make that one in several hundred million," I corrected. "You okay now?"

She nodded. "I'll see you later. I think I'll see if Rei's still interested in a round of *nicardi*."

I hoped she would be. The Erian martial art seemed to be especially good for venting negative emotions. Rei always said she found the yelling particularly liberating.

I thought I might give it a try, myself.

Chapter 5 — Lanar
Exes Past and Present

I LEFT THE docking level of FarView after Luta returned to the *Tane Ikai*. I'd detailed Linna Drake to show Viss to some temporary quarters, and he'd asked if he might have a tour of Engineering and see what the maintenance crews were doing, which I should have expected. I told Linna to see to it, and then took one of the stairwells down to the entertainment level in search of some food. This was always the busiest part of FarView, and it felt good to be part of the bustling, busy crowd just going about their normal day. Shops were open and adboards cycled through brightly-coloured promotions of new merchandise and services. The holotheatre proclaimed the first run of a new production "outside Sol System!" And delicious smells wafted out of every restaurant's open door, making my mouth water. There wasn't anything wrong with the meals on the *Cheswick*, but anyone can appreciate a little variety once in a while. I stopped in to one of my favourite eateries whenever we docked at FarView, a little bistro called Lukoreon's, with a beautiful starwise view and a *chok'to* and prosciutto panini I'd literally cross space for.

I gave my order to the pleasant Vilisian at the counter and sat at a small table near the door to wait. From some hidden source, a bluesy guitar filled the air, adding to the relaxed atmosphere. A man poked his head in at the door, quickly glanced around the room, and crossed to the order counter himself. He hadn't appeared to notice me, but I stared at his back in surprise. I was sure it was my niece Maja's ex-husband, Taso. But what would he be doing on FarView? In an area as big as Nearspace, it was extremely rare to "run into" someone you knew unless you worked with them or planned the meeting well in advance. It just didn't happen. But here was Taso, I was sure of it. I'd had a good look at his face as he scanned the room, and the lean build and longish, light-brown hair were right. Not that I'd spent much time with Maja and Taso, but we'd met enough times for me to feel quite certain. When he turned his head to look over the menu board, I spotted a small tattoo on the side of his neck and I was sure. It was a spiral galaxy, and I remembered it from their wedding. I'd joked to Luta at the time that I should get something similar, only perhaps a wormhole, to signify the countless times I'd made a skip between systems. She'd said dryly that she didn't think a round black spot made for very interesting ink.

I waited until he'd finished his order and then went up and put a hand on his shoulder. "Taso?"

He jumped violently and swung around to face me.

"Whoa, sorry," I said, holding my hands away. "Didn't mean to startle you. It's Lanar, Maja's uncle, remember?"

He relaxed so visibly I thought he might actually collapse onto the floor. "Lanar, of course," he gasped. "Sorry, I just wasn't expecting there to be anyone here who'd know—anyone I'd know," he said. He chuckled, but it sounded forced. "I guess with the Protectorate, you could turn up anywhere, anytime, huh?"

I smiled and nodded. "Pretty rare to just bump into someone I know, though. What brings you to FarView?"

"Oh, just doing some travelling," he said lightly. "Heard there might be some opportunities for teachers here on the station, thought it might make a nice change."

"I was sorry to hear about you and Maja," I said, although I knew full well it had been Taso who left her. It seemed more awkward not to mention that I knew about the breakup, though.

"Uh, yeah." He looked uncomfortable and jerked his shoulders up in a shrug. "These things happen."

"Coincidentally, the *Tane Ikai* is docked here now, too, if you can believe it," I said. "Maja's still with her mother, if you wanted to say hello."

"No! I mean, that might not be the best idea," he said. "It's a little awkward. You know. If I happen to run into her, that's one thing, but I don't think I'd go looking."

I nodded, and the waitress called my order. "Sure, sure," I said.

"I mean," he hurried on, following me over to the pickup station, "you might not even want to mention that you saw me, really. If you're talking to her. Because then she might think it was weird that I didn't try to see her."

I took my panini and double caff. "No problem," I reassured him. "I'm off on a mission shortly anyway. Nice to see you, and good luck with the job hunting. FarView's an interesting place to spend some time."

"Thanks, Lanar. Good to see you, too," he said. He didn't offer to shake hands since mine were full.

I took my order to my table and gave most of my attention to the sandwich. I did notice, though, that Taso got his food and left the bistro quickly, without glancing in my direction. The whole encounter had been . . . strange. Definitely something I'd mention to Luta, no matter what I'd told Taso. Family sticks together, and I didn't really consider Taso in that category anymore.

I mulled over Taso's odd behaviour as I left the bistro and headed for the stairwell since the elevator was crowded. It was only three levels up to the docking arms, anyway. I'd gained the first landing, the station's mercantile level, when the lower door opened and shut and footsteps sounded on the stairs below me. Someone was in a hurry, and I moved to one side so they could run past me. But a rough command made me turn to face the person coming up.

"Mahane! We need to talk."

I forgot all about Taso as I watched Mauronet approach, and suppressed a sigh. He was red-faced, probably not used to taking the stairs. I had to conclude that he'd been following me, waiting for a moment to catch me alone. To talk, or to continue what we'd started outside the meeting room? I stepped back to give him lots of room on the landing and balanced myself in case he rushed me.

"How can I help you, Admiral?" I kept my voice calm, and afforded him more courtesy than he'd shown me.

He drew level with me, but he didn't look primed for a physical fight. The fading bruise on his jaw was livid again on his suffused face. "Where are you headed?" he demanded.

"Back to my ship, at the moment."

Mauronet glowered at me and shook an accusatory finger. "Not what I mean and you know it. Where's the *Cheswick* headed? Into Chron space? Are you taking a force?"

Now I understood. He thought Regina was sending me on the mission he wanted—to attack the Chron.

I shook my head. "It's a retrieval detail," I told him, "and just the one ship. No force."

He looked like he might spit on the floor, then thought better of it. "As if you'd tell me," he said. "Holles won't listen to reason—at least to my face. But she can't be that complacent about the Chron threat. As soon as I heard you were shipping out, I knew where you must be going."

"You've got it wrong, Mauronet," I told him. I didn't care to keep this argument going, but I wasn't about to turn my back on him and continue up the stairs. "You can watch us leave if you want. The *Cheswick* is heading out on her own."

"Sure, that will prove it, because there aren't any Protectorate ships you could rendezvous with after you leave FarView." His voice was rough with sarcasm. A face glanced into the stairwell through the window, saw us, and hurried away.

"You're playing a dangerous game," I said. "It's not your place, nor mine, to second-guess the Fleet Commander."

He ignored that. "You met with Southwind. Is he going with you?"

Bastardo. He must have been following me, or having me followed, ever since the meeting. *All the way to Kiando and back?* Was he really that paranoid? I fought down the urge to punch him again and crossed my arms to make restraining myself easier. "Stop imagining enemies inside the Protectorate, Mauronet," I said. "We have enough to worry about from the outside."

Then I pushed open the door and stepped out onto the busy mercantile concourse. If he wanted to follow me and make a public scene—maybe even start another physical altercation, I'd have plenty of witnesses to call at his court-martial.

I walked about ten feet and looked back when I heard the stairwell door swing shut. Mauronet hadn't followed, but stood glaring at me through the door's window. He made an obscene gesture, and I answered it with a Protectorate salute, then turned and walked toward the next stairwell leading up. I'd have to tell Regina about the encounter, although I hated to add fuel to their already inflammatory relationship. But Mauronet was starting to feel more like a threat than an annoyance, not just to me, but to the Protectorate and the larger safety of Nearspace. His ideas about the Chron were straying towards irrational.

I didn't like to think he'd disobey orders. But I hadn't liked the anger raging in his eyes through that window, either.

I WAS ON the Engineering deck of the *Cheswick* later, checking up on the maintenance progress, when I got a text-only message from Regina. I'd messaged her briefly about Mauronet when I'd returned to the ship, but left the details for when we could talk in person. Now she asked if we could meet, and when I replied in the affirmative, she sent me a suite number on the upper habitat level. She must not be willing to risk another confrontation with Mauronet or anyone else in the Protectorate offices just now—or perhaps she wanted this to be unofficial. I considered that as I walked down the docking arm and rode the elevator up a level. There could be others who shared Mauronet's opinion of what we should be doing about the Chron. Those at the meeting when I'd volunteered Luta to go to the Corvid system hadn't voiced agreement—but they might have simply been keeping quiet in the face of Regina's obvious opposition to his ideas. I'd have to ask Regina how she thought the other Fleet Commanders felt. I knew the other four, and thought they were level-headed and reasonable, but I didn't know any of them as well as I knew Regina.

Well, I thought with a wry smile, there were few people I knew as well as Regina.

Mulling over the possible things Regina might ask me to do while on my rescue mission to the Corvid system, I found the suite number and knocked on the door.

"Come in," she called, and I swiped my ID implant close to

the door's keypad. She'd given me access and the door slid out of the way. I stepped inside.

Living suites on the upper docking level of FarView station were not exactly luxury accommodations, but they were spacious and well-appointed, several levels of improvement over my quarters on the *S. Cheswick*, and I found those comfortable enough. Regina's suite offered a view out the starwise side, a portion of the view wall now covered by long, creamy drapes. It wasn't this view she was enjoying, however, but a faux fireplace with burning logs projected on the room's hubside wall. Regina sat on a curving, dove-grey sofa, nursing a glass of what I guessed was her favourite *jarlees* wine. Her hair was down, the way she'd worn it at the academy, and she'd changed out of her Protectorate navy blues into a flowing tunic of transform fabric. It cycled slowly through a soft palette of blues and greens.

"Fleet Commander," I said with a nod, stopping just inside the door as it closed behind me.

"Never mind that silliness, Lanar," she said, smiling. "There's another glass for you, and you should have changed out of the uniform. This meeting, as far as I'm concerned, is not happening and never happened."

I shrugged out of my jacket and hung it over the high back of an oversized pale green armchair standing at right angles to the sofa. "What about those security cameras you warned me about? I'm sure there's a record of me, stepping in through that door thirty seconds ago." I picked up the second wineglass from the table and held it out. She poured from the bottle, and I sat in the armchair.

"Yes, but remember who reviews all the security recordings."

I sipped and smiled. "Your one vice," I said, saluting her with the glass. The fruit-sweet scent of the wine drifted in the air, reminding me of the expanses of vine trellises on Kiando.

"I wish," she said dryly, "but at least I'm consistent."

"How'd it go with Mauronet today? I wondered if you'd have to put him out an airlock."

"Don't sound so enchanted by the idea. No, in the end we agreed to disagree."

"Meaning you told him to shut up and take orders."

She grinned over the lip of her wineglass. "Something like

that." Her grin faded quickly, though.

I leaned forward and rested my elbows on my knees, holding my glass in both hands and swirling the deep purplish liquid inside. "You're worried. More worried even than you're letting on."

"Aren't you? What did he say to you this afternoon?"

"Accused me of going off on a secret mission to fight Chron. Apparently, I'm taking a force of other ships along, and Harle Southwind is coming with me. Which doesn't even make sense, since Harle's Investigative and doesn't even have his own ship at the moment!" I ran a hand over my face. "Obviously, he's angry at being excluded from this imaginary mission."

Regina closed her eyes. "I told him flat out that no-one in the Protectorate was taking the fight to the Chron. Why is he so hung up on this?"

I shrugged. "People are scared and angry. The Chron War wasn't so long ago that we've forgotten about it. I guess Mauronet would rather see us taking action than waiting around for the hammer to fall."

"Is that how you see it?" she asked sharply.

"No. I think you're handling it the right way. But we're a military force. There are bound to be more than just Mauronet sharing his opinion."

"Mmmm," she said, neither confirming my suspicions nor dispelling them. I didn't like that, but she continued before I could press her. "Harle Southwind told you what we suspect PrimeCorp is up to?"

"Yes, but I still don't see how PrimeCorp thinks it's going to control interactions with the Chron. They're putting all of Nearspace at risk, if it's true."

She sipped from her glass, holding the rim between the fingertips of both hands. "It's treason, if it's all true. This is top priority, Lanar. You must find out everything you can from the Corvids or anyone else while you're on this mission."

I nodded. "I already asked Mother if she still had any connections inside PrimeCorp. She didn't think there was anyone who'd be useful, but she didn't dismiss it out of hand."

Regina looked at me sharply. "Did you tell your Mother everything about our suspicions?"

"Pretty much, but I thought that's what you wanted. Harle

said it was your idea."

She blew out a long breath. "Well, it was. I just get antsy when I think about too many people knowing what we suspect, and it somehow getting back to PrimeCorp."

I chuckled. "I think if there's anyone you can trust to *not* leak anything to PrimeCorp, it's my mother."

Regina smiled then and seemed to relax. She set her empty wineglass on the table with a soft clink, and made no move to refill it. "Are you seeing anyone, Lanar?" she asked softly.

I quirked a half-smile. "You know me, Regina. Too old for the young ones, too young for the ones my age."

"Nice problem to have," she said, then she quickly shook her head. "No, I don't mean that. It hasn't actually been a nice problem to have, has it?"

I considered the dregs of wine in my glass. "It has its moments," I said, "but on the whole . . . I'm not sure it's all it's cracked up to be."

She rested her chin in her hand. "I do wonder, though. What would have happened if we'd stayed together. Your sister and her husband seem to have made it work. But I wonder if it's different for a man to be with an 'older' woman."

I shrugged. "If two people want to be together, it's no-one else's business."

She smiled. "We did get that part figured out a long time ago," she said. "At least we think we did. People still talk."

I got up and sat beside her on the sofa, putting an arm around her shoulders. She leaned back and against my side with a sigh, dropping her head to my shoulder.

"Remember that time on Vele, when we flew the training recon mission for Admiral Walamar?" I asked.

She nodded. "And you got us lost trying to fly by 'instinct' and not the coordinates? I'm not losing my memory yet. At least not that one."

"And *you*," I argued, "got us lost. We landed on the beach to get our bearings. That little lagoon with the giant blue seahorse things. And you tried to catch one."

"*You* tried to catch one," she laughed, her body shaking against mine.

"Oh no." I squeezed her shoulders. "I'll take responsibility for getting us lost, but you were the one in the water."

"They were so amazing, but I didn't catch one." She reached up and rested her hand against my cheek. "But you warmed me up afterward."

"It's probably just as well you didn't catch one. We would have had a hard time explaining that one to the admiral."

"We caught hell as it was," she said. "But it was worth it."

"Well, that's who you are to me," I said. "And always will be. The woman from that day."

She reached up a hand and touched the pure white streak in her hair. "Right," she said, "and this is just a fashion statement."

I shrugged. "It might as well be. I've lost a lot of people in my lifetime—some to death, some to my particular . . . situation. You're a constant, one of the few. And that's why I think for me, you don't age. Not really. And maybe that's the way it is with Luta and Hirin."

She was quiet for so long I thought I'd said something wrong, and then she reached up and brushed away a tear. "You're damned good for the ego, Lanar Mahane," she said, "I'll give you that."

Then she sat forward and turned her face towards mine. "But will you put your money where your mouth is?"

I smiled at her, meeting those brown eyes; the eyes of a woman who'd never grown out of my heart, even if she passed me in years. "I will, if my mouth is here," I said, and put my lips firmly on hers.

Chapter 6 — Luta
Old Friends and Enemies

FOUR DAYS AFTER my meeting with Lanar, we made our first cargo dropdown on the planet Cengare. The Protectorate shipyard had been extremely efficient, and the repairs to the *Tane Ikai* completed right on time. I wondered if they would have been so quick if Viss hadn't gone off with Lanar; likely he would have practically camped out at the repair site, sticking his nose in everywhere and questioning everything they did. The thought made me miss my absent crew members even more keenly, and I pushed it firmly to the back of my mind.

The population of Cengare was smaller than that of its sister planet, Kiando. Kiando was a busy mining colony, but it seemed like Cengare had been colonized just because someone could do it. It was a nice enough planet, in the cooler end of the habitable zone but still pleasant. The relatively small colonized area offered several ocean-side cities with spectacular surfing waters, so tourism was a mainstay of the fledgling planetary economy.

The Protectorate may have been keeping rumours about the Chron quiet, but security was on edge. Docking officials double-checked every ID sig and document, and an air of watchfulness hung over the docking station like a pall of smoke.

Baden rolled his eyes. "What are they expecting? That we might be Chron in disguise? Kind of hard to cover up those bone crests, I would have thought."

"They're just nervous," Maja said. "Rumours get everyone stirred up, but they don't know what to do about it."

"Well, maybe they could find something a little more sensible to do with all that nervous energy," Baden grumbled. "If they get the docks all tied up in red tape, they'll have more than just the Chron to worry about."

There was another message from Taso waiting for Maja when we downloaded the deliverable-in-proximities. I saw it on the list, but decided I'd wait this time before mentioning it to her, let her come to me about it if she wanted. I didn't want her to feel I was prying.

And Rei had a message from Gerazan Soto, whom we'd just left back on FarView after our Corvid-space foray. I couldn't resist teasing her a little.

"He couldn't wait to talk to you again, apparently," I said. "But have you told your mother about him yet?" Rei had confided to me a while back that her mother would be horrified if Rei ended up in a long-term relationship with someone other than an Erian, or in a marriage that hadn't been arranged according to Erian custom.

"What she doesn't know won't hurt her," Rei replied with a careless shrug. "I'll tell her, when and if it becomes necessary. I hear there's a shopping complex near the docking station. Maja and I were going to go and check it out while they're unloading the cargo. Want to come?"

I shook my head. "No, thanks, you two go on. I've got some things to do here."

While we'd been talking, I'd noticed the yellow message light on my datapad begin to blink. That meant I had a message of my own waiting, and I thought it might be from Lanar or Mother. I was doomed to be disappointed. It was from Alin Sedmamin, the Chairman of PrimeCorp himself and my old nemesis. But it wasn't a DIP, it was realtime, which meant he had to be here in the Mu Cassiopeia system, too. That was strange. I'd never encountered him anywhere but on Earth. It was also marked high priority. I had no love for Sedmamin after everything he'd put me and my family through in the past, but I had to admit I was curious. I hadn't heard a word from him since he'd sent Jahelia Sord to cause trouble for me, and she'd ended up on my side—at least, sort of. I wondered if he was calling to chew me out for ruining his operative. I took a moment to compose myself and then opened the comm link.

"*Saluton*, Chairman," I said politely. "How can I help you today?"

Sedmamin didn't look good; even worse than the last time I'd seen him. He'd lost weight, but not in a good way. His skin hung in loose folds around his face, a pale greyish colour that looked anything but healthy. Deep, dark bags sagged under his eyes, and his washed-out blond hair was unkempt. Perhaps the rumours that he'd been taking heat for PrimeCorp's current troubles were true.

"Captain Paixon, I need to speak with you," he said without preamble. There was none of his usual insincere heartiness. I almost thought he looked—frightened.

"We're speaking. About what?"

He licked his lips. "Can we meet? I'd like to ensure this is a private conversation." He glanced away from the screen, to one side and then over his shoulder, like a character in a holovid. I'd never seen Sedmamin like this, unsure and almost paranoid. It made me uneasy.

"Where are you?" I asked. "You must be in Mu Cass system somewhere since we're realtime."

He nodded. "I'm on Cengare, same as you. Please, Captain— Luta—I'll meet you anywhere you want."

Of the many attempts Alin Sedmamin had made to cajole me into meeting him, it had always been on his terms, on his turf, and, even when he wouldn't admit it, for his gain. Now he just sounded desperate. I didn't think it was any kind of a ploy. Sedmamin had never been a good actor.

I still hesitated to invite him onto my ship, though.

"We're docked at Havernough, and I hear there's a shopping complex nearby. I could meet you there sometime today or tomorrow, but I can't stay longer—"

"I know it," he said eagerly. "An hour from now?"

Dio! He had to be right here in the same city, or just outside it.

"*Okej*." The absurdity of the situation hit me. "Chairman, are you sure you can't just tell me what this is about?"

He looked directly into the screen then, intense and worried.

"It's about things that have gotten out of my control," he hissed. Suddenly he flashed a grim smile, one I thought was genuine. "I know we've had our differences, but strangely enough, you're currently about the only person I trust."

If that was true, he must be in even worse shape than he looked. "All right then, an hour, at the main entrance," I said.

He nodded and closed the connection. I spent a minute wondering what the hell was happening, then got up to go and find out.

I FOUND HIRIN on the bridge, playing around with configurations for some of the new weapons systems he'd installed. When I told him I was going to meet Alin Sedmamin at the shopping centre, he just stared at me.

"I know what all those words mean," he said slowly, "but not when you use them together like that. You're going where? To meet who?"

"Very funny." I sat down in a skimchair beside him and quickly sketched my conversation with the PrimeCorp chairman. "I don't know details yet, but Sedmamin's in some kind of trouble."

"Good," Hirin said with a snort. "That actually makes me very happy. I *want* Sedmamin to be in trouble. The more, the better, as far as I'm concerned. He's caused you—caused *us*—enough of it."

I sighed. "I know. But I'm awfully curious to know what it's about."

"This could be a trick. I don't trust that man as far as I could jettison him out an airlock."

I ran a hand through my hair. "I know, I know. I don't trust him, either. But I honestly think he's scared of something. And I want to know what." I leaned back in my chair, letting the servos massage my back. The hum of the tiny motors was soothing. "I can't think of any reason he'd try to trick me into meeting him now. Mother's released her data onto the public nets. If it's about what we saw in Otherspace—"

"Are we really calling it 'Otherspace'?"

I stuck out my tongue at him. "Until someone comes up with something better, yes. If it's about what we saw there, our statements are already on record with the Protectorate."

"Maybe they want to bully or threaten us into recanting."

"It's a little late for that. And why would they take a chance on making things worse?"

"Maybe they think we're not telling everything, and they want to torture you to find out."

I rolled my eyes. "Slightly melodramatic, even for PrimeCorp, don't you think?"

Hirin fixed a very husbandly eye on me. "Well, you're not going alone."

"I had no intention of it, don't worry. It's only a matter of deciding who to take with me. Rei and Maja have already gone over there, although it's just to shop."

"Don't spoil their fun. I can go," he volunteered, but I shook my head.

"You're busy here already. And I'm not altogether sure I can trust you not to come barging in if you imagine something's going wrong."

"You wound me," he said mildly.

"I'll ask Baden. He's good at being inconspicuous. Not that you aren't," I added, holding up a hand to forestall the protest I knew would follow. Hirin likes to think he's at least competent at just about anything. Honestly, he's probably right.

He grinned. "I'm okay with you taking Baden. I know he'll look out for you. Just remember I'll be waiting with bated breath to find out what Sedmamin wants with you."

I kissed him. "I can't wait to find that out myself," I told him, and went to collect my communications officer.

Baden and I walked to the shopping centre, since it was near the spaceport and Sedmamin had given me lots of time to get there. In this sun-drenched city, I'd left my jacket on the ship, and the heat felt lovely on my bare arms. I wished I'd changed out of long pants, as well. The locals and visitors on the tree-lined boulevard appeared to be in full vacation mode, strolling and chatting in brightly-coloured beachwear. I couldn't remember the last time I'd felt that relaxed. Hirin and I would have to get that vacation soon.

Baden walked in silence beside me, which was unlike him. He tended more to the chatty side than the strong, silent type.

"How's everything with Maja?" I asked him, since we rarely had a chance to talk one-on-one lately. Mainly because he was always with my daughter, so I suspected I knew the answer, but I like my crew to feel that I'm interested in their lives. And honestly, I wondered if she'd told him about the message from Taso. I wanted to ask, but if she hadn't, that would be disastrous.

He kept his eyes ahead, strangely impassive, but said, "Perfect, from my perspective. Unless you know something I don't."

I glanced at him, willing him to turn and meet my eyes. He did, after a moment, and I asked, "What is it?"

He shrugged. "I know she got a message from Taso."

I took his arm and leaned close to his ear. "She's not in love with him anymore, you know."

He flashed me a grin then, although it didn't touch his eyes. "Marriage—it's a pretty strong bond. All that shared history? Wouldn't do to discount one too easily."

I laughed and shook my head. "I spent a lot of years away from Maja, but honestly, I don't think she's ever been happier."

"Part of that is because the rift between you two is healed," he said. "I think that bothered her more than she'd ever even admit to herself."

"That's good, then." I studied him. "But what happened to that ladies' man who used to work my communications board?"

He snorted a laugh as we skirted around a Vilisian mother with a child in a hovercart. "Don't rub it in, Captain. This is all your fault, anyway."

"My fault?"

"She's your daughter," he said, as if that explained everything.

"I'll take that as a compliment," I said. "Don't worry too much, okay?"

"We have enough to worry about as it is," he said with a wry smile.

"Ain't that the truth," I told him, and released his arm. I was supposed to be going to this meeting alone, after all. If Sedmamin was watching, I didn't want to make it too easy for him.

We returned to a comfortable silence the rest of the way, then entered the shopping centre separately. I just went on ahead and let Baden work it whatever way he wanted. Although

I expected Viss would have more experience with this kind of thing, I trusted Baden to handle it. He knew my history with Sedmamin and PrimeCorp and appreciated the possible—if remote—implications of the meeting.

I didn't see Sedmamin inside, so I crossed to a huge luminescent fountain in the middle of the lobby and waited. The building was mid-afternoon busy, with shoppers obviously on their way home from work mingling with tourists, off-duty Protectorate types, and family groups. The crowd was mostly human or human-origin colonists, although I spotted a few gliding Vilisians and lightly bouncing Lobors in the crowd. Glowing e-boards descended from the ceiling, ads cycling through various pitches as different shoppers passed beneath them. The boards read data from their ID chips and served ads accordingly. A family got ads for toys, office workers saw the latest in datapads and implants, soldiers were reminded of deals in restaurants and other entertainment venues. Curious, I wandered over to one to see what it would show me. I got several ads for clothing stores and one for a hair stylist. I tried not to take it personally.

Sedmamin showed up then, appearing across the wide corridor and beckoning to me to join him. I was shocked by how thin he looked. It was more obvious in person than over the vidscreen. His dark blue business biosuit looked baggy and ill-cut, although it must have been expensively tailored when he bought it. His skin still looked grey, even worse under the pale, flickering light from the adboards. I took a quick scan of the area, just trying to be careful, but I really didn't see anything that made me nervous. I crossed to meet him, weaving through the flow of hurrying shoppers as I went.

"Thank you for coming," he said briefly, although to my relief he didn't make any move to shake my hand or take my arm. It was difficult for me to come to terms with the notion that Alin Sedmamin was anything less than an annoyance, if not an outright enemy. "Shall we talk over a caff?"

"Sure," I said, and we made our way down the mall, threading our way through busy shoppers to a cafe. I didn't look around for Baden. I knew he'd be around, blended inconspicuously into the crowd.

"I'm sure you didn't come alone, Captain," Sedmamin said,

as if he had read my mind.

"You're familiar with my prudent nature," I said with a smile.

"I would have expected nothing less," he said. "Although I assure you it wasn't necessary. I have much more pressing concerns than your bioscavengers now."

"I won't say I'm glad to hear it, since those concerns are obviously causing you some distress," I answered, matching the formality of his tone.

He didn't answer right away, since we'd reached the cafe. It was open to the main corridor of the mall and had an upper level, festooned with artificial greenery, where one could enjoy their beverage while shoppers passed beneath them. Plenty of the tables up above sat empty, so we each brought our own drink and headed up there. Sedmamin climbed the steps ahead of me like an old man, carefully and hyperaware of the danger of tripping.

Settled at a small round table with a recently-wiped imitation-wood surface, I took a sip of caff and asked, "*Okej*, Chairman, I'm ready to hear why you wanted to talk to me." I managed not to grimace. The caff was horrible, somehow managing to be both watery and bitter at the same time.

"It's painful for me to say this, but I need your help, Captain," Sedmamin confessed, after sampling his own drink. He didn't look anymore pleased with it than I was with mine.

I didn't say anything, just raised my eyebrows for him to continue.

"I'd like you to believe that I misjudged Dores Amadoro when I gave her the authority to deal with you," he said first. "She was completely out of control and not acting under any sort of instruction from me."

I didn't believe that, but nodded anyway. Amadoro wasn't a problem for me any longer, so why argue about her? "*Okej*."

"And I also want to state that I had no knowledge of any PrimeCorp dealings with the Chron." He regarded me intently, watching for my reaction.

Merde! Was he admitting it? That PrimeCorp had secretly been in collaboration with humanity's greatest threat? I tried to keep the surprise out of my face. "But you've become aware of it now?"

He held up a hand. "I've become aware of rumours to that

effect—all right, perhaps more than rumours," he added when he saw my face. "I have no personal knowledge, so I can't confirm or deny anything."

"It's a pretty important thing for the *Chairman* not to know about," I said carefully, wrapping my hands around my warm mug. The inside of the mall was a chilly contrast to the heat outside.

"You're completely right about that. I do take some responsibility, because I believe it was my . . . er . . . views on certain situations . . . that made others believe the Chron could be used to our ends."

I suspected he meant his previous obsession with my mother's research data and my own nanotechnological secrets, but I let it pass. I wasn't here to antagonize him over past problems. If he had anything to say about the Chron, I wanted to hear it.

"But now," he went on, "there are elements within the corporation who are trying to cover their own misdeeds." He leaned toward me, his pale brown eyes dark and serious despite the sagging skin around them. "To put it bluntly, they want me to go down for this."

"You wield substantial power as Chairman," I noted. "There must be some people who would continue to back you."

He glanced around the café, as if he thought he might have been followed. "There's been an internal power struggle at PrimeCorp for years now. Various factions, trying to promote their own interests. It's the way the corporations work. It starts out small; someone has a project they'd like to see go ahead. They start rounding up support for it. Looking to cut funding to someone else's project, or get ahead of them in the timeline. The internal structure of the corporation fragments; there's no longer a common good or a common goal. Just infighting and backroom deals." He sighed. "Eventually it reaches the highest levels, if it didn't start there. If it's splintered enough, there are entire cadres working at cross-purposes. And then everyone starts to think that if someone else were Chairman—"

"There'd be a better chance to promote their own agenda," I finished for him. It did explain some things I'd wondered about in the past, like how sometimes the left hand of PrimeCorp didn't seem to know what the right hand was doing.

"There are enough factions now that want me out," he said simply. "There's no avoiding it."

"And they're not offering a nice fat retirement package? A golden handshake and a titanium datapad?"

He pinched his lips together. "Hardly. The best way to get me out is to make me take the fall for everything the corporation has done wrong lately. Or ever. Some of the things I'll be accused of will probably date back to before I was born," he said bitterly, "but they'll still argue that I knew about it and am to blame."

I took another tentative drink of my caff. It hadn't improved. "I still don't see how I can help you, though."

"I want to get to a friend I have on Nellera," he said.

"Why would that be a problem? Surely, you're free to move around Nearspace however you want," I said. "You're here, after all."

"I'm here with the clothes I'm standing up in," he said wearily, "and a small bag at a hotel. They don't just want me out of PrimeCorp. They want me ruined—or even conveniently dead, because then I can't argue my case. I'm what you would call 'on the run'. I have funds I can access in the future, but I won't risk doing that until I'm in a secure location." His lips twitched in distaste.

"So, you want me to somehow help you get to this friend, along with, I'm assuming, some of your worldly possessions." He started to say something, but I said, "Just wait, you can finish explaining that part in a minute. What I really want to know is, why do you think I would help you now? You have to admit you've made my life unpleasant for a long time."

And *unpleasant* was an understatement. He'd hounded me, tricked me, infected me with a virus, had me kidnapped and knocked out, almost caused an irreparable rift between me and Maja, might have been responsible for the virus that had made Hirin sick and confined to a nursing home for so many years, and set Jahelia Sord on my tail. Granted, some of those things could have been initiated by other people in the corporation; I couldn't be sure he was the driving factor behind all of them. But I knew he'd had his fingers in enough to make me question again why I was sitting here talking to him.

But I knew the answer well enough. *Damne* curiosity.

"I'll grant you that, if you'll believe it was all just business." He grinned crookedly. "Nothing personal—although you were damned aggravating at times."

"It's always personal, or it should be," I said. "And I take some comfort in knowing that I got under your skin. But that's irrelevant. I still want to know why you think I would help you now."

His eyes narrowed, and I saw a glimpse of the manipulative man I'd always known him to be. "Because I have information your brother the Admiral would very much like to have. And the only way I'll divulge it—the only way I can *get* it—is if you help me. You, and Jahelia Sord, and that very competent crew of yours."

I sat back in my chair, letting my fingertips play with the handle of my mug. "My brother is not exactly one of your biggest fans either. You'd have to have something . . . exceptional . . . for him to even want to speak with you."

One side of his mouth stretched up as if it wanted to scratch his cheek. "I know that. Your family and I have simply had the misfortune to be on opposite sides of a shared interest. But that's behind us." He leaned forward and lowered his voice. "I know it had to be Jahelia Sord who took some files from PrimeCorp; I know she handed them over to your brother, or at least to you. No-one at PrimeCorp has figured out how they were leaked yet, and it's driving them crazy. They're in the hands of the Protectorate now, but with that illegal provenance they won't be of any useful effect. They won't be admissible in legal proceedings and the Protectorate must hate that. They'll be desperate at being unable to act on them."

"And you're willing to help the Protectorate against PrimeCorp now? That's a remarkable shift in loyalties."

His voice dipped almost to a snarl. "They have no loyalty to me; why should they have mine? If I don't do this, I'm going down, Captain—a very long way down. I don't think I deserve it, and I'm willing to do anything to avoid it."

The desperation in his eyes was an almost palpable thing. Apparently, rising to the top of PrimeCorp was not an achievement that came without dangers. "Well, what do you have to offer my brother?"

He studied me with narrowed eyes for a moment. "You're

willing to help me?"

Every ounce of sense I had was telling me to walk away and leave Sedmamin sitting here in his sagging clothes and the ruins of his career. But if I could help Lanar—and Nearspace, too—maybe it was worth putting up with Sedmamin for a little while. It was satisfying to know that he'd lost the power to intimidate or hurt me.

I kept my face neutral and shrugged. "I might be. I'm not expecting you to spill everything to me, but I have to know you've actually got something that Lanar would want."

"Only—everything," he said, just above a whisper. "Everything PrimeCorp knows about the Chron. Everything they're planning now. All those files Jahelia Sord took and more—but from a legitimate source, a whistle-blower, who can still obtain them legally and turn them over to the Protectorate." He sat back and tapped his chest. "Me."

For a moment, I couldn't speak. "I thought you said you didn't know anything about PrimeCorp's involvement with the Chron?"

"Oh, I didn't—at the time. Trust me, since I've seen which way the wind is blowing, I've made it my business to dig deep into everything while I still had access to it."

"And all that information is—?"

"Back on Earth," he said. "It's all together. The things I want, and the things your brother will want."

"Convenient," I said.

He shrugged. "I didn't get to be chairman of PrimeCorp without learning a few things." He drank off the rest of his caff and grimaced. It surely hadn't improved by growing cold. "So?"

"You didn't think of just turning your information over to the Protectorate in the interests of avoiding a war with the Chron and maybe saving lives?" I asked him.

"I could do that," he agreed. "But the way I see it, I'm fighting for my life, here, too. If you help me, it benefits everyone."

"Uh-huh." I stood. "Well, I'll take it to Lanar. How can I reach you?"

"I'll get back to you. I think I'm going to FarView station, but I may end up on Rhea or Renata, instead. How long before you'll have an answer for me?"

"Not sure. Lanar shipped out on a mission a few days ago, so I'm not sure where he is," I said. I wasn't telling Sedmamin that Lanar might be in Otherspace, trying to retrieve Yuskeya and the others. Let him sweat a bit if I couldn't get in touch with my brother right away. I turned to go.

"Captain?"

"What?"

"You wouldn't think of just helping me in the interests of maybe saving my life?" he asked, the wry grin on his face making it clear that he was deliberately echoing my own words.

Briefly I thought back to everything Sedmamin and his minions had done to make my life miserable, and the decades they'd chased my mother from one end of Nearspace to the other, simply because she had ethics and they didn't.

Only for a few seconds. "Nope," I said, "I can't seem to work up much interest in that." And I left him.

I DIDN'T HAVE any intention of sending a message to Lanar, because he'd left two days previously for the Corvid system. What I did want was a chance to think about Sedmamin's offer, and I didn't mind the idea of Alin Sedmamin having to cool his heels in some poky little motel room for a while. I guess that was mean, but I can live with myself. Baden rejoined me when I reached the mall entrance, appearing magically out of the crowd. We pushed outside. The breeze had kicked up, but it was still warmer out here than inside the mall.

Baden said, "That man does not look well. What did he want?"

I shook my head. "He really doesn't. He offered me a job, but I have to give it some thought."

Baden raised his eyebrows, but didn't press me for anything more. I knew the curiosity must be killing him, but I wasn't ready to talk about the whole crazy idea just yet.

Back at the *Tane Ikai*, I went looking for Hirin. I found him in the galley, having apparently finished whatever machinations he'd been up to with the weapons systems, and rewarding himself with some cinnamon *pano* and tea. I pulled a mug of double caff for myself and took the last slice of *pano*.

Hirin watched me with his eyebrows raised, waiting for the report.

"Let's talk in our quarters," I told him, picking up my plate and cup, and he followed me down the corridor. I settled at the desk and he sat in the big armchair, setting his mug on the corner of the desk.

"Must have been quite the discussion," he observed.

"I just need to talk this through with you before anyone else hears about it," I said. "I didn't see it coming, I'll tell you that."

"Don't keep me in suspense."

"Alin Sedmamin wants to hand over information to Lanar. Information about PrimeCorp and the Chron. Everything."

Hirin just stared at me. It wasn't often I made him speechless.

"It's true," I said, after a sip of caff. "PrimeCorp has decided that heads must roll, and Sedmamin's is the first head scheduled for the block. But he's got other ideas."

"He's getting back at them by going to the Protectorate? I don't know how much trust they'll put in anything that comes via that route." Hirin was frowning now, his snack all but forgotten.

"It's not exactly that. He wants a favour from me, and he'll give them everything PrimeCorp has regarding the Chron—past and present—in exchange. He says he didn't know the contact with the Chron was even happening now."

"And you believe him?"

I snorted. "Hardly. But I think whatever he's going to turn over—it's probably genuine. He really wants this favour."

"Which is?"

"He wants us to get him to Earth and help him retrieve his personal stuff, then get him away safely again. He has a place to go to ground, and funds he can access from there. He's not planning to lie down and die just because some of the factions at PrimeCorp want him to take a fall."

Hirin pursed his lips. "Sounds tricky—probably even dangerous. Why did he come to you with this?"

I'd been wondering the same thing, and I thought maybe I had an answer. I nibbled at my *pano*. "He obviously needs us to get whatever he's after. If it was easy he'd do it himself. And no-one at PrimeCorp is going to suspect me or the *Tane Ikai* of helping him." I shrugged. "Maybe all those years I spent avoiding him has given him a rather inflated notion of what we're capable of."

"Whatever his notion is, I'm sure it's not inflated," Hirin said with a half-smile. "You've run circles around PrimeCorp more than once, and we've got the crew for backup. Look how they pulled you and Maja out of that warehouse on Rhea. That's probably exactly the kind of thing he's thinking about."

"Well, I hope we'll be able to pull it off. The Protectorate needs all the information they can get on the Chron."

Hirin seemed to remember his tea and took a long drink, then followed it with a bite of bread. He chewed reflectively. "The Protectorate could probably squeeze it out of Sedmamin anyway," he mused. "Turn Sedmamin over to them, and we wouldn't have to do anything beyond that. If it's important militarily—"

"I know, but he says he actually doesn't have the information, and I believe him. It's all in the files, still on Earth. And they'd have a stronger case with the files as evidence, anyway."

"Sedmamin's cagey. You say you believe him, but can you trust him?"

I smiled. "I don't trust him, not entirely. But I wouldn't feel right just turning him over to the Protectorate. He did come to me for help. It would be like I'd sunk to his level."

Hirin chewed his lip a moment, obviously thinking it over. "I don't like this if it's going to put you—or any of us—in danger. You know PrimeCorp has lost whatever scruples it might once have had."

"None better, and I don't think they had any to start with—at least, not at the executive level. But we'll be careful. And it would be so nice to be able to hand this to Lanar when he gets back with Yuskeya and the others."

"You won't wait and discuss it with him?"

I sighed. "I don't mind making Sedmamin sweat a bit, but we don't know when Lanar will be back. And if PrimeCorp really is after him, time could be short." I didn't want to tell Hirin the other reason I didn't want to wait for Lanar's blessing—he might think it was too dangerous, and say no.

Hirin nodded, then leaned back in the armchair and sighed. "Well, I don't love the idea, but whatever you wanted from me, permission or advice, I guess you've got it. When did you tell him you'd have an answer?"

"I didn't. He's gone to FarView—at least that's what he said; it could have been a cover for all I know. He said he'd get back in touch with me. With luck, it could be done by the time Lanar gets back from Otherspace."

Hirin grinned and snapped off a brisk salute, Protectorate-style. "Very well, Captain. I guess you're back in the Protectorate's service again. Are you sure you wouldn't like a commission? I'm sure your brother could arrange it."

I grimaced. "*Merde*, don't put it that way. You know better than anyone that I was never cut out for the military, and I'm far too set in my ways to change now. Let's just say I'm doing my civic duty and leave it at that."

"That'll do. I learned long ago not to argue with my better half."

"If only that were true."

His face went suddenly solemn, worry lines tightening at the corners of his eyes. "Luta—we do have to be careful, though. I don't trust Sedmamin. This could be part of something bigger. He could be playing us."

I got up and went around to sit on my husband's lap, putting my arms around his shoulders. "If you'd seen him, I don't think you'd say that. If he's acting, it's the most convincing performance I've ever seen." I kissed his cheek. "But we'll be careful, yes. And Nearspace isn't big enough for Sedmamin to hide if he's playing me for a fool."

Then I steeled myself and went to tell the crew what I'd gotten us into this time.

WE COULDN'T MAKE any money hanging around on Cengare waiting to hear from Sedmamin again, so I decided to take a couple of cargo jobs for FarView. If I didn't hear from Sedmamin there, I could always bring a quick cargo back to the Mu Cassiopeia system—it was only one skip and the in-system times were reasonably short—and drop in on my mother on Kiando. The crew could have a bit of downtime and then we'd head back to the station to wait for word from Sedmamin. It would all be a good distraction to keep me from worrying about Lanar, Viss, and Yuskeya, and we shipped out a day later with two cargo pods full.

We'd just made it through the wormhole into Delta Pavonis when the pirates hit us.

I've said before that piracy isn't unheard of in Nearspace, but it isn't all that common, either. Uncommon enough that for years I hadn't carried a single weapon outfitted on the *Tane Ikai*. We kept a well-stocked weapons locker, it was true, but that was only prudent, and most of the time what started out in the locker was still in it at the end of the run. Times had changed. I certainly hadn't expected trouble this close to a busy wormhole, where ship traffic was frequent and regular.

Rei and Baden were on the bridge when it happened, and the rest of us were having supper.

"Captain," Rei said over the comm circuit, her voice crisp and businesslike, "You might want to have a look at this. Incoming ship, possibly not friendly."

"Please tell me it isn't Chron," I said as I got up from the table, before I could help myself. Maja gave me a worried look, and I tried to laugh it off as a bad joke, but I could tell from her eyes that she wasn't buying it.

"No, it's definitely a Nearspace ship," Rei said. "But they're—*merde!*"

"What is it?" I ran down the corridor to the bridge, speaking into my implant. The others were right behind me.

"They fired a warning shot across our bow, Captain," Rei said, the anger in her voice humming like a room full of bees.

I didn't bother responding, since everyone knew what they needed to be doing as we arrived at the bridge. Baden was already at the communications console, his fingers flying over the screen, looking for chatter. If the raiders signaled us at all, he'd find it. Hirin went straight to the empty console we'd converted into a "weapons station" and began tapping things on the screen. Maja slid into the navigation station, looking pale. I wished Viss were here to run drive checks, but since he wasn't, I did that.

"You've got full maneuvering, burst drive ready to go when you need it, Rei," I said. "Baden, anything on the comm?"

He shook his head. "They seem to be content with body language," he said, as another torp skimmed past the nose of the *Tane Ikai*.

"I'm getting annoyed with these people. Hirin, let's send our own message, shall we?"

"No problem, Captain," he said, and I felt the deep bass thump from the bottom of the ship as the torpedo launched. It didn't hit, wasn't intended to, but skimmed close enough that I saw the shields on the vessel flash.

"Nice shooting. Baden, send a keep-away message, would you? Let's make it perfectly clear that we're not putting up with their shenanigans."

"I have the drive signature," Maja said. "Running it through the database now."

"Message coming through. I'll put it on the ship's comm."

"—to see you again, Captain Paixon," a voice said. "Don't worry, the torps were just my little joke."

That voice I recognized only too well, as did everyone else on the bridge. Hirin met my gaze and rolled his eyes. Rei threw her hands up in the air and sat back in her skimchair. The smaller ship maneuvered to drift alongside the *Tane Ikai,* matching our trajectory.

I sat back in my chair, worry evaporating as annoyance took its place. "I didn't catch all of that, but I'm not sure it's a pleasure to encounter you, Jahelia Sord. I'm still miffed that you left without saying goodbye. And with more in your pockets than I'd expected."

She chuckled, her voice coming over the speaker low and throaty. "I did leave you everything, too, Captain. Well, almost. I couldn't bring myself to make a copy of Pita. She's one of a kind."

"Did you know that the data from the Corvid datachip was corrupted when you copied it?" I asked icily. "Or did you do that on purpose to the copy you left me?"

There was a brief silence on her end, and then she said, all trace of humour gone, "No, I didn't know that. To be honest, I haven't looked at the one I . . . have. Please believe me, Captain. I left you that copy in good faith."

The damnable part of it was, I *did* believe her. "All right, so what brings you into my path today?"

This time the pause went on for so long I wondered if she was still there.

"Sord? Did you fall asleep on me?"

"I'm still here. This might seem like an odd question, but

have you heard from Alin Sedmamin lately?"

Well, that was a surprise. I crossed my arms reflexively. "Not working for PrimeCorp again, are you, Sord?"

"No, definitely not. But Sedmamin has left me a rather odd message—just a static deliverable-in-proximity. I haven't talked to him. I wondered if he might have contacted you, too."

I met Hirin's gaze and raised my eyebrows. He shrugged.

"In fact, I have heard from him. What does he want from you?"

She sighed loudly enough that I heard it over the comm. "He wants his ship back, for one thing. However, he's going to be disappointed there. I seem to have lost the *Hunter's Hope,* but I picked this one up for a song on Vele."

I looked a question at Maja. She whispered, "This one is registered as *Shadow's Eclipse.* Drive sig is slightly different from her other ship, but it's probably the same one."

"Looks like a different ship to me," I said, because when it came down to it, I still liked Jahelia Sord better than I did Alin Sedmamin. "Although of course I couldn't swear to it."

"Of course," she agreed, and I sensed the grin behind her words.

"So, what else does Sedmamin want?" I asked Jahelia Sord, because she hadn't really answered that. I wasn't quite ready to tell her about my own conversation with Sedmamin.

"Good question. He wants to talk, said if I could meet him on FarView Station, he could make it worth my while."

"But you didn't want to meet him without checking in with me first? I appreciate that, Sord."

I thought she was grinning again. "He did say he'd broken ties with PrimeCorp, if that made any difference to me, and he asked if I had any idea where you are or how to get in touch with you. Says it's a matter of life and death."

"Sedmamin always liked to lay it on thick," I said. "Did he mention *whose* life?"

"No." She hesitated. "But he didn't sound like himself. You know that arrogance you could always practically smell coming off him? Gone. He sounded—well, just a little bit desperate. Maybe even scared."

"What do you plan to do?"

There was a pause again. "I'll admit I'm curious about the

whole thing. You're about the last person I'd expect Sedmamin to turn to if he really needs help. I messaged back that his best bet was to leave you a DIP same as he did for me."

I really did appreciate Jahelia Sord's decision to track me down before contacting Sedmamin. I'd asked her not to deal with PrimeCorp, and she seemed to be taking her promise not to do so seriously.

"We're headed for FarView, if you want to tag along," I told her. "It might be interesting to see what Sedmamin has in mind. Get in touch with me there once you're settled."

"See you on the station, then," Sord said. "Say hi to Gramps for me."

I caught Hirin's eye roll at Jahelia's "pet name" for him, as the little ship broke off from formation and pulled ahead of us. I had no doubt she was headed for FarView. But Jahelia Sord was not one to "tag along."

Chapter 7 — Lanar
Into Otherspace

ALTHOUGH LUTA AND others had described it to me, I'd never skipped through the wormhole into Woodroct's Star. The system, discovered by the Protectorate, connected Nearspace to the Corvid system Luta and her crew had been the first to report back from. Although Luta and her crew had devised a naming protocol for the systems they'd passed through on their roundabout way back to Nearspace, the common name was already in circulation in the Protectorate. It would eventually be formalized, in honour of the Admiral who'd lost his life, his crew, and his vessel in the first known Chron attack in a century and a half. I sombrely noted as much in the logs, as we passed through.

I also noted the unchanged state of the original wormhole from Delta Pavonis into this system, the one that had been severely damaged by a Corvid particle weapon. It glowed a deep crimson as if a fire burned in its depths, occasionally spitting sparks. Brief, lightning-like flashes arced between the sides like pale bridges for superheated plasma to slither across. No-one with any sense would consider it traversable, or want to get close enough to try.

"Let's give that a nice, wide berth, Commander," I told Linna Drake.

"Aye, *Admiralo*," she confirmed, not taking her eyes from the viewscreen. Her nimble fingers guided the *S. Cheswick* along our course as casually as if she were strumming a guitar.

I'd invited Viss to join us on the bridge, and he'd found a seat at the secondary communications console, redundant and empty most of the time. He'd been generally quiet, sipping from a steaming mug he'd brought with him from the galley, but now he whistled low. "Doesn't look anymore inviting than the last time I saw it," he said. "But the Corvids did say the effects could last for years."

"I don't suppose you have any theories about why the Corvid weapon would have that effect on it?" I asked him.

He pursed his lips but shook his head. "I can tell you how a Ford-Roman field works and what it does," he said, "but beyond that, my understanding of wormhole physics is just about enough to fill this." He held aloft the mug he'd been drinking from. "And that's *with* the caff inside."

"We'll leave it for better minds than ours, then," I said. I was just as pleased not to keep looking at the malevolent-looking, angry red eye of the wormhole.

Once I'd torn my eyes from that, there was plenty else to look at. The star in this system was a faraway, blue-white glow, casting the near side of an adobe-coloured planet into shadow. Closer, a particle cloud hung against the deep velvet backdrop of space, shading though oranges and auburns but flashing a pop of bright purple specularity in the centre. The planet caught several moons in its orbit, one of which I knew was the Chron artifact moon, identifiable by its tiny size. I searched the viewscreen but couldn't spot it. It must be circling the other side of the planet.

"You have the coordinates for the wormhole into Corvid space?" I asked Commander Drake. It should be only twenty minutes away at our cruising speed.

"Yes, sir."

"Take us in to about a thousand klicks, then send the preliminary message through," I said. Our message would be brief. It would let them know we were coming, ask for the coordinates to navigate the protective asteroid field we knew tumbled at the other end of the wormhole, and give my identification both as a Protectorate Admiral and, probably more importantly, as Luta's brother. With luck they'd respond quickly, because if they didn't, we might have to risk the passage without their help. We couldn't sit on this side of the wormhole forever, waiting for a welcome message that might never come.

The asteroid field presented a considerable concern. Although the *Cheswick*'s shields were ten times the strength of the *Tane Ikai*'s, we were also a much larger vessel. It would be tricky to navigate safely through the field without the "key" from the Corvids. I was prepared to try shooting our way through with the particle beam, but I wasn't sure how effective it would be, or how much we might get banged up in the process. I told my sensors officer to log everything he could about the system as we passed through it—there's no such thing as too much data—and watched for the next wormhole to become discernible on the screen. It remained hidden until we were almost at the thousand-klick limit. At least it had not been turned into a hellmouth like the other one, for which I was fervently grateful. I'd been worried that the Chron could have damaged this one to cut off connections to the Corvid system.

We fetched up at the designated coordinates and Lieutenant Medenez, the comms officer on duty, said, "Permission to send the message through the wormhole, Admiral?"

"Go ahead," I told him. "All channels open for a reply."

"Aye, sir."

And we waited. A minute, then two, with no answer from the Corvids. Linna Drake turned from the pilot's board to look at me, concern clouding her face. There were any number of reasons the Corvids might not reply, but there were a couple in particular I didn't want to think about.

"Re-send, in case the asteroids are causing a problem," I said. "Viss, the station was actually fairly close to that end of the wormhole?"

He nodded. His voice was tight when he answered. "It'll be visible as soon as we're through the wormhole and clear the asteroids. Should get a quick response."

"Send a tracer scan, as well," I directed. That would normally be a precaution to make sure no other ship was in transit through a wormhole, but in this case, it might tell us if the way beyond was clear or not.

Medenez complied, and we waited only about thirty seconds

before he said, "Tracer scan is back. Looks like the wormhole itself is clear, but there's definitely something on the other side of it."

"That," Viss drawled, "would probably be an asteroid. Or several."

Damne. Just what I didn't want to hear.

"Thank you, Mr. Medenez."

We waited in silence for a full ten minutes more without any answer to the comm message. Finally, Linna Drake said, "Admiral, if we're going through without the asteroid field key, we should divert everything we can to the shields as soon as we clear the wormhole."

It was one of the few drawbacks of the Ford-Roman system for traversing wormholes that energy shields had to be disabled inside the wormhole. "I'll switch the shields on myself once we're through," I told her. "You'll be busy flying us and nav will be looking at the asteroids, too." Luta had told me the tale of how she and Rei had navigated these same asteroids by working in tandem from the two pilot's boards, but I didn't think that would work with a much larger Pegasus-class cruiser. Fortunately, Linna Drake was one of the most competent pilots I'd encountered in the Protectorate. She flew a ship through some strange synergy between herself and the vessel. I couldn't explain it, but I did trust it.

"Admiral, if I might," Viss said. "I can switch on the shields. Why don't you keep yourself free to assess whatever we find on the other side?"

I grinned. "Don't trust me, Mr. Feron?"

"I just like to be useful," he said, grinning back, and I transferred the controls he'd need to his console.

"Send it one more time," I told Medenez. "We'll wait five more minutes for a reply. Commander Drake, alert engineering that we'll be switching the shields to full as soon as we exit the wormhole. I want a Level 2 brownout in effect so there's lots of juice available."

I didn't really expect an answer from the Corvids now, but I thought we might get third time lucky. But the comm board stayed silent, and so five minutes later, I ordered Drake to take us in to the wormhole.

Skipping through a wormhole is an experience that never

grows old, just as sunsets and sunrises never grow old. The swirl of light and colour is breathtaking, its beauty sharp-edged, otherworldly, and dangerous. "A hundred rainbows spinning down a drain," Luta had once described it to me, and I never skipped without hearing her words. The sensation that always accompanied a wormhole skip was somewhat less pleasant. I've heard many people say that it doesn't affect them, but even after countless skips, I still feel it—a tug on the bottom of my stomach, a silent protest at the back of my eyes. I'm not really complaining. It's another reminder that after all this time, I'm still alive.

Commander Drake piloted us through with deft fingers, so smoothly that the sense of vertigo was slight. "Coming out of skip," she said.

"Shields to full," I said automatically, still engrossed in the play of cosmic forces across the front viewscreen.

Dankas dio, Viss had been right to suggest I might need all my attention on the end of the wormhole. I'd given the shields command, but I wasn't expecting the bone-shaking impact that waited for us at the end.

As the impact rattled the ship the viewscreen exploded in a blast of light. The ship yawed starwise. Another impact battered us from that side and I bit the inside of my cheek, hard. I clutched one arm of my chair, shielding my eyes with my other hand as I tasted the hot, coppery tang of blood.

"*Fek, fek, fek!*"

I heard Linna Drake swear just above a whisper as she fought to right the *Cheswick*. Nav had been knocked half out of his chair but was snapping low instructions at her. I caught the word *asteroids*.

"Cut all drives. Weapons, fire particle beams, wide array," I ordered. "No target, just spread."

Another impact came from above, and the Cheswick dropped away under me for the space of a few heartbeats. My stomach lurched as the artificial gravity compensated. As the light from the initial explosion faded from the viewscreen, I saw the problem. The asteroids were not moving, and a huge one had been parked almost directly in front of the wormhole's mouth. We'd barely emerged from the skip when we plowed directly into it, knocking an enormous chunk of the rock free. The explosion had been a combination of the impact and the intense flare of the shields. Now we bounced around between the static chunks of rock and ice like a drunkard trying to navigate an unfamiliar living room.

No wonder the tracer beam had bounced straight back at us. But it hadn't encountered a phalanx of tumbling asteroids, just a massive one parked in front of the wormhole's mouth. I mentally smacked myself on the forehead.

"They're not moving this time," Viss said. "And they look like they've been shot to hell."

"Reverse thrusters; cut our speed," I ordered, finally leaving my chair and stumbling over to the auxiliary piloting board. "Commander, I'll get us slowed down, you deal with evasives."

"Aye, sir," she breathed, her hands flying on the board. We still darted forward, smaller impacts sounding and flaring around the ship, but she'd straightened us out and managed to avoid some of the larger obstacles.

Slowly I realized that the asteroid field was not simply static—that wasn't what Viss meant. As opposed to the orchestrated gauntlet of tumbling boulders, as Luta had described, this was a drifting field of debris. Someone had tried to destroy the asteroids—some had been pulverized almost to dust, while others sported ragged gouges as if a hungry monster had rampaged through, biting and clawing at will.

"Sensors, are you getting all this?" I asked.

"Yes, sir!"

"What happened here?" Linna Drake asked, her voice and hands now steadier as she wove us through the obstructions. The shields still flared, but less intensely, and fewer impacts rattled the ship.

"Someone shot the place up," I said. "Tried to destroy the whole asteroid field, or at least make it so that the Corvids couldn't use their technology to form a barrier to the wormhole."

"I was thinking the same thing," Viss said. Something in his voice made me look up, but his face was impassive.

"So, was it the Corvids? Funny for them to want to shoot up their own defences," Linna Drake asked.

I glanced at her profile and saw her chew her bottom lip, a

sure sign that she was worried or pensive.

"You think any Chron went through that wormhole?" she asked. "If they were the ones who tried to blow it up?"

I drummed my fingers on the edge of the console. "If so, where did they go? We've had a patrol on the Nearspace side of the replacement wormhole since before the diplomatic mission went in. No-one's come out except the *Airavata* and the *Tane Ikai*."

"They could be in the in-between system," Viss said. "We've only been in one small corner of it, after all."

"True. If they're there, they must have moved deep in-system, because we didn't pick them up on scans when we passed through."

"Coming up on the edge of the debris field," Drake announced, and we left our musings about the Chron for the time being. A moment later we cleared the last of the shattered and pock-marked asteroid remains and emerged into the clear dark space of the Corvid system. In the distance, a dim orange star threw off heat that would dissipate long before it reached here. Reddish light reflected off an interstellar dust cloud, painted with haphazard brush strokes of sulfurous yellow. There were no planets, at least not in this sector of the system. Only the Corvid station waited for us, dimly lit in the weak reflected sunlight.

I hadn't seen the station personally before this, but I'd seen images of it from the sensors aboard the *Tane Ikai*. What waited for us now beyond the edge of the debris field was immeasurably changed from the visuals Luta had brought back. Sweat bloomed cold and damp on the back of my neck and the palms of my hands as I tried to make sense of what I was seeing.

"*Merde*," Viss muttered.

"It didn't look like this in the pictures I saw," I said to Viss.

It wasn't really a question, but he answered. "No, sir. Very different. But it doesn't look—exactly—like damage."

Where the station had previously sported gelatinous-looking extrusions or spikes in varying sizes, it was now almost perfectly spherical. It looked more like a small, round moonlet than a station, hanging silent and alone and limned with red light. At first, I'd thought the change had been effected by the Chron forcibly, by somehow shearing off the spikes—but Viss was right. It didn't have the look of violence—no scorch marks or ragged edges or gaping holes. Considering what Luta had told me about the extreme adaptability of the Corvid environment suits and the malleability of the station itself, it was possible the Corvids had transformed their habitat on purpose.

While it was an interesting consideration, I found that I cared about the answer only insofar as it related to the health and well-being of Andresson, Didkovsky, Summergale, and Yuskeya Blue. The pressing question was only *are they all right?*

"Keep the shields up, and take us in slowly toward the station," I ordered. "Medenez, broadcast our intention message, please. Keep it looping unless and until we get a response. Commander, take us on a slow circuit of the station so we can attempt to determine its status."

The bridge was very quiet as we made our approach to the station and began to move around it. Medenez said nothing, which I assumed meant no reply from the station, but I didn't want him to tell me that outright. No response could mean there was no-one left to respond.

On closer inspection, it became clear that our first impression had been wrong; the station had suffered massive damage. At intervals around the strangely gelatinous-looking exterior of the *uruglat*, fractured sections danced with yellow arcs of energy like chain lighting. In some, eyes of xanthous fire burned, shifting variably to white or red. They couldn't be actual fires, I reasoned—no oxygen to feed them—but they contributed to the overall feeling of desertion and destruction the station engendered. The protrusions the Corvids used to control the asteroid fields didn't appear to have been sheared off or destroyed. More likely, they'd been drawn or absorbed back into the main body of the station itself.

We had made perhaps a three-quarters circuit of the station when Medenez blurted, "Response from the station coming in, Admiral."

"Switch it to bridge comm," I said, trying to keep the profound relief out of my voice.

"—extend our warmest greetings to the brother of Luta Paixon," a static-riddled voice said. The words were studded with pauses for breath, as if the speaker required more oxygen than was currently available. "We are in distress and recovery mode, but if you will proceed as directed we can offer you reception."

Medenez looked at me. I nodded.

"This is Admiral Lanar Mahane. We will proceed as directed," I replied. "Do you have news of our people who were separated from our ships in the Chron attack? We've come to take them home."

There was a long silence before the breathless voice came again. "I will share all I know," it said finally. "But I must tell you with great sorrow that they are not here."

THE DIRECTIONS TOOK us to a sector of the station where, since we'd passed it a few minutes ago, a large rectangular section had changed—smoothed and flattened, carving a chunk out of the spherical shape. Intermittent flashes of blue light outlined it. It was roughly the size of the *Cheswick,* although I was slightly mystified about what we were to do with it. There was no spot to set down.

Viss chuckled. "Wait for it."

The voice came again. "If you will station your ship close to the designated area, I will attempt to offer docking facilities," the Corvid explained. "Our systems have suffered extensive damage, and I fear we cannot extend the hospitality of a compatible environment inside the *uruglat,* but if you have suitable mobile enclosures you will be able to move about freely."

"Mobile enclosures" had to mean enviro suits, of which we naturally had plenty. I fought an urge to tell the Corvid that we'd rather he—or she—simply tell us what had happened so that we could get to wherever the others were. But the Corvids might need our help, too, and they were freshly-acquired allies against the Chron.

I instructed Commander Drake to take us into the position indicated, and once we were there, the station did the thing Luta had described to me. Even having it described didn't come close to the experience, though. It was . . . stunning, and terrifying, to see it happen. The body of the station flowed and elongated a dark pseudopod toward the ship, enveloping it in inky blackness as it slid and rippled over the viewscreen. Our internal lights didn't go out, so the darkness was more a feeling than a physical thing. And then we *moved*—in a way that a ship should not move—until the dark matter flowed away from the viewscreen. We'd been transported to a docking bay.

"*Sankta merde!*" Medenez breathed.

As soon as we'd stopped moving, I stood from my chair. I'll admit my legs felt watery, as if I'd been stationary for hours and the muscles had cramped up. "I'm going EVA," I announced. "Commander Drake, you have the chair, and I'll have a comm open the entire time I'm off the ship."

She turned and might have protested, but I held up a hand. "Mr. Feron, Doctor Ahmed, and Lieutenant-Commander Galwan will come with me. I don't expect we'll be long, but we have to have this conversation and I want to get an impression of the extent of the damage if I can."

Viss and I headed for the corridor to the EVA lockers, and I pinged Ahmed and Galwan, my head of security, as we walked. Annicket Galwan reached the lockers before me and had her suit half on when Viss and I arrived. She looked up and gave us a nod, her brown eyes bright with excitement. No-one loved an exploration into the unknown as much as Galwan. She was a tall, well-muscled and agile woman, and wore her dark hair cut in a close military skim. She'd had my back in more than one tight situation in the past, and I could count on her to be level-headed and smart in any crisis. Not that I expected a crisis, but I didn't take chances.

Doctor Louis Ahmed puffed up as I was closing the front of my suit. Despite being one of the best doctors I'd ever met in the Protectorate or outside it, he tended to skip physical training and exercise sessions, mandated or not, whenever he could plead out of them by saying he was needed in the med bay. Ahmed had a round head atop a rounded body and when he wore an envirosuit, he reminded me of an ambulatory snowman. He carried a medunit and an emergency medkit and set them on a bench with a shake of his head.

"I hope you don't expect me to treat any of these aliens," Ahmed said as he pulled an EVA suit from a locker, "even though I brought those along. I can treat humans, Vilisians, and Lobors, but beyond that—"

I held up a hand to placate him. "Don't worry. I'm told we

won't find our missing people here, so I doubt you'll need anything, but you're observant. Just keep your eyes and ears open, okay? Both of you."

Galwan nodded and gave me a thumbs-up, because she already had the helmet of her suit in place and locked down. Viss was ready to go as well, and he and Galwan went through the partner suit check routine. Ahmed and I hurried to catch up, checked each other, and then we all went out the airlock and into the Corvid station.

Luta had told me about the all-black decor, but I realized as I stood in the docking bay that I'd thought she was exaggerating. Not so. Everything was black, black, and more black. Other than that, it looked like every docking bay I've ever stood in, except for one other detail—it also looked like it had been the site of a major earthquake. Some of the walls buckled in a way that made me think they weren't supposed to be like that, even given the oddness of the station overall. Irregular patches broke the smooth surfaces of walls and floor. I knelt to examine one. It revealed broken arrays of small, hexagonal-shaped discs. They obviously should be seamlessly connected, but holes gaped where sections were missing or discs jumbled in snarled clots. Occasional sparks or rivulets of yellow energy erupted in these damaged areas.

Viss squatted beside me. "That's not normal," he confirmed. "Not that I understand 'normal' here, but that's not it."

"Looks like they took some heavy hits."

We had only a moment to take in these details before a Corvid hologram materialized near an exit door and beckoned to us. I knew from Luta's sensor data what they looked like, but I was still struck by the alien's height. I crossed to the door, Viss at my side and Ahmed and Galwan following behind. The hologram winked out. The door opened when I stretched out a hand to it, sliding into the wall on the left-hand side. Although "sliding" sounds like a mechanical or electronic movement, and this was—not. It gave the impression that the door had been absorbed into the wall, not merely retracted inside it.

Beyond lay a corridor in similar disarray to the docking bay, but traversable. The floor slanted downward away from us and curved in a lazy arc to the right, so we followed it, delving deeper into the station. Glowing rods ran lengthwise down the ceiling of the corridor, providing a muted, organic illumination. The light itself was a pale yellow, warmer than we humans would generally use. At intervals, the damaged hex discs appeared in larger conglomerations, but they didn't appear to be getting worse. The damage was done, but seemingly under control. Although I had my external mic wide open, the only sound it picked up was the occasional crackle or static-like sound from a damaged section.

After perhaps a minute of careful walking, we fetched up at an apparent dead end, but when we stopped in front of the wall it slid aside as the docking bay door had done. Beyond lay a room about half as large as the docking bay, still resplendent in unrelieved black, but populated with actual Corvids. The room was a control centre, although it lacked the physical screens or consoles one would find on a Nearspace station or ship's bridge. Instead the Corvids used a technology similar to their hologram representations. From horizontal cylinders on the floor, sheets of blue-white light projected upward, displaying darker blue images and symbols that must be the Corvid language. The Corvids interacted with them by breaking the light pattern in certain spots. I learned one thing that I don't think any of our ambassadors or diplomats had discovered on their sojourn here—what the Corvids' hands looked like. By all reports, they had kept their hands hidden during all encounters with our people, inside pockets or folds in the front of the long robes they wore. When asked, they replied that it was merely a cultural tradition in the presence of guests, and naturally the diplomats had not probed further.

Now, though, the crow-like aliens had been forced to set aside the niceties. Few even gave us a glance as we stood in the doorway to the room, so engrossed were they in the task of trying to repair and maintain their station. And none attempted to hide their hands. They extended from open sleeves and had the same sleek, dark colouring visible on the Corvids' heads, although for some it lightened along the length of the hand. Each hand had three long, bony fingers, thinner and more flexible than human fingers—in fact, they had twice as many joints as ours. The "palm" was much smaller in relation to the length of the fingers, and on either side, a pale, wicked-looking claw curved out and down. The claws were so at odds with the calm, restrained, and polite nature I'd come to associate with the Corvids both from Luta's encounters with them and the diplomats' reports, I felt an involuntary spasm clench my gut. *A swipe with one of those could open a human throat*, I thought, and then wondered what had prompted it. Some instinctive, primal reaction, left over from a more primitive time. I swallowed hard and hoped my face hadn't shown the obvious recoil I'd felt.

One tall Corvid had turned when the door opened and now glided toward us. At first, I thought it wore a hat, then realized that one side of its head and an eye were completely covered by a thick, coarse bandage. The one visible eye, however, was bright and intense in its gaze. As the alien approached, it tucked its hands away, and I felt a strange relief at the disappearance of those claws.

"Brother of Luta Paixon," the Corvid said, and inclined its head in a brief bow. "I am Fha, and you are welcome to our sadly damaged *uruglat*."

So, this was the Corvid who had helped Luta. Her voice resonated with a sadness so profound it was almost a physical thing. "You have my deep thanks for the help you gave my sister, and we're sorry to find you in such trouble," I said. "Can we offer any assistance?"

Yuskeya and the others were my priorities, but it was inconceivable not to offer help to such a voice.

The Corvid inclined her head to me. "We have repairs well underway, thank you. And it is your own people who concern you. We understand."

I nodded. "You—or someone—told me that they are not here. What happened to them?"

A look passed over Fha's face—a face so alien that it would be difficult to believe one could identify emotion. But it held a deep and painful distress.

"Come," she said, and turned back into the room. Her invitation encompassed the group, so the four of us followed as she moved smoothly to a light screen and, keeping her hand partly hidden within her sleeve, poked a long finger into several spots in the display. Moving images replaced the symbols, and although the display was mainly monochromatic, I realized that it was a video representation of the Chron attack. The ships that dove toward the station launching torpedo-like missiles were the same as those the *Tane Ikai* had recorded. There was no audio.

After several seconds, the playback switched to the interior of the station, and I recognized what must be the figures of Andresson and Didkovsky. They huddled against a dark wall in full Protectorate EVA suits—it could have been anywhere in the station, from what I had seen—and a third figure crouched near them. Summergale, judging by the elongated helmet that accommodated the Lobors' distinctive head shape. A Corvid stood nearby, interacting with a small light display that sprung from a device it held in a long-fingered hand. Then the scene shuddered violently as the station suffered an impact, and the Corvid staggered and fell hard, one arm twisting unnaturally as it landed. The screen device flew from its hand and smashed into the wall. Summergale made a motion as if to go to the fallen alien, but another EVA-suited figure arrived from off-screen and got there first.

My mouth felt suddenly too dry. *Yuskeya.* The arm patch on the suit clearly identified it as the *Tane Ikai's.*

She helped the injured Corvid sit against one wall. One of its long-fingered, clawed hands hung limply to the floor, but it seemed otherwise all right. Yuskeya and Didkovsky put their helmets together for a brief conversation. The image flickered and re-formed frequently—probably every time the station took a hit. I wondered where, at this point in the scenario, Luta had been. Making for the wormhole, I guessed, and feeling terrible.

Before the trio made any further move, I saw Andresson startle and bump back against the wall. Then five figures moved into the view of the camera, and the discomfort I'd felt at the sight of the Corvid claws was nothing compared to the raw, gut-clenching fear those figures inspired.

A hundred and fifty years hadn't changed the armour in any significant way, unless it was to make it sleeker and deadlier.

The five newcomers were Chron.

Chapter 8 — Luta
Nothing but Trouble

WE ARRIVED AT FarView Station without further incident and had the docking technicalities worked out by dinnertime. I told everyone to go off and enjoy some R & R, since there was really nothing to do until Alin Sedmamin contacted me. Well, I assumed Jahelia Sord would track me down to have a chat once she'd looked after docking her own ship. Or PrimeCorp's ship. You couldn't convince me that it wasn't the same one she'd claimed Alin Sedmamin had given her, but it was none of my business. Hirin and I were the only ones who stayed aboard the *Tane Ikai*. Most of the food businesses in the hub would deliver up to docked ships, so we ordered honest-to-goodness pizza and lounged in the big galley armchairs to eat it. Hirin put one of the FarView music feeds on through the comm system and a soothing instrumental filled the room.

"*Dankas dio*, it's actually quiet in here," Hirin observed. "Why is it that we keep meaning to have a vacation and we never actually do?"

I nodded. "I sometimes think I'd be happy living in less interesting times."

"Ha! You'd be bored within a week," Hirin chortled, and I threw a chunk of pizza crust at him.

"It would take at least a month," I retorted. "Maybe it's the fault of the crew. Did we get into this much trouble when it was just the two of us flying this thing around?"

"I think we did," Hirin said around another bite of pizza. "But we were younger and better able to handle it then."

"Speak for yourself, old man."

"I am, darling."

We ate in contented silence for a few moments, but with so much weighing on our minds, it couldn't last. "I checked in with Regina Holles, but Lanar's not back yet," I told Hirin. "I wonder where he is? And if he's picked them up yet. He's been gone a long time."

"Longer than I'd expected."

"They might have stayed to help the Corvids," I said, nibbling at the crust. There were other possibilities—that someone was too badly injured to move right away, or the Chron had attacked again. I didn't want to consider those.

"I'd rather he was back in Nearspace if we're going to start ferrying Alin Sedmamin around." Hirin frowned at his pizza as if it were arguing with him.

I licked pizza sauce from my lips. We hadn't really talked about this much since my initial conversation with Sedmamin. "Are you starting to think I shouldn't help him?"

He considered. "No, it's not that. Helping Sedmamin is for the greater good. The way you have to take horrible-tasting medicine with sugar or honey sometimes, because it will make you feel better in the end."

"But it's still not pleasant."

He fixed me with a skeptical stare. "Having that man on this ship will be less than 'not pleasant'. It will be a supreme test of my self-control not to beat the living—"

My ID implant beeped. Since there was no-one else on board I'd routed all incoming calls there. I pulled my datapad off the table and transferred the message. "Oh, great," I breathed.

It was Jahelia Sord. I hadn't expected her to contact me so promptly. My impression of her was that she preferred to operate as a lone gun—or at least, with her enhanced datapad AI as her primary companion. But I did encourage her to get in touch with me, after all. Maybe she'd read between the lines and realized I knew more about what Sedmamin wanted than I'd said. I arranged my face into something that wasn't obvious dismay and opened the connection. "Hello, Sord. I take it you've arrived at the station?"

Her face could never seem to be free of that slightly mocking look, but she smiled. She no longer wore the Erian *pridattii*. I'd been quite sure they were an affectation or an attempt at a disguise when she wore them before, so their absence wasn't a complete shock. She'd also abandoned the striking profusion of black-and-white curls, and her hair now hung caramel-brown and straight to her shoulders. It swung as she nodded.

"I'm on docking arm C, so whenever you'd like to have that conversation, I'm free," she said with casual indifference.

I glanced over at Hirin and he shrugged. "I have a couple of slices of pizza left here, if you haven't had dinner yet," I said. "We could chat over that or double caff."

She half-smiled. "Nice attempt at playing the hostess, Paixon," she said. "I've eaten, thanks, but I'll take you up on the caff. Fifteen minutes all right?"

"That'll be fine. Dock 25-B. I'll meet you at the door."

"Got it," she said, and broke the connection.

Hirin grimaced at me. "And I thought we were going to have a romantic evening alone, with all the kids out playing."

"Hey, you could have said no!"

"It's all right. I doubt you two will be able to talk for more than half an hour without getting into a fight, and I can amuse myself for that long," he said. He pushed out of his chair and took his plate to the scrubber. "Will I store the leftovers?"

I popped the last bite of pizza into my mouth, and got up and helped him clear away the remains of our supper. Then I started a fresh cycle of caff brewing and went to our quarters to change. Okay, I put on a clean white t-shirt and brushed my hair. I wasn't too worried about my appearance for a heart-to-heart with Jahelia Sord. Hirin kissed my cheek and said he would stay in our room and read.

And I went off to wait for Jahelia Sord on a very different footing than the last time we'd met.

AT THE AIRLOCK, I opened it and stepped out onto the dockway to wait for Sord. It was busy, clotted with merchants and civilian travellers going to and from ships docked along the station's B-arm. Any military ships docked at the station would be in the A section, on another arm, while the C section on the third arm would be mainly freighters, cargo-only, and maybe a few smaller ships that overflowed from B. So I didn't see many Protectorate uniforms, but I did see humans in family and business groups, lupine Lobors with their slightly bouncing gait and colourful, flowing clothes, and tall, amber-skinned Vilisians who seemed to glide rather than walk. Everyone hurrying or strolling about their own business. Everyone potentially affected by the favour I was going to attempt for Alin Sedmamin. A shudder ran up my back, and it had nothing to do with the temperature-controlled dockway.

Even in that crowd, Jahelia Sord stood out. Tonight, she was dressed in tight black pants and knee-high dark blue spacer's boots, a fitted navy-blue jacket that skimmed her hips, and a crimson shirt with a high collar that hugged her throat. Her lips were the same colour as her shirt, and even without the *pridattii* and striking black-and-white curls, she still looked dramatic. She caught sight of me waiting and flashed a hard-to-read smile. When she was close enough, she put out a hand to shake.

I took it, feeling a bit awkward, as if she'd taken control of the encounter already. "It's good to see you," I said automatically.

"Is it?" she asked with a quizzical smile. "I thought my presence probably fell more into the category of 'necessary evil'."

"Oh, it does. I was just trying to be polite." I smiled, though, and motioned her inside with a wide sweep of my hand. "You know how I insist on politeness."

"I don't remember that," she said playfully as we turned the corner toward the galley. It felt a little strange, how well she knew the layout of the ship, although it made sense—she'd spent enough time on it. "But I could be remembering wrong since I was essentially a prisoner at the time."

"A prisoner who refused to stay in her prison, as I recall. Double caff?"

"Delighted."

I fixed the hot drinks for both of us and turned back to her. She'd seated herself in the chair that Hirin had recently vacated, so I returned to mine and passed her the caff. We both sipped hesitantly, and I felt as if our banter had both dealt with the preliminaries and cemented our positions. We weren't friends, but we could manage to get along when the occasion warranted it.

Jahelia Sord must have felt the same way because after a sip of caff, she said, "So. Sedmamin. What is up with him? He looked like *merde*."

I sipped and tilted my head to one side. "He's in trouble—apparently PrimeCorp wants him to take a fall this time, and it's a big one. He wants me—my crew—to help him out. I assume he has a role for you to play in his scheme as well."

She raised an eyebrow. "He said as much to me—but that's all he said. No details. So, if I knew what he wanted from you, it might give me a clue."

"Why'd you agree, if he wouldn't tell you what he wants?"

She laughed. "Who said I'd agreed? I told him I'd think about it. He told me he'd be on FarView when I was ready, and if I couldn't find him, to get in touch with you." She stirred the liquid in her cup and watched steam curl lazily up from it. "He sounded pretty confident that you'd help him out, but he kind of pissed me off, to tell the truth. Seemed to think I still owed him something."

"But you don't see it that way?" I leaned forward. "Just between you and me, I suspect your new ship isn't all that new, and that it originally came from Sedmamin."

She leaned in, echoing my movement. A half-smile quirked the side of her mouth. "Just between you and me, I think I stopped owing him anything when he got me stranded in Otherspace with hostile aliens."

I grinned. "You have a point." I leaned back again and took a sip of my drink. "Well, here's what he wants from me." I briefly outlined Sedmamin's request that I get him to Earth and help him retrieve files and personal items, then see him to somewhere he considered safe.

"Huh," she said, and sipped at her drink. "Well, that does give me an idea of what he might want from me. When I was participating in the 'trials' for Pita—my AI, remember?"

I remembered the AI well. She'd helped save my life and my crew, and given me a glimpse into Sord's personality, after whom she was modeled. I nodded.

"He gave me access codes for some restricted areas of the

PrimeCorp facility—and I had the feeling that maybe he didn't have complete authority to do that. He as much as told me to keep it under my hat, and to take . . . precautions, anytime I used them."

"Precautions like, not being seen?"

She grinned like the only cat aboard a mouse-ridden far trader.

"And you still have those access codes, and maybe he needs them to get in, because probably he's been locked out of the system since he's now *persona non grata* around PrimeCorp."

She smoothed a hand over her hair, which didn't need smoothing. "That would be my guess."

I swirled my own drink, seeing how close I could get it to the rim without spilling. "That makes you pretty integral to this plan. Will you do it?" I asked. "Because if you're out, it probably isn't worth the risk for me to try and help him at all. I certainly don't have special access to anything involved with PrimeCorp."

She sighed and got up from her chair, shucking her jacket and hanging it over the back of the seat. She walked around the room for a moment as if she were a potential buyer assessing the amenities of the ship, running a finger along the countertop. Finally, she stopped and leaned against the large table, crossing her ankles and her arms. "Sedmamin did intimate that he'd pay me for my part in the plan. I expect he's got some secret resources around Nearspace. He offered you files. Why would you help him, if you do?"

I shrugged. "Because there's more riding on this than just Alin Sedmamin's health and welfare. I honestly don't care that much about that. But the files—that could have huge repercussions over all of Nearspace. My brother would leap at the chance to have copies of those that weren't . . . ahem . . . stolen."

"Yeah, that's what I was thinking." She hoisted herself up on the table and scooted backwards, pulling her knees up to sit cross-legged. She rested her chin in her hands and her elbows on her knees and regarded me in silence for a moment. Her head tilted to the side as she considered me, a slight frown dimpling a line between her eyebrows. "Do you ever get tired of thinking about other people before yourself?"

I snorted, and for a moment I didn't know how to answer.

"Where did that come from?"

She lifted her shoulders. "I don't know. I watched and listened, you know, when I was on board the ship before. And when we were on that Chron station. You're often kind of flip about it, but you really care about everyone—your family, your crew, that Lobor—and it extends even further than that. Like now. You're thinking about all of Nearspace when you should be wondering if you're going to get caught helping Sedmamin—a man who's made your life absolute *hell* from what I can tell—retrieve data from a secure, restricted facility where he has no legal business going. Me," she said, sliding her hands behind her on the table and leaning back against them, "I think about what's in it for me."

I got up abruptly and took my mug to the scrubber, then turned to face her. "I don't really know how to answer that," I said slowly. "Yes, Alin Sedmamin has been nothing but trouble for me, for most of my life. But this is not about me, or about him, really, the way I see it. I don't have a good answer except it's just the way I am, I guess. That sounds kind of lame, though." I put on a half-smile.

She shook her head. "No, not lame. I'm not sure what it is. But the annoying part about it is that you make *me* want to do this thing, too. Because of everyone else in Nearspace, and not *just* because of what might be in it for me." She mock-glared at me. "That pisses me off more than anything else."

I laughed. "I think there's more to you than that tough exterior you show the world, and you don't want to admit it."

She gazed off over my head, into the far distance at something only she could see. "Well. I guess I'll see what I can do to help, if that does turn out to be what Sedmamin wants. It should be interesting to hear what he has to say, anyway."

Jahelia Sord slid off the table and brought her empty mug over to me. "Thanks for the caff."

I took a second to change mental gears. "There's one other thing," I said as I took the mug and set it inside the scrubber.

She raised her eyebrows. "The other shoe falls."

I smiled. "Nothing too serious. But it's about— the nanobioscavengers," I said.

Her face went very still. The look was gone in an instant, but I'd seen it, and I knew the casual lightness of her voice when she spoke was at least partly a put-on. "What about them?"

"I talked to my mother about you. She thinks you should see her to get checked over and maybe—probably—get an infusion of newer, better bioscavs. If mine could fail, so could yours, anytime. They're about the same age, even if they might not be the same prototype."

Her face still had that closed-off look, even as she kept her tone casual. "I've never had any problems," she said, "but tell your mother, thanks for the offer."

I frowned. "Don't just shrug it off. Your parents both died— you told me that. Theirs failed. Given the time frame, yours can't be all that different."

She crossed back to her chair to collect her jacket. "Thanks for the caff, and the gossip about Sedmamin," she said, shrugging into the coat. "I'll get in touch when I hear anything from him, and you can do the same. You know how to reach me. In the meantime, I'm due some rest and relaxation, and FarView's a good place for that."

"But you'll think about it? The nanobioscavengers?"

She didn't answer right away, just buttoned up her jacket and pulled it down over her hips. Then she turned a bright, false smile my way. "Thanks, Paixon. I'm sure we'll talk again soon. I know the way out."

Without waiting for me to answer, she turned and strode out of the galley.

Two days passed without any word from either Sedmamin or Jahelia Sord. I'd never admit it to Viss Feron, but what I missed most was Viss asking my permission to tear apart this system or that intake, since we had some "down" time. I wondered what he and Lanar were doing all this time. I wondered if they'd found Yuskeya and the others. I wondered when we would hear something. I wondered if I was going to go crazy waiting.

Rei and Maja did their best to distract me—hell, they were distracting themselves, too, and they knew it as well as I did. We went shopping on the mercantile level, and between them they made me buy more new clothes than I normally would have in a year. I was sure some things would be consigned to a drawer and never seen again. We all went out and dined in some of the restaurants, trying to keep the conversation light and fun. We took in entertainment; a play adapted from a Tali Shonen novel I'd read, and a blues band playing in a poky little club. Twice I saw Jahelia Sord out and about on her own errands, but apart from a smile and a nod, she made no move to join us or strike up a conversation.

It was the longest sojourn I'd ever made on FarView—usually we might drop in to offload or pick up some cargo, or make a one-night stopover so that people could get off the ship and physically and metaphorically "stretch their legs." The station was home to about six thousand residents, with another thousand travellers, tourists, and visitors likely to be aboard at any given time. Many of the permanent residents worked in scientific research for one corporation or another, because none of the Corps owned FarView—it was maintained by the Worlds Council and governed by the NWAC, and was mandated to offer equal opportunity to anyone who wanted to live, work, or trade there. The three docking arms extended from the top of the central hub, which in turn was comprised of habitat, mercantile, entertainment, cargo, administrative, food production, and laboratory levels. Each arm was capable of docking ships on four sides, so there was rarely a problem obtaining a docking assignment.

The Protectorate maintained administrative offices on FarView, partly because it was responsible for station security, and partly because it was a convenient hub in the system. So Protectorate uniforms mingled in the crowds of civilians on all of the levels. I kept an eye out for Regina Holles, since Lanar had said she was here, but beyond our initial conversation our paths didn't cross.

On the third day after we'd arrived, Hirin and I had left the *Tane Ikai* to seek out a bit of lunch on one of the mercantile levels. We found a little cafe with a view wall on the outer rim of the station offering a lovely overlook on the vista of star-studded space. We were lingering over dessert—cinnamon *pano* studded with dried *jarlees* fruit that made me lonely for Yuskeya—when the station klaxon startled everyone around us.

"Lockdown protocol initiated," a calm but commanding voice intoned over the ship's comm system. "Please proceed to refuge stations."

Around us, chairs scraped the floor as people began to move

toward the cafe's exit. They stayed calm, but concerned faces and whispered questions flurried all around us. *Solar flare? Radiation pocket? Micrometeoroid dust cloud?*

Hirin looked a question at me and I raised my eyebrows, pushing my own chair back. The comm system continued to issue instructions in that clear, unruffled voice.

Residents, please return to the habitat levels or proceed to a designated refuge station. Visitors, please return to your ships or proceed to the nearest refuge station. Refuge stations are identified by a red ring or circle icon.

"Should we try to get back to the ship? Or find a refuge station?" I asked Hirin.

"We're three levels down from the docking arms," he said, one hand firm on my elbow as we joined the flow of people leaving the cafe. The crowd jostled us along with it. "I think we'd better look for a station."

I thumbed my ID implant and pinged Maja. "Where are you?" I asked when she answered.

"On the ship, with Baden," she said. Her voice was controlled but an undertone of worry gave it a sharp, clipped edge. "You?"

I had to hold the implant close to my ear to hear her over the announcement system and the worried murmurings around me. "Mercantile. We're heading to a refuge station. Any idea what's happening?"

"None," she said. "Where's Rei?"

"I'll try to find out. Stay put and stay safe," I told her. I pinged Rei. She didn't answer.

I'm not sure what made me turn my head and look back into the cafe. Maybe I just wondered how many remained inside, maybe it was a premonition. But as I did, my eyes sought the dark of space outside the cafe's view wall. A flash of light sparked in the void—a flash I knew all too well. The flare of a ship's shields responding to impact. No explosion followed, so the shields had held. But that was a dogfight. Headed this way.

I caught at Hirin, turning him to look.

"*Kia inferna?*" he muttered. "Who's that?"

"I don't know, but we'd better get to that refuge station." Part of me wanted to stay here and watch, but common sense vetoed that idea. We joined the throng of people again, and I pinged Rei. Still no response. I wondered how many pings flew around the station and if anyone could hear the notifications above the din of worried people.

Chaos threatened to blossom out in the main corridor. The thin veneer of calm rubbed off as folks made decisions about where to run—home, work, refuge stations. I spotted the red circle over an open bulkhead perhaps twenty-five metres down the corridor, on the hubward side. People scurried in through the opening. Could we make it there through the sea of bodies before the space was filled and they shut the door? We had to try.

The klaxon continued its incessant, grating bleat. The calm, cadenced instructions coming over the station's comm hadn't changed in frequency or intensity, but the repetition underscored the urgency of the situation. This was no false alarm. Something bad was happening outside, and anything that included ship-based weaponry had the potential to—

The first impact hit the station. We'd made it only halfway to the refuge station. FarView's own shields flared with an intensity that flashed in through every view wall visible from the corridor. I closed my eyes involuntarily against the light and felt Hirin's arm slip around my waist as the decking shuddered under our feet. Screams and shouts reverberated off the walls of the corridor. The refuge station's bulkhead door slammed closed. We were out of time.

Someone is attacking the station. My brain knew it, but I couldn't accept it. This could not be happening. How could this be happening?

"Luta." Hirin's voice was hard and low, his breath soft against my ear. "*Run!*"

Chapter 9 — Lanar Aliens and Rescues

EYES RIVETED ON the grainy video, I felt my hands clutch into fists inside the enviro-suit, the creases of fabric digging into my flesh. My throat tightened, making my breathing harsh and rasping in my own ears. Beside me I sensed Viss go very, very still. What nightmarish thing was about to happen to Yuskeya and the others? *What is this Corvid showing me?*

Yuskeya looked up, startled at the entrance of the five Chron figures, and I saw her hand dart involuntarily to draw a weapon she wasn't wearing. The Chron had their backs to the camera filming the scene, so I couldn't see their faces, but every Protectorate member knew the sleek outlines of Chron armour. Didkovsky, also unarmed, launched himself in front of Andresson and Summergale.

Then the entire tableau froze or paused. No one moved, and Yuskeya continued to kneel next to the injured Corvid, looking up at the Chron. I glanced at Fha, but the Corvid kept her uninjured black eye fixed on the playback.

On the screen, Yuskeya suddenly nodded and stood, then turned to speak to Andresson and Didkovsky. I realized belatedly that the video hadn't paused—one of the Chron, or more than one, had been *speaking* to her. Andresson nodded, although Didkovsky's face, cloudily visible through his helmet, looked defiant. Yuskeya spoke again, leaning toward him with an intensity I recognized all too well, and after a moment he nodded, too. What happened next shook me. Together, Yuskeya and one of the Chron helped the fallen Corvid to his feet, an arm draped over each of them, although the taller alien had to stoop to make it work. I realized when the Corvid began to move that one of its legs must also be injured. The smooth glide that usually characterized the crow-like alien's motion was gone, replaced by a struggling limp.

Didkovsky helped Summergale to stand, and I realized that the Lobor had suffered an injury as well. The video jittered and the image blurred, presumably as the station suffered another strike. One of the Chron put out a hand to steady Yuskeya as she almost stumbled. Moving together, the group slowly exited the camera's range.

I turned to Fha, frowning, and she regarded me with one bright eye. "Those Chron helped them," I said slowly. "They were not the ones who were attacking the station."

Fha clicked her beak-like mouth. "No, they were of the peaceful Chron your sister learned about. They came with several ships to help us, because their network for gathering intelligence on the violent faction indicated the attack was going to happen. They helped save the *uruglat* from destruction."

I swallowed. "And what of my people? What happened to them?"

Fha turned from the now-static video display and walked slowly away from it, back toward the central display where she'd stood when we entered the room. Viss and I followed. Dr. Ahmed and Lt. Commander Galwan took a few steps, then hung back, surveying the rest of the room.

"The *uruglat* suffered heavy damage—so much so that we knew, should your people's environmental suits fail, we would not be able to provide proper atmospheric conditions for them. The Chron took them onto their own ship, and away to safety," Fha said. She pulled a spindly hand from inside her robe and held something out to me. Despite my revulsion at the proximity of those terrible claws, I put out my gloved hand, and she placed the item on my palm. It was a datachip. A very familiar-looking datachip that could have come straight from Nearspace.

"This holds a message for you, from the one who travelled with your sister and stayed with the peaceful Chron."

"Cerevare?" Viss asked. "She was here?"

Fha nodded. "The—Lobor, you call them?—was the one who brought the message to me. She left it so that when someone came looking for your people, they would know where to go."

Viss sighed heavily. "If Cerevare has them, I feel better already."

I nodded and slipped the datachip into a pocket of my envirosuit, securing the pocket closed carefully. "And what about you? Is there any way we can assist you?"

The tall, crow-like alien bowed slightly. "We appreciate your offer, *Admiralo*," she said, "but in reality, there is little you can do for us. We have reconfigured the *uruglat* so that we may make repairs, and we have supplies enough. Others of our kind are on their way to help."

I opened my mouth to answer, but she put a long-fingered hand on my arm. Her grip was firm although the bones of her hand felt too fragile to hold such strength. I tried not to think about her talons. "Without the *uruglat*, we cannot control and maintain the asteroid barriers. Some of them were destroyed by the Chron ships, and we cannot restore or reconfigure them at this time."

I nodded. "The one we came through was pulverized."

"That means your Nearspace—as well as other systems for which we acted as a guardpost—are at risk. If the Chron come with the means to easily clear away the debris from that wormhole, or ships that can navigate it without damage, they are one step closer to your systems. We will continue to do what we can, but this severely impedes our ability to keep the Chron constrained."

"I understand." I put my own gloved hand over hers. "We will set a guard on the wormhole on our side. And the one in Tau Ceti. They will not be able to come without our knowledge."

Fha looked down at me, her one visible eye dark with what I felt was a pitying look. "The Chron will come where and when you least expect it, my friend. Do not be complacent, thinking they have no way in."

"You mean the ghosted wormholes?" I nodded. "My sister has told me about those."

"Yes. You must be prepared for what you cannot even see. They are ruthless and implacable. Do not underestimate them."

"Thank you for your wise words, and your help," I said. "When we return through the wormhole, we plan to deploy communications beacons to more easily maintain a connection with you here. We will still have to pass messages through the intermediary system, but it will make communications somewhat easier. Are you amenable to the idea?"

She nodded and took her hand from my arm, slipping it into her robe again. "That will be most agreeable," she said. "I can have one of our communications engineers give you devices to install at beacon points in the intermediary system. That will speed the transfer of messages."

I hesitated. "I—can't wait long. I have to go after our friends."

"Your people are safe, and the beacons can be readied within a day," she said. "It would be faster were we not in such disarray. But I think you can delay that long. And then, you must return to your Nearspace as soon as you have your people. Others must know to be on their guard."

"I will," I assured her. "Thank you for all your help. Can we assist you in any way while we wait?"

"No, but thank you for your offer," Fha said. "I believe our alliance with Nearspace will be a good one."

"I think so, too," I told her. Then I turned and collected the others with a nod, and we wound our way up the black hallways to our ship.

Viss strode beside me, Ahmed and Galwan trailing us as we made our way back to the *Cheswick*. We didn't need a guide since it had just been one long hallway, but I suspected that since the Corvids could "reconfigure" their station, it wasn't always necessarily that way.

"*Dios!* Did you *see* them?" Galwan breathed. "They're magnificent!"

"I should put in a request to study them from a medical perspective," Ahmed mused. "It would be fascinating to see what basic physiology they share with us, and how they differ."

Viss caught my eye, and I let them chatter, knowing it was a tension release after a stressful few minutes. I touched the outside of the pocket where I'd slipped the datachip, feeling the comforting presence of its square outline. I wondered what message it held from Cerevare Brindlepaw.

"The professor must have gained the full trust of those peaceful Chron, if they were willing to take her on a mission with them," I mused to Viss.

He nodded. "And, since she'd already been to the Corvid station, I suppose it would make sense to have her along."

I wondered what it was like for the Lobor historian, living among the people she'd studied—and possibly hated—all her life.

Surprisingly quickly, we reached the black docking bay again. The *Cheswick* waited, half-in and half-out of the station, and I fought down an urge to sprint through the docking bay to the ship. We walked, but we cycled through the airlock without lingering or looking around the bay. It was disconcerting to see the ship partly engulfed by the dark walls, and I didn't care to study the sight for too long.

"What now?" Galwan asked as we shucked our EVA suits and hung them in the lockers.

"You two can return to your stations, and write up the encounter from your own perspectives, if you would. Put in whatever you thought or saw or anything that struck you. Mr. Feron and I will see what's on this datachip."

"You trust the Corvids?" Ahmed asked. Medical curiosity was one thing, but the good doctor had a habit of never walking into a situation with his eyes closed. He expected no less from anyone else.

I glanced down at the datachip in my hand. "They've given us no reason to mistrust them yet," I said. "This would be an awfully roundabout way to pull a fast one on us, and honestly, with their technology—"

Galwan nodded. "They could pretty much deal with us whatever way they liked. You don't have to spend long on that station to figure that out."

"Keep that in mind when you're writing up those reports," I said, and made my way to the bridge.

"*Admiralo* on the bridge," Linna Drake announced when I rejoined the crew there.

"At ease," I said, and took my chair. "Mr. Medenez, open a ship-wide channel, please."

When the communications officer nodded to me, I made the announcement I knew no-one would want to hear.

"This is Admiral Mahane. It turns out that our mission won't be completed at this station; Ambassador Andresson, Lieutenant-Commanders Didkovsky and Summergale, and Commander Blue are no longer here, although we have reason to believe they're safe. We'll have to travel further to recover them. The Corvids are preparing some communications relays for us, to be deployed in the Woodroct's Star system. They'll deliver them tomorrow. Until then we'll stay docked here. I'll keep you all informed as I know more."

Linna Drake had visibly suppressed an exclamation when I began my announcement, but she kept silent until I nodded to Medenez and he closed the channel.

Now she spoke. "Do we know where they are, sir?"

"Not yet, but I'm hoping the answers are here." I pulled the datachip from my pocket and gestured to Viss. "Let's take this into my office." I wanted to see it before making its contents widely known.

I led Viss out the back of the bridge to my office. At my desk, I pulled up an extra seat for the engineer to join me, then plugged the chip into the reader on my datapad. The chip held only two files; one an obvious message file tagged with both video and audio components and named LISTEN_FIRST, and one a text-only file labelled EMERGENCY_CONTACT. I set the video to play.

The placid Lobor face of Cerevare Brindlepaw looked out at us. Her brown eyes were huge and dark, and the concern in her voice was evident before she'd spoken very many words. The image blurred and shook intermittently. She must have been on one of the Chron ships assisting the Corvids when she made it. The image was steady enough, though, that the ship must have been docked at the *uruglat* and not in the midst of battle maneuvers. Otherwise she'd have been bouncing all over the place. The shaking came from hits to the station.

To whoever comes to rescue Commander Blue and the others, she said, *please know that we will endeavour to keep them safe. We will take them to a planet known locally as Tabalo. Exit the Corvid system via the second wormhole starwise from the one you entered through, and proceed to these coordinates.* Here she rattled off coordinates in a standard Nearspace configuration; she obviously knew how we'd parse them in relation to our entry point into the system. *I believe when we were on the* Tane Ikai *it was estimated to be about eighteen hours away from the wormhole.*

This system is not entirely controlled by the Relidae—the peaceful Chron, as we know them. This is how their name for themselves translates for us. There is a second planet, inhabited by the other Chron, whom they call the Pitromae. Border disputes are ongoing, but there is a reasonably safe route directly from the wormhole to the planet. When you are close to Tabalo, you should be able to reach me via my Nearspace ID comm, included in the emergency contact file. If not, land at the coordinates noted in that file and display it on your datapad. Show it to anyone who will look, and they'll help you find me.

The video stuttered and Cerevare looked over her shoulder. Behind her I saw the group with Yuskeya and the others come into view.

I must go so I can leave this with the Corvids, she said, turning back to the screen. *Good luck, and I hope to see you soon.*

She reached out a furred hand, and the screen went dark.

I turned to Viss, glad to have someone to talk to. "I have to make a decision."

"I probably know what you're thinking about, and you probably know what I'm going to say about it, but go ahead," the engineer said, leaning back in his chair with a lopsided grin.

I stood up and paced the small space. "We have two choices. Turn back, navigate the pulverized asteroid field again, then go back out to Delta Pavonis to warn them that the Chron threat could be imminent. Or trust that whatever protections the Corvids can offer will hold, and press on to get our people back as quickly as possible first."

"As I said, you probably know what I think."

I tapped the admiral's insignia on my collar. "This is telling me that the Protectorate needs to know extra precautions are in order. One level of protection separating the Chron from us has been taken out of play, and that heightens the threat level considerably."

Viss sighed. "And what if you send the message, and the Protectorate response is to order you back to Nearspace immediately? They could argue that Andresson, Didkovsky, and Yuskeya Blue are apparently safe and in good health. That would make it acceptable to delay their retrieval until we're certain there are no imminent threats."

I leaned against the view wall and folded my arms. "Did the message from Cerevare give you that much reassurance?"

Viss stood and joined me at the wall, looking out at the black nothingness of the inside of the station. "No, it didn't." He reached out and tapped my insignia, as I'd done. "Forget for a minute what this is telling you," he said. Then he tapped me lightly on the chest, just over my heart. "What's this telling you?"

I blinked, a little surprised at his familiarity, and also at the sentiment. The Viss Feron I knew had always presented a more pragmatic and stoic face to the world. Apparently becoming involved with Yuskeya Blue had changed something in him.

The answer to his question was easy, though. "That I want our people back, and I want it now."

He grinned. "Then I think we're on the same page. There's a third option, though. We could do both."

"What do you mean?"

He shrugged. "Compose a message for Fleet Commander Holles, and ask the Corvids to take it through to Delta Pavonis. They know how to get there, because they got the *Stillwell* back, right? Even in their current state, they should be able to spare one ship to run that errand."

If I hadn't thought it would be overly dramatic, I'd have slapped a hand to my forehead. Instead I simply shook my head. "It's a good thing one of us is thinking," I told Viss.

"Fly with your sister for a while," he said with a grin. "You get used to figuring out ways to do more than one thing at a time."

He left me to compose a message for Regina, but I didn't go back to my desk right away. I turned to look out the view wall. It still showed only the inky blackness of the *uruglat*, although if I put my head close to the glass I could make out the hexagonal discs of mysterious matter that comprised the station. I stared at those, marvelling at the precise way they fit together, how well they worked in unison to provide whatever the Corvids needed.

They reminded me, oddly, of Yuskeya Blue.

If I was honest with myself, I wasn't all that concerned about Andresson, Didkovsky, and Summergale. It would certainly be good to get them back to Nearspace, and there were undoubtedly dangers associated with being on a Chron station now. But, like Viss, it was Yuskeya I wanted to rescue, Yuskeya I was worried about. Yuskeya Blue, with her dark eyes and hair and quiet compassion and competence. Yuskeya, whom I'd foolishly sent straight into the arms of someone else when I'd assigned her to the *Tane Ikai*.

I pushed off from the view wall and ran a hand through my hair. "Not like you would have done anything about it anyway, Admiral," I muttered to myself, and it was true. Between Soranna and Regina Holles, I'd learned a lot about loss and why my situation made that an inevitable end game for me when it came to romance. I really couldn't see myself spending a lifetime—a very long lifetime, for me—moving from one younger woman to the next, only to lose them to the two implacable forces: time and death. It felt both slimy and dishonest, no matter how strong my feelings.

So, I'd sent Yuskeya Blue on an outside assignment, and she'd met Viss, and I could put that particular problem out of my mind.

Which didn't mean I could leave her trapped in what was essentially enemy territory.

I crossed to my desk to write my message to Regina, cursing myself for the fool I knew I was. But if I'd learned anything in the past eighty years, it was that I'd have lots of time later to think about it. Now we had a job to do.

I DIDN'T HAVE to go back into the station to put my plan to Fha; she answered me directly by materializing, as a hologram, inside my office when I requested a meeting. Fortunately, Luta had told me about this communication method, so I managed not to jump and scream when it happened. She agreed that they could spare a runner to take the message to Nearspace.

When I returned to the bridge after making the

arrangements, Linna Drake gave me a look that said, "when are you going to tell us more?" I pretended I hadn't seen it.

"All right. I want senior officers in the galley for a briefing. Mr. Feron, please join us."

Viss nodded.

When we'd gathered in the galley, I said, "The good news is, they were taken for their own safety to a planet, and we have the coordinates for it."

"In this system?" Commander Drake asked, her eyes narrowed.

I shook my head. "That's the downside. They're in a Chron system, the guests of the 'peaceful' Chron faction—who call themselves the Relidae, and so we will, too."

"And where is this other system?"

"Just one skip away, and then about eighteen hours in-system to the planet," I said.

Viss cleared his throat. "You'd better allow a little longer, Admiral. Cerevare remembers correctly, but the Corvids had given us an upgrade to the burst drive, which cut about twenty percent off the time. Say a full day, counting the time in this system to get to the wormhole, and travel time on the other side."

I sighed. "All right, thanks for setting that straight. Fha tells me that the asteroids aren't moving in a preprogrammed course, just drifting, so it should be an easy passage through them."

Then I played Cerevare's message for them. No-one questioned my decision to press on to the Chron system. I wanted them to hear what she'd said, though, and to understand the situation. We were walking into the middle of hostile territory, and we had to remember that we couldn't tell our friends from our enemies just by looking.

"If we make it to the planet and Professor Brindlepaw answers when I comm her, that's one thing," I told them. "En route, if we encounter Chron ships, I expect we'll be able to tell pretty quickly if they're friendly or not."

"And if they're not?" asked Lieutenant-Commander Huba Jelenka. Jelenka oversaw weapons, so I'd expected this question to come from him.

"We won't be the first to fire," I said. "No aggression on our part. There might be a war coming, but it's not started yet, and the *Cheswick* is not going to be the ship that starts it."

"If we find hostiles engaged with friendlies? What then?"

"We go to the aid of our allies," I said. "But I'm really hoping it doesn't come to that."

"Well, I'll make sure one of the launches is ready for the trip down to the planet." That was Alice Payette, the Lieutenant-Commander in charge of the flight deck. We kept two launches and I knew that with Yi in charge, they'd both be spotless, fuelled, and ready to fly on a moment's notice. "Anything else I can do?"

"No, that will be fine. Lieutenant-Commander Betany, I don't know what kind of a timeline we'll be on, so will you make sure there are quarters ready to receive our guests if they need them?" Chuck Betany was the master of stores and quarters on the *Cheswick*, and I knew he'd make room for the newcomers if he had to sleep in the galley himself to do it.

"Do you really think it will be a straightforward pickup?" Linna Drake asked. She'd been quiet up until now, a trick I suspect she learned from—or taught to—Regina Holles.

I shook my head. "I honestly don't know," I said, "but that's what I'm hoping for. We'll plan for the best and expect the worst. I'm sending word to FarView about what we learned from the Corvids, so if we run into delays, we won't have that pressure, at least. Any questions?" When none came, I said, "*Okej*, you have your orders, and everyone is dismissed. Please make sure your sections know what's happening. None of this is classified or secret."

The meeting broke up. Viss stayed in the galley to get something to eat, and Linna Drake and I walked back to the bridge together. "You're worried," she said. She had her hands clasped behind her back and she looked straight ahead as we walked, not at me.

I sighed. "Damn right I'm worried. There are so many ways this could go wrong, I can't even count them. What will we encounter on the way to the planet? When we get there? Will Cerevare Brindlepaw's friends really recognize us on sight and be happy to see us?"

"Good questions," Drake said, still not looking at me. "And you're right, we don't want to make any aggressive moves if we do run across the other Chron. In and out quickly, that's the best we can hope for."

"We need to make that happen," I said. I glanced over at her and caught the hint of a smile around her lips. "What?"

"I'm glad you can tell me what you're really thinking," she said. "You control it well in front of the others, but I know you, Admiral. You need to blow off steam sometimes in order to keep your head on straight. I'm just pleased that you feel comfortable enough around me to do that."

I used to do that with Yuskeya, too, I thought. In fact, she was probably the first Commander I'd felt comfortable enough with to do so. She never seemed to mind, which was one of the things I appreciated about her.

But it was not Yuskeya walking beside me now. She was on the other side of a whole lot of unknowns. "I'm glad, too, Commander," I told Linna Drake. "Now let's get everyone ready to head into that wormhole tomorrow."

THE ASTEROIDS GUARDING the wormhole entrance drifted lazily, no longer tumbling and spinning in their course to block the entrance. The Chron hadn't seen fit to pulverize this field, or perhaps hadn't had time before the Corvids had destroyed them. But I felt sure it was only a matter of time until they returned. I asked Linna Drake to send a tracer through the wormhole before we entered it. I didn't want to meet up with a Chron ship anywhere, but especially not inside a wormhole. It came back clear, and with trepidation—and a bit of something else—I ordered us through.

The *something else* was a thrill of excitement. Every skip that took us deeper into Otherspace re-ignited my passion for space travel, something that I realized had become a bit blasé over the past number of years. Nearspace was my home, and I felt that way about all of its great expanse and many systems, but exploring—that was an entirely different experience. Despite the danger, I couldn't ignore the spark of wonder I felt.

The Chron system expanded before us as we exited the wormhole, opening like a door flung wide. It revealed an enormous crimson particle cloud nearby, with a smear of sulfurous dust painting it like frosting on a cake. The system's yellow sun, looking not terribly unlike Sol, burned in the distance.

"Scan for the planet," I ordered. "Supposedly we should be able to pick it up now or very soon."

A moment later Linna Drake reported, "It's there, just inside the edge of our range."

I felt the muscles in my neck relax and realized that I'd been worried it wouldn't be so easy to find. "Set a course," I said. "Give me an estimate on time to reach it as soon as you can."

"Twenty-plus hours," the nav officer said. "If we use the burst drive to its full capacity." Viss had been right.

"Locate the station, too," I said. "There should be one, not too far from the planet, I think. We don't have to go there but we might as well know where it is."

In-system travel is usually boring; it's a fact of space travel. It was less so, I found, when you spent the time waiting to see if hostile aliens were going to notice your presence in the system and launch an attack. I distracted myself some of the time in my office and at the gym, but I spent a good bit of it in my command chair, watching with everyone else. The system, fortunately, provided plenty to look at, from the particle cloud we'd first seen to a spectacular nebula—probably a supernova remnant—that burst to life in dazzling colour when Linna Drake switched the viewscreen to its ultraviolet filter.

What we didn't see was any indication of hostile Pitromae, and I was grateful for it. I caught a few hours of sleep, although it didn't come easy. I expected my comm to buzz at any moment with news of trouble.

I was back on the bridge by the time I thought we might be close enough to send a message to Cerevare Brindlepaw's ID. I wasn't completely surprised when the officer on duty, Lieutenant Toor, reported no response. In Nearspace, regular relays made long-distance communications possible, but things might be different here. It still made me nervous, but I made myself wait another ten minutes without fidgeting and then asked Toor to try again. This time we got a reply—faint and distant, audio only, but it was the professor.

"Admiral, good to hear from you. I am alerting those who should know that you are approaching. Your ship will not encounter any difficulty. Will you send a launch vessel down to the planet? Yuskeya and the others are well, but the

Ambassador isn't quite well enough to travel yet. And I expect you'll want to meet some people here, anyway."

It was implied that this would be the proper course of action. I was tempted to ask further about the Ambassador, but made myself wait.

"I'm coming down myself, yes. And Viss Feron is with me. We'll have plenty of room to bring four back, when the time comes. Unless you're coming now, too? We can make room for five."

There was a pause before the Lobor historian answered. "Not yet, no, Admiral," she said, "although I am anxious to meet and speak with you, and it will be good to see Viss. I believe I am of far more use to Nearspace if I stay here on Tabalo."

"Understood," I answered. "Then if you'll send the proper coordinates, I'll see all of you shortly." We closed the connection, and I said to Linna Drake, "I'm going to change into casual clothes. The Ambassador is the official Nearspace representative, and I don't want to muddy the waters. Assign a pilot and let me know when the launch is ready, all right?"

"Will do, Admiral," she said. "Are you going armed?"

I thought about that for a moment and then shook my head. "I don't think Professor Brindlepaw would lead me into any danger, and I'm only one man, after all. If there's a horde of aggressive Chron down there waiting for me, even a plasma rifle won't help."

Viss had poked his head onto the bridge just as I ended my conversation with Professor Brindlepaw, and now he followed me into the corridor.

"Permission to accompany you down to the planet, Admiral?" he asked formally.

I grinned. "Granted. I didn't expect you to sit up here and wait. In fact, I already told Brindlepaw you were coming."

He clapped me on the shoulder. "I'll gather some things and see you in the docking bay, then."

He was a few steps away from me down the corridor when I said, "Viss?"

He turned and looked back at me.

"No weapons, I think. Shouldn't be any need for them down there."

"Well, you're no fun," he said, but touched his hand to his

forehead in a mock salute.

In my quarters, I considered my off-duty wardrobe and decided to take a page out of my sister's book. She always swore that a good pair of jeans, white t-shirt, and leather coat could take a person almost anywhere, so I tried to follow her advice. I didn't own a white t-shirt, but I did have jeans, a button-front shirt in transform fabric that I could set to white, and a short dark leather jacket. I kept my Protectorate boots on because there's nothing more comfortable than a well-worn pair of prots, as we call them. Mine had trod the dust of countless planets in Nearspace, so it felt right to wear them down to the surface of my first Otherspace planet.

I slipped a few necessities into my pockets and hoped I was ready. It wasn't a first contact, but it felt that way, and the weight of responsibility lodged in my gut. With a quick glance in the mirror to make sure I was presentable, I left my room and headed down to the docking bay.

One of the two ship's launch vessels sat with its door open, and I glimpsed movement inside. When I crossed to it and climbed in, I was surprised to find Linna Drake running through the pre-flight and chatting easily with Viss about the launch's engineering specs. Like me, she'd swapped out her Protectorate blues and now wore navy pants, a green high-necked sweater, and a many-pocketed hiker's vest.

"Who's watching the store up top?" I asked her. I realized that I hadn't ordered her to stay on the bridge when I'd left, and Linna Drake was not averse to taking advantage of a loophole.

"Commander Shule is on duty," she said unblushingly. "He was scheduled for next shift, but he was happy to take the chair so that I could pilot you down to the surface."

"I don't think I'm really in need of a *commander* for this job," I said dryly. "You might be slightly overqualified."

She threw me a grin over her shoulder as she buckled into the pilot's seat. "Technically we're escorting Council officials on the return flight, so you should be accompanied by at least one other officer of a rank above lieutenant-commander," she said. "Shall I quote from the regulations?"

I shook my head and held up a hand. "Not necessary. I bow to your superior knowledge of little-known Protectorate minutiae. Although I doubt they were written to cover this sort of situation," I added.

"Buckle up, then, Admiral, and I'll close the doors," was all she said, and although she'd turned back to face the front of the launch, I could still hear the grin in her voice. Five minutes later we dropped out of the docking bay and down toward the Relidae planet, and whatever awaited us there.

Chapter 10 — Luta Under Attack

RUN!

Hirin didn't have to tell me twice. When the first impact jarred the station, panic blossomed across the crowd in the corridor. Some because they'd seen the refuge station door slam shut, and some simply because whatever was happening was obviously bad.

I couldn't quite *run* in response to Hirin's suggestion, but I pushed quickly through the crowd, ducking and weaving to find openings between the press of bodies. I tried to sort out a plan as we wriggled through the masses.

We're three levels down from the docking arms. I tried to think calmly, but I knew my body was blasting out adrenaline and cortisol in reaction to stress, and it clouded my brain. My nanobioscavengers would clear the excess hormones quickly, but I didn't have time to wait around for that. I tried to cudgel my foggy thinking into something logical.

The elevators will shut down as a safety protocol. That leaves stairs. I know I saw a stairwell door near the elevators on the shopping level, so it stands to reason, that's where we'll find them on this level.

"Elevators!" Hirin said, close behind me. I didn't remind him they'd be shut down. At least we both wanted to go in the same direction. The elevator we'd come down in was behind us, but on the circular station, we had to come to another one eventually.

Up ahead, the red ring icon of another refuge station blinked above the heads of the throng, but the door was already closed. There was only one place I'd feel safe now.

On the *Tane Ikai*. Three levels up.

The worst thing about this corridor was the lack of a view to the outside. We were in the centre of the ring level, with shops and services lining both the spaceward and hubward sides. I wanted to see what was happening outside. However, it was obvious that the station was under attack. Before we reached the stairwell, the station had shuddered twice more under our feet, the flash of the shields reflecting through some of the open doorways into the corridor. Each one provoked gasps and cries of alarm from the scuttling, now-panicked crowd.

The elevator came into sight and I dashed for it. The elevator and stairwell bays were positioned in transport blocks in the centre of the corridor, with enough space on either side to allow foot traffic to flow around them. As I'd expected, the elevator doors were tightly closed. A young man, perhaps twenty-five, held a little curly-haired girl by one hand and pressed repeatedly on the button to open the door, with no result. The stairwell door stood on the other side of the transport block, just behind the elevator from this side. As I passed, the man balled a fist and punched the stubborn door in frustration. I put a hand on his arm and his head jerked toward me.

"It won't work. Safety shutdown," I said, looking directly into his eyes to drill the message into his head. "The stairs are right behind here."

"What's—" he started, but Hirin passed me, catching my hand and pulling me around to where he threw the stairwell door open, and I dashed inside. I felt a pang at leaving the young man, confused and afraid, but I couldn't help everyone— and I couldn't help my own people if I didn't get to my ship.

We'd circled perhaps twice up the spiralling metal stairs when I heard the stairwell door open and shut again, and two more sets of footfalls joined ours on the steps. Maybe I'd gotten through to the young man. Hirin and I pounded up the stairs, my heart hammering. I wondered how Hirin was doing, but he stayed right behind me and didn't sound too laboured—at least not yet.

Should have done less tae-ga-chi and more nicardi, I thought absurdly. Tae-ga-chi was great for muscle tone and coordination, but I could obviously use more aerobic training. And perhaps yelling.

We reached a landing where a large blue numeral 4 had been stencilled on the wall, along with corresponding symbols in other Nearspace languages, including Lobor and Vilisian. Smaller lettering underneath, again in several languages, detailed the merchants doing business on the level. A door exited to this level, and through the viewpane I saw another, less-crowded corridor. A Vilisian scurried past with two small children in tow. A man in a Protectorate uniform ran in the other direction. Maybe more people had made it to the refuge stations on this level, or maybe it had not been as busy when the alarm went up.

I wondered briefly if we should try for a refuge station here, but everything in me urged a return to the ship. We didn't stop to discuss it, just kept climbing. The habitat level lay above us, and then one more climb would put us on the docking level. Unfortunately, I suspected we would emerge near docking arm A, a third of the way around the station from docking arm B, where the *Tane Ikai* waited. But there should be fewer people on the docking level, and we'd be able to move faster. Provided we had any energy left.

The stairs shook under my feet, and I clutched at the metal railing for support. Hirin grunted, and I swung my head to check on him, but he merely scowled. "Almost slipped," he said.

"How long are the shields going to take this?" I wondered.

He shook his head. "They're meant primarily as protection against space debris, small meteorites, that kind of thing. I'm sure no-one set them up expecting a full-on attack with weapons of this calibre. And to maintain them around the entire station—?"

He didn't go further. He didn't have to. I knew the answer to my question. The shields wouldn't hold out long.

I sucked oxygen and set off again, my legs burning from the climb. Further below us, the other sets of footsteps had merged into one. I imagined the young man was now carrying the little girl. I gave myself a mental shake. Here I was complaining about the burn in my legs. I wondered briefly where they were heading—the habitat level? Surely there must be enough refuge stations on the whole of FarView to accommodate everyone who might be aboard? But the trick, at a moment like this, was finding the one that had your space in it.

Another round of hard climbing and we reached the landing of the habitat level, marked with the numeral 3. Here they'd included a numbered schematic as well, since so many tiny apartments ringed the level. Through the viewpane only a few inhabitants came in and out of view, hurrying, I assumed, to the level's refuge stations. Hirin's breath sounded louder, harsher now behind me. I stopped on the landing and turned to watch him climb the last few stairs to where I stood.

"You okay, old man?"

He nodded, sucking in a deep breath. "Old is right. Might only have one more level in me," he rasped.

"That's all you need," I said. "We'll make it."

There'd been a respite from the impacts, and part of my brain wanted to believe that the incident was over. Protectorate ships at the station would have scrambled to meet the attack, and possibly destroyed the attackers. But the klaxon continued to sound, although it was mercifully muffled in the stairwell.

As we caught our breath, the footsteps below us drew nearer, and the young man puffed into view. Red-faced, he now carried the little girl, as I'd surmised. She had her arms around his neck and her head buried in his chest. Hirin and I pulled out of the way and he approached.

"Thanks," he said to me as he passed us. "I wasn't thinking too clearly down there."

"Who is?" I replied, and tried to smile.

He put a hand on the door release and almost slammed into it when the door didn't open. The little girl whimpered.

Hirin moved to help, but I had a sinking feeling I knew what was wrong. He couldn't get it to open, either. The young man turned to look at me with wild eyes.

"What's wrong?"

I ran a hand over my hair. "They probably locked them as part of the safety protocol," I said. "Even a partial shield breach—"

"—and they'd automatically lock-seal," Hirin finished.

"All the levels?" the man asked.

I looked up the stairs that spiralled away from us. "Probably, but there's only one way to find out," I said, and started to climb again.

WE WERE MORE than halfway to level 2, the docking level, when the big hit came. This one knocked me sideways, and I would have fallen without the railing. I caught it and held on. I heard Hirin shout and the young man gasp. With his arms around the girl, he had no free hand to steady himself. He'd slipped to his knees and almost toppled onto her, but Hirin caught him. I expected the girl to scream or cry but she must have been too terrified to do either. The station shields must have failed to stop the last attack. And with the shields down—

The next hit dealt real damage to the station. I felt it in the odd dichotomy of sound—a deep, physical rumble and the high squeal of protesting metal. We found out later that it had impacted level 5, the entertainment level. The same level where we'd been seated at the cafe. Although the previous assaults had been silent, this one crashed in our ears as if the world were toppling. In a sense, it was. Shut inside the stairwell, we were shielded from any view of the explosion; the side of the station fragmenting away, pulling suddenly-lifeless bodies along with it, but in my mind's eye, I knew it was happening. The sound told me we'd been breached, and I knew what happened to living things thrown suddenly into the vacuum of space. I closed my eyes for a moment, shaken and horrified.

A hissing noise sidled up the stairwell, maleficent as a snake's warning. Something was leaking in, or leaking out, and neither prospect cheered me in the least.

"We have to get out of this stairwell," I said, keeping my voice as steady as I could for the sake of the child.

"If we get to the top, we might get someone to open the door," the young man said. He'd climbed shakily to his feet again, still clutching his daughter, and started up the stairs.

Hirin and I shared a look. We both knew that if the station had been breached, no-one would be able to override the safety lock on these doors.

I started up, but pressed my ID implant, comming the ship. "*Tane Ikai*, is there anyone there?"

"Mother, where are you?" Maja answered instantly. She must have been waiting for us to report in.

"Stairwell, almost at the docking level," I said. "But the doors are lock-sealed and I doubt we can get out on our own. And—" I lowered my voice and raised my arm close to my face, speaking into the implant, "—I think the stairwell's integrity is compromised."

"Which stairwell?" That was Rei, her voice flat and efficient.

"Near A-arm, I think, but I'm not entirely sure."

"We're coming."

That was all; no discussion, no panic, no hesitation. *We're coming.* I didn't know what they'd do when they reached us, but I felt a tiny prickle of hope.

We quickly finished the climb to the landing. Hirin tried the door, although I think we all knew it was a futile gesture. It was as tightly sealed as the one on the habitat level. I saw no movement in the corridor beyond it. By this time everyone who had been trying to gain their ships had made it or given up and taken refuge on another level. The floor here trembled slightly but I thought it wasn't more attacks—we were close to A-arm, where the Protectorate ships docked, and some of them would still be undocking to engage the enemy. They'd probably been waiting for enough crew to return to the ships.

"You might as well sit for a minute," Hirin said to the young man. "You must be ready to drop."

Since there was nothing I could do at the door, I turned my attention to our companions. The man looked as pale as milky chai, and his eyes were wide and wild. The little girl hadn't loosened her hold on his neck or lifted her own head. He nodded and leaned his back against the wall, then let himself slide down it until he reached the floor. He stretched out his legs and nuzzled his daughter's hair. "It's okay, honey," he murmured, looking at me as if he dared me to call him a liar. I wasn't prepared to do that.

I knelt beside them. "My crew is on their way," I said. I didn't share my doubts about what they could do. I just wanted him to be as comforted as I was by the thought that someone was coming to help us. I tried to ignore the hissing in the stairwell, growing louder.

A knock on the door's viewpane drew my attention. Rei's face appeared, peering through at us, and she motioned us away from the door. Baden glanced in as well, frowned, and disappeared again. Whatever they had planned, I was ready to comply with their requests.

"Over this way," I said, and the young man scooted as far from the door as he could get. He turned his body away from it, curling around the little girl to protect her. Hirin and I pressed ourselves against the far wall, but the stairwell wasn't all that big to begin with. I hoped Rei and Baden knew what they were doing. I wanted that door open, I wanted out of here—but not at the risk of endangering anyone else. Another external hit jolted the station—smaller this time but still terrifying—and the hissing noise intensified. Or maybe I was just focused on it now. It sounded louder than the still-bleating alarm klaxon. I felt Hirin's warm hand slide over mine, entwining our fingers. I squeezed. *Thank you.*

I half-expected to see curls of smoke issuing from the door, or some other breach of its integrity, but all stayed quiet and still. The suspense was, as they say, killing me. I was keyed up for something big, but nothing happened.

Until four loud *thunks* sounded from the door and it swung out into the corridor. Rei's face appeared, a wide grin stretching and rippling the inky swirls of her *pridattii*. "Well, what are you waiting for?"

I grinned back, relief making my knees feel watery. "What took you so long?"

Hirin held a hand out to help the young man get to his feet, and he wasted no time in doing so. He swung his daughter up into his arms again. "Thank you so much," he almost whispered, as if fear had stolen his voice.

Outside the door, Baden held his datapad and another techrig that didn't look familiar to me. The unfamiliar one was pressed to the wall next to the door's control pad. With a free finger, he tapped codes onto its screen.

"Should I ask?"

He glanced at me and winked. "Everybody clear?"

Hirin listened for a moment, then nodded. "We didn't hear anyone else in the stairwell, and there's nothing now. Better reseal it."

"Already on it," Baden said, and a series of clunks sounded as the lock-seals activated around the perimeter of the door.

The decking vibrated under our feet as another impact shook

the station. Hirin grabbed my hand. "Time to go again," he said, tugging me after him.

"Move, everyone," I ordered, and caught the eye of the young man with the child. "You too. Let's get you both somewhere safe."

He didn't need urging, but ran after us. I wondered belatedly, as the battle raged outside and rattled FarView, if the *Tane Ikai* would be the haven I hoped.

As we sprinted back down the docking arm corridor toward the *Tane Ikai,* another impact hit one of the lower levels and the overhead lights dimmed. I winced, waiting for the repaired stairwell door to burst open behind us, but it held. We rounded the curve and the *Tane Ikai* came into sight. Maja and Jahelia Sord stood at the airlock, Maja looking anxious, and Jahelia Sord looking—defiant? worried? Whatever it was, I'd never seen that particular expression on her before.

All along the docking arm airlocks slid shut as other ships detached, either to try and assist the station, or perhaps just hoping to put some distance between them and the fight. I wasn't sure that was the smartest move, but everyone had to decide for themselves.

"Everybody inside," I ordered, not wanting to stand around in the corridor talking to Sord or explaining how I'd managed to pick up a man and a little girl. "My crew, head to the bridge and be prepared in case we have to move. Everyone else, follow me to the galley."

Surprisingly, no-one argued. I didn't plan to go anywhere immediately—I thought the ship was as safe docked here as it was going to be in the middle of a dogfight, and I didn't see us being a huge help with all the Protectorate ships already out there. If the worst happened and the station started to break apart—but I wouldn't let my mind go there.

Sord and the young man followed me into the galley. The first thing I did was pull a double caff for the man and a cup of juice for the girl. "Here, sit," I said, putting the drinks into their hands and motioning to seats at the big table. "Hold onto these. If we get a big jolt they could go flying." Neither argued. The man took a careful sip of the caff and closed his eyes. A bit of colour came back to his cheeks.

"Where's your ship?" I asked Sord.

"As far as I know it's still docked," she said, "but there's a minor breach in that section of the C-arm and the blast doors came down. I can't get to it." She ran a hand through her straight, glossy hair, shattering the unruffled air she tried to project.

"You can stay here," I said, "as long as you have to. If you need help getting back to your ship when this is over, we'll see what we can do."

She looked almost surprised, as if she thought she'd have to convince me to let her stay aboard. I didn't have time to talk about that, though. I turned to the young man.

"I'm Luta Paixon, and this is my ship," I told him. "I haven't had a chance before this to ask your name."

He flashed a grateful smile, which transformed his pale face from distraught to handsome. "I'm Farro Grenna, and this is my daughter, Neive," he said.

"Do you live on FarView?"

He nodded. "Temporarily, at least. My partner moved here for work six months ago—"

His voice shuddered, and he broke off, glancing at Neive. "My partner works as a manager at one of the restaurants," he said. "He was at work when—"

"I'm sure it will be fine," I said, although I wasn't sure at all. The hit had felt like it happened on one of the lower levels. If he'd been on the other side of the station and the protective airlock doors had engaged, or if he'd been in a refuge station at the time—but we obviously weren't going to talk about those or the other possibilities in front of the child. "You can stay here on the ship as long as you need to, but we may have to disengage from the docking arm, depending on what happens."

He nodded. "I understand. I can't thank you enough—"

I held up a hand and smiled. "Don't thank me yet. In fact, no thanks necessary at all. Just make yourselves comfortable in here, all right? I have to go and talk to my crew and see what the situation is."

The ship shuddered, sloshing the liquids in their cups a little, but they didn't spill. "I know this is scary, but I'm sure it will be over soon," I told the girl, leaning down to her eye level and putting on my brightest smile.

Farro nodded again. Neive looked up at me and spoke the first words I'd heard her say. "Do you have any cookies?"

Farro tried to shush her, but I smiled and nodded. "I think I do." In the cupboard under the scrubber there was a container of the crunchy *solanto* cookies Cerevare Brindlepaw had taught us how to make. Rei had proven herself able to duplicate the Lobor's recipe with great accuracy, and they'd become a crew favourite; brown-sugar-sweet, flavoured with roga-nut spice from the planet Renata, and drizzled with a sweet glaze.

I put two on a plate for the girl. Her father tried to remonstrate but I shook my head. In the midst of the frightening things that were happening, a couple of cookies was the least I could do.

Then I left them, motioning for Sord to follow me to the bridge. "Have you heard from Sedmamin?" I asked her.

She shook her head. "I thought I saw him the first day I arrived, but it was across the hub and I wasn't sure. Nothing since then."

I couldn't believe I was worried about the man who'd caused me so much grief, but if he'd been caught in the explosion—whatever he'd had to offer us to help against the Chron would be gone, too.

"Well, let's hope he's safe, or we're both out of a job," I said, but the humour didn't really work. My mind constructed horrible images of the station levels below us. I felt like I couldn't pull enough air into my lungs. The tourists. The families. People going about their daily business or having some fun. A bustling little microcosm of life the way it was all through Nearspace.

On the bridge, everyone sat expectantly waiting for me, looking either worried, nervous, or both. I got my first glimpse, out the front viewscreen, of the scene outside the station. Small Chron ships—for they were Chron, the ships matched the configuration of the ones we'd seen before—buzzed around the station like angry hornets, launching torp-like missiles and occasional particle-beam blasts. A clutch of Protectorate fighters and at least one Pegasus-class vessel, like Lanar's, harried them, trying to drive them off or destroy them. But the Protectorate ships were hampered by their need to keep the station safe, so they had to aim with care.

From this vantage point on the docking arm, the damage to the lower level was horribly obvious. Debris floated in a tumbling, lazy spray beyond a gaping hole in the station's outer wall. A shimmer of yellowish light shone in the dark hole like a beacon, the emergency field straining to stay intact every time the shields suffered another impact. I forced my eyes away from the debris, not wanting to identify bodies, which surely formed part of the mess. From the three docking arms, ships of various types disengaged, moving away from the station, whether to join the fray or distance themselves from it. Lights on some levels dimmed as I watched, as energy reserves were diverted to power the shields.

I had never felt Yuskeya's and Viss's absence as keenly as I did in that moment. The world was tumbling to pieces around us and two of the keys to my crew were absent. Maja sat, looking a little paler than usual, at the nav board, and Hirin was at the unofficial "security" station—that is, looking after the weapons that we'd never really needed a designated board for in previous years. The engineering board was conspicuously empty.

Jahelia Sord said, more humbly than I'd ever heard her speak, "Captain? With your permission, I can sub in at the engineering board if you need me to."

I hoped my surprise didn't show in my face and raised an eyebrow. "Your qualifications? I've seen your Protectorate Academy records, and I don't remember an engineering credit."

Hirin also stared at her, waiting to see what I'd say.

She grinned and held up thumb and forefinger almost touching. "I was this close to finishing the course when I left the Academy, and I've got . . . a few years of experience under my belt since then." She glanced at the others and then winked at Hirin. "I'll bet Gramps would say experience is the better teacher anyway."

Surprising me, Hirin grinned. "Your call, Captain. But she does have a point."

I wondered briefly what Viss would say—I shuddered to imagine, actually—and then nodded. "If you break my ship—"

"I'm aboard her, too, and you know how I like to look out for myself," she assured me, and slid into place at the board. It felt oddly comforting just to see the seat filled.

A blossom of energy and debris bloomed against the dark backdrop of space as a Protectorate fighter took out one of the Chron ships.

"I count six Chron left, and ten Protectorate ships," Baden said. "We have the numbers on our side. If they don't run soon the Protectorate will just keep picking them off."

"But they can still do more damage before that," Maja said, her eyes riveted on the viewscreen.

"Ten to six isn't exactly insurmountable odds," Jahelia Sord said. "You've got weapons, should we be going to help?"

"We're not a fighter, we're a far trader," I said, perhaps a little too sharply. "We can defend ourselves, but we don't have the maneuverability. We don't want to be a hindrance, more civilians for the Protectorate to worry about." Truthfully, disengaging and going to help had been my first instinct as well, but practicality kept me from doing anything about it. What I'd said was true; the *Tane Ikai* wasn't built for dogfighting, although we could hold our own when necessary. And now I had Farro and Neive to think about, too. They'd already been thrown into danger through no fault of their own.

But the Chron made no move to retreat, apparently determined, as Maja said, to simply do as much damage as they could. I watched another torpedo sing toward the station's central spire. The shields flared a protective blue and the torpedo detonated harmlessly. The yellow repair field flickered but held.

For every few that were foiled, one got through. Another tremble ran through the ship, as an impact erupted on the main hub's docking level and the energy dissipated through the station and out along the docking arms, but it felt less violent than earlier ones. I sat down in my chair and switched the servos on to massage my back. I could practically feel them bumping over the tension knots in my muscles.

And then they hit us with the big one.

Chapter 11 — Lanar Among the Relidae

My stomach dropped along with the launch as we left the relative safety of the *Cheswick* and plummeted down toward the alien city. Cerevare Brindlepaw had assured me we were perfectly safe, but I was keenly aware of descending into the environs of our enemies—or at least the close descendants of our enemies. That this particular sect claimed to seek peace and friendship was comforting, but a lifetime of conditioning had instilled fear into the very word *Chron*. I resolved to think of these Chron, the peaceful variety, from now on only as *Relidae*, the way Professor Brindlepaw identified them. The names *Chron* and *Pitromae* could stay reserved in my mind for those who sought to harm us.

This side of the planet lay under the blanketing shadow of nighttime, and the flickering glow of lights showed only small inhabited regions compared to a planet like Earth or even Mars. That made sense for a breakaway segment of the race that had separated from its more aggressive counterparts and sought a peaceful existence away from the home world. From the height of the *Cheswick*, the planet showed green and umber, suggesting deserts and oases rather than the watery blue globe of Earth. I expected the water was there—the Chron were not so different from us that they could survive without water. Our oldest investigations into their species, by way of tests performed on the few corpses left to us as a legacy of the Chron war, had provided that much information.

"Could be a Nearspace planet, coming in at night like this," Linna Drake observed.

I startled out of my reverie. "It could be, at that," I agreed. "Let's hope we get a Nearspace-type welcome."

She turned her head just enough to observe me out of one eye. "Expecting trouble? You might have warned me."

I shook my head. "Not expecting, no. But . . . wary."

"You could have said. There's such a thing as playing things too close to your chest."

"Just drive, Drake," I said, and she laughed.

Viss Feron cleared his throat. "Without saying too much, let me assure you that we're not without . . . options," he said. He didn't look at me directly.

I opened my mouth to say something, but realized that although I'd specifically told him not to bring weapons to the surface, that still left options. Viss was a man who thought outside the box. I closed my mouth. Brindlepaw hadn't warned against it, after all.

Instead I said to Drake, "Ping Professor Brindlepaw again, would you? I want her to know we're getting close, in case there's anyone she needs to notify. I'm not in the mood to be shot down as an unidentified hostile."

"Just wary, right," she snorted, but she put the message through.

"Admiral, you are cleared to land," Brindlepaw said. I punched up the video on my datapad, and her furred face appeared, liquid canine eyes bright and upright ears pricked forward. She smiled in greeting. "All necessary authorities have been alerted, and you should encounter no difficulties."

"Good to know, Professor," I acknowledged. "We'll see you shortly, then."

We came in over the city from the west, wary of dipping too low until we could gauge the height of buildings. A few other flying vehicles crossed the sky at lower altitudes, and the roadways below were also quiet. I wondered just how late at night it was, here. Although the darkness masked details, the city followed the usual structure of transportation ways networked through developed sectors. The lights that glowed in the windows were not the yellow burn that harkened back to candlelight, but ranging through blues and greens, spotted with dots of purer white. Blocks of buildings, too, showed subtle differences. There were few discrete structures; buildings crowded close together, as if a tall glass structure might share the lower part of a wall with a shorter, distinctly different building. And instead of generally square and rectangular shapes, many structures featured upward-sweeping rooflines or odd, irregular architectures. I wondered if the style was influenced by the Chron's highly individuated bone crests.

The coordinates Brindlepaw had sent carried us down to a wide landing area in front of an impressive building. Two glass-fronted sections shaped like soaring cathedral windows anchored a taller, slender, central connecting segment. Greenish light shone from the windows—or was the glass tinted? Low, neat hedges of pale green leaves lined the sides of the landing area, and an inlaid stone walkway led from it to the front of the building. The landing pad glowed with luminescent markings similar to the few examples of written language the Chron war had left with us.

As we descended, I made out three forms standing just outside the obvious doors of one of the cathedral ends of the building. A human, a Lobor, and, I guessed, a Chron. *A Relidae,* I corrected myself. As vehemently as Luta had assured me of their good intentions, I still felt a clench of fear in my gut as I recognized the form. It stood relaxed, hands clasped behind its back. The Lobor—obviously Professor Brindlepaw—lifted a hand in greeting, and the human did as well. As soon as the viridian light fell across her face, I knew it was Yuskeya Blue, and the fear was replaced by a warm rush of relief. *She was safe.*

"Shall I stay with the shuttle?" Linna Drake asked as we settled down on the landing pad and she cut the engines.

"No, come along," I said. "I doubt anyone's going to make off with the launch, and you might as well take in as much of this as you can. We're going to be writing reports forever about this meeting."

She grimaced, then nodded and unbuckled, waiting for me and then Viss to exit the ship before following. I thought she locked it up behind us.

My first breath of the alien air was . . . strange. The night had, presumably, lent a coolness that it might not have held during the daytime, but it was desert-dry as well. Unusual scents, like cooking spices from a foreign culture, wafted on the breeze, neither appetizing nor repulsive, merely different. Like the planet itself, the air seemed green and brown—it managed to hold the dusty scent of desert and sand, and verdant growth, at the same time.

Yuskeya and Professor Brindlepaw had started toward us, although the Relidae held back, waiting. Yuskeya reached us first and saluted. She wore a yellow tunic-like blouse that fell past her hips and narrow-legged grey pants tucked into soft boots. Although I knew she wouldn't have been in Protectorate uniform aboard the *Tane Ikai*, I didn't think these were her own clothes. Since she'd been here several days now, I supposed it made sense that she'd have had to find something else to wear.

"*Admiralo*, it's good to see you," she said. Although her face remained calm, I read relief and pleasure in her dark eyes. And perhaps something else, but I couldn't identify it in the half-dark. "Commander Drake," she added with a smile, and shook Linna's hand. Then she abandoned Protectorate reserve and threw herself into Viss Feron's arms. His circled her in a tight embrace and I saw her close her eyes.

The Lobor came forward and extended a hand, and I pulled my attention away from Yuskeya and Viss. The professor had come here with no personal belongings, so her clothes were not the flowing shirt and billowy trousers favoured by Lobors. Instead she wore a pale, narrow tunic like Yuskeya's and a long purplish skirt. I wondered if she'd had trouble finding clothes, considering the differences in Lobor and Relidae physiology. As Luta had told the story, Cerevare Brindlepaw hadn't had time to retrieve her things from the *Tane Ikai* when she'd made the decision to stay with the Relidae. It struck me again what a remarkable choice she'd made.

I shook the offered hand, mentally preparing myself for the unnerving heat the wolf-like aliens radiated. "No difficulties, Admiral?" she asked, her voice carrying a pleasant lilt that both the hastily recorded message and our recent communications had hidden.

"None, thank you, Professor."

"Come and meet our host," she said, and turned her soft-footed, almost bouncing gait to return to the lone Relidae who had followed Cerevare partway and then stopped to allow us to greet each other.

Bemused, I followed. It was all so natural, so casual—I could have been meeting a foreign delegate from any Nearspace planet. And yet I was about to meet one of the most feared creatures ever to have haunted a Nearspace child's nightmares. The Relidae who awaited us stood a little taller than my six feet. Light washed out of the windows, revealing pale mauve chitinous plates that molded the alien's face, creating an alien geometry of linear planes and angles. These morphed into a sweeping, almost crenellated bone crest. The head was hairless. Deep-set blue-green eyes with diagonally slitted pupils watched us approach, unreadable in shadowed eye sockets. They—no gender was obvious—wore plain dark pants and a blue thigh-length tunic with slitted side seams. White symbols proclaimed something over the right breast of the tunic, below a crest that looked a bit like an elongated yin/yang.

As I neared, the alien stepped forward and held out a hand in greeting—I assumed Cerevare Brindlepaw had taught it the familiar Nearspace handshaking ritual. I took it solemnly, careful not to flinch from the odd combination of soft, fleshy palm and the harder, chitinous plates my fingers brushed on the back of the hand. The Relidae chatter-whistled something completely unintelligible as it squeezed my hand in a firm grip before releasing it. Then, to my surprise, they smiled.

Professor Brindlepaw came to my rescue. "This is Den-Aldar. He is one of the first Relidae I met, and has been so much help to me in beginning to learn their language. He says," she hesitated only a moment, "you are welcome to Tabalo, and an honoured guest of the Relidae."

The Relidae must have understood the Lobor, because his smile widened and he gestured toward the building with a hand.

We followed him into the building. Yuskeya and Viss dropped back to walk beside me.

"Viss says everyone from the *Tane Ikai* is all right," she said in a low voice thick with relief. "When you didn't mention anything to Cerevare—"

"*Dio*, I'm sorry," I said. "It didn't occur to me that you wouldn't know. Yes, everyone's fine. They made it back to Nearspace safely, and that's how we knew to come for you."

Yuskeya smiled. "I wouldn't have been surprised to see the *Tane Ikai* coming back for us herself."

I chuckled. "Luta would have, but I dissuaded her. The Council wanted an official but unobtrusive 'rescue' mission anyway."

"I wouldn't blame Luta for not wanting to come back here too soon," she said. "Her last visit wasn't exactly fun."

We'd arrived at the door to the building, a cathedral domed shape that echoed the larger building's outline. I was surprised when it did not slide or swing in any direction, but merely dematerialized when the Relidae put a hand near it. I threw a glance at Yuskeya and she nodded.

"Their tech—some of it is amazing," she said. "We have to find a way to keep the other Chron from getting to Nearspace, sir, because we won't stand a chance against some of it."

Inside, the entryway opened into a large space on the left, obviously used for social gatherings. Bench seats covered with soft-looking fabrics, in muted shades that echoed the Relidae skin tones, offered seating. Long, tapering spindles glowed dimly above the room, suspended from the high ceiling by gossamer filaments. In the low light, the glass front wall offered a shadowy glimpse of the outside world.

Den-Aldar gestured across the room to an open doorway, and motioned for us to follow him.

"His office is there," Cerevare told us. "Den-Aldar is the administrative head of Tabalo. They govern by a modified sortition, so his title doesn't have a direct translation. The closest I can come is 'Legate.'"

I nodded as we entered a roomy office with plenty of seating. There was no desk, although a credenza stood against one wall, littered with what I assumed was the Relidae version of office clutter. Den-Aldar took a chair and gestured for us to sit. He said something to Cerevare and she relayed to us.

"The Legate wants me to explain about Ambassador Andresson," she said. "She was injured just before we left the Corvid station—while we were getting on the ship to take us out of there. The station took a heavy hit and she fell, and a section of wall toppled onto her."

"How is she?" I asked. "I wondered what had happened when you said she couldn't travel right away."

The Lobor looked discomfited, her ears tilting back. "Perhaps I should have explained more. She is recovering well under a doctor's care here, but the doctor advises another day or two of rest before she's moved."

The delay was disappointing, but I nodded. "Of course, if that's what's best." I was suddenly very glad I'd sent the message to Regina via the Corvids.

Den-Aldar chirp-whistled another few sentences to Cerevare, who nodded.

"In the meantime, you are welcome to stay in accommodations here, or return to your ship," she continued. "Den-Aldar hopes you and some of your crew will attend a reception tomorrow afternoon. He has several matters to discuss with you, but since it's late tonight he thinks it can wait until then."

"Please give the Legate our thanks," I told her, nodding to Den-Aldar to acknowledge his offer as best I could. "I think Commander Drake and I should return to the ship so I can let the crew know the situation." I looked to Viss, who sat next to Yuskeya, holding her hand.

"He'll stay here, with me," Yuskeya said, not waiting for Viss to speak. "I want to show him around tomorrow."

I smiled. "Sure. I'd like to visit the ambassador tomorrow, if I may. Professor Brindlepaw, would you message me when it's appropriate to come?"

The Lobor smiled. "I'll be happy to. You'll want to see Emar and Jolah, too." Obviously, their shared adventure had made friends of the professor and the Protectorate officers she'd helped rescue.

With little else that needed discussion, Linna Drake and I soon found ourselves lifting off in the launch alone. As the sparse lights of the city disappeared below us, she blew out a sigh.

"I still can't believe that I just met a Chron. And he seemed like a nice guy," she said.

"He did. And I think they deliberately just made it him and us. Casual, welcoming."

"The professor knows how anyone from Nearspace is going to feel about them at first. She's probably advising him, and he's listening. Smart guy."

I looked down at the lights disappearing below us. "But I don't like this delay. I thought we'd make a quicker turnaround."

She looked across at me. "You think there's something they're not saying?"

I shook my head. "It's not that. Fleet Commander Holles will be worrying when we're not back. The run into the Corvid system should have been a couple of days at most."

"What about the message you sent her? Did you tell her we had to go into Chron space to get them?"

I felt my face warm and hoped the semi-darkness inside the launch cabin masked the flush. "I told her they'd been taken to a nearby planet for safety. I didn't exactly say, 'Chron space.'"

Linna Drake grinned, not looking at me. "Wow, withholding information from a superior officer. And Regina Holles, at that. At least you got to visit an alien planet before your court-martial."

"Just drive, Drake," I said, but I could still feel her smiling all the way back to the *Cheswick*.

I WAS READY in the morning when Cerevare's message came in. We had a small group of officers on board who had either diplomatic training or experience, so I'd briefed three of them to come down to the surface with me. Linna Drake would pilot us again, since she'd been there last night. The whole thing made me nervous, though—this was not the mission we'd set out on. The rumour of PrimeCorp's hand in starting the first Chron war cycled through my mind at annoyingly regular intervals. I didn't want any misstep on our part to put the *Cheswick* in the same situation.

The weather was auspicious as we arrived back in the city, however. The buildings that had looked mysterious under the shroud of night still appeared alien in bright sunshine, certainly—but no more different than any of the various styles that cropped up around Nearspace. We set down in the same courtyard as the night before, and Cerevare, Yuskeya, and Viss were there to meet us.

"Admiral, it's good to see you back," the professor said as I stepped down out of the launch. "I've arranged to take you to see the ambassador, and Yuskeya will show your crew members some of the city. Then we'll meet back here. Is that all right?"

"That sounds perfect," I said, although I felt a momentary trepidation at being separated. I told myself that was silly. I could trust Yuskeya to look after everyone else.

Cerevare and I crossed to a smaller, flitter-type vehicle parked at the other edge of the courtyard. Its vaguely insect-like shape, with a long sloping front and twisting, spindly-looking legs, gave me another of those gut-twitching moments of revulsion. When a side door slid open and a smiling Relidae motioned us inside, however, it dissipated.

We lifted off smoothly and flew low over the city. Raised monorails, which I hadn't noticed last night but had seen as we descended this morning, sped their passengers along at extraordinary speeds. Below on the streets, other vehicles moved at a more leisurely pace, and pedestrians filled sliding walkways. We passed a few other flitters as well. It was all so utterly like any Nearspace city I'd ever visited that I began to relax.

We touched down on the roof of the medical building, and Cerevare led me to an elevator. I could say if you've seen one hospital, you've seen them all, and it wouldn't be far wrong. The smells were different and yet still suggestive of antiseptics and medicines. The hallways were characterized by muted colours and voices. Relidae medical personnel wore pale green uniforms as they hurried about and consulted one another. I wished I could understand their clicking, whistling language. It was the one thing that kept me at bay and made me feel like a true outsider.

Cerevare knocked on a half-open door and stuck her head inside. "Feel like visitors?" she asked.

A faint female voice from inside said in welcome Esper, "Certainly! Come in, Professor!"

I followed Cerevare into the room. A pale blue light suffused it, although a window in the far wall allowed sunlight to pool on the floor inside as well. The bed was set at a full-body slant, partially covered by a clear half-dome on which readouts and statistics flickered. On the wall above the bed, a full electronic panel displayed much more information, in the curving symbols of Chron script.

I knew Ambassador Bele Andresson by sight, with her slight build and fall of dark hair, now spread across a pillow. Her skin, always pale, looked almost translucent in the room's lighting. I wondered if her condition was worse than Cerevare had intimated. No wonder the Relidae doctors were advising against moving her. Tiny electrodes on thin, hair-like filaments scattered along her hairline and along her bare arms, which lay atop a daffodil-yellow sheet. A smaller panel curved up from the side of the bed and covered her midsection.

She smiled when she saw me. "Admiral . . . Mahane, isn't it? Excuse me if I don't get up."

Although her voice still sounded frail, she looked cheerful enough, and her blue eyes were bright.

"No need, Ambassador. I can see you're a little busy. Professor Brindlepaw tells me you're on the mend." I smiled, and she lifted a hand for me to shake. Her grip was firmer and stronger than I'd expected.

Ambassador Andresson nodded. "That's what they tell me. And I believe I have your sister to thank for that."

"Luta?" I didn't catch her meaning. "In what way?"

Before she could explain, though, a tall alien entered the room. Dressed in the green uniform of the medical personnel, this one had camel-coloured skin and a ridged and knobbly parietal crest. It smiled at me, deep brown eyes examining me closely. Then it spoke to Cerevare in a quick series of whistles and chirps. She nodded.

"Admiral, this is Doctor Chy-Loren. She's the doctor who helped Luta when we were on the Relidae station. She says to please give your sister her regards when you see her."

I put out a hand and the doctor shook it. The sensation of those smooth, seemingly jointless fingers was a bit unsettling, but I didn't pull away. "Tell her I'm very grateful to her for helping Luta."

The doctor didn't wait for Cerevare's translation, but nodded as if she understood me.

"This is what I meant about Luta," Ambassador Andresson said. "Because Dr. Chy-Loren had treated Luta on the station, she knew much more about human physiology than she would have, otherwise. That knowledge allowed her to quickly figure out what internal injuries I'd suffered, and how to treat them."

The doctor chirped something to the ambassador, who laughed and said, "Indeed." I stared, not understanding how they could possibly communicate so easily. The ambassador had been with the Relidae for even less time than Cerevare had, and the Lobor had intimated that her command of the language was still rudimentary.

My confusion must have been evident, because Cerevare said, "Oh! I forgot to give this to you." From a pocket in her skirt, the professor withdrew a small disc, with a short tube, perhaps six inches in length, attached. It looked like something a techdog hacker might put together—functional, perhaps, but not polished or mass-produced. She offered it to me and explained.

"It is a rudimentary translator," she said. "We began working on them soon after I arrived, because we could see the future necessity for a way to communicate with Nearspace folk. They already had the trans-cymatics sound library and the language database from . . . from long ago," she said delicately, obviously loath to mention the Chron war. Perhaps they were sensitive about it. "So, with my help and the files from Jahelia Sord's datapad, we've been able to correlate and update the translator so it works reasonably well. It was not a full database to start with, and both languages have certainly changed over the course of a century and a half, but it will allow you to converse with a minimum of difficulty, and without the need for my stumbling translations."

I accepted the gadget and immediately thought to attach it somehow to my ID implant, but Cerevare put a warm hand on my arm. "It actually goes in your ear," she said. "The disc can adhere behind it, and the flange on the end of the tube should fit reasonably well into your ear. Don't push it in too far," she cautioned with a smile. "The disc contains a pickup device, so it will 'hear' what's being said and feed the translation into your ear."

I noticed, now that I looked closely, the clear tube running from the ambassador's ear into the dark hair behind it. So that explained her ready conversation with the doctor. Since the Relidae had no obvious ears, I wondered how it worked in reverse, and asked Cerevare.

She said something to Dr. Chy-Loren, and she smiled and bent her head forward. I spotted a similar disc tucked inside the hollow of the bone crest, near the back. I assumed that the vibrations must resonate through the hard crest via bone conduction.

I tucked the small, flexible flange inside my ear and jumped. The murmur of whistles and chattery noises forming the hum of the hospital's background noise resolved into conversation fragments—all in Cerevare Brindlepaw's voice. I caught only bits of the dialogue, but suddenly it was like being in any Nearspace building, with an added background of bird and small animal sounds. I looked back at the professor in surprise, and she grinned.

"I forgot to tell you, Admiral, that mine is the voice you will hear. Naturally, there are no other Esper speakers to provide the translated words. It will likely be a bit disconcerting at first, but I hope you'll soon get used to it."

I chuckled. "I hadn't thought of that. Yes, it gave me a bit of a start. But it makes sense."

The doctor had moved to examine the information on the wall display, occasionally tapping one or another of the lines of data. "The professor tells me you should be up and about in another couple of days," I said to Ambassador Andresson.

She nodded. "The doctor confirmed that this morning, so long as nothing else crops up." She motioned me closer, and when I leaned over her, she whispered, "Between you and me, I'll be glad to get to the galley on your ship, Admiral. The care has been wonderful here, but the food is not to my taste."

"I'll see that we have something particularly good for your first meal aboard, then," I said with a grin.

"Admiral, we should get underway," Cerevare said. "The reception will be starting in a bit, and I believe Den-Aldar wanted to speak with you privately first."

I gave the ambassador my hand again. "I'll see you soon, Ambassador. It looks like you're receiving excellent care."

She nodded and smiled. "I'm sorry to delay everyone."

"Not at all. We're just glad you're all right."

The flight back was as pleasant as the one to the hospital, and I watched the intriguing and unfamiliar city unroll beneath us. No-one waited outside for us this time, although citizens crossed the square on various errands. Cerevare and I walked alone to the building. Inside, a few Relidae moved around the room we'd passed through last night, obviously preparing it for the reception later. They greeted Cerevare but didn't make conversation. On our foray to the hospital I had begun to understand the wide range of colourations Relidae could have, and it was borne out here as well. One had caramel-coloured skin peppered with small bluish dots, and one a slightly deeper mauve than Den-Aldar. A third was shorter than the other two, with deep brown skin and an impressively elaborate bone-crest that flared upwards and out to each side. A fourth, teal-skinned Relidae emerged from a door in the back of the room, bearing a tray full of glasses, rounded like the bowls of wineglasses but without the tall stems.

The door to Den-Aldar's office was closed this time, but swung open as the professor raised her furred hand to knock. The tall alien smiled a greeting and motioned us inside.

"Admiral Mahane has his translator," Cerevare told him, and Den-Aldar smiled and answered. After only a slight delay, the professor's voice in my ear said, "Excellent."

The Legate motioned us to a grouping of chairs in one corner. They clustered around a low table bearing a tray set with glasses of deep amber liquid. I looked to the Lobor historian with a question. She nodded and a smile stretched over her muzzle.

"It is both safe, and generally agreeable to humans," she said. "Not so much to the Lobor palate, but we have discovered other drinks that I can enjoy."

I raised one of the glasses to my lips, sipping tentatively at the drink. It was surprisingly warm, and held hints of peach and mint, along with a flavour that was unlike anything I'd tasted before. It was, as Brindlepaw had suggested, quite agreeable. Den-Aldar poured a pale raspberry-coloured drink from another carafe and handed it to Cerevare.

"Admiral," Cerevare said, "the Legate and I agree that it is vital for the safety of Nearspace that you understand what is happening with their Chron counterparts, the Pitromae. They currently pose a grave threat to Nearspace."

Den-Aldar clasped his long-fingered hands in his lap and

spoke in a rapid string of Relidae. The translator lagged only a few seconds behind before feeding the Esper translation into my ear. "*Jk-kaa'lin* Mahane, we are gravely concerned about the actions and intentions of the broken ones," the voice of Cerevare Brindlepaw said into my ear.

I nodded. "Please tell me more."

"We intercept some of their transmissions," Den-Aldar continued. "That is how we knew of the plan to attack the Corvid station."

The alien's use of the word "Corvid" startled me, until I realized that Cerevare Brindlepaw would have provided it.

"We also knew from their chatter that your envoys were present and could be in danger, so Honoured Cerevare was concerned for their safety. Although we could do nothing to thwart their plan, we knew that if we were present, we could assist in the defence of the station and possibly be of other assistance. As we ultimately were," he said.

Cerevare looked at me, obviously anxious to know how the translation system was working.

"We are very grateful for your help, and the kindness you have shown our people," I said. "We will be relieved to bring them home with us. But we do fear for the continued safety of Nearspace."

He nodded. "As you should. The broken ones have plans to further harass your worlds, but the true threat comes from within your own borders."

"What do you mean?" I felt a prickle across my scalp and the hairs rise on the back of my neck.

"The broken ones work in concert with the first explorers. They have made *ink-luk'cha* with them."

I shook my head as the word failed to translate and the Relidae's voice filled in the spot where no word of Cerevare's matched. I also didn't know who the "first explorers" were.

Cerevare asked, "What is it?"

I told her the word problem, repeating what I'd heard inexpertly but well enough that she nodded. She pulled out her datapad and consulted it, flicking through a few screens, and scanning them intently. "It means a reciprocal agreement, I believe, but it's more nuanced than just a 'deal'," she said finally. "It's a deal between equals, where there's no power differential."

"So, who are the first explorers?"

She exchanged a few words with Den-Aldar in the Chron language, tapped her screen again, and showed him the display. He nodded. The Lobor turned the datapad so I could see the PrimeCorp logo displayed there. The letters *P* and *C* bracketed a stylized atom with a red nucleus, underscored by a dark red line.

"The first explorers are the ones who made first contact with the Chron back before the Chron war in Nearspace," Cerevare confirmed. "PrimeCorp."

I swallowed. There it was. First-hand confirmation.

I turned back to the Relidae. "And what have the first explorers agreed to give them in return?"

"We know of only one thing for certain." The tall Relidae looked grave, the chitinous plates on his face cast in sharp relief. "Us."

DEN-ALDAR'S ANSWER momentarily confused me. "I'm not sure what you mean," I said slowly, giving the translation program lots of time to keep up with what I was saying. "PrimeCorp is going to deliver you to the—broken ones? The *Pitromae*?"

The tall Relidae nodded again. I set my drink down on the table between us. Pleasant at first, after a few sips it had tasted overpoweringly sweet.

"You may know that our society suffered a break—a rift—many years ago," Den-Aldar said. He spoke with care, allowing the translation program time to work. "It became increasingly clear to some that the aggressive intentions of many in our culture was damaging to us as a whole—many needs of the larger society went unmet to fuel ongoing conquests. There were those who did not share the desire or need to participate in the conquest of other worlds and peoples."

He sighed, a very human sound that needed no translation. "I will not bore you with a long tale of how our people foundered on these shoals of discontent and strife. There was war among us—civil war, you would call it—and for a time all that aggression and need for conquest was directed inward, to our own people. Eventually, a portion of the society, calling themselves *Relidae*, or 'seekers after peace,' left the homeworld in search of new places to settle. They thought that, if they could not change the minds of the broken ones, at least they could remove themselves from that life." He swept a hand outward in an encompassing gesture. "They were the ancestors of all who live on Tabalo, and some other planets as well."

"And that was only a small number of the Chr—of your people?" I asked.

"Somewhat less than half the population of our home world left it when the rift occurred," the Relidae said.

"But your population has grown. The colony on Tabalo seems large, and my sister mentioned the orbital station you've built, as well."

He shrugged. "The population of the Pitromae has grown as well in the time we have been separate. And they have not forgotten us, as we might have hoped."

"Sometimes problems aren't left behind—they follow you," I said.

Den-Aldar nodded. "The Pitromae eventually couldn't abide the notion that we had separated ourselves from them. We were no longer true to our species, in their eyes, and the same compulsion to overcome other beings drove them to come after us again." The Relidae smiled, the chitinous plates on his face sliding and shifting. "I believe your colloquialism is 'a thorn in the side.' Our existence, apart from them and pursuing a different way of life, irks them, and now they have determined to do something about it."

I frowned. "But there's still something I don't understand," I said. "The Pitromae seem determined to attack Nearspace again, maybe even start another all-out war. The Corvids say they can hardly hold them back any longer. Why would they take on two enemies at the same time? It would make more sense to unify themselves—or deal with your people in whatever way they plan to—before taking on Nearspace, too."

Den-Aldar sipped his drink. "But that is the thing," he said. "Once we realized their threat to us was real, we took action to defend ourselves. We have infiltrated some of their ships; we monitor their messages. That is how we knew to go to the Corvid system and help the aliens there. How we knew your people were there, apparently consulting with them. It is also how we know this: the war against your Nearspace may not be what it seems."

"In what way?"

The Relidae canted his head from side to side. "I cannot say for sure. On one hand, it seems to be a plan of harrying attacks only, mounted in order to fulfill an agreement with the PrimeCorp."

I leaned forward, resting my elbows on my legs. This was what Harle had suspected, but I wanted the Relidae's take on it. "What would be the point of that? PrimeCorp stands to suffer as much as anyone if Nearspace comes under attack. Why would they orchestrate such a thing?"

At that, Den-Aldar had run out of answers. He lifted his hands, palms up. "That, we do not know. The PrimeCorp must have reasons for wanting to cause fear and distress among your people. They have recruited the Pitromae to their cause. To all appearances, the PrimeCorp intends it to be only a minor incursion. Almost, a distraction. The Pitromae will leave Nearspace alone once the terms of the agreement have been met."

"When PrimeCorp helps them defeat you," I said.

He sucked in a breath. "There is more than that—some technology exchange is hinted at. But that is all we know."

I wanted to race back to my ship and head to Nearspace to tell Harle he was right and let Regina know that maybe the threat was not as dire as we feared. But that flash of relief faded quickly. If the safety of Nearspace was built upon the destruction—or at the very least, subjugation—of these Relidae, who had shown themselves more than once, now, to be our allies, it was not acceptable. No matter what technology PrimeCorp was getting from the Chron, even if it would be positive for Nearspace, the price was too high.

Before I could say anything, the Relidae went on. "But understand: the Pitromae cannot be trusted. Their word, even in *ink-luk'cha*, is suspect. They will alter their plans without notice if they have reason to change their minds. Whatever agreements the PrimeCorp has made with them—" he spread his hands again. "They may find things do not proceed as they planned."

I thought it might serve PrimeCorp right to be double-crossed, but not if it meant Nearspace suffered.

"I'll be ready to testify against PrimeCorp when I return to Nearspace," Cerevare Brindlepaw said, her dark eyes flashing. "I know all the individuals involved in starting the Chron war are long dead by now, but there must be some way to hold the corporation accountable—"

"Whoa," I said, holding up a hand. "Den-Aldar said PrimeCorp made first contact, but starting the war? Luta said you thought something like that, but—" I felt myself almost start to rise from my seat, an involuntary motion, and made my body settle back. Honestly, I'd discounted the idea as too far-fetched. Something that Cerevare had misunderstood. If I'd thought myself immune to surprise about anything PrimeCorp might do, I'd been wrong.

Cerevare flicked her left ear in agitation, reminding me sharply of Harle Southwind. What was my old friend going to think of all this? He'd wanted information about PrimeCorp— well, I was certainly going to be able to deliver on that request.

"The Relidae have been remarkably open in letting me study their historical documents since I've been here," she said. "Although it's been slow going, since everything has to be translated as I go. I suppose," she said with a hint of irony, "I do have to thank PrimeCorp for that. Without them, we wouldn't have that handy dictionary that has made it possible for our communication attempts to progress so far, so quickly."

"I doubt they ever intended it to be used by anyone but themselves," I said, "so you probably don't have to feel too indebted to them."

She smiled. "True. At any rate, in the documentation, it's plainly recorded that the Chron war with Nearspace was a direct result of PrimeCorp's contact with the Chron. An interaction that was outside Nearspace's accepted rules for first contact."

"They were directly responsible?"

Cerevare Brindlepaw nodded. "According to the records— and what Den-Aldar and his people have always known or believed to be true, PrimeCorp was the first to make contact with the Chron. It happened in a system PrimeCorp had discovered and explored, but obviously never reported to the Council.

"We didn't know, however, that there was some experimental trade between PrimeCorp and the Chron," the

Lobor professor continued. "It was apparently a tentative relationship, although there was enough communication to allow the development of the dictionary. I don't know what the Chron would have wanted from PrimeCorp, and the records don't say. But it doesn't take much imagination to see what PrimeCorp saw—the vast possibilities of alien technology."

I laced my fingers together tightly, fighting down my anger. "I can't believe they could do something so dangerous. They put all of Nearspace at risk."

Cerevare sighed. "I'm sure they didn't envision their actions posing any threat to the safety or security of Nearspace. They saw a golden business opportunity; a chance to pull far ahead of any of their corporate competition. But that's PrimeCorp—thinking they are always right, can do no wrong."

"What did go wrong? Do we know?"

Den-Aldar took up the narrative. "We do not know for certain what happened between the two parties—in some accounts the PrimeCorp caused the destruction of one of our traders and all aboard it; in others, it was an accusation by our people that they were being cheated. Whatever the truth, it led to hostilities between the sides, and when your people retreated to Nearspace, our ancestors followed them." He made that odd head shake again. "And then there was no stopping them. They saw the wealth and resources of your worlds and their aggressive, conquering nature took over. Only when they were physically stopped from entering Nearspace would they give up the fight. That is when the Relidae knew for certain they had to remove themselves from the larger society."

A knock sounded at the door of Den-Aldar's office, and I realized we'd been closeted in here for some time. I became aware of the faint hum of conversation and the clink of dishes from beyond it. Apparently, the reception had started without us.

As we moved to join the others, I wondered what Regina Holles, Harle Southwind, and Mother were going to make of all this.

Chapter 12 — Luta
Departures and Arrivals

As I GRIPPED the arms of my command chair and watched the attack unfolding outside the front viewscreen, I was struck by the utter silence on the bridge. I wasn't sure when the *Tane Ikai* had been so quiet with so many people on board.

A Chron ship, larger than the others, loomed up from below my line of sight and launched a pounding assault on the main station hub. The impact caused the shields to flare a deep blue, but the colour shaded to an angry red and dissipated. I quickly counted levels and thought it must be nearest the administrative level. The only thing that saved us was that the shields had absorbed most of the impact before they failed. The remainder of the jolt affected the Leighzing stabilizers, because the whole station jerked and wobbled, suddenly affected by the movement of every ship pulling away from it, every impact from a weapon. Without the stabilizers, it couldn't hold a lock position relative to everything else. We lurched dockward and I reflexively clutched the arms of my chair even tighter so I wouldn't be thrown from it. A creaking screech sounded from the airlock, where the flexible dockway strained to its limits as the docking arm pulled the *Tane Ikai* after it.

"Release the dockway," I almost shouted, and Rei's fingers flashed on her board. The ship righted itself, but out the forward screen, the station continued to sway. For the people inside and the stationary ships still docked, the station would seem wobbly until they got the stabilizers back online and stopped the motion with maneuvering thrusters.

"Take us away from the station," I said, more calmly. "Try to keep away from the worst areas of fighting, but get us clear. We don't want to be in the way."

"Are you going to—" Jahelia Sord began, but I cut her off.

"Hirin, all weapons on standby. If we're engaged, we'll fight back, but only in defence. Sord, reroute everything you can to our shields."

She bit off whatever else she might have said and concentrated on the board. Sord taking orders without comment? That was a surprise. I hoped she was as good as she claimed to be at the engineering station, and that I wouldn't regret installing her there.

"What's happening?"

I turned to see Farro and Neive standing at the entryway to the bridge. The girl clung to her father's hand, but she looked around the bridge wide-eyed with curiosity, not fright. Her curls framed her face like a dark halo. The young man, understandably, sounded worried. I left the command chair and crossed to him.

"We're not going far," I assured him, "just trying to put some space between us and the hostilities."

"Who is it? The Chron?"

He was looking past me at the viewscreen, his own eyes as wide as his daughter's.

"I think so. They look like Chron ships. But the Protectorate is taking care of it." I didn't think the girl should be here watching any longer than necessary.

Farro nodded, swallowing hard and licking his lips. "I'd heard rumours . . . so this is it. Another Chron war is beginning," he said in a voice that was little more than a whisper.

"Not necessarily. This could be an isolated incident. If the Protectorate—"

"*Sankta Dios,*" he breathed suddenly. He'd seen the gaping, ragged holes in the station, on the entertainment and admin levels. "Is everyone—"

"No," I said firmly. "The blast doors would have closed off the affected section; the rest of the station is safe as long as the shields hold. If there's another breach, they'll seal off that section, too. There are so many redundancies built into a station like this—"

"But no-one was planning on a war when they built it," he said, a hint of bitterness in his voice. "I told Bructa we were safer on Vele, but oh no, he wanted to experience the majesty of space. And now maybe—"

I put a hand on his arm. "We don't know anything yet, and he's probably perfectly safe," I said, with a meaningful glance down at Neive. She gaped around the bridge with interest, and didn't seem to be paying much attention to our conversation. With kids, though, you never knew what they were taking in. "Go on back to the galley and make yourselves comfortable until we can return to the station."

He met my eyes and nodded, although I could read his thoughts. *If there's a station to get back to, once this is over.* He didn't say it, though. He just took Neive's hand a little more tightly and said, "Let's go get another cookie, *karulino*." They made their way back down the corridor and I turned back to the bridge.

Rei had us moving slowly, trying to edge us away from the station without attracting undue attention. A bright flash signalled the end of another ship, but I didn't see the explosion itself. I really hoped it was a Chron ship, and not a Protectorate one.

I managed to sit in the command chair before Baden said, "Captain, incoming message for you from Alin Sedmamin." He turned his skimchair and raised one eyebrow at me. "You want me to ignore it? He's a headache we don't need."

It was tempting, but I felt a pang of guilt. "Actually, Baden, I'll take it. Route it to my datapad. I might as well hear what he wants."

"If we do many more favours for the Protectorate, I'm putting in for an honourary rank and a pension," Baden said, but he put the message through.

Sedmamin's face filled the screen. "Captain, where are you? I need to get to your ship."

"That'll be a little difficult at the moment, I'm afraid."

"I'm in the upper habitat. I'm fairly certain I can get down to docking."

I shook my head. "You're better off staying where you are. We had to move off from the station."

His small, dark eyes widened. "Move off? You've undocked?"

"It got too dangerous when the station lost its stabilizers. Look, don't panic. We'll dock again as soon as things settle down."

"You don't understand." He put his face closer to his own screen, and it grew to outsized proportion on mine. I didn't enjoy getting this up close and personal with him. "Someone's here—I think someone is looking for me. Someone from the corporation."

Trust Sedmamin to think he was the most important person on FarView. "I expect they've got other things to worry about, like getting somewhere safe and staying there," I said pointedly. "As you should. If you're in a secure area, stay there."

"But don't you see? This would be the perfect time to—to eliminate me, and have it look like an accident! Just another casualty of the attack."

As if to emphasize his words, the station took another hit. The image jittered and static overlaid Sedmamin's next words.

"You have to come back and get me!"

I looked out at the battling ships, darting and buzzing around the station. "I can't. You'll have to wait."

On my screen, his face flushed with anger. "If anything happens to me, you'll never get—"

A bright flash surrounded FarView station, fading to the telltale red of failed shields. And the connection with Sedmamin went dead.

BY THIS TIME Rei had us turned completely away from FarView. "Baden, put the rear cameras up on the main screen, would you?" I asked. Part of me didn't want to see what state the station was in now, but I couldn't ignore it. I had to know what was happening.

"Aye, Captain," he said, and the screen flashed as the station came into view. One more ship explosion flared, debris shooting out to join the already substantial amount of flotsam and jetsam the attack had produced. And with a shock of relief I realized that the Chron ships were gone.

"Broad feed message from FarView," Baden said.

"Put it on. Bridge only," I added, thinking of Farro and Neive in the galley. Best to wait until I knew what was going to be said.

"This is FarView Station Admin," the voice said. "All unfriendly ships have been neutralized. I say again, all unfriendlies neutralized. FarView Station is in lockdown mode while we effect emergency repairs. If you have left your dock, please contact Station Admin to arrange for re-docking. Do not return without first contacting Station Admin. Lockdown disengage will begin shortly."

The message began to repeat and Baden cut it off.

"Route it to the galley and let it play through once," I said. "I expect we'll see our guests back up here soon after that. Then contact Admin as they asked. Go wherever they ask us in the queue."

Hirin left his weapons board and came to stand beside my chair, slipping an arm around my shoulders. "What did Sedmamin have to say?" he asked in a low voice.

I sighed and ran a hand over my face. "He was demanding that I go back and get him," I said. "And then—the connection went dead."

Hirin tightened his arm around me. "You couldn't have gone back even if you wanted to."

"I know. It was too late when he contacted me." I looked up and into Hirin's blue-grey eyes. "But if anything's happened to him, we just lost any hope of accessing that information."

"If it's gone, it's gone," Hirin said philosophically. "I can't say I was looking forward to having him on this ship."

I was mildly shocked at my usually forbearing husband. "But you don't hope something happened to him!"

He grinned crookedly. "No, not really. But stop beating yourself up about it—hey, I can tell you are," he added, when I would have protested. "You couldn't do anything but what you did. So, stop with the guilt."

I reached up and squeezed his hand, then shut my mouth and watched out the front viewscreen as Rei guided us back toward the docking arm we'd left such a short time ago. All around the station, other ships began to move in the same direction, sometimes weaving through debris and wreckage. I wondered briefly how much of it was from Protectorate ships, then tried to shake that thought out of my head.

"It's all right?" Farro's breathless voice came from the bridge entryway, and I turned with a smile.

"Seems so," I said. "We're going back to the docking arm, but we might have to wait a bit for instructions to dock again. Then you can see about getting home."

He held up a small datapad he must have had in his pocket. "I heard from Bructa," he said, relief softening his face. "He's all right. They were locked down in a refuge station near the restaurant."

I closed my eyes briefly and sighed. "I'm so glad to hear that," I told him. "There are free chairs here on the bridge, if you'd like to sit and watch while we wait to dock again."

"Yes, *patro*! Please, can we?" Neive clung to her father's hand, jumping lightly from one foot to the other. Her curls bounced with each hop. I was reminded of Maja as a little girl, full of exuberant energy.

"*Okej*," he said, smiling down at her. I thought he'd probably agree to just about anything at that moment. Neive settled herself in the co-pilot's chair, next to Rei, who gave her a quick, indulgent smile.

"*Tane Ikai*, this is FarView Station Admin," said a voice over the ship's comm. "You are queued for docking in thirty minutes. Please proceed to your previously assigned dock and await further instructions."

Baden replied in the affirmative, and Rei continued our slow return. So many ships moved around the docking arms that we couldn't have gone faster anyway.

Farro stayed next to my chair for a moment, as if trying to make a decision.

"Captain," he said hesitantly. "Just now—when they said the name of your ship. I realized that I'd heard a man asking about it the other day on the station."

I raised my eyebrows. "Really? I was supposed to pick up another passenger here. Was he a bit shorter than you, heavier, with thin pale blond hair and brown eyes?"

Farro shook his head. "No, this man was younger, probably a little older than me, although Vigor-Us makes it harder to judge. But he had light brown hair a little long, down over his ears, and his eyes were blue, I think. He was slimmer than I am, and he had a small tattoo on the left side of his neck. I wasn't close enough to see exactly what it was."

I frowned. "That sounds a lot like my ex-son-in-law," I said, "but I didn't know he was on FarView." What would Taso be doing on FarView station? He'd only just messaged Maja that he was thinking of coming out from Earth. Could he have made it here already? No. He'd have to have started as soon as he'd sent the message, and not waited to hear any response from her. But that didn't make any sense. How would he know where she might be?

"I only noticed him because he looked nervous. Kept glancing back over his shoulder and fidgeting, as if he was afraid someone was going to walk into the room and see him there."

"Where was this?"

"In the Nearspace database offices, on the Admin level," he said. "I work there. He didn't come to my station, but the one next to me. He was so unsettled, my colleague and I spoke about it after he'd left. But he was perfectly polite to her."

It made a certain amount of sense. If Taso was trying to track Maja down, he'd check the nearest database office and ask them to run a search. The Nearspace database doesn't always have the current whereabouts of every ship, but commercial vessels like traders and cargo haulers are expected to file flight plans. Not that there's much in the way of actual enforcement of those regulations—Nearspace has simply become too big. But filing your flight plans can be beneficial in my business, since sometimes satisfied customers will look you up to see if you might be in the vicinity when they need a particular job done. I knew Baden had filed our plan for the last haul to Cengare with a tentative return to FarView Station, and our docking information would certainly have been updated by the station when we arrived back here. No-one could dock anonymously on FarView. So Taso must know we were here.

I looked up to call Maja over from the navigation board. She had her head down over the board as if she were concentrating hard on what she read there, but past the fall of her blonde hair I saw her cheeks stained with a pink flush. She might easily have overheard what Farro and I had been saying; neither of us had spoken in a particularly quiet voice. But why would our conversation have discomfited her? Was she simply worried that Baden would overhear us as well? But he was the comm officer—he had to know she'd received messages from Taso recently. I changed my mind about calling her over. Better to defer this until we could talk in private.

"Thanks for the information, Farro," I said instead. "He might be trying to get in touch with my daughter. He'll know we're here now, at any rate, so I'm sure he'll track us down."

Farro smiled as Neive skipped over to us and tugged at her father's sleeve. He bent low to listen as she whispered in his ear, and nodded. "Bathroom run," he told me. "I think I noticed the head down near the galley?"

I nodded. "Third door on the left."

"Thanks." Farro took Neive's hand and led her off the bridge again.

Maja had her eyes on the front viewscreen now, watching our slow approach to the docking arm, and didn't look back at me.

DURING THE RE-DOCKING process, the station admin asked if everyone on ships or in habitats could remain there for the next three hours, while the casualties were assessed, the station ran through safety checks, and the maintenance teams secured the damaged areas. That would also allow time to get people out of the cramped refuge stations first. After that time, the rest of us could move about the station as well. Since Farro and Neive hadn't returned to the bridge, I went looking for them and found them back in the galley. They'd curled up in one of the big armchairs, her head on his shoulder as he read to her from a book on his datapad.

"You'll have to remain our guests for a little longer yet," I said, crossing the room to pull off a glass of water since I was here. "We're safely docked, but they don't want the corridors too busy while they check for damage. If you'd like, you can have the use of one of the passenger cabins while you wait. Take a nap, or use the computer there."

Farro looked up and smiled. "I think we'll be fine here," he whispered.

I glanced over and saw that Neive had begun to doze, eyelids drooping even as she fought to stay focused on the story. I winked at him and whispered, "That's fine. Let me know if there's anything you need, and don't leave without saying goodbye."

Emerging from the galley, I nearly ran into Maja. She stood with arms crossed next to the door, her eyes worried. "Can we talk?" she asked.

"Let's go to my quarters," I said, and she followed me in. When the door closed behind us, I asked, "What's up?"

She stood behind the big armchair, resting her hands on its back. "I overheard what Farro said. He's right, Taso is on FarView."

"I knew he'd messaged you a second time when we were on Cengare. He must be trying to catch up with you?"

Maja shrugged. "He wanted my help with something—but I told him no. I didn't see any reason to bother you with it. It's no big deal."

"I thought it *was* kind of a big deal when he first messaged you. You were unsettled by it."

For some reason, she wasn't meeting my eyes, although her voice was neutral. Her fingers kneaded the back of the armchair lightly. "I was just worried that Baden might take it the wrong way. But I wanted you to know that it's nothing you need to be concerned about."

Maja and I had been a long time with only minimal communication, but we'd grown close over the last months. I was sure there was more that she wasn't telling me. The problem was, I didn't want to risk a return to those days of estrangement by pushing her too hard. "*Okej*," I said easily. "If it's not a big deal, it's not a big deal. Just let me know if anything changes, all right? I'll help out if I can."

"Captain?" Baden's voice came over the comm. "Incoming message for you on the bridge. And the caller is rather . . . insistent."

"Duty calls," I said, and Maja turned to leave with me. I caught her hand and squeezed it. "I mean it, though. Let me know if you need my help."

She squeezed back and smiled at me. "I will. Thanks."

But something hung in the air between us, something that hadn't been there before. I didn't much like the space it filled, but neither of us spoke as we hurried back down the corridor to the bridge.

When we arrived, Baden rolled his eyes at me. "Your old pal Alin Sedmamin," he said. "Just as cheerful as ever."

I felt a brief flash of relief that our information source was still intact, but it battled with irritation at the man's demands. "Put him on my screen," I said, and sat in my skimchair, swiveling the screen over in front of me. In a second it was filled with the former PrimeCorp Chairman's face.

"Captain, I need to get to your ship immediately," he said. His face glistened with an unpleasant-looking sheen of sweat and his eyes had sunk deeply in their sockets.

"I believe there's a three-hour moratorium on movement around the station," I said. "Well, a little less than that now. As soon as those restrictions are lifted, you're welcome to join us."

Hirin caught my eye and grimaced at the word *welcome*, but I kept my face neutral for Sedmamin.

"That's outrageous!" he huffed. "I could be in danger here, and they want to keep me locked down—"

"I can't change the station restrictions," I interrupted him, holding up a hand. "And the operative word there is *locked*. If you're in your quarters with the door secured, you should be perfectly safe."

He almost pouted. "I thought I could slip onto your ship while it was quiet, with not too many people about. In three hours it will be bedlam all over the station. Anyone could sneak up on me in a crowd and—"

I interrupted again. The man still got my back up, even when I was trying to help him. "If you want, I'll have someone come and collect you when we're allowed to move around the station again," I offered. "Just tell me your habitat number and we'll get you to the *Tane Ikai* safely."

He looked for a moment as if he would protest some more, but he must have realized it was futile. Moving around the station when it was in lockdown might make him even more noticeable, and he didn't want to end up in the custody of security. "I'll message you again when the lockdown is lifted," he said, and closed the connection without saying goodbye.

"Such a pleasant man. I'm so looking forward to having him as a guest," Hirin drawled. "Do we have to put him in a guest cabin? I could put a sleeping mat in one of the cargo bays and we could lower meals to him on a rope from the catwalk."

"It'll be one of those 'grin and bear it' jobs," I agreed. "But I'm afraid you'll have to just close your eyes and think of Nearspace."

ONCE FARVIEW ADMIN announced an end to the lockdown, I sent Baden to collect Alin Sedmamin. It wasn't until that moment that I realized how spectacularly uncomfortable it was likely to be, having Sedmamin aboard. Hirin hated the man. He had duped Maja, leading me into a trap. Sedmamin and Jahelia had each used the other for their own ends. Baden disliked him by association, but at least they'd had no direct dealings, so he seemed like the best one to send.

After Baden left, Farro and Neive arrived on the bridge. The little girl looked bright and full of energy after her nap. Farro looked exhausted but relieved.

"Captain, I guess we'll be going," Farro said, holding out a hand to me. "Thank you so much for taking care of us. I don't know how I can repay you, but if there's ever anything—"

I shook his hand but brushed aside his thanks. "No repayment needed," I said, as Neive wrapped her arms around my legs in a shy hug and then hopped back beside her father. "I'm glad we were in the right place at the right time."

"Well, let me at least treat you and your crew to dinner at Bructa's restaurant," he said. "It's the least we can do. Drop in anytime; I'll tell Bructa to watch for you. It's the Blackstar, on Level 5."

"That sounds wonderful," I said with a smile. "We might just take you up on that. I do have a crew that loves to eat."

They headed for the bridge airlock and I went the other way, down the corridor, to make sure Alin Sedmamin's quarters were ready. The room was clean and empty, and I briefly considered disconnecting the computer access. But I realized with a bit of a start that I didn't expect Sedmamin to do anything nefarious. I actually—sort of, for the moment—trusted the man.

Baden and Sedmamin arrived back at the ship about twenty minutes later. I'd just been starting to wonder what was taking them so long, and if I shouldn't have suggested that Baden go armed. Sedmamin had, after all, expressed the concern that someone was after him, and I could have unwittingly sent Baden into the middle of something bad. But my implant vibrated and when I answered, it was Baden.

"We're just about there," he said. "Thought I'd give you the heads up."

"Thanks, Baden. Take him to the rear airlock, would you? I'll meet you there."

I'd been sorry to see Farro and Nieve leave the *Tane Ikai*, I mused as I followed the corridor from the bridge to the rear airlock. I didn't view our new visitor with any of the same emotion.

Although when I opened the door to Baden and Sedmamin, I felt a twinge of pity for the man. Anger and apprehension mingled on Alin Sedmamin's face, and both washed away in a flood of relief when he saw me. It felt ridiculous that the man would be so glad to see me or to come aboard the ship, considering our previous relationship.

He released a long sigh when the door slid shut behind him.

"Welcome aboard the *Tane Ikai*," I said formally. I wasn't ready to shake the man's hand, but I motioned him inside graciously. He still wore the clothes I'd seen him in when we met at the shopping centre, and they looked the worse for wear. He carried a battered duffel bag over one shoulder and a briefcase in his other hand. His face, still too thin and carved out of sharp angles, had softened when he stepped inside the ship. He looked at me with a pathetic hopefulness. I realized that until this moment, Sedmamin hadn't really believed that I would help him—or that he'd make it here. I felt a sudden surge of power, and I didn't like myself very much for feeling it.

"Thank you, Captain," he said. "I'm glad to be here safe and sound." He managed to make it sound just a little bit accusatory, and I stopped feeling bad.

"I'll show you to your quarters, and in the morning, we'll discuss what's next," I said. "We're all drained." Sedmamin accepted that with a nod. Baden raised his eyebrows in a question and I nodded. He could go; I'd look after Sedmamin myself from here.

The guest quarters he'd been assigned were just around the corner, and he looked around the tiny space with a sigh. "It's small, but I don't mind. It's worth the inconvenience just to feel safe," he said.

"You really think there was someone following you, looking

for you, on the station?" I leaned against the door frame and folded my arms.

Sedmamin put his bag down on the floor and sat on the edge of the bed. "I did. They're not going to let me just walk away, as I told you. And if they could get rid of me out here, far away from PrimeCorp Main, make it look like an accident—" He shrugged. "Problem solved, for them."

"Well, you're valuable to the Protectorate, and everyone on the *Tane Ikai* will do what they can to protect you," I assured him.

He quirked a self-deprecating half-smile. "Everyone? Your crew doesn't like me anymore than you do, Captain. I'm fully aware of that."

"Not everyone on the *Tane Ikai* at the moment is even part of the crew," I told him. "Jahelia Sord is here, too, waiting to see what you want from her."

"Does my door have a lock?" he asked.

"It does. But trust me, there's not a lock on this ship that will hold Sord back if she puts her mind to it, as I know from bitter experience." I shrugged. "I guess I should amend my assurances. Everyone will protect you from outside threats, but it's up to you to keep on the good side of those aboard. My advice is keep your head down and try not to antagonize anyone. I'll ask everyone to play nice, but if your tongue gets you into trouble while you're on board, that's your lookout."

Sedmamin ran a weary hand through his thinning hair, as if he'd gotten tired of the banter. "I'm just looking to get out of this alive. Will we be able to leave tomorrow?"

Startled, I said, "I don't have my full crew aboard. I'd thought we'd wait until I got them back—"

Sedmamin reached out as if he might take my arm. "There isn't any time to waste, if this plan is going to work. My ability to access the files could change any day."

I blew out a sigh. Leaving again without Yuskeya and Viss—particularly on this mission—hadn't occurred to me. I didn't like it. On the other hand, if Lanar wasn't here, he couldn't try to talk me out of helping Sedmamin. I could leave a message to let him, and Yuskeya and Viss, know that I'd be back soon.

"Then I guess we'll go in the morning, as soon as we're cleared," I said finally.

Alin Sedmamin ran a hand over his face. "I haven't slept well in weeks. But I might tonight. I finally feel safe."

I hoped he wasn't putting too much faith in me.

"I'll leave you to it. The galley is just there," I said, pointing over my shoulder, "if you want something to eat."

"Thank you," he said earnestly. "I can't wait to get away from here. I think this station is bad luck."

Leaving Sedmamin behind me as I headed for the bridge, I had to wonder if he might be right.

MIDWAY THROUGH THE next morning, Sedmamin finally made an appearance. Hirin, Jahelia and I gathered in the galley to see what he had to say. I'd warned everyone to be civil, but I could tell it was a struggle at times. I'd pulled hot drinks for everyone and set out a plate of *solanto* cookies and chocolate *pano*.

"I assume you have a plan?" I asked Alin Sedmamin. "You spoke as if you've orchestrated things pretty closely, so if you don't have one I'll be disappointed."

"Of course, I have a plan," he said mildly, wrapping his hands around his mug of milky chai. Steam rose and dissipated from it, and he hadn't tasted it yet. He looked like he really had slept well. I wouldn't say he looked good, but his face was slightly less drawn, and his eyes not so sunken. He'd showered, combed his hair, and traded his wrinkled suit for a pair of dark pants and a navy transform sweater. "It's this: get into my old office at PrimeCorp Main, retrieve my files, and get out again. A stop-off at my apartment so I can gather some things. Leave the planet and everything PrimeCorp." Now he lifted the mug and sipped. "I'll review the files, tie them all up in a neat, incriminating package for the Protectorate—after removing anything that unnecessarily implicates me—and after I turn everything over to your brother and sign whatever they want for authentication, you deposit me at the safe haven I've set up."

Jahelia Sord snorted. "Sounds easy enough," she said in a voice thick with sarcasm. "Of course, you're *persona non grata* at PrimeCorp now and they probably have alarms set to go off if you set foot on the premises, but we'll just walk in—"

"Not *we*, Jahelia," Sedmamin broke in. "You. And Captain Paixon. I'll be present only as a voice in your ear."

I raised an eyebrow and a hand. "Hang on, Sedmamin. If you

think Jahelia and I are going to break into PrimeCorp Main—"

He shook his head. "I didn't say break in, I said walk in. You'll be going to a prearranged appointment, but on the way there, you'll detour to my office. The appointment will be fake, so you'll never actually be expected anywhere, and no-one will notice when you don't show up. Once you have the files, you'll leave with them and no-one will ask any questions at all."

"You sound extremely sure of yourself," Jahelia Sord observed, "while I see so many holes in this plan I could drive my ship through a few of them."

"It's not your ship," Sedmamin retorted.

"Prove it," Jahelia said, showing him her teeth in a predatory grin.

"Luta is not taking that kind of risk, no matter what you say or the Protectorate needs," Hirin said quietly.

I frowned. Hirin rarely presumed to speak for me on anything—but I ascribed it to his obvious dislike of our involvement with Sedmamin at all. I looked at him quizzically and he met my eyes with determination.

Trying to be diplomatic, I said, "Why don't we hear all the details before we make any decisions? I assume you've laid some of the groundwork, Chairman?"

Sedmamin flushed a little. "Not Chairman any longer, Captain, or none of this would be necessary. Yes, I've made sure of the plan. I have someone inside PrimeCorp who's willing to help me. Not to the extent of removing files for me—that would put her into direct jeopardy and I won't ask her to do that. But she will set up the bogus appointment that will get you into the building. And she'll make sure my old office is empty when you go there."

"Can she be trusted?" Hirin asked. "If she's willing to betray her employer, what makes you think she won't betray you?"

"We have an arrangement," Sedmamin snapped. "It's not like I'm risking nothing here. My future—my life, if I'm right about how badly they want me to take the fall for this—depends on how well this goes. I'm actually paying her quite well, and she's already disposed to help me because we were friends. I trust her. She could have gone to the Board when I first contacted her, but she obviously didn't."

Hirin said nothing more, but I felt his disapproval like a

physical heat radiating from him.

"Unless she did, and they're waiting for you to make your move. But let's not go there just now," Jahelia Sord said. "Let's review. Captain Paixon and I march boldly into PrimeCorp Main for a bogus appointment, detour to your unguarded office, I use the passcode you gave me to access your locked-out files, and we bring the data back to you."

Sedmamin smiled thinly. "Your passcode won't get you deep enough for the files I need. You'll need that very useful and experimental AI to do that."

"Pita? Well, she is one of a kind, I'll give you that."

"We'll connect through your ID comm unit or an implant, and I'll talk you through the files to find the right ones."

"You know," Jahelia said idly, "I—well, Pita—copied a *lot* of files off the PrimeCorp Main computers already. Maybe we already have what you want."

The ex-chairman shook his head. "You won't have these. You'll need a decryption chip to find them."

I leaned forward. "And we get this decryption chip, where? I didn't hear you mention that part of the plan."

"It will be in my office by the time you get there. It changes every day, so there's no point in trying to get one beforehand. You'll need that and Jahelia's datapad AI in order to do this."

"And if the chip isn't there when we arrive?"

He leaned back and swallowed the last of his chai. "Then you turn around and leave, just as planned but without the data. I go on the run and Nearspace—maybe—falls to the Chron."

"Why does Luta have to be part of this at all, if Jahelia and her AI friend will be doing all the work? Why don't we just send her in alone?" Hirin asked.

"Wow, thanks, Gramps," Jahelia said. "Nothing like throwing me to the wolves." Hirin ignored her as Sedmamin answered.

"Because Luta's name won't trigger any flags on entering the building. She's made visits to Main before—no, not a lot, but she's in the system. Trust me, no-one will suspect she's doing anything to help me. Her loathing for me is well-known. But she'll still be in the general database."

"And Sord won't?"

Sedmamin quirked a secretive smile. "Jahelia Sord's visits were . . . a little more circumspect."

"In other words, I was top secret," Jahelia said. She looked pleased about it.

"So, I could go in alone, and take Pita with me," I said. "She and I worked together before, on the Chron station."

"Hey!" Jahelia said. "I am not loaning you my datapad again, and you're not leaving me out of this. I deserve a little fun now and then."

"Fun, right." I tapped my fingers on the tabletop. "You make it sound easy, Chairman. Too easy. I don't like it."

Sedmamin shrugged. "I've done everything I can to *make* it easy. But it's your call. You don't like it, I can't do anything about that. Unless you want to take a more aggressive approach, go in there with guns blazing or something—"

"Sounds like even more fun," Jahelia drawled. I felt like she was deliberately baiting him. "But we'll try it your way. If it doesn't work, guns are still an option." She grinned and winked at me, and I knew she wasn't serious.

Rei's voice came over the ship's comm. "FarView admin has cleared us to leave any time, Captain," she said. "Whenever you're ready, let me know where we're headed."

I thumbed my ID implant. "Looks like we're going to Earth. Check with Maja on supplies and have Baden try to get us a berth at Central Mass."

When I looked up, Sedmamin looked smugly pleased, and Hirin was staring at me.

"What? We have to dock somewhere," I told him. "What we do when we get there . . . well, we can keep talking. We have the whole run to think about it."

But I think he knew as well as I did that we were going to try it. Jahelia was game, and I certainly wasn't going to be the one to let Nearspace down.

Chapter 13 — Lanar
Long Road Home

After two days on the Relidae planet, I was tired of being a diplomat.

Don't get me wrong—the Relidae were kind, friendly people who welcomed us and wished us well. They hosted receptions, showed my crew around the city, explained their cultural beliefs, and generally impressed us as a people we would welcome into the Nearspace alliance. But the unrelenting pressure of not wanting to make a mistake, or have any of my crew make a mistake, was draining.

So, it was with a light heart that Linna Drake and I left the *Cheswick* that morning, on what I expected would be our last sojourn on Tabalo for a while. Cerevare had sent a message that Ambassador Andresson had been given the go-ahead to leave the hospital by Dr. Chy-Loren, on strict instructions to continue her regimen of rest and recovery. The professor had instructed us to meet them at the usual courtyard. Yuskeya and Viss, as well as Jolah Didkovsky, had already returned to the *Cheswick*, but Emar Summergale had chosen to remain on the planet while we waited.

I knew as soon as I climbed down from the launch and saw Cerevare's face that there was trouble. My immediate thought was for the ambassador.

"What is it?" I asked, striding to meet the Lobor. "Has she had a setback?"

Cerevare held up a leathery palm. "No, the ambassador is fine. She's inside with Den-Aldar. But there have been reports of heightened Pitromae activity in the system. We don't believe it is safe for you to leave today."

Linna Drake had followed me, and the three of us went into the big building. The room usually reserved for social occasions held a few knots of people. Den-Aldar was there, in conversation with two other Relidae in military uniforms. Ambassador Andresson, still looking pale but upright and composed, sat on one of the benches, speaking in low tones with Lieutenant-Commander Summergale. Three more Relidae bent over a handheld device that I'd learned fulfilled the same functions as our datapads.

Den-Aldar saw us arrive and crossed to greet me. "Admiral, you've heard the news?"

I nodded grimly. "How bad is it?"

He spread his hands. "There is substantial activity in the system. I could not guarantee that you would reach the wormhole back to Corvid space undetected."

"Any idea what it's about?"

The tall Relidae spread his hands. "We do not have sufficient information yet. But I urge you to delay your departure even for a day or two. You are more than welcome to remain here, or even to dock at the orbital station. There are no indications that an assault there should be expected."

Ambassador Andresson rose and crossed to us, giving me a tense smile. "Admiral? What do you think we should do?"

I appreciated her asking me, when really, she could have made the decision herself. "I don't want to risk your safety, Ambassador. There's no pressing need for us to leave today. I think caution is best, especially with you on board."

She snorted and shook her dark hair. "Oh, I'm no more important than any member of your crew," she said. "But I do agree. Let's give it a day or two and hope things settle down."

I swallowed and turned back to Den-Aldar, inclining my head politely. "Legate, we're in your debt and we'll take your advice. We'll remain your guests for a couple more days."

But it wasn't a couple of days.

Three, then four days passed with no decrease in the Chron activity. On the fifth day came a report that Chron ships appeared to be massing near the Pitromae planet, which I'd learned was a comparable distance from Tabalo as Mars was from Earth. The next day the news was that part of the force had moved to take up station near another wormhole out of the system.

"Does that mean they're going somewhere else, not to Nearspace?" I asked a Relidae named Hin-Garan, who'd been assigned to me as a liaison and kept me updated on the intelligence reports coming in, explaining anything I didn't understand.

I felt a little guilty as soon as I'd asked the question. It wasn't that I wanted the Pitromae to attack anyone else. It was just that if they were elsewhere, maybe we could make it home.

Hin-Garan shrugged. He had skin the colour of rose quartz and an asymmetrical bone crest. One side had a ragged edge, dark with scorch marks, where a chunk had been torn away. I hadn't asked him about it, but he'd volunteered the information that it had happened when the Pitromae attacked the orbital space station. I swallowed. That was the battle Luta and her crew had been present for, when she'd been so sick, when the Pitromae and their PrimeCorp allies had tried to overrun the station. Sitting here with this Relidae who'd been there, been injured there, made me shudder. Luta's ordeal felt suddenly very close.

But it was the next day that everything changed.

I WAS SITTING in Den-Aldar's office with Linna Drake, Cerevare Brindlepaw, Ambassador Andresson, and Hin-Garan, speculating about how long we'd continue to be locked down here. After a brief knock on the door, a Relidae with mint-coloured skin and a worried face entered the room and hurried over to Den-Aldar, leaning close to speak to him. I saw the Legate's face change, and my translator picked up his low reply.

"Send word to Mar-Heden. We might intercept some on their way back, if any remain. I'll tell our guests."

Mar-Heden, I knew, was the chief of the planet's military force. I'd met her at several official functions since we'd been here. When the messenger hurried away, Den-Aldar stood, and

Cerevare and I did as well. The look on Den-Aldar's alien face was grave.

"My friends, I have received worrisome news," he said. "The Pitromae have launched another attack in Nearspace, this time against one of your stations. Although I believe it is still dangerous, I will understand if you wish to leave immediately."

I swallowed. We had five large habitat stations scattered around Nearspace, and a few smaller research and scientific bases. "Did they know the name of the station?" I asked. It shouldn't have made a difference to me. I was duty-bound to care about and protect them all. But it did.

Den-Aldar looked rueful. "Not a name. But it is in the star system you would have left on your journey to come here."

There was only one station in Delta Pavonis. FarView. Where I'd left both Regina and Luta. Cold sweat prickled the back of my neck and my gut clenched as if against a punch.

I'd had a mug of a sweet, tea-like drink the Relidae served at any and all occasions, and set it down on the table with a hand that felt a little shaky. *What if Regina hadn't gotten my message? What if they'd been caught completely unaware?*

We'd been away far too long.

"Thank you for your hospitality and your help, Den-Aldar," I managed to say, "But you are correct. I think it's time to take the chance. We'll be leaving immediately."

THE TRIP FROM the Relidae planet back to Delta Pavonis and FarView Station felt like the longest of my life. We'd spread the word quickly among the others, and encountered only a slight delay when we gathered together. Lieutenant-Commander Emar Summergale stood to attention in front of me, saluted me formally, and said, "Requesting permission to remain on the planet to assist and protect Professor Brindlepaw, Admiral."

I glanced at the Lobor professor but her face showed surprise as well. "The Professor seems safe here, Lieutenant-Commander," I said. "Do you have a particular reason for your request?"

Summergale stood even straighter, if that was possible. "No, sir. But I respectfully submit that it may be in the professor's interests to have a member of the Protectorate with her. As well, I can continue to act as a Protectorate liaison with the Relidae.

You're aware of my diplomatic experience, sir. It's why you sent me along with the envoys in the first place."

Well, that was true enough. "Very well, Lieutenant-Commander." She'd been staying on the planet anyway, so there was nothing to fetch from the *Cheswick*. We'd brought her personal belongings from the *Tane Ikai* with us and delivered them as soon as we arrived, along with Cerevare's things.

Den-Aldar, who had listened quietly to the discussion, now said, "We would be very pleased to entertain another Nearspace guest, Admiral."

Summergale saluted me. "Thank you, sir. My experience while we've been here leads me to believe that we'll be looked after."

Den-Aldar and I had already discussed the establishment of a communications relay between Tabalo, the Corvid station, and Nearspace, although the plan had been derailed by the Pitromae activity. He assured me that they would do everything possible to coordinate with the Corvids and set it up. I had the feeling that even Cerevare and Lieutenant-Commander Summergale would feel better knowing it was a reasonably simple matter to get word to us if the need arose.

Then the rest of us said hurried goodbyes and reiterated our thanks to the Relidae. Worry gnawed at me as we piled into the launch. I knew it, and this frantic race home, were both futile. Whatever had happened was long over now. Nothing would change dependent on when the *Cheswick* crossed back into Nearspace. Still, the drive to get home, to see Luta and Regina and assure myself they were safe, was fierce.

Once aboard the *Cheswick*, we set course for home. It wasn't until we were underway that I sat back in my chair and wondered how the hell I was going to fill almost two days until we arrived at FarView.

I was in the library, hunting for some holovid I hadn't already watched a million times, when Yuskeya and Viss found me. It was a small room that held a few workstations and small tables and chairs and a wall rack of datachips—books, videos, games, and other entertainments—for the ship's crew to borrow as they wished. Much of the task of patrolling Nearspace, after all, consisted of long in-system stretches where nothing much happened. Not that I was complaining about that. I'd rather a hundred uneventful patrols than the events of the past few weeks.

The walls here, unlike much of the rest of the ship, had been painted in a soothing blue, and the furnishings were intended for comfort rather than pure utility. Tucked between the crew quarters and the galley and recreation area, it provided a quiet and reasonably private spot for research, de-stressing, or small group discussion. By silent consent we gathered around one of the small tables. Yuskeya said, trying for a light tone, "Viss and I have discussed it, and we've decided that Luta and everyone are fine."

"Absolutely," Viss said. "They might not even have been there when it happened. The Captain isn't one to sit around when she could be hauling cargo."

I realized my leg was bouncing with agitation under the table, and forcibly stilled it. Neither of them knew the depth of worry I had for Regina as well, but I kept quiet about that. "You're right," I said, forcing a tense smile. "These in-system travel times are just hell sometimes."

"So, let's talk about something else," Yuskeya said, leaning back in her chair. "What in the worlds do you think PrimeCorp is up to with those Chron?"

I hesitated a moment, thinking of Harle's request that I keep the results of his investigations close to my chest. But Yuskeya certainly wasn't the mole in the Protectorate.

"Something big. Whatever deal they've made with the Chron, PrimeCorp's also managed to get a sizable number of ex-employees into high positions at several other corps—too many to be pure coincidence," I added, when Yuskeya looked like she might object. "I have a feeling that it's all tied together. But after talking to Den-Aldar, I wonder if even PrimeCorp knows what they've gotten mixed up in."

"I don't see what PrimeCorp can hope to gain by allying itself with enemies of Nearspace," Viss said. "I mean, it has to be financial gain; that's what PrimeCorp is all about."

"It could go deeper than that."

"We don't have anyone on the inside anywhere, who could poke around?" Yuskeya asked. She didn't come right out and say it, but I assumed she included connections Mother might have in the question.

I shrugged. "We're considering some possibilities. Nothing yet." I tapped my fingers on the tabletop. "The Relidae seem almost too good to be true, but I can't help it—I trust them."

Yuskeya thought for a moment, then nodded. "I do, too. Cerevare was already completely won over by them, when we arrived, and she certainly had no love for the Chron as a species before. I think we can count on them as allies."

"The NWAC will want to establish formal relations with them soon," I said. "They'll recognize that we need all the help we can get to cope with the Chron threat, just like we did in the last war."

"It'll be interesting to see how the PrimeCorp ambassadors like that idea," Viss said. "If the corporation is in league with the Chron."

I pushed my chair back and stood. "They'll likely go along with the program and keep quiet," I said. "But they don't know we suspect something bigger is happening. We'll just have to see that we put all the pieces together while there's still time to stop it."

"If it's not already too late," Yuskeya said, with uncharacteristic pessimism.

"It's not," I told her, with a conviction I didn't feel. "We'll make sure of it. Now let's go and find something to eat."

THE LESS SAID about the rest of that trip, the better. It felt achingly slow, even though I let everyone know we were to move with all speed, and we ran the burst drive almost the entire way. Yuskeya and Viss and I stayed close, united in our worry for the *Tane Ikai*.

I sent a message to Fha and the Corvids when we passed their station—it was still curled into a protective ball as they worked on repairs. I asked if they'd been hit again by the Chron passing through on their way to attack FarView, but she sent back a puzzled reply.

"Admiral, there have been no further incursions through this system since you left us."

I shot a glance at Linna Drake. "We got word of an attack in Nearspace when we were with the Relidae," I said. "I assumed they would have had to pass through this system to get there." That had been stupid of me. I had never asked the Relidae if they knew precisely how the Chron had entered Nearspace.

On the screen, the Corvid's bright black eyes radiated worry. "This means they have another access point into your Nearspace," she said. "I will try to find out if another of our protective systems has been compromised, or if this is something new."

"Thank you. We'll look forward to any information you can give us," I said automatically, but I felt a creep of fear in my gut. If the Chron hadn't passed through the Corvid system, where had they come from? The only other wormhole into Nearspace that we knew about was in Tau Ceti, but that one was now under heavy Protectorate guard. I couldn't imagine an attack force getting past them and making the three skips it would take to reach Delta Pavonis, undetected. Just another reason I had to get back and talk to Regina as quickly as possible.

Once we'd reached Corvid space, I could send a message to FarView via the new relay beacons. I felt a rush of relief when, after a couple of tense minutes' wait, Regina herself responded.

"Got our stray sheep?" she asked me with a tight smile.

"Safe and sound," I said. "Everything all right there?"

Her smile faded. "I wouldn't say that, but we're still standing. What's your ETA?"

"Less than four hours now."

"All right, report to me as soon as you can once you dock," she said. "I'm in medical. Come find me here."

I opened my mouth to ask what was wrong, but she quelled me with a look and a brief, "Glad you're back. See you soon, Admiral." Then she closed the connection before I could even respond and left me staring at a blank screen.

I tried messaging Luta, but the only response was a notification that she was not in the Delta Pavonis system, and that it would be relayed as a deliverable in proximity. I wondered if she'd left me any kind of message about where she was going, but I'd have to wait until I was close enough to a relay point to get my own DIPs for an answer to that question.

I heaved a sigh and went to the gym to kill some more time.

WHEN WE FINALLY got in range, a deliverable-in-proximity message came in from Luta—but it was maddeningly brief and vague. She said only that she and her crew were all fine after the

Chron attack and that they'd left on a run out-system. She asked me to let Viss and Yuskeya know that she'd be back soon to collect them, and to have a little rest and relaxation on the station in the meantime.

I wasn't sure R & R was very near the top of their priority lists, though, once FarView station came into view. Yuskeya, Viss, and I were all on the bridge with the duty crew when we caught our first glimpse of the pale yellow temporary seal closing off the breach in the station's hull. It pulsed gently, neither bright nor opaque enough to hide the gaping, ragged hole left by the Chron attackers. Debris still hung in a wide ring around the damaged area, and small shuttles moved with funereal slowness as tethered forms in EVA suits gathered bits and pieces by hand. There must have been bodies initially, but they would have been retrieved first.

Sharp pain flickered along my jaw and I had to deliberately unclench it. I still hadn't heard an official number for casualties of the attack, but I knew there had been deaths. Everyone who ventured into space knew there were risks involved, although we'd become, as a whole, quite casual about those risks. But no-one expected to die this kind of violent, senseless death in what should be one of the safest environments we could construct. Whatever the Chron were doing, and whatever part PrimeCorp had in this, we had to stop them.

Viss had discreetly put a hand next to Yuskeya's when the destruction came into view, and she had taken it. Her face was resolute and sombre as her dark eyes took in the scene, perfect Protectorate protocol, but I knew she'd feel this affront as keenly as I did.

It flitted through my mind that this might be a good time to recall Yuskeya back to regular Protectorate duty, but I knew how close she and Luta had become. It didn't seem fair to make that move without discussing it with Luta first. And I knew that maybe a little part of me just wanted to take her away from Viss, which was not only mean-spirited, but dishonourable.

Viss caught my eye, and I felt an uncomfortable flutter in my gut, as if maybe he knew what I was thinking. But his eyes flicked back to the hole in FarView station. "*Bastardos*," he said flatly, just stating a fact. "I'll stay aboard as long as I'm needed, Admiral."

"Thanks, Viss," I said. "As soon as we're docked, I'll see what Fleet Commander Holles has in mind for us. Luta's probably going to be anxious to get you both back aboard the *Tane Ikai*, though."

Did a flash of relief cross Yuskeya's face? If so, it was so quickly there and gone that I might have imagined it. But she must have wondered if she'd find herself back aboard the *Cheswick* in the wake of these new developments. It would only make sense. And if she was needed here, her duty would be to fulfill that need.

However, duty wasn't everything, as I knew better than most. So I said nothing more about it, pushed those thoughts away, and went to see Regina. Lieutenant-Commander Didkovsky left the *Cheswick* at the same time, reporting back to the Protectorate Admin on the station. He thanked me again for bringing him back to Nearspace, and we parted ways as I took the elevator down to medical.

The medical bay occupied one third of the lowest level of FarView Station, along with labs and research areas that were theoretically shared among all the corporations and governments scattered around Nearspace. Occasional complaints held that funding and space allocation moved into the realm of politics, but it wasn't a Protectorate matter and I paid little attention. Considering all the current questions surrounding PrimeCorp, though, I was curious to know if they were currently using any station resources. I made a mental note to ask about it as I watched the levels crawl past the descending elevator. The side walls were glass, allowing glimpses of corridors or public areas as they slid past. I was glad to see that life on the station appeared to be carrying on as usual, but that fantasy dissipated as I passed the level that had suffered the most damage in the Chron attack. The corridor on one side of the elevator shaft was littered with repair materials, and on the other, the golden glow of the temporary shield flickered, securing the blasted-away section of station hull. Workers in full EVA suits toiled to repair the damage. I swallowed. Life was not proceeding as usual for a lot of people, no matter what facade they presented to the world.

The destruction slid past and I arrived at the medical level. The walls here offered a pale yellow that I suppose was meant to be cheery and soothing. I followed the curving corridor to a desk and asked for Regina. The nurse gave me a look that held just a hint of martyrdom, and asked me to follow him along the antiseptic-smelling hallway. Behind his back, I suppressed a smile. Knowing Regina as well as I did, I had no illusions about what kind of a patient she'd make. The not-so-patient kind.

The nurse stopped outside a door numbered 9-4 and knocked lightly. Regina's voice called, "Come in!" and he pushed the door open and stepped aside for me to enter. He didn't follow me in.

Regina nodded brusquely when she saw me, and I felt a flood of relief to see her sitting up in the bed, datapad in hand. She'd pulled her hair back even more severely than usual, and her face looked drawn, as if she were in pain or had been recently. Her brown eyes snapped with energy, though. Energy, and something else—pent-up frustration, I thought. The sheet traced a much larger lump for one leg than for the other one, so it must be encased in a brace or cast. She didn't mention it.

"Thank you for reporting in, Admiral. I'll want to hear your report from the Corvid system right away."

I turned and shut the door behind me so that we were alone, then held up my hands. "Slow down, Regina. I want *your* report, first. What happened to you? Are you all right?"

"Of course, I'm all right. I'm perfectly fine," she snapped.

I looked pointedly at the lump under the cool white sheet and folded my arms.

She rolled her eyes and reached down to rap the leg with her knuckles. It made a hollow knocking sound. "It's broken in two places," she admitted grudgingly. "This is a walking brace, although for some silly reason there's to be no walking for another two days. So here I sit, while Nearspace just waits for the next Chron attack. And apparently even my subordinates feel like they can take the opportunity to ignore direct orders," she finished, mimicking me by crossing her arms over her own chest.

I crossed and sat on the side of the bed, tapping the leg brace experimentally with my knuckles. "You have to give the bones a chance to start healing before you put your weight down," I said, "which you know very well. The trauma nanos can only do so much, so fast. I'm sure they'll let you up as soon as it's safe, because I'm also sure you're making life a living hell for anyone trying to help you out here."

Regina's eyes widened, and I felt sure she was about to blast me, but suddenly she laughed. "Lanar Mahane, you are the most insubordinate—"

"What happened, anyway? Were you on the level where they breached?"

She shook her head wearily. "No, I was on the admin level. But when the stabilizers failed, I fell—and I did it spectacularly badly. So now this," she added, disgust edging her voice as she knocked her knuckles against the brace again. "It will heal, but it'll take a while."

I wanted to lean in and kiss her forehead, but even with the door closed, this wasn't the place for that. I contented myself with patting her hand, instead. "All right, report accepted. So, about my trip to Corvid space. It went well. The Corvid station was badly damaged and they're still in repair mode, but willing to help us any way they can. They gave me some valuable information, which I'll get to in a minute. But Yuskeya and the others weren't there when we arrived. They'd been rescued by some of the friendly Chron—they call themselves Relidae—and we went into the next system, the one Luta's crew called GV5, to collect them. The Relidae planet there is Tabalo."

A tiny frown line had appeared on Regina's brow. "Yes, we received the message from the Corvids. I don't remember clearing you to go into Chron space."

"No, ma'am. But we didn't know it might be necessary when I left Nearspace. I made the decision myself, and I take full responsibility."

She tapped a finger pensively on the edge of her datapad. "It might have gone badly if you'd encountered enemy Chron."

I nodded. "I considered that. But we didn't encounter any of them, only Relidae. I suggest we start calling them by that name, since it's what they prefer. They've been spying on their aggressive cousins—the Pitromae—in hopes of countering or avoiding their attacks. But they're a minority population against the Pitromae Chron. And they think the Pitromae want to see them wiped out. I think they'll be an excellent source of intelligence, though."

"What delayed you? Sheer distance?"

I shook my head. "Initially, we had to wait for the ambassador to recover—she was injured in the attack on the Corvid station. Then there was increased Pitromae activity in the system and no-one thought it was safe for us to leave. But then they heard about the attack on FarView—"

"And you forgot about caution."

I reached out and gave her hand a little squeeze. "You can't blame me for worrying about my sister. And the ambassador insisted, too."

"And Professor Brindlepaw? Is she still with them?"

I nodded again. "And I left Lieutenant-Commander Summergale with her as well. With the help of the Corvids, we're setting up a line of relay beacons to make communication easier and quicker."

"That's good news," she said, then must have read something in my face. "But there's something else, too."

"The Chron have another way into Nearspace," I said. "The Corvids said, when we were coming back, that none had passed through their system. But somehow they got here to attack FarView."

Regina nodded. "We figured that out. We still have the guard posted on the known wormholes out of Nearspace, here in Delta Pavonis and in Tau Ceti. We just haven't figured out where else they're coming through."

"How bad was it, here?" I asked. I wasn't sure I wanted to know the answer.

Regina pressed her lips together in a thin white line before she answered. "It could have been worse. Thirty-five dead, seventy injured. I got your earlier message, so although we didn't know where the threat was coming from, or what the target might be, at least we were on the alert. We spotted them incoming and scrambled a squadron. Took out a few before they even got to the station."

And still they'd managed to penetrate the shields and do the damage I'd glimpsed as we approached the station and when I came down in the elevator. I suppressed a shudder. If the station hadn't been alert and watching, how much worse might it have been?

"We've deployed scouts to follow the drive signatures back to where they came into Nearspace, but they fade out before leading anywhere definitive. I've already recalled them," she said.

I blew out a sigh. "So, what now?"

Fleet Commander Regina Holles, pale in her standard-issue med bay gown, looked past me, her eyes fixed on the daffodil-coloured wall. I knew she didn't find it soothing in the least. She looked like she wanted to kick it in with her super-hardened leg brace. Finally, she sighed.

"The other Fleet Commanders and I are meeting here in three days' time," she said wearily. "And I expect we'll fight about just that. I'm afraid more of them will share Mauronet's view that we should take some sort of initiative against the Chron, instead of concentrating on defences."

"Which is still your preference," I said. It wasn't a question.

She nodded. "Not just my preference, but what I see as the only sensible course of action, considering our numbers." She turned a bleak look on me. "If we knew where they were coming from, it could make all the difference. I want you to tackle that, Lanar. Get help from the Corvids and the Relidae if they can offer any, but find out how the Chron are getting into Nearspace."

Chapter 14 — Luta
No Good Deed

I HAD SO many misgivings about Sedmamin's plan that it would have taken me longer to detail them than to make the actual visit to PrimeCorp Main. Hirin still suspected a setup, but he calmed down when I reminded him that Sedmamin would stay in his sight the entire time Jahelia and I were gone. I said if we were double-crossed in any way, Hirin could shoot him. Sedmamin's eyes grew wide and he spluttered a bit, but he agreed to the terms.

I wouldn't really have let Hirin shoot him—for Hirin's own sake, since I didn't want him spending time in prison—but it was fun to make the suggestion and watch them both react.

And I didn't expect to have any fun on the mission itself. I would have to steel myself to walk into PrimeCorp Main again. The place didn't inspire a warm and fuzzy feeling in me—more like stress, fear, and frustration. I'd spent most of my life assiduously avoiding doing this very thing.

The only bright spot in that trip was a new wormhole between Delta Pavonis and Lambda Saggitae. After months of observation and testing, the Council had declared it stable and opened it to general travel, which meant that it took us only five days and a few hours to reach Earth, compared to more than twice that. Considering the level of tension on the *Tane Ikai* with Alin Sedmamin on board, the time still dragged until we docked at Central Mass, but I could keep reminding myself that it could have been much worse.

From Central Mass, Jahelia and I rented a flitter for the morning, to take us inland to PrimeCorp's sprawling corporate headquarters. Jahelia had dressed for the occasion in dark pants, low-heeled boots, and a tailored blazer in red synthwool. A black turtleneck completed the outfit, and created an intriguing impression of casual power. She carried an oversized bag in soft black fabric studded with tiny mirrors. I wasn't sure I'd achieved the same level of unselfconscious sophistication. Maja and Rei had both insisted on consulting with me on my wardrobe, making me wonder just how awful they thought I usually looked. With their guidance, I'd chosen navy suit pants with a pale mauve blouse of Maja's and a tailored, asymmetrically-cut dark blue jacket belonging to Rei. They'd also insisted I wear my hair up, at which point I agreed but told them they'd have to style it themselves. I am quite aware of my own limits. The outcome had looked good to me in the mirror on the *Tane Ikai*, but I wasn't sure how it stood up next to Jahelia's cool and seemingly effortless style.

Glancing over at her in the passenger seat of the flitter, I wondered if any of that casual confidence had to do with a weapon she might have concealed somewhere, but PrimeCorp's headquarters had sophisticated detector systems. She'd never get inside with it. I asked her about it once our flitter had lifted into the air.

"If you have a weapon, you might as well leave it here," I said. "We'll be thoroughly screened at PrimeCorp Main."

She nodded, but continued to stare out the window. Light rain fell, the droplets streaming in wriggling trails across the flitter's windows. "I've been there before, remember? I know all about their 'restrictions'."

"Oh, right." I felt silly for having forgotten that she'd visited Sedmamin there. "But didn't you say you were a 'secret'? I thought maybe you weren't used to using the front door."

Jahelia flashed me a grin. "Well, not with this name. But no system is failsafe, either," she said, but wouldn't explain what she meant. I stopped trying to pry it out of her after about five minutes, and we spent the rest of the flight in relative silence.

PrimeCorp Main was built to be impressive, and I had to admit it fulfilled its mandate. It sprawled over every building on a full city block, and this was just the administrative and research arm. The corporation had offices, labs, factories, and warehouses strewn over almost every corner of Nearspace.

In the centre of the block, the previous building had been demolished and a new centrepiece constructed on the site. It stretched more than sixty floors skyward, taller than anything else in the vicinity, and glistened with green-tinted, solar-receptive glass. Although we didn't fly over it, I knew the building's greenroof sported a garden that supplied vegetables for the in-house cafe. PrimeCorp knew how to put its best foot forward no matter what was happening behind the scenes. Glass-walled skyview elevators, offering vistas of the surrounding city and beyond, crawled up and down both the east and west sides of the building. We left the flitter at a nearby parkade and walked the last block to the complex. The city streets bustled, as city streets tend to do, with a mix of humans, Lobors, and Vilisians that felt so natural, it was hard to believe humans had ever inhabited Earth as the only sentient species. City-dwellers, more than most, seemed to accept the blending of the three alien species as natural, inevitable, and hardly deserving of notice. They walked, talked, argued, shared food, and even held hands. It was nice to disappear into this sea of people, anonymous for a short time. It was also easy to forget the looming danger lurking just beyond the borders of Nearspace, to believe that the concerns of space stations and aliens who wished us harm was very far away. And I suppose it was, by some measurements. By others, it was far too close.

Jahelia Sord walked silently next to me, apparently lost in her own thoughts. We were in sight of the PrimeCorp Main doors when she said, suddenly businesslike, "I expect you'll do most of the talking. I'm just along for the ride, right?"

"Sure," I agreed. "According to Sedmamin, it's my name that will get us inside. I hope they don't pay too much attention to it. Find it on a list, wave us in, and forget about us."

"And if it doesn't go quite that smoothly," she said, "we have each others' backs, right?" She'd turned to look at me, brown eyes serious and dark.

I wasn't sure what she was getting at, and felt my forehead

tighten in an involuntary frown. "Well—yes. What do you mean?"

She looked away, ahead to where PrimeCorp waited, and shrugged a little. "Never mind. I know we're good. I'm not used to doing this sort of thing with anyone else. With a partner." She half-smiled.

"Oh, we're partners now?" I grinned back. "I guess we are. So how often do you do 'this sort of thing'? By which I assume you mean, gain access to a corporate building under false pretenses, with the intent to steal something from the premises."

She mimed counting on the fingers of both hands. "Not all that often, really. Considering how old I am."

I laughed. "Considering how old I am, I guess it's more surprising that I haven't done it before."

"First time for everything," Jahelia Sord said, and opened the glittering glass front doors of PrimeCorp Main.

WHATEVER I THOUGHT of PrimeCorp, I had to admit the lobby of their main headquarters was an impressive sight. The floor of the vast space shone, pale, polished marble with the corporation's atom logo inset in the centre. Overhead, a huge glass dome vaulted skyward three stories. Full-grown trees stretched leafy boughs up to catch the light, lining a boulevard that channeled visitors and employees to a bank of escalators and elevators at the far end of the room. A thin stream of people moved toward and away from the elevators. A curved desk, also marble, presented visitors with no fewer than three receptionists, all bright, smiling, and ready to assist. The woman in the middle spoke to a tall Vilisian, and the Lobor on the left side of the desk was apparently in conversation with someone via a headset implant.

The young Vilisian on the right side of the desk caught my eye, and I moved toward him.

"Good morning, and welcome to PrimeCorp Main," he said, smiling. "How may I help you?"

"Luta Paixon," I said, hoping I sounded both confident and a bit bored. "We have an appointment."

Sedmamin had assured us that we wouldn't be asked who our appointment was with—that would be considered intrusive. The only information attached to my name on a visitor's list would be the building floor or section I'd be looking for, so the receptionist could offer directions if needed.

The young man nodded and consulted a screen set into the top of the desk, tilted just slightly toward him so that he could read it easily. He typed a few commands on an input device I couldn't see, and then nodded. "You're on the sixtieth floor, main tower," he said. "The last two elevators on your right at the back of the lobby will be the fastest."

From behind the desk he pulled two badges marked "Visitor" and handed them to us. "Please keep these visible while you're in the building, and return them to me when you're leaving," he said. "They alert our security staff that you've checked in and are cleared to be here."

"Thanks for your help," I said, handing one badge to Jahelia and clipping the other to my lapel. "We'll see you in a bit."

We rounded the desk and headed for the elevators he'd indicated.

"Well, that was easy," Jahelia said in a low voice.

"We're not even on the elevator yet," I said. "Let's not get ahead of ourselves."

"He said sixtieth floor, but Sedmamin's office is on sixty-one," she said. "Do you think they'll monitor where we stop?"

"We stop at sixty, and walk up one. Even PrimeCorp has to have stairs in case the power goes out."

We stepped into an elevator with a bored-looking Lobor, a woman in a dark green power suit who didn't take her eyes off her datapad, and a man who smiled noncommittally at us and then stared at the floor progress screen. They got off at the fifteenth, twenty-eighth, and fortieth floors respectively, and we were on our own for the last twenty. We rode mainly in silence, since the elevator would undoubtedly have video and audio surveillance. Around floor fifty-two Jahelia said, "Contact" to me in a low voice to let me know that she had Sedmamin on her implant comm. I wasn't one for implants myself, beyond the forearm ID that everyone in Nearspace had, so Jahelia was the one with a direct line to Sedmamin.

We exited at the sixtieth floor and were confronted by a massive wall-mounted screen, directing us to offices, departments, and labs. We ignored all that and found the nearest stairwell. Most offices had their doors open and people milled about in the hallways, so we just looked like we knew exactly what we were doing and where we were going, and everyone ignored us completely. I thought Sedmamin must be asking Jahelia for a progress report, because I noticed her mutter a low phrase a couple of times, and she certainly wasn't talking to me. She caught my eye and rolled hers, so I knew my assumption must be correct.

The stairwell was deserted and we climbed easily. Once on the sixty-first floor, Jahelia led the way. I'd had the dubious pleasure of visiting Sedmamin's office a couple of times in the past, but that had been in the old building. We followed a long, straight corridor, richly carpeted in a colour I thought of as "PrimeCorp red," and at the very end reached a double glass door marred by patches of adhesive where a name plate had been recently removed. Jahelia raised her eyebrows at me, took a visible breath, and opened the door.

The long, angled secretary's desk and seating area were empty, as Sedmamin had promised. We stepped in and closed the door behind us, and Jahelia dipped a hand into her bag. She brought it out and pressed something tiny next to the doorknob.

"What's that?"

"Motion sensor. If anyone opens this door now, I'll get a ping."

I wished I'd thought of that. I glanced around and saw the closed door that led, I presumed, to the inner sanctum.

We crossed quickly and opened it, stepping inside and closing it behind us. I was surprised to find that we were in a small antechamber containing a single desk and three chairs. Another closed door led further inside.

"When you don't rate the big office, you get to have your meeting here," Jahelia said.

"And did you rate the big office?"

"Always," she said with a grin, and opened the next door.

Sedmamin's office—or former office—was huge and sleek. Windows wrapped two walls and looked out over the greenroof of the slightly lower second PrimeCorp tower, and beyond that, the city. A corner sofa in white leather offered seating for cozy business chats, while a long conference table waited for more serious discussion. Tall plants added dashes of green to the room, and the floor was a warm, striated green tile. Sedmamin's desk, a white and black monstrosity, was flanked by a touch-table. The room, elegant as it was, had a deserted feel. I felt certain that in other parts of the corporation, a war for this space was already being waged.

Yet another door, closed, was set into the far wall. I listened at it, heard nothing, and opened it to peer inside. As I'd expected, it was an executive washroom, complete with shower and sauna as well as the usual amenities. "Washroom," I told Jahelia, closing the door again.

"Let's do this," Jahelia said, as if relieved to finally be able to speak. Sedmamin had assured us that his office was not monitored, although I didn't have absolute faith in that belief. Sedmamin's current position was proof that he hadn't been pulling all the strings at PrimeCorp Main, and surveillance chips could be minuscule. In and out fast, that's how I wanted this to go.

As promised, the smooth white surface of Sedmamin's desk held a single data chip, and I snatched that up as Jahelia stood at the tabletop screen and double-tapped it to bring it to life. Her fingers danced over the surface as she entered her passcode and the file system resolved on the screen. She let out a sigh and flashed a grin at me. "I'm still in here," she said.

"I didn't know you were worried about that."

She shrugged. "You never know."

I handed her the chip and she slotted it into the table. The outer rim of the tabletop screen turned green and another layer of files displayed.

"Perfect." She opened her bag and took out a chipcase, extracting the one Sedmamin had given her and slotting it into another port. While it ran through a handshaking routine, she pulled her datapad out of her bag, too, and set it on the desk. "Say hello to Luta, Pita."

"Good morning, Captain Paixon," said a cheery voice from the datapad.

"Good morning, Pita." Intellectually, I knew that Pita was nothing more than a very sophisticated AI, but I thought of her as more than that. Her interface was based on Jahelia Sord's own personality, and she'd been instrumental in allowing me to interact with the first of the friendly Chron we'd encountered. After that "bonding" experience, I'd secretly been sorry to give her back to her rightful owner. Although from time to time she was a bit of a pain in the ass, from which, Jahelia had told me, her name derived.

"Yes, I'm doing that now," Jahelia responded to her implant.

Jahelia hurriedly entered commands, her fingers flying nimbly over the screen. "Pita, you should be able to interface with the database now." Then, to Sedmamin, "Yes, I see that. Everything in that sector? All right." She stood straight and put her hands on her hips, staring down at the tabletop screen.

"Okay Pita, start the download when you're ready."

"Download initiated," Pita said after a brief pause.

"The files are downloading now," Jahelia relayed to Sedmamin. "All right, now let's deal with that other little matter," Jahelia said, keying something else into the tabletop screen

The first alarm bells rang in my head. Sedmamin had given us clear instructions on what we had to do, and they'd involved only one task.

"Should you be distracting Pita with anything else?" I asked carefully. "No offense, Pita."

"None taken, Captain. But I am an extremely efficient multitasker."

Jahelia didn't answer me, only said, "Never mind, Chairman, it's nothing about you."

"What are you doing?" I leaned down to make her look at me.

She grinned. "Just fixing a little something while we're here anyway. Don't worry about it." She typed a couple more things.

I wasn't sure if she was talking to me or Sedmamin. "How long will it take?"

She shrugged. "Not long. Pita, how's it going?"

"Searching the database, Jahelia," the AI told her.

"Look, Sedmamin, if you don't shut up about that I'm shutting the implant down," Jahelia hissed. "I told you it's not your concern."

I glanced at the door. I couldn't shake the feeling it would open any moment and we'd be caught. I had no doubt what Sedmamin was demanding to know, and I felt the same way.

Jahelia reached up and pressed a spot behind her ear.

"Did you just—"

She looked at me defiantly. "He deserved it. He wouldn't shut up. And we don't need him anymore now."

"Okay, what's Pita up to? We came here with one job, and you're doing that."

Jahelia threw me a catlike grin. "I couldn't pass up the chance to fix one little item while we're here."

I folded my arms and narrowed my eyes at her. "Your ship."

"Look, it's not taking any extra time. Pita's going to find it and just delete its existence from the database."

"You already changed the drive signature and the ship's registration," I said. "They're not coming after you. Are you feeling paranoid?"

She shrugged, completely unapologetic. "Sedmamin still owes me," she said. "He can't fix this for me anymore, so I'm doing it myself. That's my ship, Captain, and I don't have any intention of letting anyone take it from me. I want every trace of its existence out of the database here. I'd expect you, of all people, to understand that."

And I did. I sighed. If Sord felt even a little bit about her *Shadow's Eclipse* the way I felt about the *Tane Ikai*, I had to let her do this.

"As long as it doesn't put us at any greater risk," I said, unwilling to give in too easily.

"It's already happening, and it won't," she said.

Her ID implant pinged softly, and she looked at me with sudden concern.

"Someone just opened the outer door."

WE FROZE. IN the seconds available to us, my mind ran through the possible options. *Wait to see if they come into the inner office. Hide in the washroom. Quietly knock the person out and run.*

I hoped Jahelia wasn't considering anything more drastic. I'd never felt more conscious of her potential volatility.

Then the need for a decision was out of my hands. A voice called out, "Luta? Can we talk? I know you're here."

Jahelia turned wide, slightly dazed eyes in my direction, and I realized absurdly that I'd never seen her so taken aback. My own heart raced so loudly in my ears I wondered if she could hear it. The cold of shock drained heat from my hands and face.

Jahelia mouthed one word at me. "Who?"

I swallowed. I knew the voice, but I couldn't seem to get the word out. And in the next heartbeat, it didn't matter, because the inner door opened and my ex-son-in-law, Taso Tacan, poked his head into the room. He hadn't changed much since the last time I'd seen him, and he threw us a lazy grin when he saw our shocked faces. I almost put a hand up to check that my jaw hadn't dropped open.

"Hey, don't look so worried," he said, putting up a placatory palm as he came all the way into the office and closed the door behind him. "No-one else knows you're here. I want to keep it that way."

"Great. That means no-one will know what happened to you," Jahelia said. I glanced over and saw that from somewhere she'd produced a tiny, palm-sized oval disk. She held it toward Taso threateningly. It was only partially visible in her hand, and I didn't know what it was, but I knew Jahelia. This might not end well.

"Whoa, okay, let's calm down," I said. "Jahelia, I don't know what that is, but let's not make the situation worse."

She raised an eyebrow. "We might have different definitions of *worse*, but I'm listening. You know this guy?"

Heat flooded my extremities now, and I felt my face flush. My legs twitched with adrenaline, shouting at me to do something, but I managed to fight it. Instead I crossed my arms casually and leaned back against the edge of Sedmamin's monstrous desk. "Jahelia Sord, meet my former son-in-law, Taso Tacan. Taso, I'm assuming you already know who Jahelia is."

He shrugged. "Not really. It's you I'm here to see. Pleased to meet you, though, Ms. Sord."

"Can't say I feel the same."

Taso ignored the jab and turned his full attention on me. "Look, Luta, I know this has to be short, and I'm happy to make it that way. I want to make a deal with you, and I don't think you'll find it difficult to say yes."

I noticed then that Taso wore a PrimeCorp ID badge on the left side of his shirt. Unlike mine and Jahelia's, though, his did not proclaim him a "Visitor." None of this made sense. What connection did Taso have with PrimeCorp? I swallowed.

"Keep talking. I'm listening."

"I know you've got Alin Sedmamin with you on the *Tane Ikai*," he said rapidly. "And *you* must know that PrimeCorp wants him."

I said nothing and kept my face neutral as my thoughts spun. Had Maja told Taso that we had Sedmamin? Why would she? Or had Taso been monitoring us that closely? At least Jahelia had shut down her implant. It probably wouldn't be great to have Sedmamin listening in on this.

Taso went on, "I don't really know why you're here, and I don't care. All I want is Sedmamin."

I frowned. That was surprising enough to make me ask, "Why?"

He smiled and rubbed the thumb and fingertips of his right hand together in the classic gesture for *money*. "They'll pay me big time to deliver him. They came to me because of my connection to you."

My brain was still not up to speed. "But why would they think I'd even be involved? They know better than anyone that Sedmamin and I have never been friends."

Taso shrugged. "He didn't go to anyone else they thought he would. They figured there was a chance he had something on you—some leverage he could use—to force you into helping him get away."

Yes, that would be PrimeCorp's thinking. They'd never consider that I might help Sedmamin for altruistic reasons, or because he had something that *I* wanted. Or maybe even that he'd sell them out in exchange for freedom. That classic PrimeCorp hubris.

"So that's why you were in touch with Maja. Did she tell you Sedmamin was with us?"

Taso barked a short laugh. "My dear ex-wife wouldn't tell me anything, don't worry. I thought maybe I could still charm it out of her, but I guess I've lost my touch."

I wanted to punch him, and also tell him that he was out of his league getting involved with PrimeCorp. I decided to save my dignity and my breath. He'd been the one to cut ties with my family and Maja obviously hadn't been taken in by him again. And as for PrimeCorp, he'd made his choice already. I didn't owe him anything. I played along, but I couldn't make it too easy for him or he'd be suspicious.

I shrugged. "Say that's what happened. If you knew we were coming here, why didn't you just tell PrimeCorp and let them deal with it? If they caught me here, they'd have all the cards. You know my crew would hand Sedmamin over to cut me loose. All you had to do was make a call."

Taso's blue eyes narrowed and a smug look crept over his face. "And they might not feel they had to pay me if all I did was tip them off. No, I want to physically hand Sedmamin over myself, so they can't squirm out of our deal."

I knew all too well that PrimeCorp would do whatever it took to cancel a bad deal, and that the safest place to be in that case would be far, far away from their sphere of influence. But I merely asked, "So what's this about? Why are you here?"

"I'm here to make a deal," Taso said.

"You let us walk out of here, and we hand over Sedmamin to you," Jahelia said. "That's pretty obvious."

Taso continued to talk to me. "Look, I know you hate the guy. Whatever reason you have for being here, you're not looking out for his health. Just promise you'll hand him over to me. That's all there is to it."

I laughed. "And you'll take my word for it?"

He cocked his head at me and one side of his mouth twisted up in a smile. "I know you and Maja had your issues," he said. "There were times I thought she downright hated you. But she always said that once you said you'd do a thing, you'd do it. She didn't always mean it as a compliment. But I don't think you'll lie about this. You hate Sedmamin anyway. And if I found you once, I can find you again. PrimeCorp has ample resources I can call on."

"I could take care of this, Captain," Jahelia said in a terrifyingly rational and detached voice. "I can put three bioplas flechettes in his throat in less time than it takes to suggest it. We'd be out of here long before anyone discovered the body."

I pretended to consider, and my mind truly was racing, trying to figure the best way to deal with him. The main thing was that Jahelia and I walk out of here with the files. Giving Jahelia free rein to use her little gadget would be one way—I believed she was totally serious. But I didn't want to leave a mess behind us if I could help it. We had enough to deal with.

And I didn't think the situation warranted murder.

"I can't give him to you right away," I said. "What we're—collecting—here . . . he's got to have time to deal with it or my investment is worthless." I kept it vague, hoping he'd interpret that to mean that I was making money on this enterprise. And that his loyalty to PrimeCorp didn't extend past his own self-interests.

He held up a hand. "Hey, I get that. You've got an operation going here, I don't want to mess it up for you. I just want the same consideration from you."

I looked away from him and at Jahelia, who glanced at me and shrugged. Her arm, pointing the deadly gadget, hadn't wavered while Taso and I talked.

"I'm supposed to deliver Sedmamin to FarView Station," I told Taso carefully. "But after that I promised him I'd take him to a safe haven. We could make an unscheduled stop at Rhea or Renata. Your choice. I won't do a handover at FarView. Too many people in too small a place, and too much Protectorate presence."

Taso nodded gravely. "That'll work. I'll send you an aliased ID code where you can reach me when you're back in Delta Pavonis. I'll arrange the details and tell you where to meet."

"And come up with a story for me to tell Sedmamin?"

"I'll leave that part up to you. You're a smart lady. You'll come up with something." His face and his voice hardened then, and I wondered what had become of the young man I'd been happy to see Maja marry, long ago. "Don't try to break our deal, though, Luta. This has been amicable—" he glanced at Jahelia— "for the most part. But it won't stay that way if you double-cross me."

I shrugged and kept my voice light. "Hey, you've got it right. Sedmamin's nothing to me, once this job is finished."

He nodded. "Then let's get out of here, shall we, ladies? Ms. Sord, you can put that thing back in your pocket now. I guarantee you won't need it."

"I'll just keep it handy, thanks," Jahelia Sord said in a bored drawl. "Let me get my datapad." She retrieved Pita from where the datapad still lay on Sedmamin's tech-table, after a glance at the screen. She ejected the two data chips and slipped them and the datapad into her bag, then turned and nodded to me. She kept the oval disk in her right hand.

"All right, we're done here. Let's go," I told Taso.

He stepped aside and motioned us out the door and I went, feeling like someone had painted a bulls-eye on my back.

But Taso kept his word and escorted us uneventfully down the corridor, to the elevator, and inside. We didn't talk as the car carried us smoothly and swiftly down to the lobby level, stopping only a few times along the way to collect and disgorge passengers. When the doors opened at the bottom, I nodded to Taso without smiling and headed across the sprawling lobby toward the exit. Jahelia kept an easy pace beside me, but she kept one hand in her pocket, and I knew she still clasped her tiny weapon inside it. We stopped briefly at the desk to return our badges. I fully expected guards or alarms at any second, but it didn't happen.

We didn't talk until the doors of PrimeCorp Main had closed behind us and we were a city block away. Jahelia paused near a storefront filled with colourful bio-weave jackets and pulled Pita out of her bag.

"Pita? You got it all done?"

"Absolutely," the AI answered. "Files accessed and copied, and one ship effectively erased from existence."

"Excellent." Jahelia slipped the datapad back into her bag, and we resumed walking. Her next question was directed at me. "You have no intention of giving Sedmamin to him, do you?"

I shook my head. "Not in the least."

She turned to grin at me. "I noticed that you didn't actually *say* you'd do it. He only thought you did."

I returned the grin. "I learned a long time ago that sometimes people hear what they want to hear. Now, tell me about that very interesting device you kept pointed at him that whole time."

Jahelia Sord held out the disk and pressed a tiny button on the side. It opened like a clam shell, and she proffered it to me. Inside was a scattering of small white pellets.

"Mint?" she asked, her eyes dancing. "I learned a long time ago that sometimes people see what you want them to see."

Chapter 15 — Lunar Mistrust and Rebellion

I KNEW THAT Regina wouldn't have set me an impossible task deliberately, but asking me to figure out where the Chron were slipping into Nearspace felt like one. I went back to the *Cheswick* with a promise from her that she'd send me all the information the scouts had gathered. She was as good as her word. I'd barely been back aboard the *Cheswick* long enough to file the first of several reports when the datapacket from Regina arrived with an urgent notification ping.

The scouts she'd sent out to attempt a trace on the drive signatures of the Chron ships came back with little helpful information. They'd followed signature traces that led to the vicinity of the Split, but that didn't make sense. The Split, a malformed wormhole that few pilots would even attempt to traverse, opened into an uninhabited system, GI182. This system had been well-explored for years, since the Split didn't afford an easily traversable connection, and every wormhole explorer out there would have loved to be the one to find a viable alternative. It seemed unlikely that GI182 held an undiscovered wormhole from Chron space.

I'd never traversed the Split myself, but I knew Luta had made the skip at least three times—possibly more, during the shadowy years when I wasn't always entirely sure what my sister was up to.

I hit my implant and called the bridge.

"Commander Drake," Linna answered. "What can I do for you, Admiral?"

"Would you find out where Viss and Yuskeya are now?" I asked her. When I'd left the *Cheswick* to go and meet Regina, they'd gone to book temporary accommodations until Luta and the *Tane Ikai* returned. They'd both experienced the Split firsthand, so they might have valuable input for me. If they weren't sick of me by now. They deserved a break, but I needed them.

"I'll ping them," Linna promised. "What's the message?"

I considered. "Ask if they'll join me for dinner in my quarters," I said. "Something's come up and I really need to speak with them."

"Direct reply to you?"

"Yes, thanks, Linna."

I spent a little more time perusing the reports, but Yuskeya messaged me promptly. "Thanks for the invitation, Admiral," she said. "I'm assuming this is more than just social."

"I'm sorry, Commander, I know you thought you were rid of me for a while."

Yuskeya smiled. "Admiral, please."

"Well, I could use your opinions. I promise I won't keep you long this evening."

"No need to apologize. We'll see you then."

I made sure the dinner would be worth their while, ordering an Italian pasta and sausage dish I knew Yuskeya liked, salad, fresh-baked *pano*, and cheesecake for dessert from one of the station restaurants. It arrived, hot and delicious, at the same time as Viss and Yuskeya, so we sat down to eat right away. We talked through the meal.

"You've both been through the Split with Luta," I began once we'd loaded our plates.

They nodded. Viss said, "And I have a bit of previous experience as well."

Yuskeya raised her eyebrows at him over a bite of pasta, but said nothing.

"All right. Here's the thing," I said, forking salad. "Fleet Commander Holles put a trace on the drive signatures of some of the Chron ships, to try and figure out how they're arriving in Nearspace. The attack on FarView didn't originate through the wormholes we know about. Not the one in Tau Ceti, and not the one the *Tane Ikai* has traversed."

"We've found another entry point?" Yuskeya asked, pausing with her hand on her wineglass.

I shook my head. "Unfortunately, no. The sigs seem to lead to the Split, but they haven't been able to find anything corresponding in GI182."

"Probably just dissipated," Viss said. "I'm assuming the Protectorate ships didn't go through the Split themselves? So, by the time they got someone to go in from Eridani—"

I shook my head. "One of the scouts actually did go through," I said. Viss looked surprised. I nodded. "I know. No-one does it lightly. But they got the go-ahead from Regina. He came right out in GI182, and there was no trail there to pick up."

Yuskeya frowned. "There can't be an operant moon or an activator in GI182. There probably isn't a better-mapped system in Nearspace. Everyone would love to find a hidden wormhole there. Surely any Chron artifact in that system would have been discovered."

"I know. What do you think is going on there?" I asked. "That's why you're here. I need ideas, and I thought getting them from someone with actual experience of the Split would make sense."

Viss frowned as he chewed thoughtfully. "We have readings that put them around this end of the Split, but not the other. Only two possibilities come to mind."

"They exit through the bad side?" Yuskeya asked. "There's nowhere else to go *inside* the wormhole."

Viss pointed his fork at her. "That's one. The other is that they're 'ghosting' a wormhole with an operant device and an activator drive. Making a second wormhole that mirrors it but comes out elsewhere. In this case, near the Split."

"But like Yuskeya said, there's no operant moon in GI182. Or here, at this end of the Split. Unless it's invisible, and in that case, we might as well give up now," I said.

"They're not ghosting the Split," Viss said, tapping the tines of his fork on his plate. "They're ghosting a wormhole on the other end, and making it open near the Split. Or maybe even sharing the terminal point."

"Is that even possible?" I'd read the reports on the Corvid's ghosting technology, but I had to admit I hadn't absorbed every detail.

Viss shrugged. "Have to ask a Corvid that."

Yuskeya looked thoughtful. "Didn't the Corvids say that using that ghosting technology caused wormholes to have problems, become unstable or changed in different ways? Time effects and other things? Maybe that's why the Split is the way it is. Maybe the Chron ruined it long ago."

Viss nodded. "And we already avoid the Split because it's an unknown, and anyone who's gone through the bad side has never returned. Nothing scares us like the unknown. They could be pretty certain of not running into anyone around either end of the Split in Nearspace."

"Or maybe Yuskeya's right, and it *is* the bad side," I said. "There could be a Chron base in some system you might reach by sliding off that side of the Split, and we'd never know it."

"I think it's entirely possible," Viss said. "It might not even be hard to do—just let the ship slide off the safe side and you're through, right? But it's a damn hard thing to investigate or verify."

"Because who's going to take the chance?" Yuskeya finished his thought. "The Protectorate wouldn't order someone to try it. It could be a suicide move."

I nodded. "I don't think Regina would approve such a mission, even if someone volunteered. Not without a lot more evidence that it would be survivable."

"Well, I've got skip data from at least two runs through the Split in the *Tane Ikai*'s computer," Viss volunteered. "I've never really had the chance to study it, but it's there. Could be something in it that would help."

"But that's not accessible until Luta gets back," Yuskeya said. "Any point in going out there and just seeing if there's anything new to see?"

"I'm not taking the *Cheswick* into the Split," I said automatically, then laughed ruefully at myself. "See, it's a knee-jerk reaction."

"Well, I didn't mean we had to go into it," Viss said. "But maybe go out there and look at it with different eyes, see if there's something we haven't noticed up until now. Send a data-collector probe through."

I set down my fork. "An excellent idea. And since you say 'we,' I assume you mean you'll come along for the ride?"

Viss and Yuskeya shared a glance. "I don't really have a choice, Admiral, do I?" Yuskeya asked with a half-smile. "I'm still a Protectorate officer."

"I'll go where she goes," Viss said, "but yes, I'd actually like to come along. We could take readings that I could compare with the data on the *Tane Ikai* when we get it."

"Except that we're not going *into* the wormhole," I reminded him.

Viss laughed. "Not yet."

I TOLD REGINA our plan the next day and filed a survey route to the Split. We'd stay only a day. Earlier that morning word had arrived of a Chron incursion into Beta Hydri and an attack on Damyadi Station there. There was no explanation for how the Chron had managed to get to that system, although it gave credence to Viss's theory about the use of the Corvid ghosting technology.

"I don't know how we stop them if that's the case," Regina said over a secure connection. I was in my office, alone, and she in her hospital room on FarView. "You didn't hear that from me, Lanar, but I don't know what else to do. It's the Chron war all over again, and even if we had the same technology, how do you stop an enemy who can appear anywhere, anytime?"

"We could find out more about that technology from the Corvids," I suggested. "Maybe there's a way to block it, and we just don't know."

"It would be worth asking." She tugged at the silver lock of hair agitatedly, pulling it down from its loose coil and winding it around her finger. "I'll see to that. We need to stop the Chron getting into Nearspace. They've got us on the defensive, and you and I both know that's not the way to win a war. But we can't risk making an offensive move, either, no matter what Mauronet would like to see."

"We don't even know enough about their space to know where to go," I agreed. "But maybe with the communications relay set up to the Relidae and Professor Brindlepaw we could remedy that. If we pool our knowledge it could benefit everyone."

She nodded. "I'm working on that. We need all the information we can get."

"*Okej*. And maybe we'll get some answers at the wormhole." For once, I wanted to end this conversation with Regina as quickly as possible. It was difficult to look at the despair in her eyes and know that she might see the same thing mirrored in mine.

Viss and Yuskeya met me on the bridge, eager to go and glad to have something constructive to do.

From FarView, it was only a matter of hours to reach the Split. Despite the brief transit, the crew seemed on edge; perhaps they thought I was planning a secret foray into the dangerous wormhole.

From the outside, the Split looks like any other wormhole—a darker splotch against space's ebony backdrop. Despite all my years in the Protectorate, I'd never skipped through the Split. It wasn't forbidden—it was simply so dangerous that no-one attempted it without a very good reason. It was almost always a better idea to go around the long way. I knew that Luta had traversed it three times in her life, and there was a tiny, deeply-buried seed of envy in me for that.

Not that I had any desire to take the *Cheswick* into that dark eye at the moment.

We arrived and took up a stationary hold a little distance from the wormhole, and Viss and Yuskeya joined me on the bridge. If we initiated the Ford-Roman drive the wormhole would become stable and open in front of us like a doorway. Instead it was simply a dark blot in space. If you looked closely enough with the screen magnified, you might see a swirl of darker tendrils of matter within it, but that was all.

Viss and Yuskeya had a conference with my chief science officer at her station, setting up scans. Although Viss had said he hadn't had a chance to study the readings from the *Tane Ikai's* skips through the Split in any detail, he'd obviously reviewed them to some extent. He was detailing to Lieutenant-Commander Alice Payette the data he wanted to collect, and I caught myself marveling again at the sheer range of the man's knowledge. It was a shame he'd never become a full member of the Protectorate. Or maybe it wasn't, I mused. It might be better for us to have the benefit of his expertise when we needed it, and be able to call on him to work outside the lines when the necessity arose.

After the scans were started, things got . . . boring, fast. Waiting while data is collected isn't the most stimulating part of being in the Protectorate.

It didn't stay boring for long.

"Ship on the long range," Linna Drake reported. "Coming from the direction of FarView."

I swung around to face her. "Can we identify them?"

After a pause, she said, "I have a drive signature. It's a Protectorate vessel."

I felt some of the tension drain out of my shoulders. "Particulars?"

"Working."

I flicked the display on my screen to show the blip of the approaching ship.

"It's the *NPV Dorland*," Drake said. "Admiral Antar Mauronet, commanding."

I frowned. Unlikely that Regina would send Mauronet, of all people, out here to join me. So, what was he doing here? I didn't have to wait long to find out. As soon as the *Dorland* drew close enough, he messaged me.

"Admiral," I acknowledged when I opened the connection. Mauronet's face filled my screen, looking smug. "What can I do for you?"

"Just here to assist, Admiral," he said with an insincere smile.

"The *Cheswick* is collecting wormhole data," I told him. "Not really a lot we need assistance with."

Admiral Mauronet cocked his head and regarded me. "Whatever you say, Admiral. I suspect you're here for a lot more than that. And the *Dorland* stands ready to help."

"You still think I'm heading off on some secret mission to attack the Chron, don't you? This obsession is going to hurt your career, Mauronet."

"I'm not concerned about *my career*, Admiral Mahane. I'm concerned with the safety and security of Nearspace."

"So you're following me around? Not the most productive

use of your time."

"I'll be the judge of that."

I shrugged. This was going nowhere. "All right, Admiral. Stay and observe as long as you like. Just don't interfere with the wormhole."

"I wouldn't dream of it," he said, and I signalled to the comm officer to close the channel.

"Is he as crazy as I think he is?" Linna Drake asked me.

"I don't know how good your imagination is, Commander," I told her. "But I'm guessing the answer is yes."

MAURONET BACKED THE *Dorland* off to the opposite side of the wormhole and sat in silence. Every time I glanced out the viewscreen and saw him sitting there I grew more annoyed, but I kept it to myself. If he wanted to sit there and waste time, that was his call. I updated my logs with our activity and his message, and tried to find something else to do.

After a couple of hours, Viss messaged me. I'd gone down to engineering for a chat about wormholes and ghosting technology with my chief engineer.

"Scans are finished," Viss said. "Payette and I would like to do some comparisons with the readings the scouts collected. Then later, maybe we can fire up the Ford-Roman drive and—"

"We're not going through there."

He laughed. "No. I was going to say collect some more data with the mouth open, that's all. Then when your sister's back, we can get the comparison data."

Yuskeya said in the background, "We should try to get one of the Corvids to come and look at this. They know more about wormholes than any of us, right? And ghosting, and operant moons, and all the rest of it."

"I already spoke to Regina about that. She's going to see if we can pry one of them away from the repairs on their station. I'm coming back to the bridge now."

Once there, I told Linna we'd be running the skip drive but on no account skipping.

She nodded to the viewscreen where the *Dorland* hung, presumably watching us. "Are we going to tell our friend our plan?" she asked me with a straight face.

I shook my head and gave her an evil grin. "Let's let him

freak out a little first, and then—" I broke off. Something out the front viewscreen had grabbed my attention.

Without warning, the wormhole's dark eye grew a bright, flickering edge, a thin glow that quickly brightened to white-hot. Glowing plasma streamed in arcing tendrils from the edges toward the centre.

"Did someone start the Ford-Roman drive?" I asked. I hadn't given any such order.

"No, sir," Linna Drake said sharply. "It's not us."

"Is it the *Dorland*?"

"Negative. Something's coming through the wormhole. No tracer ping."

I was on my feet. "Back us off, Commander. I want distance between us and that wormhole." If no tracer had come through, that meant it wasn't a Nearspace ship on the other side. We had strict protocols to ensure that ships never entered opposite ends of a wormhole at the same time, or would exit and collide with someone else about to enter.

The *Cheswick* veered off and I clutched at my chair to keep my balance. I glimpsed the other ship moving as well and wondered if Mauronet realized what was happening. "Engage shields. Open a channel to the *Dorland*," I barked at comms. Damn Mauronet for making me look out for his *azeno* when he wasn't even supposed to be here.

When the channel opened, I said shortly, "No tracer ping, Admiral."

"Were you expecting this?" he demanded.

"Don't be an ass. Close the channel," I ordered comms in disgust, and left him without another word. If he couldn't let go of his absurd conspiracy obsession for one minute—

A Chron ship, spidery and black and utterly deadly looking, emerged from the wormhole at speed. It banked left when it saw the *Cheswick*, swerved right and saw the *Dorland*, and turned nose up ninety degrees away from us. Mauronet's ship darted after it in pursuit.

"Go after it," I ordered, but Linna Drake said, "Wormhole's not closing, Admiral."

"Belay that order." If the wormhole hadn't closed when the Chron ship came through, then something else was transiting. Another Chron ship? "Back us off from the wormhole another fifty klicks."

While we moved, the centre of the wormhole continued to arc and writhe, and then the second Chron ship came through. This one reacted more quickly to our presence, launching an energy weapon even as it bore down on us. The shields flared as it impacted, but it was a weak hit. The Chron ship careened off after its partner and the *Dorland*.

"Engage—" I started, but glanced out the viewscreen to be sure. "*Damne*," I swore. The wormhole hadn't reverted to normal.

"How many of them are there going to be?" Yuskeya asked. She and Viss had moved to empty stations and settled in chairs. Neither of them had a job to do on this bridge at the moment, so they'd calmly gotten out of the way. Viss, however, was doing something at his screen. I left him to it.

"We can't wait around to see," I said. "Can't leave Mauronet without any support. Follow the other ships," I told Linna Drake. *And if it's another Chron ship, maybe we don't want to wait here in full view.*

The Cheswick leapt under Linna's control, arcing to follow the others. Bright flashes burst against the dark velvet of space as energy weapons spurted and shields responded. We weren't close enough to tell if any of the ships had suffered damage yet.

"Third ship through the wormhole," Nav reported. Linna Drake had her hands full piloting, so Lieutenant-Commander Payette stepped in to monitor the wormhole. "Readings show it's closing now. But Admiral," Payette said, looking up to catch my eye, "that third ship? It's got a PrimeCorp drive sig."

It wasn't a shock, but it was a surprise. They were getting cocky, following Chron ships so closely out of the Split. Obviously, they hadn't expected anyone to be sitting right outside the wormhole, but this showed little concern about being caught.

That worried me almost more than anything else.

Ahead, both Chron ships had managed to get behind the *Dorland,* and the Protectorate ship's shields flared under the heavy fire. "Weapons," I ordered, "let's try to get them off Mauronet's tail. Distract them, take them out if you can. Fire at will."

"Aye, Admiral." My Lobor weapons officer, Lieutenant-

Commander Huba Jelenka, concentrated on the targeting screen, her ears pinned back. Her hands, dark-furred across their backs, were sure and precise as they locked in on one of the Chron ships.

"PrimeCorp ship is in pursuit," Lieutenant Hablar reported. "It's a corvette, possible weapons up to full torps."

"Armed?" I asked. Surely, they wouldn't engage. No-one in PrimeCorp could be stupid enough to take on two Protectorate Pegasus ships right here in Nearspace.

Could they?

"Scans show a particle beam coming online."

I made a quick decision. "Concentrate on the Chron," I said. "Don't engage the corvette unless we have to. I want to talk to someone on that ship, and we can't do that if we blow it up. Commander Drake, full shields and evasive maneuvers. Jelenka, take every opportunity you get at those Chron ships."

I glanced over at Viss and Yuskeya. They both looked ready to jump out of their chairs and take over the stations they'd normally hold. But this wasn't their ship, and I had good people in all my positions. I couldn't help them out. They'd just have to sit and watch.

"Open a channel to the *Dorland*," I told my comms officer. "Tell them not to target the PrimeCorp ship. I want it seized once the Chron ships are dealt with."

Comms sent the message, waited a moment, then said, "The *Dorland* doesn't reply, sir, although they must have received."

"Don't worry about it. They are a little busy at the moment," I said, biting back on my annoyance. I felt sure Mauronet was ignoring the message deliberately.

Even though I half expected it, I still felt a jolt of shock when the PrimeCorp ship took aim at us with the particle beam. I wasn't worried; the shields were rated to take a much rougher barrage than the beam would deliver. If they became damaged by something else, it might be a different story. But for now, we had little to worry about from the PrimeCorp ship. Their temerity in targeting us made me blink.

Wheeling past each other in a mad dance, the Chron ships and the *Dorland* engaged in a bright, silent exchange of energy weapons and torpedoes. The *Dorland's* shields flashed under the impact, but didn't seem to waver. Mauronet's gunner was so far too slow in targeting the Chron ships, and the missiles they fired went wide.

We joined the general melee with the PrimeCorp ship blasting away at our rear shields. We ignored them, a bull pricked by a mosquito. I told my comms officer to let me know immediately if any of the ships tried to make contact, but the channels remained quiet and still. Not even a word from Mauronet on the *Dorland*, and I would have expected him to coordinate with us. I supposed he was either distrustful or angry with me, or maybe just too stubborn to do anything but battle it out on his own. It was a stupid attitude to take when we were outnumbered.

The shields flared around us, and Linna Drake said, "Direct hit from a Chron missile. Shields weakened but holding."

"Bring the rear weapons array online as well," I ordered. The five ships engaged in this battle formed a tight, whirling mass now, increasing the risk that one of us would hit an ally. The Chron ships were sleeker and more agile than our heavier Pegasus cruisers, which gave them a distinct advantage. If the third enemy ship had been another of those and not the PrimeCorp corvette, we might have been in trouble.

A torpedo flew from the forward array and caught one of the Chron ships in mid-turn, as it spun to take another long run at the *Dorland*. It was a beautiful shot, and I knew in the heartbeat before the blossoming explosion that it had gone true. My crew was too well-trained to cheer, but I caught a quick flash of satisfaction cross Linna Drake's face as she nudged the ship upward and back for another run.

That's when the PrimeCorp ship surprised me, and it was completely my fault. I knew damn well it was possible for a corvette to be outfitted with full torpedoes, but when they powered up that particle beam, I assumed that was their top-level weapon.

It wasn't. The corvette swung in close, and their torpedo punched through the aft shield and the hull like they weren't even there. The force of the impact shuddered the ship and I clutched at the arms of my chair. Viss swore loudly and Yuskeya lurched in her seat. Linna Drake barked an order about the shields.

"Damage report!"

It took a moment, but reports came in. Shields were back online, and the hull damage had been minimal. "Looks like the skip drive is out of commission, though, Admiral," Lieutenant Hablar told me from engineering. "No wormholes until we can get a closer inspection."

"*Konfirmi*," I told him. There were no wormholes in my immediate plans, anyway. "Bring us around, Commander Drake. We might have to take the corvette out after all, but I want her disabled if possible, not destroyed unless we have to."

But as we turned, the *Dorland* sent a spray of wasp missiles directly at the PrimeCorp corvette. I watched as the first three flared against the shields. Then the shields themselves flashed bright, white-hot light which died instantly, and I knew they'd overloaded. The next two missiles punched through the hull like bullets, and the ship exploded in a mass of brilliant light and arcing debris.

"*Damne*," I swore again. Mauronet must have known the corvette couldn't withstand an intense attack. He hadn't acknowledged my message to leave the PrimeCorp ship alone, so he'd deny ever having received it. But he must have done this on purpose, just to defy me.

I was going to have to punch him again, the next time I saw him.

I was distracted from this pleasant thought, however, as the remaining Chron ship suddenly spun and shot back in the direction of the wormhole. Mauronet's ship jumped in pursuit, firing a volley of missiles at the retreating ship, but they skimmed above the darting form.

"Go after them," I told Linna. "We'll catch the *Dorland* at the Split even if the Chron ship makes it through, and then he and I are going to have some words."

But I hadn't realized just how obsessed Mauronet had become. The Chron ship led the *Dorland* on a breakneck race to the wormhole, evading everything Mauronet threw at it. From a distance behind them, I saw the wormhole begin to shimmer as the Chron ship activated its equivalent of our Ford-Roman drive, opening the wormhole to allow access.

"They're going to get away."

And the Chron ship slipped inside the wormhole and disappeared from our view.

But the *Dorland* didn't stop at the entrance to the wormhole, as I'd thought it would. Viss realized it at the same moment I did.

"Wormhole's not closing," he said, standing up from the skimchair where he'd managed to stay seated through the encounter. "That idiot's going to follow the Chron ship through."

"Has Mauronet ever flown the Split before?" Yuskeya stood too, her smooth brow creased in a frown as she watched the cruiser careen toward the wormhole.

I shook my head. "His pilot, maybe. I don't know. And look at the speed!"

"Without an experienced pilot he won't make it," Viss said.

"Open a channel," I barked at comms, and when he nodded to me I said, "Admiral Mauronet! Do not enter that wormhole! You won't make it!"

He answered me, audio only. "I'm taking the fight where it belongs, Mahane," he said. "Tell Fleet Commander Holles I expect her to do the same."

And then the *Dorland* was swallowed up by the shimmering blackness of the Split.

Chapter 16 — Luta
Revelations and Betrayals

UNDER THE CLEAR blue sky of Earth, I spent the walk back to the *Tane Ikai* waiting for a clutch of PrimeCorp thugs to appear out of nowhere and take us down, or at least try to steal Pita. Jahelia didn't look nervous, but her alertness was almost palpable. Occasionally one of us would stop to look in a store window, point out something to the other. A casual charade of two friends out on a window-shopping stroll. But in reality, neither of us would relax until we were back aboard the ship.

We did talk about one thing in low tones—I told Jahelia that I was not going to mention our conversation with Taso to Alin Sedmamin. "And I don't want you to say anything about it, either," I said.

She pursed her lips. "Oh, why not? I wanted to see his face when we told him that all his worst fears were real, and PrimeCorp really is gunning for him."

I shook my head. "That's just it. I don't want him rattled when he's trying to review these files for the Protectorate. Or when he's trying to erase things that make him look bad. I don't want him accidentally deleting something important."

"Come on, don't you want him to suffer just a little bit? You know he's sitting up there on the ship, disgustingly smug over the way this is all working out for him," Jahelia said persuasively.

I paused to buy us ice-cream sandwiches from a street vendor. When we walked on, I said, "It doesn't bother me to see Alin Sedmamin uncomfortable. But I don't want him making any mistakes."

She sighed and nibbled at her own ice cream. "I suppose you're right. But if you're not planning to turn him over to Taso, what *are* you going to do with him?"

I walked in silence for a moment, savouring the treat. "Give him to the Protectorate and wash my hands of the whole thing, if that's what they want. Or just take him to Nellera like I said I would. Now that he's no threat to me, I find I don't care so much about revenge. I'd really just like to be through with him for good, and that'll be enough of a perk for me."

Jahelia stopped in her tracks. "Seriously?"

I shrugged. "Seriously. Now, let's get him working on these files so we can be rid of his charming company." I quickened my pace toward the *Tane Ikai*, and we made it the rest of the way without incident.

We found Sedmamin in the galley, reading on his datapad and polishing off a plate of pasta in cream sauce. He looked up and frowned at Jahelia.

"That was rude."

She shrugged. "You were being annoying."

"Well, you're back intact. I suppose that's the main thing."

Jahelia Sord pulled out one of the chairs, swung it around backwards, and sat down, the chair back forming a small wall between her and Sedmamin. She pulled Pita out of her bag and slid the datapad across the table toward Sedmamin. "This is a loan," she said, "conditional on your taking very good care of her, and returning her to me when you're finished. If you don't think you can handle that, say so now."

Sedmamin gave Jahelia a sardonic grin. "If I recall correctly, I *gave* you this AI," he said.

Jahelia put a hand on the datapad. "The operative word there is *gave*. You told me she was mine to keep, regardless."

He rolled his eyes. "I did. Your AI is safe with me," he said. Then he turned to me. "Captain, if we could just retrieve the things from my apartment now, we'll be able to leave this system entirely and head back for FarView. I know you'll be anxious to speak with your brother."

"Sure. Give Rei the directions and we'll see what we can do. Will there be guards or lookouts on your apartment?"

He drew a deep breath and blew it out. "Quite possibly on the building. But if I stay hidden in the ship and one or more of your crew go to collect the things, I think it will be all right. They'll be watching from outside, but they won't be looking for you or your crew, and once you're inside it should be easy."

I hesitated. Depending on how much Taso had shared about where Sedmamin was and who he was travelling with, there could well be someone on the lookout for us. But I still didn't want to tell Sedmamin about that, or that I'd promised to turn him over to Taso. "All right, then," I said finally. "Tell Rei where to go, and Baden and Hirin what to get. They'll just have to try to be inconspicuous."

Sedmamin got up and fastidiously disposed of his dishes and utensils. Then he took Pita from the table. "And I'll start working with Pita to decode and collate the files," he said. "Congratulations, Captain. Everything's running smoothly so far."

I thought of that moment of sheer disbelief when Sedmamin's office door and opened and Taso appeared. "Let's hope it continues that way," was all I said.

MUCH AS I didn't want to do it, I figured I had to tell Maja about Taso. Although he'd told me she hadn't helped him or told him anything, I felt as if I had to hear it from her. And she deserved to know what had happened with her ex-husband at PrimeCorp.

I found her in Stores, running down a list of supplies and checking it against what was in a stack of storage crates. Her shoulder-length blonde hair was twisted up in a knot and secured with a silver clip Baden had given her. She turned when she heard me enter the cargo pod and smiled.

"Need a break from our favourite ex-Chairman?" she asked. Sedmamin had tricked her into almost betraying me once before, and she'd assiduously avoided him as much as possible since he'd been on board.

"I need a break from more than Sedmamin, but I'm not going to get it anytime soon," I said. I took a seat on a low, sturdy-looking crate and sighed. "We need to talk about Taso."

Maja frowned. "Taso? Why?"

"What did he really want from you, when he got in touch at FarView?" I asked her.

A pink flush rose slowly on her cheeks. "I told you, he wanted my help with something, but I told him no."

"He was trying to find Alin Sedmamin."

She looked startled. "That's right. He had some scam he wanted to run on him, now that Sedmamin's been discredited, and he thought I might have a way to get in touch with him still. Since that other time when I—" She broke off and pressed her lips tightly together. She sighed and sat on a crate near mine, balancing the datapad on her knees and looking down at it instead of at me.

I knew she didn't like thinking about how our relationship had almost been irreparably damaged by her actions, and held up a hand. "It's all right. We don't have to talk about that. The thing is, Taso was lying to you."

She shrugged. "Not that big a surprise, considering. What about?"

"He wanted to find Sedmamin, all right, but not to run a scam on him. Taso is working for PrimeCorp, looking for Sedmamin so he can turn him over to them. For a big payoff, apparently."

"PrimeCorp?" she whispered, going pale. "He didn't tell me that. But I didn't tell him anything. Nothing about Sedmamin, or where he was, or what we were doing—"

I nodded. "That's what Taso said. But why didn't you come and tell me what he was after?"

The flush rose again. Maja picked up the datapad and hugged it to her chest. She looked at me, a little defiantly. "At first, I thought I *would* help him. Scam Sedmamin out of something, hurt him? When he's done so much to hurt us? That sounded good to me. I thought maybe someday I'd tell you about it and we'd have a laugh." She sighed. "I didn't tell you because I guess I didn't want to be reminded that I'd helped Sedmamin once. But if I did help hurt him, I could go to you and show you that we'd gotten a bit of revenge. Make up a bit for what I'd done."

"You don't have to—"

"I know. But I wanted to do it, and to handle Taso, on my

own. It didn't seem like there was any danger in it." Maja shook her head. "Then you came to us and said you'd agreed to actually *help* Sedmamin. For the good of Nearspace, I know, but there it was. So, I told Taso I wasn't interested. I figured whatever he was planning would fall through now, anyway. If Sedmamin was going to disappear so that even PrimeCorp couldn't find him, I didn't think Taso would have any chance of tracking him down."

"Well, Taso got along without your help, anyway." I leaned back against the cool metal wall of the pod. "Somehow he tracked Sedmamin to us and then followed us to PrimeCorp Main. He confronted us in Sedmamin's office and made me agree to turn Sedmamin over to him when we're through with him. In exchange, he'd let us walk out of PrimeCorp Main."

Maja's eyes went wide. "You agreed to that? I thought you promised Sedmamin to deliver him to somewhere safe. I thought that was part of the deal."

"It is. And I didn't agree to do it." I grinned. "Taso only thinks I did."

She blew out a long breath. "Sounds like there's more to this story."

"I also left out the part where Jahelia threatened to kill him with a box of mints," I said, getting up from the crate. "I'll tell you all that later. For now, though, if Taso gets in touch again, tell me about it, okay? There's too much happening for us to keep any secrets from each other."

Maja got up and gave me a quick hug. "It's a deal. I'm sorry. I just thought I could handle it on my own."

"We're family. You don't have to keep secrets, okay? I don't know where you get these ideas," I teased her, thinking guiltily about my own decision to deal with Sedmamin without waiting to talk to Lanar.

"Right," she said with a wry grin. "Must be from Dad."

"I won't tell him if you don't," I said, and went to see if Sedmamin had given Rei the directions to his apartment.

I WAS FINISHING up a round of *tae-ga-chi* when someone buzzed my door. Hirin had gone down to the galley in search of lunch and I'd planned to join him there in a few minutes. I felt a slight buzz of irritation as I called, "Come in!" I wiped my face with a towel as the door slid open, and Alin Sedmamin stood, hesitating, just outside.

"Captain," he said, but didn't make a move to come into the room. His normally pale, greyish skin was flushed and his eyes bright with nerves.

"Chairman," I said, although he'd told me before not to call him that. It was an old habit, and a difficult one to break. "Come in, please," I repeated. "What's happened?"

He came in slowly and the door slid shut behind him. He held a datapad, and when it said, "Hello, Captain," I realized it was Pita.

"Hi Pita," I said. "Still working hard?"

"File decryption is just one of my many talents," the AI drawled, sounding so much like Jahelia Sord that I almost smiled.

"That's why I'm here," Sedmamin said. "We've found something that I think you should know about."

"Okay." I sat at my desk and motioned him into the big armchair. "I'm listening."

Sedmamin stared down at the datapad for a moment, apparently gathering his thoughts. "It's worse than I thought," he said finally. "PrimeCorp—what they've been doing, with the Chron. There's a conspiracy here that's so huge, and goes back so far, even I can't believe it."

I leaned forward in my chair. "Enough to bring them down?"

He barked a short, humourless laugh. "More than enough. Definite references to dealings with the Chron. They're circumspect, but with these files, it becomes obvious. But that's not actually why I'm here. There's something else."

"Coordinates," Pita piped up. "Very interesting coordinates!"

"At this point, I'll believe just about anything," I said. "More wormholes we don't know about?"

Sedmamin snorted. "Try coordinates pinpointing a location on an unnamed planet. Some kind of a base, we think. There's something important there—a top secret research project. But I can't identify the planet or the system, and neither can Pita."

He turned the datapad so I could see it, but although I recognized them as latitude and longitude, the mere numbers meant nothing to me. The description of the system went on in some detail, but didn't sound familiar. "Pita? Can you tell if this is somewhere in Nearspace?"

"If it was in Nearspace, I could tell you where," the AI said with some asperity. "There's a description of a binary star and identifying points about the system. The only binary in the Nearspace system is Keridre/Gerdrice, and this isn't it. The planet is referred to as *Orbis Latet*, but that's just Latin for *hidden world,* so no help there. Not a Nearspace name or nickname and I can't match up the description to anything in Nearspace. But they went to some lengths to pinpoint a location on the planet. Defined a prime meridian using a geographical feature—the highest mountain peak in the northern hemisphere—and then used latitude and longitude to locate it."

"But what's there?"

Sedmamin shook his head. "Whatever it is, it's big. Big and vital and secret."

"But you can't tell how to get there. Pita?"

The AI said, "Not enough data, Captain. I'm certain this is a planet outside what we define as Nearspace. If we were there, we could use the coordinates to find the base. But I don't know how to get there."

"Here's the thing." Sedmamin leaned toward me, eyes serious. "I did not know about this, and I am not taking the fall for it. You've got to protect me, Captain. I'm bringing this to you, and you can do whatever you think is best with it, but none of this is on me."

I nodded. I'd never thought much of Sedmamin's veracity, but I believed him this time. This went far beyond the treachery he'd been part of or even dreamed about.

"I want you to take me to Nellera now," he said, his voice finally cracking a little. "I want out. I've gone through the files. They're ready for your brother. I have nothing to add." He ran a hand over his face. "I just want out."

I could see Sedmamin's point. If there was anything iron-clad by the Nearspace Authority it was the protocol for new system exploration and discovery, and this looked like at least twice PrimeCorp had broken it. But it put me in a bad spot. I'd thought I had a loophole in my promise to Taso through Lanar and Regina Holles—that they'd want a chance to question Sedmamin, find out more details than what might be in the files, and he'd pass from my hands to theirs and that would be the end of it. I'd tell Taso I would have turned Sedmamin over to him, but the Protectorate got in the way and I didn't have a chance. Taso would be angry, but I could deal with that.

But if Sedmamin wanted to go to Nellera now, maybe I had to let him. He hadn't steered us wrong on any of this, he'd delivered what he promised, and I had the files. I'd had no intention of doing what Taso thought I'd agreed to. This just meant I wouldn't have an easy excuse.

"Okay," I said. "But look, keep working on the files with Pita while we're en route, in case there's more about the location of this mysterious planet. I'll start us toward Nellera. You still have your contact there?"

"I hope so." The flush had left his cheeks and been replaced by the wan grey tone that was his usual colour of late. He looked more tired than I'd ever seen him. "I haven't had a response to my last message, but I'm going to send another one."

I nodded. "All right. I'll tell Rei to forget FarView for now, and head for the wormhole into Keridre/Gerdrice."

WHEN WE ENTERED the twin star Keridre/Gerdrice system, the wormhole deposited us nearest to the planet Stana. It was still distant, a softly glowing orb in the reflected light of the system's double suns. Our destination, Nellera, was the system's fifth planet, just barely squeaking into the habitable zone. Much more removed from the suns and it would have been too cold to offer colonists a hospitable welcome. However, Nellera's equatorial island chains were warm and hospitable, making it a popular tourist escape for inhabitants of Stana and Tarcol and even planets from other systems. I never visited Nellera without feeling a bit of a pang, though. We'd lived here when my mother had gathered her things and quietly left one night, hoping to leave us to a better life without PrimeCorp constantly on our tail. Seventy years later, we'd finally been reunited. That was the important thing, but Nellera always left me disquieted and sad for what had ended here so long ago.

This visit was disquieting for another reason; as we transited the system, Sedmamin's contact on Nellera still hadn't answered his messages. The strain told on him—he became even more quiet and withdrawn, keeping to his quarters sometimes even at mealtimes. He hadn't exactly become fast friends with the crew; there was too much history for that. But we'd managed to maintain a cordial co-existence within the confines of the ship.

I knocked on the door of his quarters when we were a day out from Nellera. He called for me to come in. When the door opened, he was at the small desk, his datapad and Pita on the surface while he hunched over them. He didn't even look up.

"Chairman?"

"Come in, Captain. I suppose I'll just stop asking you not to call me that."

"Sorry," I said. "Old habits. Still no word?"

He heaved a great sigh and turned to look at me. His face was gaunt, his eyes red-rimmed and sunken. He shook his head grimly. "Nothing."

I let the door close and leaned against it, crossing my arms. "Is there any sense in going further?"

"If I don't go to Nellera . . ." he paused and started again. "If I can't go to Nellera, I don't know where else to go."

"Surely you have friends—"

He stopped me with a vehement shake of his head. "No. In my position, you don't have friends, only allies. And when they stop being that, they're enemies."

I stayed silent for a moment. "When's the last time you messaged?"

"This morning."

"The Protectorate will probably offer you asylum," I suggested. "Set you up somewhere—"

"*Fek* the Protectorate," he snarled. "I don't want their pity or their makeshift life. I wanted to deal with them—fair exchange—and then be left alone."

I fetched a deep breath and let it out slowly. "Seems to me that life under protection is still life. If you're worried about being assassinated by PrimeCorp, it's a viable alternative."

"Why do you care?" he asked me in an exhausted voice

I shrugged. "You haven't exactly been a force for good in my life, Sedmamin. But, well, I can afford to be gracious. You're helping us out. I'm trying to help you. Does there have to be more to it than that?"

He grunted and slumped further in his chair. "Maybe not. I'm not—"

He broke off as his datapad dinged with a DIP message.

I raised my eyebrows.

He didn't ask me to leave, just pressed the screen to bring up the message. He read it and sighed. "She's there. It's all right."

"She say why she hasn't been responding?"

"She was off-planet. Didn't expect me this soon," he said.

"Well, all right then," I said. "Tell her we'll be in orbit by late afternoon tomorrow, and we'll order up a shuttle to take you down."

"Thank you, Captain." He didn't look up, already typing out his reply.

"Find anything else about that mysterious planet?" I asked. I assumed he'd continued to go through the files. He'd been closeted in here with the datapad and Pita, barely emerging for meals.

"No. Nothing more about where it is. But the files I haven't gone through, I'll just include in the package for your brother. I don't care anymore what's in them," he said recklessly. "I'll be beyond the reach of anyone who cares, anyway."

"*Okej*. Why don't you join us for dinner tonight, since it'll be your last night aboard?"

He turned a half-hearted smile my way. "Don't pretend you're going to miss me, Captain. The one thing I've always admired about you is your honesty."

I chuckled. "I didn't say I was going to miss you," I told him. "Just trying to be the perfect hostess. You know how much my reputation means to me."

"I can't say you've treated me any worse than I deserve," Sedmamin said, suddenly serious. "And thanks. Maybe I will see you at dinner, Captain."

SEDMAMIN DID JOIN us for dinner and the meal was actually rather pleasant. Maja had found a supply company that made stores-packaged food that reconstituted beautifully, and we enjoyed miraculously fresh teriyaki chicken and rice, washed down by *jarlees* wine. There was a celebratory feeling in the galley, perhaps because delivering Sedmamin safely to Nellera signalled a successful end to part of this undertaking. On the other hand, it might be more to do with getting rid of him, but everyone was civil.

By the time we were in orbit around Nellera the next day and Sedmamin joined us on the bridge, he looked much better than he had the afternoon before. He'd cleaned up, shaved, and changed his clothes for one of our inconspicuous shipsuits, which I'd told him he could keep. He'd returned Pita to Jahelia with grave thanks, and she'd accepted her datapad and AI graciously. Everything he owned fit into two bulging duffel bags that lay at his feet as we watched Nellera spin slowly below us, wreathed in clouds.

"Last chance to stay with us and go into protection," I said lightly as we waited for the shuttle we'd ordered for Sedmamin. Nellera didn't have planetside docking facilities for a ship as large as mine, and no orbiting station, either. So shuttlecraft were kept busy ferrying passengers to and from orbiting ships. There was talk of a space elevator sometime in the future, but that time hadn't come yet.

"I hope you're joking," Alin Sedmamin said. "The likelihood of my wanting to spend any amount of time in the company of the Protectorate is about as remote as . . ." He trailed off, apparently unable to think of anything that unlikely.

"As remote as the chance you'd ask me for help?" I suggested.

"Or that you'd acquiesce," he returned, and half-smiled.

I can't say I liked Alin Sedmamin, but I didn't loathe him quite as much as I had before. That had to count for something in my stock of private karma, didn't it?

Hirin had not come to the bridge to see Sedmamin off, but Rei was at the pilot's board and Baden on the comm. Jahelia was, I assumed, down in Engineering, taking her job as Viss's fill-in quite seriously. I wondered if she'd have trouble turning it over to him when we finally got Viss and Yuskeya back. I had no doubt that my crotchety engineer would roust her out of his chair quickly enough and spend at least a couple of weeks complaining about all the things she'd managed to mess up.

I'd struggled with the question of whether I should tell Sedmamin about Taso. As things stood now, he'd probably never have to worry about running into my ex-son-in-law. Taso was not a particularly skilled operative; that wasn't why PrimeCorp had picked him. It had been his connection to my family, and probably his willingness to do their dirty work in return for a quick payment. If Sedmamin's connections were as good as he thought, no other PrimeCorp operative was likely to find him, either. Still, it went against the grain with me not to let Sedmamin know he'd been right to watch his back.

"Look, Chairman," I said, swiveling my skimchair to face him. "There's something I should tell you."

"Should I sit down?" He looked vaguely amused.

"I don't think it's that serious. But you were right about PrimeCorp sending someone after you."

All traces of amusement, and most of the colour, left his face. "What?"

I sighed. "I don't think you actually have to worry about this, but I don't feel right not warning you. I left out a little detail about the day Jahelia Sord and I went into PrimeCorp."

There was no sign of Sedmamin's shuttle yet, and he pulled one of the vacant skimchairs over from a console to sit near me. "Tell me."

So, I told him how Taso had followed us into the building and into his office. His expression didn't change much as I related the conversation, but by the time I'd finished, the rest of the colour had drained away.

"But I had no intention of turning you over to him," I reiterated. "I intimated that I would, so we could get out of there with the files, but I didn't have much choice. If he chose to interpret what I said as a promise, that's not my fault."

"How did he know?" Sedmamin asked in a low voice. "How did he know where to find you, and when?"

I shrugged. "He just said he'd followed us. I thought he might have put a tracker on Maja when they'd met, but she was sure he hadn't touched her or any of her things. I got Baden to sweep the ship just in case, but he didn't find anything."

"You don't think you would have noticed someone following your ship?"

"Maybe, maybe not."

"And you didn't file a cargo manifest for Earth?"

"No. We had you on board by then, and I wasn't broadcasting where we were headed. I didn't even tell Lanar in the message I left for him."

Sedmamin got up from the chair then, and stood, spinning it idly under his hand. "And your son-in-law—"

"Former son-in-law."

"Conceded. Former son-in-law is not a trained operative."

I shook my head. "Not as far as I know. Just an opportunistic guy who couldn't turn down the deal PrimeCorp offered him. He came to FarView to find Maja, thinking she might help him find you, and got lucky because you were actually there."

"I suppose it could be coincidence . . ."

"What are you thinking?"

Sedmamin turned and stared out the viewscreen at the slowly spinning planet beneath us. A small craft, probably his shuttle, had just come into view, heading our way. "My contact on Nellera," he said slowly, "is the sister of the person who left my office open for you at PrimeCorp and got the decryption chip. But if she—my helper at PrimeCorp—found out what Taso wanted and let him know when you'd be there . . ."

"Why would she double-cross you? I thought she was a friend."

"Money's a better friend. She could do what I asked and take what I paid her, then tell Taso how to find me and also presumably share in whatever PrimeCorp's paying him."

"So, in that case, your friend on Nellera—"

"Could very well not be my friend at all," he finished, his voice bleak.

"Because if you turn up here, it means that Taso didn't manage to get you his way, and they can let PrimeCorp know where you are themselves."

"Collecting the full reward and leaving Taso out in the cold." He heaved a deep sigh and put his hands on his hips. "I can't go down there."

I shook my head. "Not with those kinds of doubts. I'll get Baden to put in a call and cancel the shuttle."

Sedmamin didn't answer. Well, he was watching his carefully constructed plan for the rest of his life crumble. That had to be rough.

"Captain?" Sedmamin said suddenly. "Did you tell Mr. Methyr to cancel the shuttle yet?"

"No. You'd have heard me."

"Then why is it turning around and heading back to the planet—fast?"

He was right. The shuttle I'd pegged as his had turned tail

away from us.

"Captain, priority message coming in from Orbital Admin," Baden said.

"On screen."

"—ships in orbit around Nellera. Be advised of possible hostile craft approaching the planet. Protectorate craft are scrambling to meet any threat but you must remain on alert. All ships in orbit around Nellera. Be advised—"

I motioned to Baden to cut the repeating feed. "Rei, anything on the scan?"

"I've got a handful of blips on the short-range, moving fast," Rei said.

"PrimeCorp?" Sedmamin wondered, unease evident in his voice. "Maybe they followed us here—"

"They're not PrimeCorp ships," Rei said. "I wish Yuskeya were here, she's better at this drive signature stuff than I am." She keyed commands into the screen.

"Chatter on the public Protectorate channel says they think it's Chron," Baden said.

"Drive sigs?" I asked.

"That, and general configuration," Baden answered. "And apparently there's nothing else like this scheduled to come in today."

"Let's get moving, folks," I said. "Sedmamin, take a seat." I touched my own screen. "Jahelia, we're moving out of here, and fast. Any reason not to?"

Her voice came after a pause. "Everything in order down here, Captain. What's happening?"

"Unwanted visitors to Nellera," I said. "Give Rei whatever she asks for."

"Got it."

From the surface of the planet a scattershot of ships surged up and away, heading to intercept the interlopers. One passed across the big viewscreen in close enough magnification for me to see the Protectorate emblem on its side. It was too fast for me to read the words, but I knew what they said: *In Astra Pax.* Peace Among the Stars. It had been mostly true for a long time, but those days were quickly coming to an end.

"I'm a little surprised you don't want to stay and help out, Captain," Sedmamin said with the hint of a sardonic smile. "You have a reputation for altruism."

"Not today, Chairman. Top priority is getting those files to Fleet Commander Holles."

As Rei turned us in the direction of the wormhole to Delta Pavonis, the rear viewscreen showed a bright flash of shields as the Protectorate ships and Chron engaged.

Chapter 11 — Lanar
All About Control

I COULDN'T SAY we limped back to FarView Station, because there was nothing much wrong with the *Cheswick* except for one hastily-patched hole in the aft hull and a disabled skip drive. But it felt like limping. A subdued air permeated the entire ship, and even Viss and Yuskeya were quiet. I'd messaged Regina immediately to tell her about the Chron ships coming through the Split, and what Mauronet had done, but I didn't mention the PrimeCorp ship. That would wait until we were face-to-face. We had the wormhole data we'd gone to collect, and no Chron ships had made it past us into Nearspace, but it still felt like a failure. We had no idea where Mauronet and the *Dorland* might be, we'd lost the PrimeCorp ship and our chance to interrogate its crew, and had suffered damage.

Regina summoned me to her office as soon as we'd docked. I was only slightly surprised that she'd managed to get herself off the med level so quickly—I'm sure they were only too happy to let her get back to her desk. Viss, Yuskeya, and I left the *Cheswick* together. Viss had requested permission to use the Protectorate data station to start analyzing what we'd collected at the Split, and Yuskeya had the necessary permissions to get him in there. I'd found out what he'd been doing at that empty station on the *Cheswick*'s bridge during the Chron incursion.

"Started the data collection module up again once the wormhole opened and the first Chron came through," he'd told me laconically after Mauronet had chased the Chron ship through the Split. "I thought we might get something different when it was active. Couldn't pass up a chance like that. There'll be a lot of interference from all those weapons, but I might be able to clean some of it up."

Now we'd find out if his hunch had paid off. We rode down in the elevator from the docking level to the Administrative level on 3 in relative silence. In some areas, through the glass panes of the elevator, we glimpsed repairs still being effected. I wondered dully if it would do any good, if the Split was going to spit out more Chron fighters every time we turned around.

Viss and Yuskeya turned off in one corridor, and I continued along to Regina's office. When I knocked, she called, "Come in!" and I pushed the door open.

The auburn-haired woman who turned from Regina's guest chair to smile at me was a surprise, and I almost blurted "Luta!" before I realized that it wasn't her—it was Mother. Even more shocking.

She stood and came to give me a hug while Regina smiled benevolently at us. "I'm so glad you're back! Fleet Commander Holles tells me you encountered Chron ships?"

Regina still didn't know about the PrimeCorp ship, so I merely nodded. "Two of them. One was destroyed, but the other one went back through the Split."

"Along with Admiral Mauronet," Regina said, her smile slipping as a frown took its place. "I can't say I'm terribly surprised, although I'm mad as hell at him for taking that risk."

Mother let me go and returned to her chair, and I sat in the other one next to her. "Now that it's just us, I'll add that there was a third ship that came through after the Chron—a PrimeCorp ship," I said.

"After the Chron? You mean in pursuit of them?" Mother asked.

I shook my head. "No, following them through. It actually joined in the attack on the *Cheswick* and the *Dorland*. They were the ones who took out my skip drive."

Regina sat back in her chair. "That was bold. They're not concerned with hiding their involvement with the Chron anymore, then."

"They probably didn't expect anyone to be sitting right outside the Split," I said, "and once through, they could break off from the others. We were just in the right place at the right time to see it. And then they had to try and take us out."

Mother sighed. "I still don't know what PrimeCorp is playing at."

"Did you think of anyone with ties to PrimeCorp who might be able to help us figure it out? Is that why you're here?"

Mother pursed her lips. "I have some information I thought the Protectorate should have."

"We're just waiting for Harle," Regina said. "He's on his way over."

"There's something else, too," Mother said. "We've had Chron incursions in Mu Cassiopeia. Gusain's been able to handle it with the Duntmindi forces stationed on Kiando and Cengare, but if the assaults get much heavier, they won't be a match. They've got some corporate corvettes and runners they use to patrol for pirates and smugglers, but they're not warships."

Regina's frown deepened. "This is my fear. If we have to dispatch Protectorate ships to defend every planet in Nearspace—"

"Maybe it won't come to that," I said. "Maybe Admiral Mauronet will take out every Chron in Otherspace before he comes back. He was quite enthusiastic."

"Very funny," Regina said, but she didn't smile.

A knock at the door signaled the arrival of Harle Southwind, and he came into Regina's office with his slightly bouncing Lobor gait. As soon as he saw me he said, "Heard you had a little dustup out there. Chron coming through the Split? That's new."

"I have a couple of people working on readings we took before the wormhole opened up, and then again after it did," I said. "Not sure what it might tell us, but if Mu Cassiopeia's being targeted too, that might tell us something. It's only one skip from Delta Pav, and this is where we've witnessed them coming through."

"The Split is an essentially useless wormhole for Nearspace navigation anyway," Regina said. She limped over to a cabinet and pulled it open, offering hot drinks to all of us. I knew better than to offer to help her. "Maybe we should consider blowing the damn thing up."

"Luta's information from the Corvids suggests that might not be a long-term solution," I said. "But we could ask her about it again."

Regina introduced Mother to Harle and he shook Mother's hand gravely. "I hear you might be able to help us," he said.

"I don't know if you'd call it help, exactly," Mother said. "But I do have information I think you need to have."

Mother glanced at Harle. The Lobor smiled a bit uncertainly, but Regina seemed to understand Mother's hesitation. "Harle can be trusted, Emmage. You can speak freely."

But Mother ignored her and turned her attention to me. "It involves the . . . family secret," she said after a moment.

The nanobioscavengers.

WELL, AS FAR as I knew, Harle didn't know about Mother's research and our longevity, although Regina did. Mother and I held a silent conversation for a couple of heartbeats and I knew what she was asking. *Can I talk about this in front of him?*

I thought about all the people who now knew about our functional immortality—Luta's crew, Regina, a few others in the Protectorate, Gusain Buig, an indeterminate number of people at PrimeCorp—and shrugged. "I trust Harle," I said. "Go ahead."

The Lobor laid a hand on my shoulder. The fervid heat of his normal body temperature reached through my uniform coat and warmed my skin. "Thank you, Lanar."

I reached up and patted the back of his hand with its covering of soft fur. "Brothers in arms," I said with a grin.

The drinks were forgotten as we waited for Mother's revelation. She bent to the large carryall at her feet and pulled out a datapad. "I think I know what PrimeCorp is up to. The whole thing," she said. "And it's even worse than we thought.

"I took the list of executives Lanar gave me and went over it, thinking at first that I'd look for connections that might link me to some of them," she began. "That went nowhere, so I went through it again, paying more attention to the corporations they'd moved to." She called something up on her datapad and turned it so we could all see. Regina, Harle, and I all leaned in, studying the screen. It showed three columns. In the first were names, presumably the executives who'd left PrimeCorp and moved to other jobs. In the second were corporations and divisions. In the third were words I didn't recognize—some looked medical, some technical.

"What is it?" I peered at her notes, but they were gibberish to me.

She tapped the datapad. "All these corporations? They have one thing in common."

"What's that?" Regina asked, peering at the lists.

"They're all manufacturers of, or control resources used in the manufacture of, nanobioscavengers. Not just the everyday ones. All of them," she said pointedly.

"So PrimeCorp wants to control the medical market?" Harle twitched an ear. "That's not so surprising, is it? Pretty lucrative business."

"The nanobioscavenger market includes some applications that haven't been widely known or utilized before this," Mother said. "There's new research that's going to turn much of what we know on its head, and PrimeCorp is positioning itself to be able to take advantage of—actually, *control* is a better word— those applications."

"Okay," Harle said slowly. "I agree that we don't want PrimeCorp controlling important medical resources. And these are important applications?"

"Harle," Regina said, taking a deep breath. "What if I told you there was a type of bioscav that would make you, for all intents and purposes . . . immortal?"

The Lobor Admiral's ear twitched reflexively a few times. "Immortal? You're saying this technology is imminent?"

"More than imminent," I said. I stuck out a hand for Harle to shake, and he took it automatically. "Nice to meet you. My name is Lanar Mahane, and I was born in 2204."

Harle stopped shaking my hand, although he continued to hold it. "2204?" His voice was incredulous. "Lanar, you're *eighty* years old?"

I nodded to Mother. "And my mother is a hundred and twenty-eight."

He took Mother in with wide eyes. "Luta?" he asked in a slightly dazed voice.

"Eighty-four."

Harle swallowed a couple of times and looked over at Regina. She smiled and touched a hand to her shock of white hair. "Not me. Lanar's family is it. I have exactly the number of years you think I have, not that you need to actually name that number," she said. "Emmage was the researcher who developed the technology, and spent decades trying to keep it out of PrimeCorp's greasy fingers. Now her research is freely available, so PrimeCorp can't put a lock on it. But I guess they figure they can do the next best thing—control the resources."

I frowned. "But PrimeCorp started moving people years ago, according to Harle. They couldn't have known that Mother's research would become available."

Mother tapped the edge of her datapad. "No, but remember, they did have the research data up to a point. And they knew Schulyer Group was working on something similar—there was industrial espionage going both ways with PrimeCorp. Many of the components are the same for all nanobioscavengers anyway, and they've definitely been moving to put a lock on those. I can tell from some of the other corporations they've targeted that they were making certain assumptions. Reasonable ones. So now they're well-placed to control the market, if they control the corporations."

Regina steepled her fingers and tapped them together. "Here's a question. Would your super bioscavs work for different races?"

Mother nodded. "They function at the cellular level. We may have different genomes from other races, but the bioscav programming can be changed to accommodate differences. When it comes down to it, they're just tiny machines, after all. We were working on a Vilisian line when the breakdown in the project happened."

"So they'd work for Chron."

Mother looked startled, then nodded. "With the necessary alterations in programming, I can't see any reason why not."

Regina slumped in her chair, looking every minute of those years she'd just joked about. "Can you imagine," she said, "what a self-healing, non-aging Chron army would look like? If PrimeCorp has allied with them, there'd be no stopping it."

I stood up then; I felt an absolute need to be on the move. Regina's office wasn't large enough for truly satisfactory pacing, but I could stride back and forth in front of the desk.

"All right, we need to regroup," I said. "The Chron incursions are getting worse, and PrimeCorp is obviously allied with them; after what Mauronet and I encountered, I'd say there's no longer any doubt. PrimeCorp is positioned to take over both the Nearspace Authority and the manufacturing of the nanobioscavengers. Mother," I turned to her. "When you talked to Schulyer group about their anti-aging tech—will it be a viable competitor for PrimeCorp?"

She nodded. "It definitely has the potential, but they'll rely on the same resources that PrimeCorp is locking up. That'll kill any competition before it even gets started."

"All right. So, we're looking at complete domination of Nearspace by PrimeCorp within a few years, if we don't stop it now. And the Protectorate doesn't have the manpower or the ships to mount an adequate defence."

"Thanks for making us all feel better, Admiral," Regina said bleakly.

Harle put two furred fists on the table. His ears angled back in a way that I knew meant he was angry. "Well, what next? I'm not about to sit back and let PrimeCorp walk all over us on the way to the Nearspace Council."

I paced again. "This is what Commander Blue and Viss Feron and I talked about. We know the Split is key. The Chron are coming into Nearspace through it somehow. But not from the GI182 end. So that leaves the damaged side or a ghosted wormhole."

"They're not coming through the wormhole in Tau Ceti," Harle agreed. "We have that one shut down tight."

"Maybe Viss's readings of the Split while it was closed and after the Chron ships began coming through will tell us something. He says he also has data on the *Tane Ikai* from when they traversed it. There must be something there."

"You're sure we can't just blow it up?" Regina asked. "I know they have an access route through the Corvid system and Woodroct's Star, but if we work with the Corvids we can probably shut that one down again. And whatever other ones the Corvids can tell us about."

I shook my head. "According to the Corvids, if we disable the Split, another replacement wormhole will appear. We saw that with the one leading to Woodroct's Star."

Regina ran a hand over her hair, dislodging some strands. They fell around her face, making her look vulnerable. "What about the ghosting? Anything there we can use?"

"I don't know if there's any way to block one. We'd have to ask the Corvids."

"Okay, so we bring the Corvids fully into this," Harle said. "See if one or more of them will come here, examine the Split, see if they can give us any advice. They seem to be the experts."

"Already in the works," Regina said.

I stopped walking. "What about the Relidae, too? They might be able to help. They know the Chron better than anyone else." I looked around the room. "Get everyone together, pool our resources and knowledge."

"I had a message from Luta this morning," Regina said. "She's en route from Nellera and should be here by tomorrow. Said she's bringing some very interesting information. Maybe it will be something we can use."

She straightened in her chair and I could see the fire come back into her eyes. "All right. We have the start of a plan. We also need to know what happened to Mauronet, but that ties in to what we find out about the Split, and I'm not sending anyone else through it until we know more." She turned to Mother. "There are a few other people in the Protectorate who know about Lanar's—uniqueness. I may need to tell others about the nanobioscavengers. I have to make the full scope of the possible threat clear."

Mother took a deep breath. "It's all right," she said, glancing at me. I nodded. "I think it's time we came out of the shadows anyway. I still won't broadcast it—and we'll have to see how Luta feels about it—but if it has to come out in order to save Nearspace, then there's no question. Talk to whomever you need to about it, Regina."

MOTHER AND I had dinner at the Blackstar restaurant, on the fifth level of FarView. They had sustained only minor damage in the Chron attack, being on the opposite side of the hub, and normal operations had resumed. Everything on the surface, at least; it was harder to repair the fear that had gripped everyone on the station. An undercurrent of unease ran through every level now, and it couldn't be dispersed even by the finest *jarlees* wine and pasta *primavera.*

We tried to talk mainly of trivialities, but weightier issues continually intruded; I asked about Gusain and Mother said he'd stayed on Kiando—mainly because he wanted to oversee the defence of the system if the Chron threatened again. Mother asked about Luta and I gave in and told her about what had happened on the Corvid station, because she was bound to hear it eventually now and I preferred she hear it from me. Whatever new course we attempted to set for the conversation, it inevitably wound back to the threat we were all facing.

We'd finished our wine when my ID implant buzzed. I took the call on my datapad, but it was text-only, from Regina. *Please come to my quarters if you're free after dinner.* That was it, no intimation of why. It wasn't an official order, but neither did it have the feeling of an invitation to another dalliance.

"I'm going to my quarters now, anyway," Mother said. "I've only just realized how tired I am." The tiny lines around her eyes, usually so faint, seemed deeper and more firmly drawn tonight. She was tired. No wonder. The technology that she'd so eagerly developed to help all of Nearspace, then sacrificed so much to keep hidden away for years to prevent its exploitation, had now taken on the potential to be an active threat. I wondered if she'd be able to sleep at all.

We rode up the elevator together in silence, and she got off at level three, the main habitat level. I continued up to the top level, above the docking ring, where Regina had her suite, and knocked at the door.

She had changed out of her uniform from earlier, into black tights and a long, pale green sweater. One leg of the tights was rolled up above the level of her walking brace. Her hair was still up in its no-nonsense pins, although a few more strands had come free and now curled around her face. She stood at the view-wall, a glass of wine in one hand. Beyond the glass, a few ships came and went from the docking rings, but most lay quiet, settled for the artificially-induced night of the station.

"I want to know what you really think of our plan," she said, motioning me to sit on the sofa. She sat across from me, not beside me, and raised her glass in a mute question, but I shook my head. The wine I'd had with dinner was enough for the evening.

"I think it's as good as we can do," I said. "There's too much we still don't know. We need the input from the Corvids. And the Relidae. We need whatever Luta's bringing. Where was she, anyway?"

Regina shook her head. "I don't know—nowhere I sent her."

"I think we'll have to send someone through the Split," I said. "Off the side. You can't put it off forever."

She nodded wearily. "I know. But I need more before I can do that. I'm not sending anyone to their possible deaths on a guess."

"You might not have that luxury."

"Oh, Lanar." She smiled at me. "Always ready to make me face the hard truths I'm trying desperately to avoid."

"That wasn't my intention," I said, but she put a hand up to stop me.

"I know, and I needed to hear it. But I'm also facing up to another hard truth, too, which is why I asked you to come over."

I felt a pang of fear. Was she sick? Something beyond her injuries from the Chron attack? I'd never seriously contemplated something happening to Regina until the station had been targeted, and now the spectre of it loomed everywhere I looked.

"Don't look so stricken," she said with a smile. "I'm not dying or anything."

"Well, that's good to know. Not that I was worried," I said lightly. "You're too stubborn to do that anyway."

"Charmer."

"I try."

Regina sighed. "That's the problem. You *are* charming. And the other night was . . . lovely." She swirled the wine in her glass and took a sip.

"It was."

She stood and moved toward me, bending to put a hand on my cheek. "Yes. And I may have read more into it than you meant, but I have to say this anyway. It's not going to happen again."

I said nothing. She turned away and walked to the window again, setting her glass down on the counter as she passed and crossing her arms, hugging herself.

"We tried this before, Lanar, and we both know there's no future in it. And, neither of us can afford to be distracted."

I joined her at the window, standing close but not touching her. "You were never just a distraction. But it does seem like bad timing again," I said. "We never seem to get it right."

She rested her head lightly on my shoulder. "I don't think we ever really had a chance at that, Lanar. Time—and timing—were against us from the beginning."

Beyond the glass wall, ships glided against the dark velvet background pricked by beckoning stars. Looking across it, it was almost possible to believe that time could stretch forever, that you could set sail across its ocean and never reach the end. But we both knew that ocean was finite, and that its shorelines differed for everyone.

"Time doesn't care one way or the other," I told her. "We made our choices."

"We made some. Others were out of our hands," she said.

It was true. I'd had no say about my nanobioscavengers, and there were times I'd wished Mother had left well enough alone.

Chapter 18 — Luta
Enemies and Alliances

"WE JUST DON'T have the luxury of waiting around on this," Lanar said. I rubbed a hand over my eyes. I think it was the third time I'd heard my brother say the same thing, and every time the discussion just went around and around and didn't end up at any clear plan of action.

We were closeted in a boardroom in the Protectorate's administrative space on FarView Station. The Protectorate contingent consisted of Fleet Commander Regina Holles, Lanar, his friend Harle Southwind, a Vilisian Vice-Admiral I'd never met before named Mare Ker, and Yuskeya's friend Jolah Didkovsky. He looked none the worse for his encounter with the Chron—they'd been the peaceful ones everyone now called *Relidae*. Hirin and I and Viss and Yuskeya were there from my ship, and I'd been happily surprised to find Mother waiting on FarView, too. Alin Sedmamin was in attendance to explain the files we had obtained from PrimeCorp Main. Jahelia was there with Pita, to explain the information she'd decrypted in those files that pertained to the Split.

It had been a long day of explaining.

There'd been a couple of bright spots—seeing Mother was one, and she hugged me tightly for a long moment. The other, strangely, had been introducing Lanar and Jahelia Sord.

She'd looked him over from head to toe, and I'd been surprised to see my brother discomfited by the inspection. "Even without the uniform, I'd have guessed Protectorate," she said. "Must be the famous brother, even though I don't see the family resemblance too strongly." She looked at each of us in turn with a calculated impertinence.

"Admiral Lanar Mahane, meet Jahelia Sord."

Lanar recovered his composure; he grinned and stuck out a hand. "The equally famous rogue element," he said, and left his hand there long enough that she eventually reached out and shook it.

In a more serious tone, he added, "I'm honestly glad to meet you. I understand you were instrumental in saving my sister's life a few weeks ago."

Jahelia looked taken aback. "If she made it back, I made it back," she said diffidently, dropping his hand and folding her arms again. "But you're welcome. Your sister is all right."

Lanar slid his arm around my shoulders in a half-hug. "I like her," he said. "She puts up with me and hardly ever complains."

"Not to your face," I said dryly. "*Okej, okej.* You two have met, and we've all formed a mutual appreciation society. Maybe we could just send the two of you off to make friends with the Chron."

It was a weak joke, and not very funny, but I felt a bit flustered. Something strange hung in the air between Lanar and Jahelia, and I couldn't put my finger on what it was.

But I soon forgot about it as the council of war started. And went on for a long time.

It wasn't that we'd made no progress; we'd pooled our knowledge about the Split, the Chron, Sedmamin's files, and PrimeCorp. Alin Sedmamin had been closely questioned by Fleet Commander Holles and Admiral Southwind. Holles hadn't spared him anything. She might be grateful that he'd turned over important information, but she couldn't forget that he and PrimeCorp had been a thorn in her side for a long time. Although he'd made a couple of blustery attempts to characterize this questioning as illegal, Holles had shut him down pretty quickly. In times of potential war, protocol goes out the airlock. And I think Sedmamin himself knew that whatever his treatment at the hands of the Protectorate, he could expect worse from PrimeCorp.

It was my first time learning about PrimeCorp's plans to clandestinely move executives into other corporations, with a view to controlling both the Nearspace Worlds Council and the resources needed to manufacture and control the nanobioscavengers. I sat somewhat stunned, trying to get my head around all the ramifications, while Holles and Southwind put their suspicions to Sedmamin. He initially hedged, and then confirmed that it was all true. Not an idea that had originated with him, he hastened to assure us, but one that he had known about and yes, tacitly approved. I didn't think anyone believed his protestations, but there was little point in arguing about that now. The pressing concern was what to do next.

Fleet Commander Holles advised that she had already sent a message to the Corvid system, with an urgent request for someone with wormhole expertise to examine the Split and advise how we might stop the Chron using it as a conduit into Nearspace. We knew destroying it was useless, but maybe there would be another way. She'd also set up a cordon around both terminal points of the Split, both here in Delta Pavonis and in GI182. "It might force them to come through in Tau Ceti," she said, "but we're waiting for them there, too. We'll wait and see what happens."

Lanar had said, "If we look at what happened to Mauronet's ship—it didn't come out the other end of the Split, so it went *somewhere else*—and the information in the PrimeCorp files about a base outside Nearspace, I think it's clear we need to consider sending someone through the Split to investigate further. We don't have the luxury of time on this."

That was the first time he'd said it. Now he'd repeated it for the third time and I was about to stand up and volunteer to take the *Tane Ikai* through.

It wasn't as crazy as it sounds. It was logical to assume that Lanar was right, and the *Dorland* had followed the Chron ship back to wherever it had come from. *How* they'd done it remained to be discovered, but we weren't going to figure that out sitting here. Holles also made it clear that the Protectorate was stretched to the limits of its capability with two new cordons and increased demands for protection from many planets in Nearspace. And we'd run the Split not long ago. We weren't going to be freaked out by its inherent weirdness and make a mistake.

But before I could do that, Regina Holles fixed Sedmamin with an icy glare. He'd been sitting quietly since his initial questioning, staying out of the ongoing conversation unless asked a direct question.

"And what has PrimeCorp been doing in this mysterious system?" she asked him. "From what Admiral Mahane and his sister have observed independently, it seems you've developed quite a cozy relationship with the Chron."

Sedmamin paled but shook his head. "As I've already stated," he said in an aggrieved voice, "I knew nothing about that side of operations. I've never had direct contact with any Chron myself, nor ordered any."

That was his story and he appeared to be sticking to it, but Holles didn't ease off. "Please, Mr. Sedmamin, I'm not a fool. You may not have been directly involved, but you must have some educated guesses, now that you do know."

Sedmamin licked his lips. A muscle twitched erratically on his jawline. He did know something, I thought. And he was weighing whether or not he should mention it.

"Spill it, Chairman," I advised. "I could always call Taso."

He shot me an evil glare. "I'm really not sure. I'm guessing."

"Guess away," invited Regina Holles. "I won't hold it against you if you turn out to be wrong."

He swallowed, still trying to decide. Finally, he said, "I did always wonder where some of the breakthrough technologies came from." He picked up a mug of caff that must have gone cold long ago and sipped from it. "There were times—I wouldn't be aware that we were even working on something, and then there'd be a major development. Over time I realized that these developments always came from a particular department. They were supposedly just a think-tank—Innovation and Advancement. You have to understand that I was much more occupied with overall strategy for the corporation, not individual departments or projects."

Lanar nodded. "But now you think these might have had something to do with the Chron connection?"

Sedmamin shrugged. "Perhaps. It was only six, seven times

in all my years at PrimeCorp. But the department predated my tenure. Now, yes, I wonder."

"So, this Innovation and Advancement group might have been responsible for trade with the Chron," Harle Southwind mused. "Whenever the corporation needed a boost, they'd get something from the Chron that they could pass off as PrimeCorp's own work or invention."

"And in return, the Chron would get what?" Regina Holles asked. "Historically, they haven't been notable for being easy to get along with."

"I can't guess," Sedmamin reiterated. "I don't even know what they'd want. You have to understand, PrimeCorp is huge. There are hundreds—literally hundreds of ways that money, goods, information could have been funneled to the Chron."

"The Corvids said they stopped the Chron attacks during the war," Hirin said. He tapped his fingers slowly on the table, thinking. "Sometime after that, PrimeCorp made contact with them again, and this time on a friendlier footing. They must have had something that the Chron wanted badly. Something they'd be willing to trade for."

I looked at him. "You don't think—even then?"

He shrugged and turned to Mother. "When you left the nanobioscavenger project at PrimeCorp—when you essentially shut it down—were you at a point where the technology could be adapted for other races?"

Mother nodded. "I just said that yesterday. We were looking at Vilisians first, but Lobors would have been next. From there it could have probably been adapted for anyone."

Hirin spread his hands. "So that could have been it. The promise of immortality. And all the Chron had to do was keep providing PrimeCorp with the means to stay at the top of their game until they tracked you down or got what they wanted from Luta."

"Which is why PrimeCorp could never give up trying to regain the data, either," Lanar said. "The promise of it could hold the Chron at bay—but only if they were seen to be actively working at it."

Jahelia had been mostly quiet since she'd explained Pita's part in obtaining the PrimeCorp files. She sat at the far end of the table, and had leaned her chair back far enough to put her feet up. Surprisingly, Regina Holles had merely looked at her for a long moment, then ignored it. Now Jahelia spoke. "So once the Chron have enough information to make their own nanobioscavengers," she said, "what's to stop them from picking up where they left off a century ago?"

All eyes turned to her. "You think they'd still want to destroy Nearspace?" Holles asked.

Jahelia shrugged. "Why not? I'm sure they don't like us any better now than they did then. They've also decided to hate half their own people. They've figured out—maybe with PrimeCorp's help and certainly with their blessing—how to infiltrate Nearspace. They seem to have lots of information about inhabited planets and stations, and they're currently testing our defensive capabilities. Why wouldn't they launch a full-scale invasion as soon as they have what they want? Or simply to get it?"

"But doesn't Admiral Southwind think the attacks are just a distraction—to keep people from noticing PrimeCorp's real endgame? Why would PrimeCorp get in bed with the Chron if the Chron were just going to turn around and attack us?" I was afraid I knew the answer, but I wanted Jahelia to keep going.

"PrimeCorp doesn't know they're about to be double-crossed." It was Lanar, not Jahelia, who spoke. "Den-Aldar warned me that the Chron wouldn't hesitate to break their deal with PrimeCorp if they had reason. And there's one thing about getting to be as big as PrimeCorp has. You think you're too big to fail. You don't expect to fail. Eventually, you don't even think you can. And you think you're always the one in control."

"So you open up the doors and let the tiger into your living room, thinking it'll be fine, because you have it on a leash," Mother said.

Jahelia nodded. "But you forget that the tiger doesn't give a damn about a leash." She lifted her boots from the table and let them drop to the floor, leaning forward to put her palms on the table. "Because it's about to bite your hand off anyway."

NO-ONE SAID anything for a long moment. I think we were all a little bit in shock at how vulnerable Nearspace had become—through complacency and the machinations of a corporation so proud, and so greedy, that they'd put all of the intelligent species of Nearspace at risk.

I glanced at Hirin before I stood up. He met my eye but I couldn't communicate simply with a look, what I was about to propose. I just had to trust that he'd go along with me.

"I volunteer to take the *Tane Ikai* to investigate the Split," I said. "It's obvious we need to get inside it."

Mother stood up, too. "Luta, no. You can't. There's not enough—"

I held up a hand. "I'm not going to leap off the unknown side—I'm not crazy. I'm saying we just take the ship through, take readings, see if we can figure anything out. Maybe there are clues to what happened with Mauronet and the *Dorland,* or how the Chron are getting in. Maybe something has changed inside the wormhole since anyone else from Nearspace went through it. But we can't find out enough from the outside."

Then everyone on the Protectorate side was speaking at once. Lanar shook his head. Viss and Yuskeya shared a glance but said nothing. Jahelia Sord was grinning at me. She looked downright approving, and that was the only thing that made me think I was making a big mistake.

Lanar said, "Luta, much as you're an asset to the Protectorate, you're still a civilian. If anyone goes in there, it should be a Protectorate ship."

"How many Protectorate ships have pilots who've actually run the Split?" I asked.

"There are some," Lanar said stubbornly. "A handful."

"Who may be days or even weeks away, somewhere else in Nearspace. We don't have that kind of time. You said it yourself."

"She's right about one thing," Viss said. "All that data we collected, even from the probe—didn't really tell us anything new."

Lanar shot him a betrayed look, but Viss shrugged. "Sorry, Admiral, it's the truth."

"What if something bad happened in there, with the *Dorland* and the Chron ship?" Harle Southwind asked mildly. His tone masked agitation, however, which manifested in the flicking of one ear. I'd noticed the same thing in Cerevare Brindlepaw when she'd been with us.

"Well, no debris exited either end of the wormhole."

"Which proves nothing."

"If there's debris inside the wormhole, we'll know what happened," I said reasonably. "And the probe should have detected that."

"I'm in, if you go," Jahelia said suddenly. She glanced at Viss. "At least, I'd like to be. I know you have your engineer back now, but I might be useful."

"She's not going," Lanar insisted. "What if you get pulled through the bad side against your will? End up somewhere else, like this mysterious system the PrimeCorp files mention."

"I consider that a possibility," I said. "If that happens, we'd deal with it. Maybe it would be a good thing."

"What will your crew think of this idea, Captain?" Harle Southwind still kept his voice calm and reasonable, but that ear kept twitching.

"My crew is always encouraged to make their own decisions," I told him. "They know they can opt to stay behind, no questions asked and no recriminations."

"I'll go," Viss said, leaning back in his chair and crossing his arms. "I need to see what shape my engine room is in." He didn't look at Jahelia, but his tone was friendly.

Mother took a few steps toward me and put her hands on my arms. "Luta," she said, "I just found you. I don't want to lose you. This seems reckless. Let someone else do it."

"There is no-one else," I said gently. "Look, the crew on my ship probably has the most combined experience of the Split of any ship in Nearspace. Even if only Hirin and I went, we've been through it three times. We can handle this. It's necessary."

Mother hesitated a moment, then nodded and released my arms.

Fleet Commander Regina Holles had been the only Protectorate officer saying nothing, as usual. Instead she regarded me through considering eyes. "I don't have to allow you to do this, Captain Paixon," she said.

"You'd have to find a way to stop her," Hirin muttered, and I almost smiled.

"No, you don't. But I'll be honest with you, I'd probably try to find a way to do it without your permission. We need to find out what's in there. It could be the key to this whole mess. And if we could have that knowledge by the time the Corvids get here—"

Regina Holles held up a hand. "If I allow this, there will be conditions. You are not, under any circumstances, to try to navigate through the malformed side of the Split."

"Agreed. I have no intention of doing that."

"If something happens that tries to force you through that side, you will attempt to counteract with any means possible."

I nodded.

"We'll have Protectorate ships stationed at both ends of the Split. They'll protect you when you emerge, if it's necessary. If you need crew members to replace any of yours who opt out of the mission, I will ask for Protectorate officers to volunteer in their stead."

"I'm fine with that."

"Your ship will undergo a complete inspection by qualified Protectorate specialists before you leave. They will carry out repairs or improvements at the Protectorate's expense."

Viss narrowed his eyes but I hastily said, "That's very kind of you."

"Admiral Mahane will go with you. So will ex-Chairman Sedmamin."

Mother looked startled and Lanar looked slightly mollified, but Sedmamin popped up from his seat, sputtering. "Fleet Commander, this is outrageous! There is absolutely no reason to involve me in this. I'm not a military person! I have nothing more to offer."

The Fleet Commander fixed him with a steely eye. "We don't know what you might have to offer, sir, because we don't know what you might find. You have years of knowledge and experience with PrimeCorp. You may have insights or knowledge that will be useful to Captain Paixon and her crew."

"I've given you the files! Everything! Willingly!" Sedmamin had summoned every ounce of indignation he could muster. "And this is how you thank me."

"We appreciate your cooperation," she said, but her voice held an edge of mockery. She knew he'd only done it to protect his own *azeno*. Regina Holles rose from her chair and placed her fingertips on the desk, leaning forward slightly. "I don't think you quite realize your situation, *Citizen* Sedmamin," she said with emphasis. "You may have made a deal with Captain Paixon. But you have not made a deal with *me*."

The full implication of her words hit Sedmamin at once. He looked a little wildly from Holles to Lanar to me and back again. He'd assumed that I'd talked to Lanar about the trade— Sedmamin's freedom for the information that he'd turned over. But I never had. And I'd never, I realized, told Sedmamin that.

I shrugged. "Sorry, Chairman, I guess you're stuck with us for a little while longer."

He sat down again and ran a hand over his face. "It looks that way, Captain," he said finally. "Just stop calling me Chairman."

LANAR CAME ON board the *Tane Ikai* two days later looking like he was embarking on shore leave, which I didn't think he'd done for at least five years. He'd traded his Protectorate uniform for organic denim jeans, a trim transform t-shirt painting itself a repressed purple, and a short black jacket. He carried a plain weekend bag and a smaller case for his datapad.

I greeted him at the airlock. "You look like you're going on vacation," I said, giving him a quick hug.

"I thought it might be less intimidating if I didn't look officially Protectorate for this little jaunt," he said.

"Intimidating to whom? Not me, I hope."

He smiled. "No, not you. But I was thinking of Yuskeya. You're her current Captain, and I wouldn't want to muddy that up."

"Well, that was thoughtful of you."

"Also, I like to get out of the uniform occasionally," he reflected. "Sometimes I think differently without it."

"Does the Fleet Commander know this?" I asked him, showing him along the corridor to the quarters he'd have while on board. We'd agreed after further discussion that the mission could involve several skips through the wormhole, from both ends, and might continue for several days. Lanar had seemed content to leave Commander Linna Drake in charge of the *Cheswick* while he'd be away.

"I don't tell her everything," Lanar said mildly. "It's a need-to-know basis."

"Uh-huh. How's she doing? With her leg, I mean?" She hadn't moved around the room while we were meeting, and I'd seen the cane propped unobtrusively against the wall behind her chair.

Lanar grinned. "Regina? Cranky. The doctor says she'll still be using the cane to get around for a couple of weeks, and she hates the thing. Personally, I won't be surprised if she ends up hitting someone with it."

"Up to giving orders, though," I said, smiling.

"Until the day she dies, I'm sure."

We had a full ship now, with Sedmamin on board, Viss and Yuskeya back, and Jahelia Sord still with us as well. The *Tane Ikai* had been subjected to the thorough inspection Regina Holles had ordered, and even Viss stopped complaining after they installed a few nice upgrades.

As we reached the door of the quarters I was giving Lanar, the door across the corridor opened and Jahelia stood silhouetted in the opening. I saw her take him in, and then slip back behind her mask of bored amusement. She leaned against the doorframe and crossed her arms. "Well, Protectorate, we meet again."

"You can't call him 'Protectorate,'" I told her. "That's the same thing you call Yuskeya. It's going to get confusing around here if you don't start learning names."

"Hmm." She nodded. "You're right. Although if only one of them is around at a time, it could still work."

"And you were almost Protectorate yourself, if I remember correctly," I told her.

"Don't remind me of my misspent youth."

"You could just call me 'Admiral,'" Lanar suggested. "I'll answer to that."

Jahelia pursed her lips and frowned in mock speculation. "That sounds entirely too respectful. I'll have to give it some further thought. Later, Protectorate." She threw a perfect Protectorate salute to Lanar and moved off toward the galley, letting the door close behind her.

Lanar watched her go. I watched him for a moment, then said pointedly, "So here's your room."

He looked back to me, a small frown creasing his forehead. "What's up with her, anyway?" he asked. "Is she like that with everybody?"

I shrugged. "Pretty much. Jahelia Sord is prickly, outspoken, apparently fearless, and entirely disrespectful of authority."

"Huh," Lanar said. "I think I see why you two hit it off."

I punched him in the arm. "I'm going to the galley for a much-needed double caff, and then I'll be on the bridge. When you run into Jahelia, just play nice and don't break anything, all right? We'll leave the Station as soon as we get the go-ahead from Docking. And you're welcome on the bridge any time." I opened the door for him.

"See you in a bit," he said, and stepped inside.

I found Jahelia in the galley, sipping caff and eating a *solanto* cookie.

She grinned. "I've decided to make life easy for you. I'll use Yuskeya's name from now on, and reserve the pet name for your brother. He hasn't earned my respect yet."

"Thanks, that's all I needed to make my life easier," I said. "Should be a walk in the park, now."

Jahelia leaned against the counter as I pulled my caff from the machine. "Your brother," she said, nodding her head back the way we'd come. "Does he know about my nanobioscavs?"

I shook my head. "Not from me. I didn't tell anyone until I told my mother, and he was back aboard his ship by then. Since then . . . well, it just hasn't come up. I don't think she has told anyone."

She nodded. "So, it's just you and your mother and your husband who know? Really know? All of it?"

I snorted. "Jahelia, I wouldn't say that any of us know all of it." I put my back against the counter next to her, so that she and I weren't facing. I wrapped my hands around the warm mug gratefully. "Maja and I know what you told each of us, and Hirin saw the message you left for me. I asked Mother about your father, so I know her side of that. I know you're about the same actual age as we are, and that your nanobioscavengers could probably use an upgrade."

She said nothing, so I shook my head. "Okay, you still don't want to talk about that. The short answer to your question is, yes, only Hirin and Mother and I know your true age. Maja probably suspects, but we haven't talked about it. I don't see any need to tell anyone else unless circumstances make it necessary, or you want to." I glanced sideways at her and grinned. "How's that?"

She nodded once. "That's fine. Thank you. I'm not—" She

broke off, then tried again. "I'm not used to anyone else knowing about me. I feel like I need to know where I stand with everyone."

I blew out a sigh. "I do know. It's only recently that my crew found out about me. So, I understand. But it's your secret, not mine to tell. And Hirin can keep a secret better than anyone else I know."

"Do you mind my staying aboard?" she asked with uncharacteristic frankness. "I said I'd help, and I meant it. But I know it's probably not the most comfortable arrangement."

I took a sip of my drink. Sweet and hot and fortifying. "Things have changed fast over the past couple of weeks. I don't have a problem with you being here." I risked a glance at her. "I do wonder a bit about your motivation."

She was silent so long, eating the last bites of her cookie, I thought she wasn't going to answer. Finally, she said, "It's a long time since I cared about anything but myself and . . . revenge. But I—now I do. I care about stopping the Chron."

"You've changed a lot since we first met," I said. "For the better, I think."

She took a long swallow of caff. "Believe me, no-one is more surprised than I am," she said. "Now let's go up to the bridge and you can find some job for me to do."

Chapter 19 — Lanar
Into the Dark

I WASN'T USED to being a mere passenger on a ship; even when I could turn the immediate bridge command of the *Cheswick* over to Linna Drake or one of my other officers, there was still an alertness, a sense of purpose in knowing that I was ultimately responsible for everything that happened. Being a passenger on Luta's ship—emphasized by the absence of my Protectorate uniform—was unnerving. I realized just how long it had been since I'd taken a real vacation. Too long, obviously.

And I was also unnerved by the presence of Jahelia Sord. That feeling was more difficult to figure out. She was a loose cannon by all reports, and although Luta told me the woman had changed considerably since they'd first met, I still didn't know whether we should trust her. She was just as prickly and insolent as Luta had said, and yet I had the impression that it was all an act. She was living up to a reputation, but at least some of the time, it rang false. I wondered if I was simply being too suspicious, or if she was planning some elaborate double-cross. From what I knew of her, it was entirely possible.

We arrived at the Split to find five Protectorate ships in place near the terminal point—two Pixiu scouts, two Pegasus cruisers, and a Bahamut support ship. It was a sorry complement if the Chron sent through a serious invasion force, but this was only one possible entry point into Nearspace, and the fleet was stretched thin. In the event of an attack, they'd have to do what they could, and get word to Fleet Command.

They'd obviously been apprised by Regina that we'd be arriving and heading into the wormhole, because the lead cruiser, the *Sophia*, sent a message of acknowledgement through to Luta. She responded and after they'd broken the connection, looked around the bridge.

"Are we ready to do this?" she asked.

It had been no surprise to me that her entire crew had agreed to be involved in the mission. I knew the glue that held this crew together was more than the duty and purpose that bonded a Protectorate crew. These folks were more like family, and had been through a lot together in the past months. Jahelia was an outsider, but they'd opened up a space for her, too. She was installed now at the secondary engineering board on the bridge, while Viss manned the main controls on the lower level. Yuskeya, Rei, and Baden were at their usual posts, and Hirin had shown me with some enthusiasm the weapons station he'd set up.

No, I was the odd man out, and it was a strange feeling.

"Where's Sedmamin?" Luta asked.

"Sulking in his quarters," Jahelia said with a grin. "I threatened to tell Fleet Commander Holles and he was—extremely rude."

"I can go get him," I said. It would give me something to do, but Luta motioned me into a seat at one of the empty consoles.

"Never mind him. He doesn't have to be here for this. We'll get him if anything unexpected happens."

"Like being pulled off the missing side of the Split?" I asked.

"That wouldn't be completely unexpected, but yes," Luta agreed.

"You lied to Mother," I said, shaking a finger at her as I crossed to sit where she'd indicated.

"You didn't stop me," Luta countered. "All right, Viss, let's get the skip drive online. Baden, send the tracer through, make sure there's nothing coming the other way."

The ping was back in a moment, and Baden confirmed we were clear to enter.

"Rei, you can take us in whenever you're ready."

"Straight through unless anything interferes," Rei said. "Anything goes weird, you tell me what you want me to do, Captain. But don't leave it too long. You know what it's like in there."

"I know, and that's the plan," Luta confirmed. "Yuskeya, Jahelia, you're clear on running scans? Keep them going no matter what happens."

They both responded in the affirmative, and the tenor of the ship's hum changed as the skip drive kicked in. After a moment, the change in the wormhole was visible as the drive acted on it. The dark mouth of the wormhole changed and widened, beckoning us in. Runnels of plasma tendrils streamed along the edges, hot and wicked-looking.

"Engaging," Rei said, and the *Tane Ikai* moved slowly toward the mouth of the wormhole.

I felt a thrill of excitement that I hadn't felt in a long time. I'd explored nearly every corner of Nearspace with the Protectorate, but like the vast majority of Nearspace inhabitants, I'd never traversed the Split.

Naturally, I'd read all the data about it, and even had Luta describe it to me. Despite not being an engineer, I know how wormhole travel works; skip drives generate a thin layer of Krasnikov matter, which keeps the wormhole from destabilizing while a ship is inside it. Alternating positive and negative energy pulses allow the ship to skip through the tunnel-like wormhole, protected by a Ford-Roman field. The field repels from one side of the hole, and the ship slides around to bounce the next time off the other side, creating a water-going-down-the-drain effect. That's the experience.

But the Split is essentially only half a wormhole. Once inside, the usual tube-like passage is more like the half-pipe used in extreme gravity sports. One half of the tube reflects the wild swirl of colour found in any wormhole. The other half of the tube, however, is simply a plain grey haze. A ship spinning over to that side would simply punch through and careen off into— no-one knew where. Wormhole spelunkers—a few—had attempted it and never returned. Nor had any probe. No sensors have picked up useful readings for what's beyond it. So, the pilot must manage to keep movement caused by the Ford-Roman repulsions constrained to a much narrower area. I'd never seen it done.

Now we had to consider that maybe something survivable lay beyond that hazy curtain.

But we were not here to find that out. We were here to run a normal skip—or what passed for normal in the Split—and take readings. That was it.

My heart beat abnormally fast as my mind raced. I turned my focus to Luta, facing the wormhole with aplomb, and felt better. I realized suddenly that I'd been taking cues from her for as long as I could remember.

Despite Luta's calm confidence, the mood on the bridge was tense. I sensed it in the clipped, intense way the crew spoke to each other, running checks. It thrummed in the air, a sense of heightened alertness. It made me wish I had something productive to do, but all I could do was sit and watch as the wormhole terminal opened and we slid inside.

The colours of the safe side of the Split blossomed before us, the cloudy side looming opposite like a crouching animal. Rei swung the ship along the safe side, coming heart-stoppingly close to the demarcation between the two sides, and then slid us back in the other direction. The ship careened side to side like a pendulum as the swirling plasma slid beneath us.

"Scans are running, Captain," Yuskeya said. She watched the wormhole unfold through the viewscreen, glancing down at the readouts on her screen occasionally. "Huh," she said suddenly.

"What?"

She turned slightly to face Luta. "Remember those grey striation lines we noticed in that first wormhole from Delta Pavonis into the system with the operant moon? They're here, too."

"Is that new? Or did we not notice them before?"

Yuskeya frowned. "Hard to say. We could easily have missed them before. It's a distracting place."

"But they mean that at some point, this wormhole has been ghosted," Luta said. "Affected by an operant device."

"Which could account for the malformed side," Hirin added. "Fha told us that ghosted wormholes sometimes suffer anomalies or damage, right?"

"And it could mean that the Chron—the Pitromae—are ghosting it now, to get into Nearspace," Luta said. "All right, that's a helpful observation, Yuskeya. Rei, anything out of the ordinary?"

"Struggling to hold us to one side," Rei said in a strained voice. "So, absolutely normal for the Split."

Moments later we emerged from the other end of the wormhole, into the quiet emptiness of GI182. I felt an odd mix of elation and disappointment. I'd been through the Split, had finally experienced the odd and dangerous wormhole first hand. But we didn't seem to have discovered anything striking that would help with the current problems.

Luta responded to the Protectorate vessel that hailed her to check on our status, then turned to Rei. "We'll go back through once Viss has a chance to re-check the drives, all right? Are you up to it?"

Rei nodded as she massaged her hands. "That'll take him an hour, if I know Viss. By then I'll be good to go. Hands need a little break, that's all."

I stood and crossed to Luta's chair. "You think there's still more to find?"

She half-shrugged. "Quite possibly. And it's still the fastest route back to FarView, right?"

Jahelia Sord stood from the secondary engineering console. "I'll go down to engineering and offer to give Viss a hand, Captain."

Luta nodded. "Come back up when we're ready to go."

After the first few exciting minutes of talk about running the Split itself, since I was the only person on the bridge for whom it was a new experience, the next hour passed as slowly as if we were stranded on the event horizon of a black hole. The only break in the monotony came when Sedmamin appeared on the bridge, asked where we were, and returned to his quarters with a sniff. Yuskeya and Rei huddled over a screen, running through the data we'd collected, and the rest of us made stilted attempts at desultory conversation. It was a huge relief when Jahelia returned and Viss assured Luta over the comm that everything was in order and the ship was ready to make the skip back to Delta Pavonis.

Luta apprised the Protectorate ships that we were ready to go, and with little fanfare, we approached the terminal point. The dark mouth of the wormhole, once again painted with streams of colourful plasma, swallowed us up.

This time I saw the grey lines Yuskeya had mentioned. I'd never observed them in a wormhole before, which apparently meant I'd never been through a wormhole that had been ghosted. This was good; it meant that few of the Nearspace wormholes had been affected by the ghosting technology.

No-one commented on anything else unusual as the *Tane Ikai* swung pendulum-like across the safe side of the wormhole.

"Rei, you all right?"

"Fine," was Rei's clipped reply. I wondered if we should have given her a longer break between forays into the Split.

"You're doing great," Luta reassured her. "The ship feels rock solid. Viss, everything okay on your end?"

Whatever Viss's answer would have been, we never got to find out.

WE'D SWUNG FROM side to side five times, which, judging by the previous skip, meant we were about halfway. I didn't expect anything untoward to happen, despite all of Regina's admonitions about what Luta should do if it did. With one uneventful skip just behind us, I'd relaxed.

I was completely unprepared for a gaping hole to open in the gauzy grey half of the Split just ahead of us, and a Chron ship to come screaming through.

We'd swung almost to the limit of a left-hand arc, so we weren't directly in its path. The offset wasn't much, but it probably saved our lives.

Rei gasped. Luta jumped up from her chair. Jahelia Sord swore. "*Merde!*"

The Chron pilot slid to our right as far as possible, but the wormhole was only large enough for one ship at a time. This was why Nearspace had strict protocols regulating the use of tracer pings to ensure that a wormhole was empty of other traffic before any ship entered. If Mauronet had destroyed the ship he'd followed—or if they'd met with misfortune—the Chron likely remained confident they had the Split to themselves. They didn't expect company.

But there we were. We clung to the side, the Chron ship swerved, but it wasn't enough. The impact was a bone-jarring shudder that resonated through the entire ship. I hadn't stood or moved from my chair, only grasped the arms when the rift in the wormhole had appeared, so I guess I was more stable than the others. They were occupied with screens and tasks, or like Luta, had stood or half-started from their seats at the intrusion. Despite the intensity of the jolt, it seemed surreal because it wasn't accompanied by the flare of shields that would normally happen when anything impacted or came close to impacting the ship. *No shields inside a wormhole*, I reminded myself. I wondered if the hull had been breached and felt a rush of relief that no siren had begun to sound. Then I realized that Luta's ship might not even have such a thing. This wasn't a Protectorate vessel.

I saw Luta stumble and Rei rock sideways in her chair, one arm flying out to try and steady herself while she kept the other one on the board. It wasn't enough. Our precarious hold on the safe side of the wormhole slipped from her grasp and the *Tane Ikai*'s aft end swung crazily toward the hazy unknown.

"Rei!" Luta shouted, steadying herself with her console. She made a lunge toward the auxiliary pilot's board, but it was too far, and too late. The ship careened past the safe zone, spun now almost a full hundred and eighty degrees. The viewscreen showed the Chron ship as it ricocheted away from us, bilious gas streaming from a truncated wing, bright fingers of plasma arcing in a web across its ebony surface as if searching for a way inside. It tumbled into the multicoloured swirl of wormhole plasma and shattered like glass. Black shards erupted from the point of impact to be swept into the maelstrom of colour.

Viss's voice resounded over the comm. "Captain! What's happening?"

But no-one answered him. We were too busy staring in horror as the *Tane Ikai* twisted around again, showing us the dark, gaping mouth in the gauzy arc of the wormhole as we tumbled toward it.

"Rei, can we—" Luta gasped as she half-fell into the auxiliary pilot's chair.

Rei had regained her balance, and her hands flew over the control board. She was shaking her head, though. "Lost it. We're completely out of control."

Alin Sedmamin's voice came over the comm, thready with fear. "Captain! What's wrong? Are we under attack?"

I wasn't sure what he expected to attack us *inside* a wormhole.

"Not now, Chairman," Luta managed. "Brace yourself and shut up."

A dozen commands clamoured for me to say them, but with an effort I clamped my mouth shut. This wasn't my ship, not even a Protectorate ship, and half the things I wanted to say probably wouldn't even make sense.

Hirin shouted, "Viss! Switch to maneuvering drives!"

Luta turned to look at him. "What about the skip drive? We'll lose the Ford-Roman field. We'll be crushed if the wormhole collapses!"

Hirin looked at the hole in the grey side of the Split. "We'll be inside that in seconds. Something else is holding that one open. We don't want to interfere with it."

"And we might need some kind of control once we're in," I said, understanding what Hirin was saying. My voice sounded like a mere croak but I think Luta must have heard me.

"*Merde!*" Luta swore. "Shut it down, Viss! The instant it's safe, I'm going to raise the shields. Rei, whatever we slide into, just try to get us out. Maneuvering only."

"Sord, keep things running. I'm coming up there," Viss grunted over the comm.

"Got it," Jahelia answered him. I looked over and saw her frown of intense concentration as she took control of the auxiliary engineering board. The hum of the skip drive died and I had just enough time to look up at the yawning hole on the viewscreen as we skidded through it and into the unknown.

THE BLACKNESS OUTSIDE lasted the space of a few heartbeats—I know because mine was pounding as if trying to fight its way out of my chest. On the bridge, the overhead lights flickered off, leaving only the eerie glow of the active boards to illuminate the space. The ship shuddered as its momentum battled Rei's attempts to bring it under control with the maneuvering drives, but I felt it catch the swirling plasma of the new wormhole and steady. Now we spun along the inside of the tunnel as we would a normal wormhole, and multicoloured streaks of plasma coiled along the inner walls of the wormhole like variegated lightning.

Viss gained the bridge and crossed with purpose to where

Jahelia sat, glancing up at the viewscreen as he went. He snagged an empty skimchair in passing and slid it next to Jahelia, but didn't nudge her aside at the board. "What's that *bastardo* done to my ship?" he asked no-one in particular. "And where the hell are we?"

"Bumped us into a ghosted wormhole—or something," Luta answered, "And I don't know. I didn't even know two wormholes could intersect."

Viss shot her a look of complete incomprehension. "That's not possible."

"Tell that to the Chron."

"We're in a wormhole with no Ford-Roman field?" Viss asked, incredulous. "We should be dead already."

"I'm sure there are answers, Viss, but I don't have them," Luta told him. "Stay tuned."

He pressed his lips together and turned his attention back to the engineering board.

It felt like a normal wormhole skip now, even without the hum of a skip drive and the curiously dark wormhole interior. The usual visual of multiple rainbows spinning down a drain had been replaced by rivulets of colour streaming across black glass. But we corkscrewed smoothly around the inside of this new wormhole.

"Damage?" Luta asked.

"I'm almost sure there's no breach," Yuskeya said. She'd been quiet up to now, and I realized that she'd been running damage checks without waiting for Luta's order. I almost smiled. That was Yuskeya; quietly proactive, seeing what needed to be done and doing it. "The dockside door into Cargo Pod One might have lost its seal, though. The brunt of the impact was there."

"No cargo in that pod that should be affected," Maja said. My niece's voice was thin, but steady.

And then we flew out of the wormhole.

"Shields up!" Luta ordered.

"Main drive coming online," Jahelia said. "Rei should have full power in thirty seconds."

"Scanning the system," Yuskeya said. "Navigation data log initiated. I've designated this system OS-05 to start. I'll add the spectral data on the stars when we have it."

I stared out the viewscreen at the system that opened around us. A planet hung not far away, wreathed in cloud layers that revealed browns, greens, and blues where they parted. I didn't immediately recognize it, but that didn't mean anything; apart from a few in Nearspace that had notable features, most habitable planets were visually similar from a distance. A star burned beyond it against the dark of space, bright white and similar to Sol as viewed from Earth; but it could have been larger and further away, or smaller and closer. After a moment, I realized that a more distant light signalled a binary star system. A largish moon, grey and pockmarked, orbited the planet, and a smaller one hung nearer the wormhole terminal point. To starwise sprawled a gas nebula, iron-red in the centre and splaying fingers of blue and green emissions into space.

"It's the system from the PrimeCorp files," I said, but no-one noticed because Yuskeya spoke at the same time.

"Two ships on long-range," she said. "Moving, possibly toward us."

"Identification?" Luta asked.

"Too far away yet."

"Nothing on any communications channel," Baden reported. "No signals coming from the planet. Start a scan for habitation?"

"Yes, and let's move away from the wormhole," Luta said after a moment's hesitation. "We don't want to be discovered here yet. Let's try to catch our breaths. Rei, get the planet between those ships and us."

"The wormhole has closed," Yuskeya added. "Reverted back to inactive."

"Let's look up the records of exactly what the Corvids told us about ghosted wormholes," Luta suggested. "Maja, would you do that?"

"Aye, Captain." Maja's fingers flew over the screen in front of her as she searched the ship's database for the information. I tried to remember what I'd read in Luta's report, but I thought that any poorly-recalled details I might contribute would not be useful at this point.

Alin Sedmamin arrived on the bridge then, looking frightened and angry and cradling one arm to his chest. I couldn't see blood, but lines of pain had etched themselves across his gaunt face. He stared up at the viewscreen. The system was obviously neither Delta Pavonis nor GI182, to anyone familiar with them. "Where are we? What happened?"

No one answered for a moment, then Luta said, "We collided with a Chron ship inside the wormhole and were bumped into another one. We ended up here."

"Bumped into another what?"

"Another wormhole."

"How is that—" Sedmamin broke off and tried again. "But where's *here*?"

"I think it's the system those secret PrimeCorp files mentioned," I repeated, when no-one else answered.

This time it got a reaction. Luta looked up sharply at the viewscreen. "Really? You think so?" After a moment, she pursed her lips and nodded. "Yes. It fits, doesn't it? And really, where else would we *expect* to wind up?"

"I thought if we found this system, it would be full of PrimeCorp ships and Chron," Hirin said. "That it would be a hub of activity."

Jahelia shrugged. "Could be more of a waystation *en route* to somewhere else. Or maybe they're all in Nearspace already."

"Don't even say that," Luta said sharply. "All right. Let's start a scan of the planet. We're here, we might as well collect as much information as we can."

"There's nothing here about how long a ghosted wormhole might stay open," Maja said, studying the screen. "But I wonder if that smaller moon is an operant device. If so, we should be able to open the wormhole again ourselves when we're ready. We still have the activator the Corvids installed."

"Can someone look at my arm?" Sedmamin asked in a surprisingly subdued voice. "I fell and twisted it when—when the other ship hit us, I guess. I don't think it's broken, but it hurts like hell."

Luta glanced at me. "Lanar, could you take over Yuskeya's board if she takes the Chairman to medical?"

I nodded, and for once I saw a slightly rebellious look cross Yuskeya's face. I didn't blame her—who'd want to leave the bridge right now to see to Alin Sedmamin? But typically, she said nothing in protest, simply stood and motioned for the Chairman to follow her as she led the way to the medical bay. On the *Tane Ikai*, she was the resident medic.

It's been a while since I ran much navigation, but I could see what Yuskeya had going. "We'll lose the ships in a few minutes, once the planet's between us, but they're still heading in this direction," I told Luta. "Not travelling particularly fast, so I'm guessing they haven't noticed us."

"Let's keep it that way for now," Luta said.

"They're probably on their way to the wormhole," Hirin guessed.

I felt my jaw clench reflexively. If the ships were Chron, and headed to the wormhole, they were on their way to Nearspace. My instinct was to intercept and destroy them, but I knew that wasn't an option. This wasn't my ship, for one thing, and that wasn't my mission, for another. But it was hard to know they were passing so close and I could do nothing to stop them. I had to console myself with the knowledge that a Protectorate force waited for them at either end of the Split.

"Planet seems uninhabited so far," Baden said. "But it's a big place. No definitive answer for a while. But nothing coming from the continent below us. Emissions in the atmosphere suggest lots of ships have come and gone."

"Jahelia," Luta said, "Could you call up those files on Pita, the ones Sedmamin said referred to a system and planet that weren't identified? I want to know for sure if this is it, and if so, what we might find here."

"Sure thing, Captain. But you could have asked me yourself." The voice made me look up, and I realized it was Pita, not Jahelia Sord, who had answered. Jahelia's datapad rested on the console beside her, and I guessed the AI was always listening. Good to remember.

Sedmamin came back onto the bridge then, his arm in a yellow plasticast. He went to the viewscreen and looked out, studying the planet. Yuskeya came after him and crossed to the nav station, which I vacated for her.

"This is the place?" Sedmamin asked.

Pita spoke up with his answer. "Captain, I've calculated a 95% certainty that this is the system mentioned in the PrimeCorp files. The description and the system data fits, and we know there's access from Nearspace. If we can find the location on the planet that's pinpointed in the file and there's anything of interest there, we'll know for sure."

"All right. Yuskeya, could you set up a scan using the data in the PrimeCorp file? Get it to define the equator and locate the prime meridian as it's described. Then run latitude and longitude lines and find the spot mentioned in the file."

"Will do, Captain,"

Luta sat back in her chair. "All right. Assuming nothing attacks us in the next little while, I think we need a plan."

"Fight Chron, find the treasure, escape back through the wormhole," Jahelia offered with a grin.

"Sounds like a plan to me," Hirin agreed. "Save Nearspace should be in there somewhere, though."

"And save Nearspace for Gramps," Jahelia confirmed.

It was the first time I'd seen Luta smile all day.

Chapter 20 — Luta
What the Mountain Hides

I TOLD REI to stay in the scan shadow of the planet until the Chron ships had time to arrive at the wormhole and skip through. Then we edged out to check. The wormhole terminal point lay closed and quiet, and the ships were gone. I let out a breath I'd been holding forever. It seemed we'd gambled right.

Everyone had gathered on the bridge. Scans of the planet had completed and Yuskeya had found the mountain peak that marked the prime meridian—it was taller than all around it by a good hundred metres. With that located, it had been a relatively simple matter to calculate longitudinal lines. The planet's rotation showed us where to place north and south poles, and with those in place we could define an equator and the rest of the latitude lines. Yuskeya laid in a course that would take us over the coordinates noted in the file, and Rei took us into orbit above it.

From up here, there was little to see.

An argument had broken out about how to run the recon. Viss, Yuskeya, and Hirin came down on the side of continuing to sweep and scan the area from orbit, looking for anomalies or anything suspicious or out of the ordinary, until we had an idea of what might be down there. I felt that this was reasonable for an initial approach, but that a ground search would soon become necessary. Lanar sided with me. The others were carefully non-committal.

"Finding something from way up here is only going to take us so far," Lanar said, drumming his fingers on the co-pilot's board. It wasn't active, so Rei was obviously trying to ignore it and not be irritated with him. I knew that part of his fidgeting was due to not being in command, an unusual and probably not-very-comfortable position for my brother. "We want to go back to Nearspace with more than an unidentified blip on a scan. We need solid information."

"This is PrimeCorp," Hirin said. "If there's something down there, the whole area could be booby-trapped, rigged, watched, or patrolled by drones or paramilitary—you can't put anything past them. If this is something so big that they've been hiding it for over a century in a system outside Nearspace, they won't have skimped on the security."

"Or it could all be a red herring," Maja said. "There might be nothing there at all. Just a hoax to keep the Protectorate occupied if they ever managed to discover it."

"I think that gives them too much credit," Lanar said.

"Or they might have been so sure they wouldn't be discovered by accident that they kept security to a minimum, knowing that it would be less likely to attract attention by mistake," I said.

"That sounds likely, to be honest," Sedmamin said. He'd found an empty skimchair and sat, cradling his plasticast-encased arm with the other. "PrimeCorp is cagey. And they have a very realistic understanding of the scale of Nearspace. The chances of a secret base on an uninhabited planet in a hidden system being discovered by anyone—that would seem almost infinitely improbable."

Lanar nodded. "So they'd keep security to a minimum, to save money and divert attention. Everything could be automated, just to keep an eye on things. Someone discovers the system—not likely in the first place—and they're quietly silenced. The security threat is very small. The Split's rarely used, so who's going to go through it *and* get diverted into the unknown system?"

"Us," Rei said, throwing a grin over her shoulder. "But we all know how exceptional we are."

"You think PrimeCorp won't even see us coming?" Viss scoffed. "You're underestimating them."

I stood up from my chair. "Well, arguing is getting us nowhere," I said. "Let's do a detailed scan of the area and see what shows up. When there's something new to look at or argue over, we'll do that. In the meantime, I want a constant scan for other ships in the area, out to the edge of our range. I want to know the instant we have any company. I want to know if anything happens with the wormhole. And now I'm going to get something to eat."

That, at least, was hailed as a good idea, and Maja came with me to the galley. We heated pasta and sauce for everyone and took it back to the bridge. We didn't talk much while we got it ready. I don't know what was on my daughter's mind, but I was seriously questioning the wisdom of what we were doing. Should we be trying to get back through the wormhole and home instead? But although we differed on how to approach the problem, everyone did seem to think investigating was the next step.

We ate in relative silence, too. I was scraping the last of the pasta sauce from my bowl when Yuskeya said, "I've got it."

She'd put her bowl down beside her console. "I'll put it up on the main screen, will I?"

I nodded. "Otherwise everyone will be breathing down your neck."

The image of the planet below us flickered. Now it showed the planet surface, but traced in layers of colour that overlapped, merged, and flowed over the topographical features of the landscape as well as delving the depths of the earth.

I studied the tracery of colours and lines, trying to read features and clues in their intricate patterns, but soon gave up. "You'll have to tell me what I'm looking at, Yuskeya," I said. "This looks like a beautiful abstract painting to me, not a secret operations base."

Yuskeya chuckled. "I wouldn't call it a base. Not like the thing is jumping out at us. But . . . an anomaly." She got up from her chair at the nav board and went to the screen. "This is a mountain," she said, pointing to an area that obviously rose from sea level green through a series of gradations to a dark rust colour at the peak. "But if you look closely here," she circled her finger in an area on one side of the mountain, "you can just make out a pocket of shadow—and it's a little pinker."

"That means hollow," Jahelia said, nodding.

"*Probably* hollow," Yuskeya cautioned. "I'm not making any promises. But it would be a logical place. And difficult to spot, even with the depth imaging, unless you were looking for it."

"What are all these shapes?" Maja asked, pointing.

"Seems like a lot of rock formations in the area," Yuskeya said. "They're too irregular to be anything constructed."

"And here?"

Yuskeya pursed her lips. "That does look different," she said. The area lay a short distance away from the mountain. "More regular."

"Could be discarded equipment, maybe," Baden suggested

"We need to get on the ground," Lanar said, "and have a better look."

"Still seems dangerous," Hirin said. "What about a closer fly-over?"

"That'll give us away entirely, Gramps," Jahelia said. "A ship randomly buzzing a mountain on the side of an out-of-the-way planet? Sure, nothing suspicious about that."

"We could be prospectors," Hirin said huffily. "Or explorers. It makes as much sense as putting people on the ground to investigate."

I put a hand on Hirin's arm. "Except that there shouldn't be either in this system. You're both right. If we're spotted, anyone is going to be suspicious, no matter how or what we're doing. The best course of action is not to get spotted." I looked around at the assembled faces. "Which means small vehicle, on the ground, being as unobtrusive as possible. While a larger vessel, say a ship, provides a distraction by appearing to look for something else if it's spotted."

It was a good plan, and they knew it. But everyone waited to hear what Hirin would say. "And who goes down to the surface?" he asked.

"Me, Lanar . . . and Jahelia," I said carefully. "And Sedmamin."

Sedmamin began to splutter and Hirin opened his mouth to say something, but I held up a finger. "If Lanar or I run into trouble, we'll heal faster than anyone else," I said. "And Jahelia and the Chairman might still have special PrimeCorp access, or other knowledge or information. They might be useful."

It was a good explanation, and Hirin could see that, too. Of course, my real reason for including Jahelia was that she had the same nanobioscavenger advantages Lanar and I had, but I wanted to keep my promise and not mention that to anyone who didn't already know about it.

Hirin contented himself with shaking his head. "I don't like it. It's a good plan, but I don't have to like it, and I don't," he said defiantly. "But all right. Let's get the ground car ready. Planetary data says the atmosphere is breathable, so you have that going for you," he said. He pointed a finger at me. "You're not going unarmed," he stated unequivocally.

"Excellent," Jahelia said, and started for the weapons locker.

"I can't use a weapon with this arm," Sedmamin complained, holding up the plasticast.

"Don't worry about it," I said, patting him on the shoulder as I passed. "I wasn't going to give you one, anyway."

I WENT TO change my clothes into something suitable for planet exploration, and Maja followed me into my quarters.

"Are you sure this is smart?" she asked, folding her arms across her chest and leaning back against the edge of the desk while I rummaged in the dresser. "Shouldn't one of you—you or Uncle Lanar—stay on board in case something goes wrong?"

"That's why I'm leaving your father in command," I told her, pulling a dark, long-sleeved t-shirt from a drawer. "And Yuskeya is here, too. Your uncle and I can heal quickly if anything goes wrong."

"I thought Dad had the same things now, too," Maja said.

I caught my breath a little. Was she waiting for the day when her grandmother would offer her the nanobioscavengers, too? Was she hurt that it hadn't happened yet? I was certain Mother would do it—in her own time, and when she thought she and Maja could talk about it dispassionately. I suppose I was waiting for the same thing, to bring it up with my daughter. Maybe it was cowardly. But there wasn't time to tackle it now.

"Your father has improved so much, it's true—so much of the damage done by the virus is gone," I admitted. "But he's still older, and he hasn't had the benefit of the bioscavs all these years. He's the best one to stay with the ship. It makes no sense to leave Lanar, and I have to—"

She smiled reluctantly. "You have to keep everyone on track," she said. "I know. That's what you do best."

"I do?"

Maja crossed the room and gave me a quick hug. "Yes. You do. So, I guess you'd better go and do it. Just be careful, all right? I hate that you're going into a total unknown."

"Not total. We're pretty sure that someone from PrimeCorp will be down there," I said, pulling on a short brown canvas jacket.

"Great. I feel so much better now," she said, and we hurried back to the bridge.

Chapter 21 — Lanar
Secrets and Allies

LUTA DECIDED TO keep the *Tane Ikai* well away from the mountain. We didn't know what we might find there, but anything PrimeCorp saw fit to hide away on an uninhabited planet inside a mountain was worth investigating. Rei set the *Tane Ikai* down about an hour's distance by groundcar from the suspect mountain. They'd stay only long enough for us to set out, then return to orbit. From there, they'd monitor what we were doing, watch for approaching ships or anything coming out of the wormhole, and scan for drive signatures or debris that might offer a clue about the *Dorland*. We could signal the ship at any time to come back and collect us.

Meanwhile, Luta, Jahelia, Sedmamin, and I would take the groundcar and, as unobtrusively as possible, make our way to the mountain. We'd find out as much as we could and retreat. That was pretty much the entirety of the plan.

If the mountain turned out to be guarded by real manpower or weapons power, we'd retreat, regroup, call the ship back to the surface to get us, and come up with another plan. Maybe just turn tail, head for the wormhole, and send back reinforcements. I wanted whatever information we could take back.

I wasn't sure about Luta's insistence that Jahelia Sord and

Alin Sedmamin come with us. Sedmamin, I expected to be more trouble than he was worth, and I didn't expect he'd have much to contribute.

I still didn't know much about Jahelia, but I'd had the impression that Luta didn't particularly like her. I'd been mildly surprised to find her still in the picture—but they appeared to get along fine now. Her attitude was . . . confusing. She pretended to be mockingly amused by everything and everyone, and yet somehow looked for approval, too. She was openly rude, and yet the crew tolerated it with no more than mild annoyance. Maybe their shared experience on the Relidae station had bonded them.

As I checked my weapon and a few other gadgets, I considered my own feelings about Jahelia Sord. They were almost as confusing as her relationship with the others. She was attractive, no doubt about it. I'd seen enough rare smiles on her pixie face to know that they transformed her. Her brown eyes held a different emotion every time I looked into them. But her personality conflicted me the most. Half the time I wanted to shake her, and half the time I wanted to—

A knock sounded at my door. "Come in," I called, slipping the laser pistol behind my back and into the waistband of my jeans.

Luta opened the door and poked her head inside. "All set?" she asked. She'd changed from a shipsuit into her trademark jeans and switched to a dark t-shirt. For a change, she'd foregone the somewhat flamboyant long dark leather coat for a shorter, closer-fitting brown jacket. I grinned inwardly, thinking of what her reaction would be if I described anything about her as "flamboyant."

"Ready to go." I put a hand on her arm, stopping her when she would have turned away again. "Luta, do you really think Sord is the best one to go with us? And do we need Sedmamin? We'd move faster on our own."

Luta crossed her arms and leaned against the door frame. "Sedmamin may have passcodes that will work down here—or there may be biometrics—or he may have more information than he even realizes. Or will admit to. I know he claims not to have known anything about this, but it's possible he's lying and it will take being on the spot to get it out of him. Jahelia is—

handy. Especially in an unknown situation. You'll have to trust me on that one."

"I know. It just seems—odd. I mean, Yuskeya or Viss, even Baden if you want to leave Hirin in charge of the ship—"

She grinned and repeated, "Trust me, Lanar. I know what I'm doing."

"And what you're doing is keeping secrets from me? Not very sisterly."

Her face fell a little and I knew I'd struck a nerve. "You know what it's like with secrets," she said diffidently. "They have to be yours to tell. I would if I could, Lanar. I will if it's necessary. Can you live with that?"

"I guess I have to." I made a mock-pouting face. "I'm discovering that I strongly dislike not being in charge."

She patted my cheek lightly. "Poor baby. Feeling naked without all the pretty starbursts on your shirt?"

"Absolutely." I shepherded her out the door and closed it behind us. "And the first thing I'm going to do when I get them back is impound this ship and throw you in the brig for being mean to me."

"I'll tell Mother," Luta warned. "She always liked me best."

"And I'll tell Regina you want to join the Protectorate."

Luta laughed. "*Okej*, let's call it a draw. I don't want to pit Regina and Mother against each other."

The door across the corridor opened and Jahelia Sord emerged. She wore dark pants tucked into low-heeled brown boots that rose almost to her knees and a dark blue jacket. She'd pulled her light brown hair into a knot low on her neck, and it made her look older—or at least more serious. The strap of a small cross-body bag stretched over her chest, and in her right hand she carried the plasma rifle she'd chosen from the weapons locker. When she saw us, she grinned.

"My two new best friends," she said. "This should be fun, going exploring together."

So much for being more serious. "Is everything a game to you, Ms. Sord?" I asked her before I had time to think about it. I'd decided earlier that I wouldn't respond to her baiting. I knew it was exactly what she wanted. Her grin widened.

"Everything is a game, Protectorate. When life gets too serious, all the fun goes away. And I'm all about the fun."

"PrimeCorp isn't, and neither are the Chron," I shot back. "If you're looking for fun, you might be in the wrong place."

She chucked me playfully on the shoulder. "That depends entirely," she said, hefting the plasma rifle, "on your definition of fun."

I couldn't think of a suitable reply to that, so I merely shook my head, edged past her, and followed Luta down the corridor to the hatchway. It led down past the engineering deck to the cargo pods below, where the groundcar waited for us to drive out onto the surface of the planet. Hirin and Viss had already checked it over, and Sedmamin stood to one side of it, looking put-upon.

I guessed that he didn't own much in the way of clothing suitable for exploring, so he'd borrowed a dark shipsuit and thrown his own jacket over it. The plasticast on his injured arm extended out of the jacket's sleeve. He looked fidgety, and I thought maybe he'd had to borrow the boots, as well. I wondered idly who would have willingly loaned them to him. No-one came to mind. Luta might have had to persuade someone to help out.

"Sedmamin," I said, nodding to him. I wouldn't call him "Chairman" the way Luta still did.

"Admiral." He glanced at Jahelia and Luta but said nothing to them. Maybe they'd been shipmates long enough that formalities were no longer necessary. "Do you think this is going to take long?"

"It'll take as long as it takes," Luta said.

"Oh, good, we have a timeline," Sedmamin snapped.

"Hang on!" Baden hurried down the ladder and crossed to Luta. He glanced at me before handing something to her with a few whispered words. It turned out to be a little gadget of illegal manufacture, and he wasn't sure how I'd react to his owning one. Technically, I could have arrested him for it, but I felt it was in the service of Nearspace to let it slide. The gadget had a few functions, including some facility in disabling electronic systems easily and from a distance. It might work if we turned it on the defence systems, scrambling their signals and allowing us to take them out without too much trouble.

Baden helped me unlock the docking clamps while Luta, Jahelia, and Sedmamin climbed in. By unspoken agreement, they left the driver's seat for me. That surprised me. I'd expected Jahelia Sord to insist on driving, but she seemed content to share the second row of seats with Sedmamin. We exchanged a few last comments and checks with the bridge via ship's comm, and then the big pod bay door slid open and bright sunlight invaded the cargo pod. I blinked, and Luta rummaged in one of the storage compartments, finally handing me a pair of sunglasses. She slipped on some of her own, and I glanced back to see that Jahelia and Sedmamin had found some as well—on consideration, I figured Sord had brought her own. The open top of the groundcar wasn't going to provide us with much protection from the elements. I was just glad it wasn't raining.

Baden had reported warm temperatures in this region of the unknown continent, and I felt the sun's heat as soon as we rolled out of the cargo pod. This region was predominantly sandy and desert-like, scattered with sparse greenery as if a giant hand had sprinkled it at random, like a garnish on an unappetizing meal. A river flowed down the side of the mountain where we expected to find the PrimeCorp setup, and ran in our direction, giving rise to a swath of verdant greenery that ended abruptly where the river's influence trickled out. Except for this defiant patch of forest, the landscape was sand-red and dusty, studded with tall hoodoos and other odd rock formations thrusting striated fingers to the sky. I worried that the groundcar would kick up a visible dust trail, but Luta thought we shouldn't worry about it until we were closer to the mountain.

"They're not crazy enough to monitor the entire damn planet, I hope," she said. "What would be the point? I'm assuming that the Chron already know this is here, so who would they even be hiding it from?"

"I'm not willing to take bets on the relative sanity of PrimeCorp," Jahelia Sord said from the seat behind us.

I pointed us in the direction of the mountain looming red and barren in the distance, and drove.

WE DROVE IN relative silence for about twenty minutes before we came upon the first ruins. These were the shapes Maja had asked about on the projection. It was plain now that these were the configurations we'd seen, the remains of a group of structures. I slowed the groundcar as we came up alongside them, so we could all get a closer look.

Sandblasted and worn by wind and elements, partly standing and partly toppled, they spoke of a long-ago walled habitation. Great chunks of stone formed platforms and foundations. Roofing that might have come from the nearby forest had long since decomposed or crumbled away.

"Seems like PrimeCorp isn't the first to have set up base here," Luta said. "Do you think this was once a Chron settlement?"

The ruins looked nothing like the elegant architecture I'd seen on Tabalo—didn't seem as if they ever could have been buildings like the ones I'd seen there. "And what happened, whether it was Chron or someone else? Are there more like this around the planet, I wonder?"

"Could have been a species we haven't encountered yet," Luta said. She'd pulled out her datapad to record some images.

"We're in completely uncharted territory here," I said, craning my neck to see more of the ruined structures. "Whatever it is and whoever built it, it's been here an awfully long time."

I'd slowed the groundcar to a crawl as we studied the ruins, which was probably why I heard the humming noise as soon as I did. It rose in volume and dropped in pitch, as if it was getting nearer. I looked around. "Anyone else hear that?"

Both women had weapons in their hands almost as soon as the words were out of my mouth, and surveyed the surroundings. "Better get moving again," Luta said. "Maybe we shouldn't have stopped."

"I knew this was a bad idea," Sedmamin said. "PrimeCorp would have security on any secret installation, no matter if it was outside Nearspace. There are others out here who could find it too, and they'd want to protect it from anyone."

I urged the groundcar back up to speed, but even over the sound of its own hum the other noise grew. Jahelia had stood in the back seat, gripping the roll bar with one hand while the other arm cradled her rifle. She scanned the sky behind us. "I don't see anything."

"I do." Luta pointed ahead of us and up, and if I squinted I could just make out a descending shape.

"Sit down!" I barked at Jahelia, and she lowered herself to the seat.

"Turn around and call the ship!" Sedmamin demanded. "You're driving us straight into danger. I'm going to lodge a formal complaint with—"

"Survey drone? Security?" Jahelia asked, cutting Sedmamin off as she leaned forward and squinted up, too. "Maybe we should cut over closer to the treeline."

But that was easier said than done. The ruins we had stopped to look at stretched on for some distance, the remains of blocky walls and toppled buildings creating an extremely inconvenient barrier between us and the trees. I'd have to slow considerably to weave between them, and slowing down didn't seem smart.

The humming increased. "There's another one!" Luta shouted as a second shadow joined the first. "Hey, maybe—" She rummaged in the pocket of her jacket and came out with the gadget Baden had given her.

"You think that might shut them down?"

She shrugged. "Possible. Worth a try." She aimed the scrambler in the direction of the drones and thumbed a switch on the top. I waited, hoping for the sound of a change in the drone's hum, but it didn't come.

"I'll change the settings, but I have a feeling it's not going to work," Luta said. "Drones probably have a blocker to stop exactly this kind of interference."

Jahelia stood again, steadying the plasma rifle on the rollbar. She aimed into the sky, but she didn't have the range.

"Too far!" I told her.

"I know that," she said witheringly. "I'm just setting up. They are going to get closer, if Baden's little toy doesn't work."

"I know. Hold on." I took a chance and turned the groundcar into a space between two collapsed buildings, where they had conveniently fallen in opposite directions and left a clear gap.

A whistling hiss split the air and Luta yelped.

"Incoming!"

Something bit into the ground ten metres from us, throwing up a blinding gout of sand and dirt when it exploded. I swerved the groundcar, but the encroaching ruins made maneuvering difficult. I worried that we'd be stuck or hemmed in, but the ruins afforded the only cover.

"If you stop for a minute I might get a shot," Jahelia yelled.

"Do not stop!" Sedmamin demanded. His voice was muffled and I guessed that he'd slid to the floor and had his head down.

"Risky," Luta argued. "It's a small target and I don't know how effective a plasma rifle will—"

Another *something* punched into the ground nearby, and I realized the drone had a larger payload than I'd thought. I hit the accelerator, and we hurtled forward past a section of ruined wall that still stood three times as high as the groundcar. I could try to get in close for cover, but with the drone overhead there were few places to hide.

"Make for the trees," Luta urged.

"I can take them out," Jahelia argued. "There are only two of them."

"For now." I didn't have words to waste as I struggled to keep the groundcar under control. It wasn't built for chases, and the wheels dragged in the soft, sandy earth.

The hum of the drone faded and then changed pitch, circling around for another run. I swerved around a pile of rubble, looking for a path to the protection of the trees.

"*Fek* this," Jahelia muttered.

"Sit down, Sord!" Sedmamin roared, and I thought he was trying to tug her into her seat. I don't know why he was so insistent that she not shoot at the things, but maybe he thought return fire would bring reinforcements. Maybe he knew more than he'd let on.

A muffled thump and a grunt from Sedmamin told me she'd kicked him off.

She stood again, setting her back and elbow against the rollbar for stability. As the drones' hum rose like angry insects homing in on prey, I heard the low *whoomp* as the plasma rifle spat a gout of crackling energy. The rising hum faltered as Jahelia whooped and a wave of heat hit the back of my head. I braked, turning to see what had happened, and one of the drones slammed into an upright section of the ruins to my right. It exploded in a burst of black smoke, and chips of stone rained down on us.

The second drone banked up and away, to circle around and return for another run.

"Can we make the treeline?" Luta asked, brushing bits of

stone and dust from her hair.

"Maybe." Another collapsed building blocked the route I'd thought would give us a clear run to the trees, and I had to turn hard left to avoid the rubble. This put us on what might once have been a road, flanked on either side by buildings in various stages of decay. If I could get to an opening—

Sedmamin had gone strangely quiet, perhaps shocked into silence by the destruction of the drone. We sped among the ruins as the sound of the second drone returning reached us.

"Keep us steady. I'll get this one too, Protectorate," Jahelia Sord told me over her shoulder.

"Not sure what you mean by steady," I replied. "This isn't exactly the boulevard outside PrimeCorp Main. If I come to an opening on the right that might lead us to the treeline, I'm taking it. I'll try to warn you."

"Fair enough," Jahelia said. "Captain, get ready to back me up if I miss. You might be able to drive it off while I recharge, which I'll have to do after this shot."

"I'll try," Luta said, but she sounded skeptical. "It would be better if you don't miss."

Jahelia Sord laughed, such an incongruous sound that even in the circumstances, I smiled.

The buzz of the drone rose, and we'd almost reached the end of the ruins. No opening had offered itself on the right, but the left-hand line of collapsed buildings ended abruptly up ahead. Going left would put us more in the open, but we wouldn't be hemmed on both sides.

"Slow down, Protectorate," Jahelia called to me over the rising sound. "I've got it lined up. Let it get closer."

Sedmamin moaned wordlessly. I thought he must be back on the floor again.

"You sure?"

"Trust me."

I didn't want to, and yet, suddenly, I did trust her. At least in this. I eased off the accelerator and let the sandy, rock-studded ground pull at the wheels, slowing us.

A burst of dust and rock erupted from the ground a mere metre from the left front wheel, peppering me with debris. The drone was too close. "Take it out!"

"Closer . . . closer . . . almost," Jahelia coaxed. I heard the whistle that signalled another projectile from the drone, and at the same time I felt the *whoomp* as Jahelia fired. The dark shape of the falling drone cast a shadow over the groundcar and I realized how incredibly close she'd let the thing get before taking her shot. I felt the impact of the missile as it hit the groundcar and heard the explosion of the drone at the same time.

"*Merde*," I heard Jahelia Sord swear, just before the world exploded and everything went black.

WHEN I OPENED my eyes, I couldn't see past the edge of the ruins. Smoke and dust hung in the air in all directions, slowly settling. I lay on my side, curled in an almost fetal position; I must have been trying to protect my head. The sky had darkened, but as I blinked debris away from my eyes I realized that airborne dust had blotted out the sun. A quick inventory, flexing muscles and moving my hands, arms, and legs in tiny increments, revealed nothing broken, and I sat up gingerly. My right sleeve felt sticky, glued to my skin with fresh blood. I pulled back the fabric and saw a long gash—probably from a piece of the shattered drone. The bleeding had already stopped, so my nanobioscavengers were working. I let the sleeve fall back into place. My laser pistol had landed only inches from my side, and I snatched it up with almost palpable relief.

Silence. No sound of drones. But nothing else, either.

Luta and Jahelia. And Sedmamin, although I didn't care nearly as much about him. I felt an immediate jab of guilt for that thought, but it was the truth. They could have been thrown any distance when the drone hit us and the groundcar rolled. No wonder so much dust and smoke filled the air. I wished the wind would pick up and start clearing it away; I couldn't see far in any direction. I risked a low call.

"Luta? Are you there?"

A low, smothered cough reached my ears. "Behind the wall. Sord's here, too."

But not answering for herself. Not good.

Keeping low, I scuttled toward my sister's voice. The half-wall I guessed she meant was only metres away, and I covered the space with as much alacrity as I could, keeping the pistol in my hand. The ruined stones made crawling impossible unless I wanted to shred my knees and hands on the sharp edges. I got my feet under me and crab-walked as quietly as possible on the sliding shards and pebbles.

When I rounded the jagged end of the wall, I found Luta leaning with her back against the rubble. Dust and sand had smeared light streaks through her dark auburn hair, and smudged one cheek and her chin. Still, when she looked up and saw me, she smiled. The relief in her green eyes shone through the smoky air.

Jahelia Sord lay beside Luta, eyes closed, head pillowed on Luta's rolled-up jacket. A dark red patch matted the hair on the left side of her head, but Luta said, "A cut, but not a bad one. Must have been a piece of flying stone. It's clotted already, so I didn't bother trying to clean it up any. Just start it bleeding again."

I nodded. Luta's weapon lay next to her knee, but I didn't see the rifle Jahelia had carried.

I was struck again by the quiet. Only the soft settling of dust and debris filled the air around us. No sound of enemies approaching, on foot or overhead. For that I was profoundly grateful. A few moments to think, that was what we needed.

"What about you? Are you all right?" I asked Luta.

She grimaced. "My right ankle has seen better days, but hey, the nanobioscavs should be moving into position even as we speak, right?"

It was true, and I let myself breathe out a long slow breath.

In the moment, I'd been thinking the way I would if I had any of my usual companions with me—people without the benefit of microscopic internal surgeons ready to go to work and fix things. If I'd had any of my crew with me, a broken ankle would have been a real impediment. Luta, however, only needed some time. If Jahelia Sord's injuries weren't too severe, and Sedmamin was all right, we could get them back to the pickup spot.

"What about Sedmamin? Any sign of him?"

She shook her head. "I didn't see him. I managed to drag Sord here so we'd have some cover, but the smoke was too thick."

"*Okej*, this is a good place for you to hunker down and wait for the crew to come and get us," I said. "You called them?"

Luta made a rueful face. "They should have been notified when I blacked out, thanks to a little something Baden set up in my implant a while back. I tried a direct call anyway. No response."

"What?" I pulled back my sleeve and activated my implant; we'd synced it to the *Tane Ikai's* comm system when I'd come on board. "Hirin? Baden? Anybody listening? We need immediate pickup."

I waited, counting heartbeats, but there was no response. I frowned at Luta. "What's wrong with it?"

She shrugged wearily. "Your guess is as good as mine. Something's wrong with the ship and they can't answer; our implants were damaged in the accident; something triggered a communications block on the planet or this area; maybe they hear us but we're just not getting their response. Take your pick."

"Doesn't seem likely that both of our implants were damaged," I said. "But maybe they're on the way."

"Maybe," she said, but she didn't sound convinced. "I think we should proceed on the assumption that there's no help coming from that quarter any time soon."

"All right. I'll look for Sedmamin." I risked standing up for a look around.

The groundcar lay on its side ten metres from us. Two tires looked intact, the other two buried in the sand. It looked like the drone had hit the back end a glancing blow, so there was twisted metal and a hole where the storage compartment used to be. I thought we could probably get it moving again. Righting it on my own would be a challenge, but if we could get it upright, we might be able to drive out of here. The question, however, was where to go? On toward the mountain, or back to our rendezvous point? And would someone—Chron, PrimeCorp, or other unfriendlies—come looking and simply follow our tracks in the sand?

On the other hand, if we stayed here, they were just as likely to investigate. No good options.

I surveyed the area. The ruins were just that—ruined. They offered no place we could shelter under or inside. I might be able to rig up some kind of roof or shade if there was a tarp in the groundcar, but again, it would make us too obvious for anyone looking. I had to do better than that.

But first I had to find Sedmamin. Keeping low again, I scuttled over to the groundcar. If he'd been trapped underneath it, it wouldn't be pretty.

Fortunately, he was on the other side, sprawled on his stomach, his injured arm flung out to the side. I watched for a moment, trying to decide if he was breathing, and saw his hand twitch. I crossed to him and knelt in the sand, putting a hand on his shoulder.

"Sedmamin," I said. "Wake up. I want to get you out of the open."

He groaned and moved his head. "*Fek,*" he managed. "I'm going to kill Sord for this."

"Not her fault," I said. "She probably saved all our lives."

"Well, I want to kill someone," he said, cradling his injured arm as he tried to get to a sitting position. "Maybe Regina Holles. If it wasn't for her I wouldn't even be here."

I almost laughed, thinking what fun Regina, a *zelendu* master, would have physically kicking Sedmamin's *azeno*, probably even with her broken leg. Keeping that to myself, I helped Sedmamin to his feet and led him, hunched over to protect his injured arm, to where Luta and Jahelia waited.

Should we still try to make the short trek to the forest and get in under its sheltering green canopy? The vegetation that sharply demarcated the edge of the desert was thick, verdant, and looked imposingly dense. We couldn't guess what kind of wildlife it sheltered, or how deadly or unwelcoming it might be. Still, we did have weapons, and we'd be out of the sun and away from prying eyes.

And probably totally lost within hours.

Frustrated, I looked down at Luta. She'd closed her eyes. The pain in her ankle must be fierce, but she must have felt my eyes on her and looked up. She smiled.

"Pain's already fading," she said.

"You'll feel better soon," I said. Even though it hardly mattered now what he knew about us, I hesitated to mention the nanobioscavengers in front of Sedmamin. Old habits, I guess. I squatted beside her. She put a hand to my face gently, and when she took it away it was bloodied.

I put a hand where hers had been and felt the wet heat,

although it already felt sticky, congealing. *"Damne*, I didn't realize," I said.

"Here." She reached inside her jacket and pulled out the hem of her t-shirt, then ripped a strip free. She passed the makeshift cloth to me and I wiped and blotted my face as best I could. It stung a little, and more blood than I'd expected came away, so I had to imagine that mother's little machines were hard at work in me, too.

I tried to hand the cloth back to Luta but she held up a hand. "Please," she said with a smile that was only half grimace, "just keep it."

I smiled back and pocketed it. "Now, as long as Sord's injuries aren't extensive," I said, "we should be able to move her once you're feeling stronger. Sedmamin can't help much with that arm of his, but we can manage her together."

Something passed over Luta's face, a look I couldn't parse. "What?"

She pulled a sigh and looked at Sedmamin again, but he'd leaned his head back against the low wall and had his eyes closed. "We probably don't have to worry about Sord," she whispered.

"What? Why not?" I looked down at Jahelia in confusion. For a moment, I thought Luta meant the other woman had died, but the soft rise and fall of her chest was evident.

"Jahelia Sord has more in common with us than you'd think," Luta said, still keeping her voice low. "Her father worked with Mother. She's only a couple of years younger than we are. As in, actual age."

I felt my throat go dry and tried to swallow, but it was as if I had taken in a mouthful of the dust and sand that swirled around us. *We weren't the only ones?*

I'd encountered many things in my years at the Protectorate, things shocking, gruesome, frightening, unbelievable. But this made the world tilt. I felt my legs go watery and leaned a hand against the ruined half-wall, hoping Luta wouldn't see.

"H—how did you find out?" I had to force my voice past what felt like a gritty blockage in my throat.

Luta looked out across the expanse of sand separating us from the trees. She shrugged. "She told me, when we were stranded in Otherspace. Her parents had them, too, and both died. Her mother first, and then her father. They didn't have the same generation, the same prototype, and her father didn't have the means to keep updating his research and creating new versions. Eventually they failed."

I gestured to Jahelia. "What about hers?"

Luta looked down at the still-unconscious woman. "I think—and Mother thinks—she's due for upgrades. Mother's willing to provide them. But I haven't convinced Jahelia yet that it's necessary." She quirked a smile. "She's as stubborn as an Erian snowcat, in case you hadn't noticed."

Before I could answer, Jahelia Sord's dark brown eyes flickered open. "I'm right here, you know. Ouch. *Merde,* what's wrong with my head?" Her hand came up to gingerly touch the matted spot. Luta reached out and caught her wrist.

"I think a piece of flying stone caught you there," she said. "It's probably healing now, because the bleeding stopped pretty quickly. But don't touch it until we're sure it's closed, *okej*?"

Jahelia dropped her hand obediently.

"How do you feel, otherwise?" Luta asked her.

After a moment of cautious consideration, Jahelia said, "All right. Nothing feels broken or otherwise in need of repair." She gasped. "Pita?"

Luta reached into the folds of the rolled-up jacket and pulled out the datapad. She handed it to Jahelia with a grin. "A few scratches, but she's still functional."

"I am, thank you, Captain," Pita said.

Jahelia sat up and brushed dust and sand from her arms. "The more I encounter them, the more I think those Chron are complete *bastardos.*"

"Huh. You think the Chron are responsible for the drones? I thought it was PrimeCorp."

"Seems to be less difference between them all the time."

I held out a hand to her to help her to her feet. She hesitated for a heartbeat and then took it. After divesting herself of more accumulated dust and sand, she turned to offer Luta a hand.

"Not yet." She pointed to her ankle. "I—twisted it, but it's starting to feel a lot better now. Another half hour or so and I should be able to stand on it."

Jahelia nodded and flicked her eyes toward Sedmamin. "Technology comes in handy at times like this," she said.

"Have you had many times like this?" I heard myself ask.

She turned amused eyes on me and grinned. "More than you might imagine," she said. "Maybe sometime I'll tell you about them."

I felt the beginnings of an inexplicable flush on the back of my neck and turned to look at the overturned groundcar. "We're not getting a response from the ship. If that thing's still usable, we could follow the treeline and see how close to the mountain it takes us. Might as well see what we can."

She scanned the surroundings and considered the groundcar. "Not a bad idea. Can we flip it over?"

I'd thought Luta might help me, but Jahelia seemed just as capable. "Sure. Luta, you're all right here for a minute?"

She grinned and lifted the laser pistol from the sand beside her, saluting me with it. "I'm not going anywhere. And I've got this. I'll be fine."

I stuck my own pistol in the waistband of my pants. The groundcar didn't look any better than it had a few minutes ago, but I didn't see any additional damage. We were fortunate that we'd all been thrown clear enough to avoid being crushed when it overturned. We trudged across to it, our feet sinking in the dislodged sand. The dust and smoke were clearing some and we had better visibility of the area around us.

When we reached the vehicle, I kicked dirt and sand away from the two buried tires. If they were busted, righting it wouldn't help. Jahelia Sord walked in circles around the groundcar, head down to scan the ground. Looking for her lost rifle, I realized.

Luck was with us and the two exposed tires looked intact. "I think we're good if we can turn it over," I said. "Just be careful around the rear. Lot of sharp edges there."

She abandoned her search and came over to me, taking up a position on the upper side of the vehicle and putting her hands on the roof edge. "Count of three?" she asked.

I nodded and made the count, and we pushed. The groundcar wobbled and lifted a bit, then settled back into the sand.

"Okay, that was just a test, right?" she said with a grin. "We can do better."

"Of course, we can."

I dug my feet into the soft ground for better purchase and counted again. This time it came up about halfway, but then slid away from us and we had to let it drop back.

"*Bastardo!*" Jahelia swore under her breath, then turned those brown eyes on me and grinned. "Swear a little yourself, it's a great stress reliever. I'll pretend I don't hear if it makes you more comfortable."

"We'll get it this time," I said. "Ready?"

"Whenever you are, Protectorate," she said, rubbing the palms of her hands on the smudged and dirty thighs of her pants.

And this time we did make it, and the groundcar rose, teetered for a moment, and then tipped over onto all four wheels, landing with a little bounce. Sand poured from the side that had been half-buried, then trickled off.

I glanced over at Luta and she gave us the thumbs-up. She still wasn't testing her ankle, which indicated unusual patience and good sense for my often impetuous sister. Either that, or it was still giving her a lot more pain than she was letting on, and the nanobioscavs were going to take longer to set her right.

Jahelia Sord walked slowly around the groundcar, inspecting it. "Banged up some, but it doesn't look too bad," she said. "If it starts."

"One way to find out." I climbed inside as Jahelia began kicking through the sand where the groundcar had lain—still looking for her rifle, I assumed. The electric motor hummed to life after only a slight delay, and I turned to catch Jahelia grinning at me. In her hand, she held the missing rifle.

"Maybe our luck is changing," she said, and swung herself up into the seat beside me.

"It'll have to change a whole hell of a lot," I said.

"Then it's a good thing I found my lucky gun," she said.

"Didn't you just get that out of the weapons locker on the ship before we came down here?" I asked.

"Doesn't mean it's not lucky," she said, and had the audacity to wink at me. "Let's go collect your sister and Sedmamin, and see what's inside that mountain."

Chapter 22 — Luta
Discovery and Unmasking

I GRITTED MY teeth as the groundcar lurched across a particularly rock-strewn stretch of sandy earth. I wasn't letting on to the others, but my ankle throbbed alarmingly even as my nanobioscavengers worked (I hoped) to heal the break. It must have been bad, because usually the small amounts of chemical nerve-blockers they'll construct are enough to reduce the pain to manageable levels. I tried to ignore it and keep my eyes on all sides, watching for more drone attackers.

Alin Sedmamin grunted in the back seat beside me as the groundcar hit another half-buried obstacle and bounced on its tires. He cradled his injured arm, even though it still bore the yellow plasticast. "Must we go this fast?" he snapped at Lanar. It was a ridiculous question, but pain made his voice harsh.

My brother didn't answer, but Jahelia Sord turned to look at Sedmamin over her shoulder. "Unless you can guarantee that there aren't anymore drone surprises waiting for us, I don't think we want to hang out here in the open."

Sedmamin didn't answer, just pressed his lips together and didn't meet Jahelia's eyes. I expected this was all quite a kick in the teeth for him, to learn that there were so many things PrimeCorp had done without his knowledge, even though he'd ostensibly been the head of the entire corporation. If I believed him about his ignorance. I wasn't entirely sure.

One way to find out, I thought. "So, you didn't know anything about this base?" I asked him over the jouncing of the groundcar.

"Not until recently," he said, and his voice held a grim simmer of anger.

"But you must have known PrimeCorp had a big secret," I pressed.

He barked a laugh. "Everything at PrimeCorp was a big secret," he said. "Even I didn't know how big."

"But the collaboration with the Chron?" I said, as the green of the forest flashed by to our right. "That's huge. I don't see how you couldn't have known about that."

Sedmamin kept his eyes on the mountain ahead of us. "Not all that long ago I learned we had some Chron tech. That sometimes we could get something from it, reverse engineer some 'innovation' and pass it off as original work. But PrimeCorp had that project underway long before I came on the scene, remember. I was told it was technology or artifacts that we'd acquired during the Chron War, and simply never reported to the Nearspace Authority. Questionable, but nothing to get too excited about."

He looked at me. I shrugged. "The Authority might disagree with that, but compared to some of the things PrimeCorp has done, failing to report spoils of war is tame."

Sedmamin went on. "That sector operated entirely separate from the rest of the corporation, and that's the way it had always been. They were described as a research branch, and there was the understanding that what they 'researched' was old Chron technology. But I realize now that anyone who got too interested was quietly diverted until they lost interest. I think that being Chairman looked like the top job at PrimeCorp, but it was still far below these people. They held the single most important asset and secret the corporation had, and they protected it against everyone else."

There was a sharp, bitter edge to his voice that surprised me. But Alin Sedmamin prided himself on being a master manipulator. It must have been the most bitter pill imaginable to realize he had been the one manipulated. That he wasn't trusted with the most vital secret of the corporation he fondly thought he controlled.

I almost felt sorry for him.

We stopped talking as the mountain loomed closer and Lanar slowed the groundcar. Everyone was on the alert now, listening for the low hum of more drones and watching for movement ahead of us or behind. Even the dense forest felt like it held many eyes silently watching us.

"No tracks along this trail," Lanar said over his shoulder, addressing all of us. "No recent groundcars, or footprints, or any other kind of vehicle or movement from this direction."

"Maybe the entrance isn't on this side," Jahelia said.

"No," I said, pointing ahead. "There it is." I'd just seen it, in a dark recess under an enormous overhang of rock. A giant entry door. No detail at this distance, but it was tall and too smooth to be a natural rock face. Metal, painted to blend in with the mountain. "Look how well that would be hidden from above, too. You'd never notice it unless you were down here on the ground."

Lanar brought the groundcar to a halt and flipped open the console between the two front seats. He rummaged inside and brought out a miraculously undamaged zoomlens. He studied the mountain through it for a moment and then handed it over to Jahelia. I tried not to feel wounded that he hadn't offered it to me first.

"It's a door, all right," he said, moving the groundcar forward again and steering us over to run right along the edge of the forest. Any advanced surveillance would see us, but more casual scrutiny might not. "And there are tracks in front. Can't tell how recent they are."

Jahelia put the zoomlens up to her eye again. "Not long ago. The wind would have scoured them away with all this loose sand and dust."

I looked a question at Sedmamin and he raised his eyebrows. "Really, I don't know," he said. "If there are recent tracks, I guess we're in the right place. There was nothing in the files to indicate that whatever was here had been moved."

Pita confirmed, "No, there was nothing like that. I mean, we had to figure out that the references in the files even *were* about a secret base, so it's not like they were going out of their way to record everything. But if they noted these coordinates, then it makes sense that if they'd moved, they would have recorded those coordinates, too."

"Unless this base was discovered, and they didn't want to take any chance with the next one," Lanar mused.

"Well, we're not going to find out anything sitting here. Just stay alert, the closer we get," I said. My ankle still throbbed, making me cranky, and I didn't feel like getting blown up twice in one day. I glanced at the sky. Still no word from the *Tane Ikai*. I didn't want to think about their silence, or why they weren't already here. When I'd been knocked unconscious by PrimeCorp operatives on the planet Rhea, the little monitor that Baden had surreptitiously installed in my ID implant had alerted the ship right away and the crew had come to rescue me. I'd certainly been knocked out in the drone explosion. Had the ship not received the same message this time?

I pushed these worrisome thoughts away and concentrated on the mountain looming ahead of us as we sped along in the shadow of the forest.

Nothing seemed to notice us. Not while we kept to the treeline, not when we stopped to study the mountain from a mere hundred metres away. Not when, throwing caution to the winds, we drove the groundcar under the canopy of trees for cover, and left it to creep cautiously on foot to that big camouflaged door. I was still limping, but the painkiller function had finally kicked in. I could put almost my full weight on the ankle now, so maybe it hadn't been broken.

The lack of security around the presumed base was puzzling. The two drones that had attacked us had been high-tech defence, although I'd assumed that they were being controlled by an actual person who had us on a screen somewhere. It was possible, I thought now, they'd been completely automated, programmed to attack intruders who crossed some invisible line and to follow certain assault paths until either the intruders or the drones were destroyed. If the base was still operative, it didn't feel like enough security.

We stood just out of sight of the doors, clinging close to the rocky side of the mountain. Sedmamin's annoyance had turned to agitation. "This doesn't feel right," he'd said as we got closer to the mountain with no sign of further interference. "They wouldn't do this—leave it unguarded. It must be a trap."

Jahelia shook her head and murmured, "You're looking at it the wrong way around. If this is a PrimeCorp installation, and they're working with the Chron, who do they need to protect it from?"

Lanar nodded. "Because no-one else from Nearspace was ever able to get here before this—"

"And presumably there's no need to protect it from their business partners, the Chron. If there are no other known races that even come to this system, then what's the point in having resources dedicated to security?"

"But what about the drones?" Sedmamin asked. "They were pretty determined to stop us."

Jahelia shrugged. "Insurance. If someone *did* stumble in here by accident—someone they didn't want snooping around— the drones are a good deterrent. And a good early warning system. They were probably programmed to deploy if anyone approached the mountain from any direction and got close enough."

I peered around an outcrop of rock to look up at the big double doors. They were as tall as those on the *Tane Ikai*'s cargo pod bays and almost as wide. Something big could move in and out of here. The sandy ground in front looked windswept, but crisscrossed by discernible wheel tracks. Some of the loose rock and sand almost looked as though it had been kicked around in a scuffle, but that might be just my imagination. The overhang of rough stone felt very heavy, looming twenty feet above our heads. It protruded far out over the doors at its thickest point, casting the area below into heavy shadow even in the bright sunshine of the day.

"So, if the drones are an early warning system—how come no-one has been warned?"

Jahelia shouldered her plasma rifle. "That's the next question," she said. "And the answer is behind these doors."

"All right, let's have a look," Lanar said. He reached into his pocket and pulled out something small, which he clipped to the lapel of his jacket. "Just so you all know, I'm recording what happens from here on in." Then he stepped around to survey the front of the doors. "Control panel on the right-hand side," he reported. "Looks like standard PrimeCorp technology. Sedmamin, Sord, this might be why we brought you along," he said, throwing a grin back at us.

"There are lots of reasons you brought me along," Jahelia said, "and most of them are more important and interesting than opening doors. But I'll give it a try if you say please."

"Let Sedmamin give it a try first," Lanar said. "And we'll save your talents for later."

Jahelia grinned at Lanar and I felt a little off-balance. Were they *flirting* with each other?

"This is not going to work," Sedmamin said, but he followed Lanar over to the control panel. A red light burned weakly above a biometric pad and an implant reader. He stood looking at the implant reader for a long moment, and I could guess what he was thinking. Using that reader might alert PrimeCorp immediately where he was, whether the panel allowed him to open the door or not. Using it could be a big risk.

"You can let Jahelia try first," I told him.

He sighed. "No use. I don't think the clearances I set up for her would work here—since I didn't even know that this existed. I'm doubtful even mine will, but I suppose it's worth a try. They might have been lazy and just copied permissions wholesale." He met my gaze. "Just remember that you're supposed to protect me, all right?"

"I'll do everything I can."

"All right then." He held his forearm against the implant reader and the red light began a slow blink. Then he put his index finger into the biometric reader, all the way to the second knuckle. The red light shifted to yellow and blinked faster. I don't know about anyone else, but I held my breath.

The light flashed green and an audible *clunk* sounded somewhere inside. With a whoosh of air like a quick intake of breath, the doors parted and began to slide sideways into the mountainside.

I DON'T THINK any of us really expected it to work. Sedmamin started visibly when the doors parted, and Jahelia hefted her plasma rifle to an easier firing position. Lanar pulled the pistol from the back of his waistband.

No alarms sounded; no-one appeared in the doorway.

"This is weird," Jahelia said. "I don't trust it."

"Me neither," I said. "Stay put for a minute." Even though

the ship still hadn't responded to my earlier messages, I sent another one, letting them know we were heading inside the mountain. Just in case they were receiving.

"That's all we can do," I said. "Let's see what's inside."

The space beyond the doors looked like an abandoned loading dock. Dimly lit, the room was a couple of stories tall and perhaps twenty metres square. On the back wall, another implant reader guarded a second set of doors as tall as the outer ones. A few large pieces of machinery sat idle next to the walls, and the concrete floor bore multiple greasy-looking stains. Despite the meagre tracks or markings in the sand outside, there were plenty in here. Groundcars and other vehicles had moved about, been parked, and come and gone, leaving their marks on the floor. Likewise, many booted feet.

"They go to a lot of trouble to erase most of the evidence of activity outside," Lanar said.

"Or it's easily swept away by the wind," I said. "It's the same question as the security—why go to any trouble at all when there's little likelihood of anyone finding the place?"

Jahelia had the rifle up, sighting around the room, but the place was quite empty. "Will we see what's behind the next door? Not much happening here."

Sedmamin stared around the space with a look of mild distaste. I imagined that as Chairman, he'd rarely had occasion to visit dirty rooms where physical work happened.

Then I started to notice things I hadn't before. "Lanar, Jahelia," I said in a quiet voice, "take a close look around this room and tell me what you see?"

Jahelia frowned at me but swung her head around, looking the room over. "Huh," she said.

One of the vehicles had a shattered windscreen, cracks spiderwebbing out from a central hole. Another had a similarly damaged side window. One rested on a flat tire. Looking up from some shards of glass on the sand-strewn floor, I saw why the lighting was low—several of the HPS lights had been damaged.

"Look at this," Lanar said, and knelt to touch a fresher-looking stain on the floor. His fingers came away stained sticky and dark.

"Blood?"

He nodded. "Looks like PrimeCorp should have spent more on security after all."

Lanar's discovery lent the quiet a suddenly discomfiting edge.

Wordlessly we followed Lanar and Jahelia to the doors at the back of the space. Jahelia stepped aside and motioned Sedmamin to the implant reader with a flourish. "Do the honours, Chairman."

Sourly, Sedmamin repeated the ritual that had opened the outer doors. The lights went through their sequence again, but this time continued to flash yellow, never moving to green. A screen glowed to life, with six input blocks. Sedmamin stared at it.

Lanar looked at me and I shrugged. "Higher security for this door? Any PrimeCorp ID might get you in the front door, but you need top clearance to go further?"

"Sounds likely. Chairman, you have a guess?"

He frowned at the input screen. "Six-digit codes are not a norm. All PrimeCorp passcodes are either five or twelve."

Jahelia said, "What about that gadget Baden gave you? Just because it didn't work on the drones doesn't mean it's useless."

Damne. I'd hoped no-one was going to ask about that. I shook my head. "Crushed in the accident. I left the remains back there."

Jahelia frowned. "I might have been able to do something with it."

"You didn't see it. It was smashed beyond recognition. A section of the drone landed on it."

"All right," Lanar said. He turned to Jahelia. "Anything your AI friend can do here?"

She pursed her lips. "Pita? I doubt it."

"Hey!" Pita piped up. "I resent that."

"Oh, calm down. I just meant that if my clearance is no good—"

"But *you* didn't download all those tip-top-top-secret files into your memory, did you?" the AI asked with a definite smugness. "I've actually compiled a database of codes, passwords, and data fragments that might be access codes, from those files. So, you might at least let me make the attempt."

Jahelia rolled her eyes. "*Okej, okej.* You're not contractually obliged to live up to your name."

Lanar and Sedmamin looked blank, but I knew Pita's name was an acronym for *pain-in-the-ass*. That wasn't what made me smile, though. It was how irritating Jahelia Sord obviously found the AI, especially considering that it was based on her own personality.

"Try this," Pita said, and rhymed off a six-digit alphanumeric string. Sedmamin keyed it in, in case there was a biometric aspect to the keypad and it was reading his fingerprint as well.

Nothing happened.

Pita offered a second code, but it bore no better results.

"How about this one, then?"

Sedmamin huffed but punched in the six digits.

This time a deep boom echoed from the other side of the doors, and like the first set, they parted in the centre. Still no alarms sounded and the place remained deserted of everyone but us.

"This is eerie," Lanar said, and I had to agree.

But sheer awe replaced the mystery of the situation when we moved carefully to the opening in the doors and looked into the room beyond. It lay in darkness, but as we moved cautiously through the open doors, motion-activated lights sprang to life around the room, illuminating the looming dark shape within. I heard Lanar suck in a whistling breath between his teeth.

It was a Chron ship.

It stood on an open grid metal platform perhaps six feet above the floor of the cavern, some of the high-powered lights trained directly on it. A single-pilot fighter from the Chron War era—Cerevare Brindlepaw had shown us images of ships from the time, when she travelled with us. It was not completely intact—parts of the fuselage had been removed, exposing the inner workings of the craft, and the body of the ship itself had been separated into three segments; nose, midsection, and aft. Scattered around the room were diagnostic consoles, minutely dismantled electronics, and piles of other mechanical parts that could only have come from the inside of the ship.

"*Merde*," Jahelia Sord said, a hint of admiration in her voice. "They had a Chron ship, and they took it apart."

"Had it for a long time," Lanar said. "This is a relic from the Chron War."

We moved toward it with halting steps, awed by the sheer improbability of its presence. Sedmamin stopped at a distance from the ship, glaring at it with his hands on his hips. I could guess what he was thinking—this should have been *his* secret. Jahelia crossed to a nearby computer console, intent, I guessed, on finding out what data it held. But Lanar and I both kept going, to stand beside the section of fuselage on the floor. Lanar put a hesitant hand on the sleek metal.

"This is a piece of Nearspace history," he said, and I nodded.

"The Chron War always seemed so long ago," I said, "but lately I feel like it's been running to catch up with us."

"I think it's been closer than we thought for a long time. Now we have to make sure it *doesn't* catch up."

"This data goes back . . . decades," Jahelia said. I glanced over and saw that she had her datapad—and therefore, Pita—sitting on the console. No doubt the AI had helped her gain access. Sometimes I thought Pita could be the most dangerous thing PrimeCorp had ever produced, and they didn't even know it.

"Copy what you can," Lanar said. "I'm going to get a closer look." He pulled himself up onto the platform and peered into the cockpit of the ship.

I caught Sedmamin's eye and he shook his head vehemently. "No. I did not know."

I believed him.

But while Lanar and Jahelia were distracted by our findings, I noted that there were two more doors at the back of the room. I didn't think we should ignore them.

"Give me your laser pistol," I said to Jahelia.

"What makes you think I have one?"

I simply looked at her, and she grinned and pulled it from her boot, handing it over without further comment. With it in hand, I went to the leftmost door and listened at it. Only silence. Carefully, I put a hand on the handle and eased it open. A light clicked on and startled me, but it revealed only the stark utility of a washroom. The room was empty of inhabitants and I relaxed.

I closed the door as Lanar jumped down from the platform with a rueful grin. "Sorry, I got a little swept away by the past, there," he said. "Good thing you're still thinking."

I was about to suggest we check the other door when it opened and a voice stopped us in our tracks.

"Admiral Mahane, how nice of you to drop by. And you brought the traitor with you." Admiral Antar Mauronet stepped into the room and shut the other door behind him. More shocking than his sudden appearance and the wild, almost manic look on his face was the handgun he held, trained directly at Alin Sedmamin.

I WISHED I'D stayed behind the shadowed tail of the Chron ship a moment longer.

"Admiral Mauronet," Lanar said easily, although I knew his mind must, like mine, be racing. Where had the admiral come from, and what was he doing here? Was he responsible for the damage—and the spilled blood—in the outer room?

"Good to see you in one piece," Lanar continued. "You followed that Chron ship into this system?"

"Lower your weapon," Mauronet said, ignoring Lanar. I realized he was looking directly at Jahelia.

"I don't think so," she said lazily. She still stood beside the computer console, but her plasma rifle was up and pointed directly at the admiral. "I don't know you or what you're doing here, so I think a nice safe standoff is how we'll play this for now."

"Was there anyone here when you arrived?" Lanar continued, as if the little by-play between Mauronet and Jahelia hadn't happened.

"Just some technicians," Mauronet snapped. "I've put them all in detention until I can figure out what's going on here. PrimeCorp has a lot to answer for." He spoke to Lanar, but he kept his eyes on Jahelia.

"Where's your crew?" Lanar asked. He hadn't moved, just stood casually where he'd stopped, but he still held his own laser pistol—he'd had it out since before we entered the outer room. He'd relaxed his arm so that hand hung just a little toward the back of his leg, making the gun less obvious from where Mauronet stood.

Mauronet motioned with his head to door he'd just come through. "I have officers guarding the detainees in the offices back there. I sent the ship on a scouting mission to look for a way back to Nearspace. Can't get the wormhole to open with a standard skip drive. They'll be back soon to get us," he said, eyeing Lanar coldly. "What are you doing here, in a secret base filled with illegally held technology, and *him*?"

Sedmamin said in a voice tinged with desperation, "I didn't know about this part of it, Antar. The Chron part. You must realize that."

Wait, *Antar?* Sedmamin had called Mauronet by his first name. They knew each other?

Lanar must have been as taken aback as I was, but he said, "It's true. He wasn't responsible for any of this. He's here on the orders of Fleet Command, assisting us in a reconnaissance mission."

"Fleet Command," Mauronet snorted, walking a little closer to Sedmamin. Jahelia followed him with her weapon. "Regina Holles, I suppose you mean. You know what this looks like to me, Admiral? It looks like maybe I wasn't the only one who put my trust in the wrong place."

Lanar shot a glance at Sedmamin, but his face revealed nothing. "I don't know what you mean, Mauronet."

"I could take him out," I heard Jahelia whisper, just barely loud enough to be heard. I was sure Lanar caught it, but Mauronet probably did, too. If so, he ignored it.

Lanar shook his head minutely but didn't look her way.

"PrimeCorp screwed us both over, Antar," Sedmamin said. "They were dealing with the Chron behind our backs."

Mauronet spat on the concrete floor. "I figured that out when the PrimeCorp ship came out of the wormhole with two Chron. And messaged me to help them! After all the risks I took—"

Lanar twitched as if something physical had hit him. "You. You were the mole in the Protectorate," he said in a flat voice. "The one who was leaking information to PrimeCorp."

"He thought what many in Nearspace think," Sedmamin said. "That the Worlds Council is ineffective and doesn't get things done, and that if PrimeCorp was in control of Nearspace it would be better for everyone."

"But you didn't know they were in league with the Chron," Lanar said.

"Shut up, traitor," Mauronet told Sedmamin in a growl. "I should shoot you right now."

"I did not know about the Chron," Sedmamin said slowly. "I'm here trying to help stop this."

Lanar had recovered his equilibrium. He spoke to Mauronet in an artificially friendly voice. "Look, Mauronet, we don't like each other very much, but we're both loyal to Nearspace. Let's concentrate on getting back there in one piece and then we can sort out all the rest. Were any of your crew wounded? We saw blood in the outer room."

"No-one was wounded but the PrimeCorp traitors," Mauronet snarled. But he wouldn't be so easily distracted. "And why should I believe you? You're not even in uniform. Sneaking around with that sister of yours, just one step short of a criminal. Maybe not even a step."

Lanar tensed at that, but kept his head. He and I—and Jahelia—might heal quickly, but we could still be killed if Mauronet decided to shoot. And Sedmamin was the most vulnerable. Our best chance was to keep Mauronet talking.

"You'll have to prove that," I said, to give Lanar time to think, "or I'll see you in court back in Nearspace. That sounds like slander to me."

Mauronet didn't have a chance to respond because the right-hand door in the back wall opened and two Protectorate officers, a man and a Vilisian woman, emerged and closed the door behind them. At this distance, I couldn't see their starburst pins well enough to determine their rank, but they took only a few steps toward Mauronet until they followed his gaze and saw us.

"I'd stop right about there," Jahelia said. "Your Admiral is having a chat with our Admiral, and it's all nice and cozy so far."

"Admiral?" one of them said uncertainly.

"Are the prisoners secure?" Mauronet barked at them.

"Yes, sir," the woman answered. "But the injured one needs medical assistance. We heard voices and thought the ship—"

They must be waiting to hear from the *Dorland* the same way we were waiting to hear from the *Tane Ikai*. I wondered if the two ships had possibly encountered each other, and felt suddenly glad I'd left Yuskeya on board. At least we had a Protectorate presence up there.

"Not yet," Mauronet snapped. "Get back in there with the prisoners. I can manage out here."

The male officer looked askance at the four of us, two obviously armed, and then at Mauronet. He was severely overmatched if we chose to make this violent, and they could see it. Then he looked sharply at Lanar. "Admiral Mahane?"

"Commander Yu, isn't it?" Lanar returned.

"Yes, sir! Good to see you, sir!" He stared at Lanar now as if he were trying to convey a very important silent message.

"Admiral Mauronet, will the Admiral and his companions be making camp with us while we wait for the *Dorland?*" he asked carefully.

"What?" Mauronet seemed about to explode, then went suddenly quiet. "Yes, of course, Commander. You're quite right. They should stay here until the *Dorland* arrives."

"We're just waiting for my ship as well," I said, "but they've been out of communication. I'm starting to wonder if signals off or to the planet are being blocked. Could we question your prisoners about that? They may know if it's a security measure."

Mauronet's face became crafty. "I'm afraid I can't allow civilians to interact with the prisoners," he said, "but I will see what they have to say about this." He pointed at Sedmamin. "Alin. Come with me."

Sedmamin spluttered. Mauronet waggled the gun at him.

"Go ahead," Lanar told him. "The Admiral is not going to harm you."

"No," Mauronet said, "We're old friends, Alin and I. Commander Yu, Lieutenant Merlian, stay with our visitors until I return. They're not to leave," he said sternly. Motioning Sedmamin ahead of him, he kept one eye on us as they moved toward the door at the back where the other officers had emerged. Sedmamin opened the door and passed through, but Mauronet paused. "Oh, stand down," he told Jahelia in an exasperated voice. "My officers aren't going to harm you." Then he turned and followed Sedmamin out of sight. The door closed behind them.

Immediately, Yu strode over to Lanar and said urgently, "Admiral Mahane, I need to lodge a formal report concerning Admiral Mauronet."

Lanar held up a hand. "Commander, I think perhaps it's not necessary. Has he been like this for long?"

"Ever since we encountered those ships that came through

the Split—the Chron and the PrimeCorp corvette. We followed the last Chron ship through to this system, and took it out. Then the Admiral discovered we couldn't activate the wormhole back to Nearspace with our skip drive," the Vilisian officer said rapidly in a low voice. "At first he acted as if the Engineering crew were to blame for that—like they had sabotaged the drive or were lying about it not working. I managed to talk him down. Then he ordered thorough scans of this planet. He was convinced the Chron must have a base here. Eventually we noticed movement in this area. He sent the Commander off to look for other wormholes while he brought a dozen of us down here with him to investigate."

"You have a ship down here?" Lanar asked.

The Vilisian officer, Merlian, nodded. "A shuttle, about a mile west. Five crew still there, five in back with the techs, and the two of us."

"We came from the opposite direction," I said. "Did you encounter security drones?"

Yu nodded. "We took down two of them. But the actual security here wasn't very tight. We pretty much just walked into the base. No real security forces, only technicians. There was a scuffle, but they weren't prepared to put up much of a fight."

"And not very many of them," Merlian added. "Only seven. The techs say the operation here is being phased out."

"You mentioned an injured technician—how bad is it?" I asked. If Yuskeya were nearby, or a medic from the *Dorland*, they could treat it.

Yu and Merlian glanced at each other. "There are actually several injured, but the worst—the admiral shot him in the leg," Yu said. "The man was unarmed. Mauronet admitted he did it more to get everyone's attention than anything else. He's—he's really not himself."

And that was enough for a court-martial, I thought. I glanced at Lanar and caught his eye, and an unspoken acknowledgment passed between us. Suddenly, this had turned into a rescue mission. We had to get ourselves, Mauronet's crew, and his "prisoners" out of here in one piece.

Chapter 23 — Lanar
Duty and Honour

IT WAS TEMPTING to get Luta and the others out of the base while Mauronet was in the back with his "prisoners." The man had obviously suffered a break with reality. Fortunately, Yu and Merlian recognized the situation for what it was—otherwise it might have been easy for Mauronet to sow doubt in the minds of some about my peculiar circumstances.

But I didn't feel right leaving Sedmamin, and I doubted Luta would agree to do that. She'd made promises, and she wouldn't abandon them. I also didn't want Mauronet to come after us— we were still stranded until the *Tane Ikai* showed up. And if I needed another reason, I had a duty not to abandon Mauronet's crew if their commanding officer had become unreliable.

So, before Mauronet could return, I turned to Luta and Jahelia. "I have to help out here."

"That guy's gone *freneza*," Jahelia said bluntly, retrieving Pita from the computer console. "I don't trust him for a second. We should get out of here while we can."

"No, Lanar's right," Luta said. "I can't abandon Sedmamin, and if Mauronet's gone over the edge, we can't leave his crew and those technicians. We have to help them get control of the *Dorland*."

Yu looked uncomfortable. "This sounds like mutiny."

I shook my head. "Mauronet's judgement is impaired. It isn't mutiny to remove an officer who's become unfit for duty."

We stood in uncomfortable silence for a moment. Yu and Merlian shared a glance. "Sir," Yu said finally, "something else. Admiral Mauronet ordered the destruction of that PrimeCorp corvette. We were both on the bridge at that time."

I nodded. "It was attacking our ships. You did nothing wrong in carrying out his orders."

"But you had asked him not to do that."

"I wanted to disable it and question the crew," I confirmed. "But I'm not your Admiral's commanding officer. It was his call."

Merlian appeared to come to a decision. "He received a very strange message from that ship, Admiral, before he ordered us to go after it. It made him very angry. He muttered something about being 'betrayed after all I've done for them.' We didn't understand it, but we didn't question." She looked down at her hands. "Perhaps we should have."

I couldn't berate them for following orders like good Protectorate officers, but this only confirmed Mauronet's involvement with PrimeCorp. "Well, all we can do now is face this head-on. We should go and speak with the Admiral—and it would be a good idea if your crew mates in the back were present as well."

"More witnesses," Jahelia agreed with a lupine grin.

At that moment, the lights winked out and an alarm klaxon began to wail. The lights blinked back on, but now they were red. Almost as one, we ran for the door through which Mauronet had taken Sedmamin.

The room beyond was large, housing multiple computer consoles and work stations. A long bench covered with electronics stood against the back wall. The room was crowded, with three Protectorate officers and four others I assumed must be some of the PrimeCorp technicians packed into the small space. One woman had an arm in a makeshift sling and was shouting something at one of the officers, and a man tugged and pounded at a door on the left-hand wall. Almost everyone was yelling. Mauronet and Sedmamin were not in the room.

"*Atenton!*" I commanded, and the Protectorate officers focused on me. "Where are the others?"

The officer at whom the injured woman had been shouting saluted me and said, "Admiral. Two officers and two prisoners downstairs in the living quarters. Admiral Mauronet and a man who looked like Alin Sedmamin took another tech and went into the control room." He gestured over his shoulder to the door the technician was trying to open, then pointed to the angry woman. "She says we should evacuate. The alarm—"

The woman cut him off. "That alarm means a self-destruct sequence has been started," she said. Her eyes flicked over me. She didn't look impressed. "If you're really Protectorate, you need to make them listen. We really don't have much time."

IT DIDN'T SURPRISE me that PrimeCorp would make plans to cover their tracks by destroying the evidence. If the woman was telling the truth, we needed to get out of here quickly.

"Luta, you and this officer get everyone from downstairs," I said. They nodded and moved toward an open door on the right-hand wall. Steps led down to a lower floor. "Jahelia—"

"I'll get that other door open," she said, and without waiting, pushed past the bodies in her way, shoving the frantic technician away from the door. Foregoing the plasma rifle, for which I was glad, she pulled a smaller weapon from a pocket in her jacket.

I turned my attention back to the woman. "Can you stop it?"

"If I can get in there, maybe," she said, pointing to the door Jahelia was planning to open. "Maybe not."

"All right. You're with me. Commander Yu, get the rest of these people out of here," I told him. "Head east, there are ruins that might provide some shelter." Without waiting for his reply, I followed Jahelia. If he was behind that door, I wanted Mauronet. The klaxon continued to blare.

Jahelia aimed at the door handle and turned her head away. I put a hand up to shield my eyes, and the weapon spat a gout of energy. Jahelia lifted one booted foot and kicked the door, hard. Metal squealed and bent. The door flew open.

The room beyond was smallish, holding only a traditional desk and a corner computer console. Other than that, it was empty. Another door in the back corner was closed.

"*Fek*," Jahelia swore. She blasted the door, but it was tougher than the one she'd just kicked in. Likely it led to the outside, although there must be at least a short tunnel into the mountain to reach it.

The female technician had followed us in and bent over the console. Her fingers skidded over the screen, and she swore under her breath. After a moment, she stood back. "It's locked down," she said. "I can't stop it. I bought us some extra time, but we have to move."

"How much time?"

She chewed her lip. "Maybe fifteen minutes."

Behind us, Lieutenant Merlian called, "Admiral, we have everyone upstairs and heading out."

Jahelia aimed another shot at the door, to no more effect than the first.

"Leave it," I told her, putting a hand on her arm. "We'll get them outside."

She glared at me for an instant, then relented. "All right, let's go."

The nameless technician had already left the room, hurrying past the derelict Chron ship toward the large entry doors. Everyone else had gained the outer room. I caught up to the woman and asked over the strident call of the alarm, "Is there a comm shield over this area? We haven't been able to reach our ship—"

She was already nodding. "I'll shut it off at the door." She glanced over her shoulder at the rooms we were leaving behind. "*Bastardo.* All my stuff is still back there. And all my work—"

The alarm continued to scream and we hurried on. Ahead of us, Luta and the others broke into the sunlight and turned east. Yu and another officer carried a man between them on their shoulders, the bandage around his leg evident. I felt a surge of rage at Mauronet. He had no business taking matters here into his own hands. I'd catch up to him. And when I did—

The woman ahead of us stopped outside the main doorway, at the keypad where Sedmamin had first put in his code. She punched numbers and turned to me. "That should take down the comm block," she said, then went after the others.

A distant whine filled the air and I spun around, seeking the source. A blur of motion to the west side of the mountain caught my attention. A wheeled vehicle much like the groundcar hurtled away from the base.

Jahelia heard it too, and saw what I saw. She squinted. "Three inside, I think. He took Sedmamin and the tech with him. Making for the *Dorland's* shuttle?"

I didn't answer, just turned and ran to where we'd left the groundcar from the *Tane Ikai*. Luta was there, helping the injured technician into a seat, but I called, "No, I need it! I'm going after Mauronet!"

Luta looked up, startled, then nodded. She and Yu helped the man out again.

"He's headed for the *Dorland's* shuttle, but the comm block should be down," I told her. "Get the ship down here. Tell Yuskeya what happened. Maybe she can raise the *Dorland* and tell them about the Admiral. You get to the treeline and make for the ruins. Any cover you can find."

Her green eyes were bright with worry. "What if it blows? You'll be out in the open."

"I don't know what to expect. Just get to whatever protection you can find. I'm going to get Sedmamin." *And take down Mauronet*, I thought, but didn't say.

Luta read it anyway. Her eyes hardened. "Stay safe," was all she said.

When I turned around, Jahelia was already in the groundcar. She raised her eyebrows as if to say, *did you really expect anything else?*

I hadn't. At least she'd had the decency to let me drive.

THE GROUNDCAR JOUNCED crazily over the uneven terrain, engine roaring. It wasn't made for high-speed, off-road pursuit. "Think he'll make the shuttle before we catch him?" Jahelia asked. I didn't have an answer for her. The PrimeCorp vehicle he'd commandeered seemed evenly matched with the groundcar for speed.

"I'm more worried about his crew and what they'll do," I said, letting the groundcar drift to the right a bit to avoid the worst of the dust trail Mauronet's vehicle kicked up. "If he didn't have Sedmamin I'd think seriously about letting him go and catching up to him later."

"No, you wouldn't, Protectorate," Jahelia said with a sidelong glance at me. "You'd still be leaving the rest of his crew in danger. That would go against your sense of honour and duty."

"What do you know about my sense of honour and duty?"

"Enough. I was in the Protectorate *akademio* for three years, remember," she said. "You lasted long enough to make Admiral. You're either completely corrupt and bought your way to the top, or you have a highly-developed sense of honour and duty. I'm betting it's the second one."

"I'm that transparent?"

"No," she grinned. "But I know your sister."

I'd have to remember to tell Luta that Jahelia Sord had given her a compliment. Even if it was sort of a backhanded one.

I wished I could figure out Mauronet's end game—what was his plan? If he reached the shuttle, or even made it back to the *Dorland*, what then? He couldn't get back to Nearspace on his own. Once the base went up, he'd have destroyed some of the best evidence we had concerning PrimeCorp's involvement with the Chron, and the ship had posed no danger to anyone. He had Sedmamin—as a hostage? But he'd collaborated with the ex-Chairman, so where did that get him? I shook my head. Maybe he was just beyond the point of thinking straight. Ultimately, none of that was my problem. I was bound by duty to apprehend him if I could and take him back to Nearspace, for judgement and treatment.

"He's slowing down," Jahelia said.

She was right. He hadn't reached the shuttle yet, but the dust kicking up behind Mauronet's vehicle had lessened. We were now closing on him rather than just keeping pace.

Jahelia adjusted the plasma rifle on her lap.

"We're not going to shoot him," I told her again.

"You're not going to shoot him," she corrected me, "and I'm not going to shoot him unless it's absolutely necessary."

"In self-defence," I clarified.

"In self-defence or other extenuating circumstances."

I shook my head. "You're incorrigible."

"Thank you."

I slowed the groundcar, because the vehicle ahead had stopped. Mauronet climbed out and stood beyond it. The technician emerged from the rear seat and slowly backed away from the vehicle with his hands in the air. Mauronet paid no attention to him. Sedmamin opened his door but remained inside. Maybe Mauronet had told him to stay there, or maybe

Sedmamin was refusing to get out. Mauronet must imagine this as his last stand. He had a weapon in his hand.

I slowed and stopped as well, turning the groundcar sideways to Mauronet. Jahelia and I scrambled out on the opposite side from him and peered over the top. "Admiral, we need to talk," I called.

"I don't talk to traitors!" Mauronet returned. "You would have left that ship there for your pals at PrimeCorp to keep mining for tech to sell to our enemies!"

"Tech that came from those same enemies," I muttered. "Hundred-year-old tech. I don't think they're interested."

"Just tell him he has to make it back to Nearspace and then he can testify all about it," Jahelia said. "He's itching to tell his story, you can see that. So, promise him someone to listen."

Worth a try. "Admiral, just let Sedmamin go and come with me. We'll get back to Nearspace, and you can make a full report."

He laughed, and even at this distance the bitterness was clear. "Oh, yes. I'm sure Fleet Commander Holles will give me her full attention."

Mauronet wasn't looking his way, and I saw Sedmamin slide out of his door and crouch next to the vehicle. I tried to keep Mauronet from noticing.

"It doesn't have to be Holles. I give you my word you can speak to anyone you choose in Fleet Command. Now, your crew is waiting for you on the ship. You're not going to let them down, are you?"

He was quiet for a moment, and I thought I'd gotten somewhere. A shadow passed over us, and I looked up to see the *Tane Ikai* high above. Mauronet must have seen it, too, and he answered me with a burst of energy weapon fire that crackled against the side of the groundcar. Jahelia and I both ducked down behind the car and looked at each other. I put a hand on her arm.

"Not yet. Let me talk to him again."

"Self-defence," she said. "I was wrong. He's not listening. He's not going to listen."

"I don't want to have to explain why we had to kill him."

She gave me a pitying look. "I'm not going to *kill* him. When did I ever say that?"

I looked pointedly down at the plasma rifle. "It's not exactly a precision weapon."

"That all depends on how you use it," she said. "Like so many things." And then Jahelia Sord frowned, leaned in, and very unexpectedly, very decidedly, kissed me.

IT WAS ONE of the most amazing, surprising, absolutely wonderful things that has ever happened to me. And I've had a pretty long life of surprising, amazing, and wonderful things. At first, I did nothing, could do nothing. Her lips were dusty and sweat-salty, demanding and sweet at the same time. As soon as I could think again, I kissed her back. On a dusty, empty planet, in an unknown system, hiding from a madman. We kissed, and I thought nothing would ever be the same.

And then she pulled away, stood up, and yelled, "*Sedmamin, jump!*" I saw him start and roll away from the groundcar. The technician, already a good distance away, dove for the ground. Mauronet saw motion and his head and weapon snapped toward Sedmamin. Without missing a beat, Jahelia aimed the plasma rifle and blasted the back end of Mauronet's vehicle. It bucked, spun away from the impact, and knocked Mauronet off his feet. His weapon flared but then flew from his hand. Jahelia Sord was over the groundcar in a lithe leap and running toward Mauronet before he stopped bouncing. I was seconds behind her. By the time I'd scooped his weapon from the sand, she stood over the downed Admiral with a grin on her face and the plasma rifle pointed at his.

I stared down into the mad, angry eyes of Antar Mauronet. His right hand clenched and unclenched reflexively in the dirt. One of his legs twisted off at an unpleasant angle but he hadn't seemed to notice yet. He was beaten. He knew it, and he didn't like it.

"See?" Jahelia said reprovingly. "I told you I wasn't going to kill him."

And then the PrimeCorp base exploded.

Chapter 24 — Luta
No Plan Survives
Contact with Reality

MORE THAN ANYTHING, I wanted to stand and watch Lanar and Jahelia Sord roar away after Sedmamin in the groundcar. I wanted to send protective thoughts to keep my brother safe in this crazy scenario. But I couldn't. I turned and caught up the injured technician's free arm, and Commander Yu and I scurried for the treeline. Yu called out to the others, ahead of us, to do the same. They straggled toward the scant cover the trees offered.

I tapped my implant. "*Tane Ikai*, can you hear me? We need immediate extraction. Baden? Yuskeya?"

"Captain!" Even over the faint and tinny reception of the implant the relief in Baden's voice was evident. "You're all right?"

"For the moment. The PrimeCorp base is set to explode or something. We're moving away from it toward our original drop-off point. Come and get us!"

The only answer was silence for a moment, as Baden presumably digested this, or relayed it to the others. Finally, he said, "On our way. Explode *or something*? You don't know?"

"Someone said 'self-destruct' and I didn't stop to ask questions," I said. "Sorry I can't be more precise."

"Forgiven. We were worried because we couldn't contact you, so we're not actually very far away. We've been skimming low, hunting for signal."

I decided not to chastise anyone for not following my orders to stay well above the planet. This time it might turn out to have been a very lucky thing.

An ache between my shoulder blades signalled how tense I was, waiting for something to happen at the base behind us. The injured man's weight wasn't helping. I wondered how far from the mountain Lanar and Jahelia were now, and what was happening with them. Maybe I should have stopped them from going off on their own. At that thought, I almost smiled. As if I could stop my headstrong brother, and Jahelia Sord, from doing anything.

Baden had been right; the ship hove into sight and settled between us and the ruins where we'd taken out the drones. Our group of stragglers rushed forward with renewed energy.

The door of cargo pod four opened for us, and there was Hirin, waiting to guide us in. He smiled in relief, and I felt a surge of guilt for making him worry about me. As we scrambled aboard, Hirin moved forward to take the weight of the injured man from me, and managed to give my shoulder a *welcome back* squeeze as he did so. I said urgently into my implant. "We're in!" I hit the control next to the door to close it.

"Everyone aboard? We heading for orbit?" Rei's voice was a little breathless, but steady.

"Not yet. Take us up five hundred metres!" I looked around the cargo pod, at the handful of Protectorate officers from the *Dorland* and the battered and stunned-looking technicians from the base. "We can't leave. Lanar and Jahelia went after Mauronet. He set the base to destruct and took Sedmamin with him. Headed for their shuttle, I think."

"Hold on," Rei said over the ship's comm, and I felt the engines rumble the floor of the cargo pod. Hirin and Yu lowered the injured tech to sit, leaning him back against the wall. He closed his eyes, pale and shaken, but I thought he'd be all right for a moment.

"We're moving," I shouted, so everyone could hear me. "I know there's not much to hold on to, but try to brace yourselves in case it's not a smooth lift off." If the explosion came now, the shock wave could hit the ship hard.

There must not have been anyone in this segment of the *Dorland*'s crew with medical training; the man with the injured leg had received the barest of first aid. I spoke into my implant again as the *Tane Ikai* rumbled. "Yuskeya?"

"Here, Captain. I tried the *Dorland*, but no response."

"All right. Please head down here with some emergency med supplies. I'm putting you in charge of anyone requiring medical attention."

The ship lurched to the right and I knew Rei had engaged the thrusters. I stumbled but headed for the ladder leading to the catwalk that vaulted over the pod. From there I could climb up to the bridge level. I needed to see what was happening on the planet, and where Lanar and Jahelia might be.

Yu broke from the crowd and followed me. "Is there anything I can do to help, Captain?"

I shook my head. "You're in charge of these officers, unless I'm mistaken," I said, and I saw the realization hit him. He outranked the other members of the *Dorland*'s crew here. While Lanar was with us, Yu had naturally deferred to him, but now that situation had changed.

He straightened a bit. "That's right, Captain. Thank you. I'll stay here and see to my crew. All your help is greatly appreciated."

"Commander Blue is on her way with med supplies," I told them, one foot on the ladder. "I'm going up to the bridge to see if I can figure out what's happening with Admiral Mauronet and Admiral Mahane."

I began to climb. Hirin was right behind me. "What happened down there, Luta?"

"Mauronet's lost it," I said briefly over my shoulder. "Looks like he was the mole in the Protectorate, but now he feels like PrimeCorp's betrayed him by dealing with the Chron."

"He's not wrong about that."

"True enough. They had a Chron ship down there—an old one—and we think they've been cannibalizing it for tech for decades. Probably got them where they are today."

"And he's trying to blow it up?"

"Like I said, I don't think he's thinking straight anymore."

When we gained the Engineering level, Viss called out to me.

"Captain, we're in good shape. The activator drive should function normally whenever you want to try that wormhole back to Nearspace."

"Thanks for the update. I wonder if we could pull the *Dorland* through after us, the way the Chron ship did," I said. I paused to hear Viss's reply to that, but he apparently had no opinion on the question. Hirin said nothing, either. I resumed my climb.

Once we gained the top of the ladder, Hirin and I sprinted down the corridor to the bridge. "Report," I said as I arrived, just a little out of breath from climbing and running.

I didn't bother to sit in the command chair. I just wanted to know where Lanar was now, and I didn't know how long I'd be staying.

"We're steady at a height of five hundred metres," Rei said. "Circling to come around and find our people."

Baden said, "I'm tracking two vehicles on the planet surface, moving away from the base."

"Show me."

Baden pulled up images on the main viewscreen and a smaller one. The main screen showed the area around the mountain and the base. A short distance away—too short for my liking!—on the smaller screen, two green dots moved at speed in the same direction. The image resolved to show the two groundcars clearly.

"All right, what can we do to help bring this to a close?" I asked. "Ideas?"

"I assume shooting is out of the question," Baden said with a straight face.

"Agreed."

"I could bring us down somewhere in front of the lead vehicle," Rei suggested, "but I couldn't safely get very close, so he could just veer off and drive right around us."

"We could set down between them and the base, take the brunt of the blast if it comes," Maja said thoughtfully. "And we do have the activator drive, that shuts things down. Fire that in the direction of his vehicle and see what happens?"

I pursed my lips, considering. "But we're not sure how long that takes to recharge, and we might want to open that wormhole quickly. Not worth the risk."

"If they reach the *Dorland's* shuttle, it's going to get more complicated," Hirin said. "The officers there don't know what happened at the base."

"And with Mauronet armed, we can't wait around for something to happen. We might not like what it is."

"Jahelia's still got her plasma rifle," Baden said. "I'd be more worried about Mauronet."

"Show me where they're heading."

Baden slid his fingers around on his screen and the image of the planet below showed what lay ahead of the two vehicles. The expanse of sandy flat would soon give way to another clutch of vegetation, and now that we were looking for it, the shuttle was visible. "Maybe we should just set down close to the shuttle and intervene there," I said.

But we didn't get a chance.

As we watched, the lead vehicle stopped and the pursuer caught up and stopped, as well. Mauronet got out.

"They're not at the *Dorland's* shuttle," Hirin said, "but why else would he stop? Groundcar break down?"

"Maybe." I frowned and chewed my lip. "But where's Sedmamin? What's Lanar going to do now? They're still too close to the base for comfort."

On the screen, Lanar and Jahelia exited their vehicle too, crouching behind it. Lanar and Mauronet were shouting at each other. Mauronet fired his weapon at the groundcar and even at this distance, the sudden flash made me jump.

And then Lanar and Jahelia had their heads together, discussing what to do next—but even as I thought that, I realized it wasn't right. I squinted at the screen, not believing what my eyes were telling me. They had their heads together all right, but they weren't talking . . . they were *kissing*.

Baden had time to let out a long, low whistle and then everything happened at once. Jahelia stood up, Sedmamin rolled out of the groundcar, and Jahelia blasted the groundcar right into Mauronet. When the dust cleared, she and Lanar both stood above the fallen admiral.

And the explosion hit.

THE MOUNTAIN STILL took up most of the main viewscreen, and the explosion wrenched my attention away from Lanar and

Jahelia. The ground shuddered violently, then crumpled in on itself as huge sections of rock slid and shattered into chunks. Thick black smoke and clotted dust roiled into the air, punctuated by hot bursts of orange flame.

I looked back at Lanar and saw with relief that although they'd ducked and covered their heads, the shockwave didn't seem to have affected them. "Let's go get them," I told Rei.

She piloted us down and set the *Tane Ikai* a safe distance away. I asked Commander Yu to take the *Tane Ikai*'s groundcar—if Mauronet hadn't damaged it when he shot at Lanar—and fetch his fellow crew mates from the shuttle; he was the best one to explain what had happened with Mauronet, and the base. We had room in one of the empty cargo pods to take the shuttle itself, too. No sense leaving a perfectly good Protectorate shuttle for PrimeCorp or the Chron.

Yuskeya and Viss and I went out with a stretcher to fetch Mauronet and the others. The fallen admiral was muttering invective when we reached him, so Yuskeya's first task was to give him a sedative. At least I assume that's how she shut him up. I was busy hugging Lanar. We weren't always a demonstrative family, but there were times when nothing else would do.

"He shot at you!" I said against my brother's neck. "We saw the whole thing."

I felt him go still for a heartbeat or two. "The whole thing?" he said lightly.

"Don't worry," I whispered near his ear. "My crew is very understanding about secrets."

He chuckled, but when I pulled back from the hug I thought his face had flushed beneath its layer of dust.

Jahelia had gone to collect Sedmamin, who was now limping as well as cradling his plasticast-covered arm. "I can't believe you told me to go with that maniac," he spluttered to Lanar as they walked slowly past me on the way to the ship. The technician Mauronet had coerced into starting the destruct sequence followed behind them, looking dazed.

"You're welcome," Lanar said. "We could have just let him keep you."

"It was Miss Sord I saw rescuing me," Sedmamin rejoined huffily. Lanar just rolled his eyes, but Jahelia shot me a wink as they passed.

I let out a long sigh. "Now what?"

Lanar turned to look at the smoldering remains of the mountain, the PrimeCorp base, and the Chron ship. "Now we go back to your ship, try to figure out where the hell we are, and take whatever intelligence we can back to Nearspace," he said.

"I was afraid you were going to say that." I looked around. "I guess it's not a great planet for a vacation anyway," I said.

Lanar put an arm around my shoulders. "That's my little sister," he said. "Always looking for the bright side."

"*Big* sister," I reminded him, and poked him in the ribs. That kiss had been interesting, to say the least. I was going to have some fun with little brother the next time we were alone.

WE SETTLED OUR extra passengers wherever we could make them comfortable, and as Rei took us up into orbit around the planet, I went to quickly shower and change my clothes. It felt like days since we'd set down on the surface, and I had to stare at the time on my datapad to convince myself that it had been mere hours. I looked longingly at the bed as I pulled on clean pants and a sweater . . . even just a twenty-minute nap would make me feel a whole lot better. I almost gave in, but resolutely shook my head and left the room. We had to find the *Dorland* and make a plan to get everyone back to Nearspace safely.

And I was damned if I was going to be the last one to show up on the bridge.

As it was, Jahelia was there before me, but I managed to make it before Lanar. Hirin slid out of the command chair without even asking me, so I sat down gratefully and let the servos massage my back.

"Yuskeya's still tending to the injured," Hirin told me, and sat down at her nav console. "Your brother and Commander Yu are with her. I think they're having a command meeting while Yuskeya cleans wounds and applies bandages."

"Where's Mauronet?"

"Lanar muttered something about what kind of a ship has no proper brig, and then they decided to keep the dear admiral sedated in First Aid," he said with a grin. "And before you ask, Sedmamin is sulking in his quarters, after Yuskeya told him his bumps and bruises could wait while she triaged everyone else."

"Captain, we're in orbit around the planet," Rei said. "No indications of any other ships in the area."

"Quiet on the comm channels," Baden confirmed.

"Rei, let's get over and scan that smaller moon—the one we suspect is the operant device. Let's confirm that so we aim the activator drive at the right place."

With a nod, Rei engaged the thrusters and the *Tane Ikai* moved toward the small moon. The brick-red clouds of the gas nebula were behind it from this vantage point, making it look impossibly tiny for something that was so vital to us at this moment.

I pursed my lips. "So, where's the *Dorland*? If they're scouting for wormholes, they should still be in range. I can't imagine they'd actually try a skip without reporting to the admiral first."

"Hope they didn't run into any unfriendly Chron," Jahelia said from the secondary engineering console. "We did see those two ships right after we'd arrived."

"It's a Pegasus-class cruiser," I said. "They should be able to handle a few Chron; if not, Nearspace is doomed before we even get started."

"True enough, but this is *their* territory," Jahelia said. "We— and the crew of the *Dorland*—don't know our way around or what's here. Perfect for ambushes, asteroid-mounted auto-defence systems, proximity mines—"

"All right, point taken," I said, holding up a hand. "Let's not dwell on those possibilities. As soon as Lanar gets here—"

"He's here," my brother said, striding onto the bridge. Commander Yu was with him and looked around with interest. "Yuskeya's just gone to take a look at Sedmamin, and then she'll join us."

"Commander Yu, there's no sign of your ship," I told him. "What were their orders when Admiral Mauronet left them to go down to the planet?"

Yu pressed his lips into a thin line and stared at the viewscreen, which showed us only the planet rolling now far beneath us, and the nearby operant moon that marked the entrance to the strange intersecting wormhole. The mouth itself was too dark to discern from here, and melted into the darkness of space around it.

"He told them to scout for and map other wormholes in the near vicinity, but not to venture into any of them," he said. "He also told comms to send a distress signal on a particular channel, and to include a certain code in it."

"What was all that about?" Lanar asked with a frown.

Yu shook his head. "He didn't explain. Just said that if anyone answered on that channel the crew should tell them he—Mauronet—was in command of the ship and ask for assistance. That they could trust them, and bring them back here to meet us."

"A PrimeCorp channel?" I guessed, and Lanar spread his hands wide.

"Makes sense. Even if he was disillusioned with PrimeCorp, he knew he needed their help to make it back to Nearspace. He might have planned to take them out once he had what he needed. Another thing we'll ask him about when he wakes up."

"So, the *Dorland* might just be out of our scanner range," Rei said. "Or there could be something between us and them blocking or messing up the signals."

"Or they could have run into Chron ships," Jahelia said again.

"Or they could have found a wormhole and decided to try skipping through despite what Mauronet said." I looked at Yu. "You think everyone was suspicious that he'd gone over the edge?"

"I do, but they wouldn't go off and leave the rest of us," Yu said with certainty, and Lanar nodded in agreement.

"No Protectorate crew would do that."

"And we can't, either," I said, managing to stifle a sigh. It would have been so nice to just spin up the activator drive and skip through the wormhole to home, hand all these problems off to someone else. But I knew Lanar would never agree to that, and my conscience wouldn't, either. I said as much. "I know we have to get back with what we've learned, and what these techs from the planet can tell the Protectorate, but we have to make an effort to find the *Dorland* before we do."

"And avoid any Chron in the area," Baden said. "Jahelia's right, we don't know anything about this system or how often they come and go through here."

"Thank you, Baden," Jahelia said sweetly.

"Captain? Scans of the moon match up pretty closely with the first one we encountered, in the Woodroct's Star system," Yuskeya said. "That's the operant device, all right."

I felt a little knot of tension at the back of my neck loosen. "Good. We're in business. Viss? Whatever you can do to make sure that activator drive is ready to go, please do it."

"Aye, Captain," Viss answered.

A thought struck me. "Hey, Pita," I said.

The AI answered from Jahelia's datapad, where it lay close to her on the console. "At your service, Captain."

It was really amazing how sardonic an AI could make herself sound when she wanted to.

"I'm just thinking . . . you have all the Corvid data Fha gave us, and the PrimeCorp files you and Jahelia, um, obtained when Sedmamin wasn't looking, all the files we got from PrimeCorp Main last week, *and* whatever you just downloaded from the computer here."

"And I *might* have picked up a few tidbits when we were with the good doctor on the Chron station," she added smugly.

"I didn't know about that, but okay," I said. "Do you think in all of that, there might be information about these systems, and some of the links between them?"

"I thought you'd never ask," the AI said. "Let me have a look and see what's here."

She went quiet, and I caught Jahelia's eye and shrugged. "Worth a shot?"

"If she finds something useful, you realize we'll never hear the end of it," Jahelia said.

I looked out the viewscreen at the slowly-revolving, tiny moon. "I'm willing to take that chance."

Chapter 25 – Lunar Incoming

LUTA HAD A good idea when she asked Pita to determine where we were in relation to the Otherspace systems we'd identified. But while the AI worked on collating the masses of data she'd accumulated, we couldn't just sit still.

"All right, let's assume the *Dorland* would follow standard procedures," Luta said to me. "What would the Protectorate protocol be for a ship exploring a new system?"

We'd gone to the galley for food and drink while we regrouped. Luta had suggested it, and I'd realized how hungry I was. So now Luta and I, Hirin, Jahelia, Commander Yu, and Yuskeya gathered around the big table with hot soup and drinks. Luta had told Rei that until we had a better plan, she should keep the *Tane Ikai* in an ever-widening orbit around the unknown planet, with long-range scanners in constant use.

I shrugged at the question. "Apart from Woodroct's Star, I can't remember it happening," I said. "There are probably protocols left over from the early days of wormhole exploration and the formation of the Protectorate, but I don't know what they are."

I looked the question at Yuskeya. "When we found ourselves in the Corvid system, it made sense to me to pick a base point, like the wormhole, and start recording data from there. Then you can work out from that and always find your way back. But what direction to go if you're just exploring, with nothing else to factor in—" She spread her hands. "That would be random."

"All right. So, all we can do is what we're doing," Luta said. "Next question is, what do we do if we find them?"

"If Pita can figure out where this system is in relation to others we can identify, we might be able to contact the Relidae," Jahelia said. "They could help them plot a course back to Nearspace."

"They could try to ride the trail of the *Tane Ikai* if we go back through the wormhole that intersects with the Split," Hirin said. "They got here that way, after all, following the Chron ship."

"We don't know if that will work with the activator drive on this ship," I said. "The Chron version could be different."

"And we don't know yet," Luta reminded us, "whether our activator drive is even going to work. So, Pita's data—if she can come up with some—could be just as important to us."

"No pressure," Jahelia said in a low voice.

"The crew of the *Dorland* could come aboard with us, and we'll all take a chance on the wormhole together," Yuskeya said. "I don't love the idea of leaving the ship here, but it could be locked down. It's more important to get the crew back, after all."

Yu looked uncomfortable but I nodded. "My thoughts exactly, but we won't abandon the ship unless it's absolutely necessary."

Rei's voice came over the comm. "Captain! I have a ship on long-range . . . coming this way and it looks like it's coming hot."

"Drive signature?"

"Too far out to tell yet."

"Be on the bridge in a minute," Luta said. She looked at me. "If it's the *Dorland*, they might be running from something. We'll have to decide what to do in a hurry. If it's not the *Dorland* . . ."

We all stood then. She didn't have to finish that sentence. Hirin said, "Go on, I'll secure everything here." He started picking up dishes and dumping them into the scrubber. Luta threw him a grateful glance but the underlying meaning of his action wasn't lost on any of us. We might be heading into a fight, or flight—or something else. And we had to be ready.

THE PLANET STILL wheeled below us on the viewscreen when we arrived on the bridge, but we were far enough away from it now that I could no longer make out the plume of smoke from the explosion. The shadowed background of space was littered with stars—an image I'd seen hundreds of time before, and yet every planet was different, and so I never got tired of the view.

"Still coming fast," Rei said as Luta slid into her command chair. I was still a bit lost on the bridge of a ship I didn't command or crew, so I just stood next to her.

"Anything chasing it?" Luta asked.

"Not so far—hang on." Rei stared down at her console for a long moment. "Yeah, there's someone on its tail," she confirmed. "Just caught it on the edge of the scan."

"But no identification on the lead ship yet?"

"I might have it," Yuskeya said. She'd gone directly to her navigation console and now looked up from the screen. "Tentative ID is a Protectorate signature, so if that's right it has to be the *Dorland*."

"Let's assume they're being pursued by a Chron ship—or at least one," Luta said. She turned to me. "What's our plan of action in this scenario?"

Before I could answer, Pita chirped from Jahelia's engineering console. "Captain, I believe I know where we are. Well, sort of," the AI amended. "In relation to some other places we've been."

Luta hesitated. Regardless of what Pita had discovered, we weren't going to be able to take much time for a discussion with the *Dorland*. "Give me the quick version," she said finally.

"All right. I think there are at least two other wormholes out of this system, in addition to the one we came through. One leads to a system we've visited, Commander Blue's designation OS-G5V-03. That's the one with the Relidae station, where we left Professor Brindlepaw."

Luta locked eyes with me. "If we could get the *Dorland* there, they'd find help."

"The second wormhole I believe leads to a binary star system with one Relidae-inhabited planet," Pita continued. "It's one skip away from the system we passed through on our way to Tau Ceti. So that route could lead them back to Nearspace, too."

I blew out my breath. "If we have enough time to set them up for either of those options. We have to deal with what's headed this way first."

"The bad news is—both wormholes are days away in-system," Pita said.

"One ship in pursuit, we can probably handle," Luta said. Hirin returned to the bridge just then and made his way to the improvised weapons station. "Hirin, your weapons systems are ready to go?"

He gave a brief nod. "We're not a Protectorate battle cruiser, but we can protect ourselves."

Sedmamin also came onto the bridge, cradling his arm and looking aggrieved. "Captain, your medic said she'd be back with something for pain for me, but she hasn't returned."

"We got a little distracted, Chairman," Luta said in a tight voice. "I'd tell you to go get it yourself from First Aid, but Mauronet's in there. Have a seat and we'll get to it when we can."

With a glare that Luta completely missed—or ignored—Sedmamin sat in a skimchair near the EVA suit bank and folded his arms. Or tried to. The plasticast ruined the gravitas of the gesture.

"*Merde*," Rei said suddenly. She swivelled her skimchair around to look directly at Luta and me. "That pursuing ship behind the *Dorland*? It just turned into a squadron."

"BADEN, HOW SOON can we get any kind of a connection to the *Dorland*?" Luta asked.

Baden hesitated. "No FTL WaVE capacity here. It's not going to be until they're within range of a short-range scan."

"All right. As soon as possible, I want a line to them. Lanar will talk to whoever's in command."

Commander Yu had said nothing to this point, but spoke up now. "That should be Commander Mattu, if nothing's changed since they left."

"Use his name, Baden, that'll help them realize they can trust us," I said.

"The question is, what are we going to ask them to trust us on?" Luta asked me. "We're not defenceless, but we're not a warship."

I nodded. The *Tane Ikai* and one Pegasus-class cruiser were not going to win any dogfights with a squadron of Chron fighters. I heard myself say, "They'll have to try to follow us into the wormhole."

I waited for someone to argue with me, but the bridge had gone oddly quiet. Finally, Luta nodded, and Jahelia said, "I don't suppose I get a vote, but that makes sense to me. Anything else, you're risking everyone."

"And the possibility of getting the information about the base and the ship back to Fleet Commander Holles," Yuskeya added. Then she said, "Captain? Another flight of ships has showed up on the long-range."

I crossed to Yuskeya's console. The ships were only a cluster of dots on the scan, but they moved as one, following the squadron behind the *Dorland*. I swallowed, tasting something sour in my throat. Either the *Dorland* had done something to mightily piss off the Chron—or this was the beginning of a full assault, heading for this wormhole into Nearspace.

"Rei, take us to the wormhole," Luta said. "Let's make sure we're in place so we can move through as quickly as possible when the *Dorland* arrives."

"What?" Sedmamin demanded, his voice thin with fear. "Why are we waiting? We need to get out of here now!"

Luta fixed him with an icy glare. "We're not going to abandon that ship. They don't have their own activator drive."

Sedmamin threw up his hands in exasperation. "You're all *freneza*. I'm going to get my own pain meds." He stomped off in the direction of First Aid.

"What if Mauronet's awake in there?" Luta called after him.

"I'll take my chances," Sedmamin threw over his shoulder at her. "If I have to, I'll hit him with my cast."

Jahelia raised her eyebrows at Luta. "You know, I think there might be hope for that man, yet."

"What if the *Dorland* doesn't want to follow us through?" Maja asked. She'd been silent through most of this, sitting next to Baden at the communications console.

"Lanar can order them through, don't forget," Luta said. "He's the ranking Protectorate officer in this area . . . probably in this entire system."

"I don't think that's our biggest concern," I said slowly.

Luta turned to me. "What?"

I pointed at Yuskeya's screen. "This. If this is the vanguard of an invasion force—"

My sister realized immediately what I was saying. "The Protectorate needs to know. Now."

Maja swivelled in her skimchair to look at Luta. "You're not saying we should go through without waiting for them? Just abandon the *Dorland*?"

In my peripheral vision, I saw Commander Yu twitch, but he said nothing. The ship and crew would not survive if we left them.

Luta didn't answer either, just looked at me to see what I'd say.

I had the power of command and was fully capable of making that decision. I hesitated, weighing options. We weren't sure this plan to pull the ship through after us would work. The *Dorland* might still meet with disaster if they tried to ride the *Tane Ikai's* tail through the wormhole. They might not even make it inside the wormhole, and be abandoned to the oncoming Chron squadron anyway.

I'd ordered ships and crews into battle, into dangerous situations, and not all of them had returned. But I had never abandoned anyone with a chance.

And yet we had to warn Nearspace as quickly as possible.

At the engineering console, Jahelia looked up and our eyes met, but hers were unreadable. If she was trying to send me a message—challenge, support, anything—I wasn't getting it. She didn't seem at all flustered by the moment we'd shared on the planet. I couldn't decide if that was a good thing or not.

"Wait. We don't have to make that decision," Baden said suddenly, turning his chair to look at me. "We know—the Corvids told us, and it worked this way when we came through—that when the activator drive opens the wormhole, it stays open for a while. It's not like our skip drive, which only holds the wormhole open when the ship is inside it. Right?"

He looked to Luta for confirmation and she nodded slowly. "It closes after a time, or if the ship with the activator gets too far away from it."

"Right. So, we should be able to open the wormhole now and send a message through—the Protectorate ships stationed around the end of the Split will get it and relay it to Farview and

Holles. Just as fast as if we went through ourselves. And the wormhole will still be open for us to go through when the *Dorland* gets here."

"We won't know for sure that they received the message, if they can't send back. It's still a risk," I said. "But one that I'm willing to take."

Commander Yu's face cleared. He must have been holding it steady, trying not to reveal his emotions, but the relief was plain now.

Luta also looked relieved. "I don't think the Corvids actually told us how much time we could count on. Viss?" she asked over the ship's comm. "How long does a ghosted wormhole stay active?"

"I'll check the information the Corvids gave us with the drive," came the response, "but it has to be a couple of hours. Time to make a surprise attack and disappear back through before the wormhole goes away. And Captain," Viss continued, "I think our best chance for success will come if we're moving at speed when we enter the wormhole."

"Why?" Luta asked.

"Because that's what worked for the *Dorland* before," Viss answered. "Let's keep as many of the variables the same as we can."

I turned to Yu. "All right, back to what Luta said earlier. Commander, I can't consult with Admiral Mauronet on pulling the *Dorland* through after us, but I'd like input from someone on your command team. What about the risk?"

The commander turned his eyes to the viewscreen for a moment, although the ship and its dangerous pursuers were far too distant to see. Finally, he said, "I think it's the best option, Admiral. They don't stand a chance in this system, now that they've been discovered by the Chron. If they could have slipped through undetected—but that's a moot point. They didn't. And if they make it through with us, they'll be on the other side to help defend against whatever's coming. Our pilot—she did it once. I'm sure she can do it again."

I nodded. "Fair enough. I'll tell them to follow us in."

Sedmamin returned from First Aid and settled himself in a skimchair, folding his arms as best he could and glaring at us all.

Luta ignored him. "Baden, Lanar will tell you what to send through for Fleet Commander Holles. As soon as that's ready, Viss, let's get that wormhole open."

Viss and Rei coordinated to maneuver the ship into the correct position to fire the activator drive at the operant moon. From here, we also had enough distance to get a good "running start" at the wormhole, as Viss had advised. I'd tell the *Dorland* to get close enough to feel the heat of the *Tane Ikai*'s engines—well, figuratively, anyway.

I tore my eyes away from the phalanx of dots moving toward us on Yuskeya's screen, and went to bend over Baden's shoulder and compose a message for Regina. As succinctly as possible, I outlined the imminent threat and told her we'd be coming through the wormhole first, with the *Dorland* in tow. I didn't want any Protectorate ships reflexively opening fire until we were well clear of the Split.

Baden keyed the message and nodded to Luta.

"Viss, ready to fire the activator drive. Whenever you're ready."

"Firing now."

A flash glimmered around the back of the ship as the drive fired, although it generated nothing visible toward the operant moon.

"Yuskeya?" I prompted.

She nodded. "It worked. The moon is generating the same rays we read in Woodroct's Star. They're streaming directly into the wormhole."

I'd never seen a wormhole activated by one of the Chron operant artifacts, and I stood transfixed. The dark shadow of the wormhole mouth began to glow blue as runnels of plasma flowed like lava around the edges. Fingers of plasma stretched inward from all sides as if drawn inexorably toward each other. When they met, the centre began a slow rotation, increasing in speed until it swirled like a whirlpool, shot through with silver. I flinched as a cone of silver-blue light reached out from its centre as if it might grasp us. Rei had kept us back, but the cone strained toward us. I had the oddest impression that it was trying to pull us in. It was stranger than any other wormhole I'd ever seen, weirdly beautiful but dangerous-looking, too. It felt . . . hungry.

Luta said, "Baden, send the message." Her words broke the

mesmerizing spell the wormhole had cast on me. I had to look away, so I glanced around the bridge. Everyone, even Sedmamin, seemed transfixed by the terrifying beauty of the wormhole we were about to fly into. I turned my eyes back to the viewscreen and waited for the *Dorland* to get close enough to talk.

Chapter 26 — Luta
Going Rogue

Baden swore under his breath.

"What is it?" I asked.

His fingers slid over the communications console. "Message to Fleet Commander Holles bounced back," he said tersely.

"Try again."

"I am."

Lanar caught my eye and we shared a moment of silent desperation. It felt like walls were closing in on us. We were all that stood between the *Dorland* and death, and all that stood between Nearspace and an onslaught they were barely prepared for.

Baden sat back from the console and clasped his hands behind his neck. "It won't go," he said. "Maybe it can't get past the intersection of the two wormholes."

"Or maybe there is no intersection," Maja said in a bleak voice. "Maybe the activator drive isn't making the two wormholes link."

I could almost feel the chill spreading over the bridge at my daughter's words. If this wormhole didn't link to the Split, we might emerge anywhere. Nearspace, Otherspace—inside a star. We were taking as big a chance as any wormhole spelunker diving in to an untested wormhole.

Sedmamin opened his mouth and I *looked* at him. He shut it again.

I ran a hand over my face. "No. I have to believe that part is working. That's our assumption and we'll stick to it. The message isn't going through for some other reason—like Baden said, maybe it can't pass the intersection." I glanced at the main viewscreen, where Yuskeya had opened a corner image of her screen, and the oncoming *Dorland* and its pursuers. The *Dorland* was just on the outer edge of our short-range scan. "We can't change the plan now."

Lanar said carefully, "There won't be time for the Protectorate to get many more ships in place." He wasn't arguing with me, just stating a fact.

"I know." I stood up. It felt right to be standing up when I said what I was about to say. "That's why we're going to blow up the Split."

I don't know if there had ever been such complete, shocked silence on the bridge of the *Tane Ikai* before. Jahelia broke it.

"*Fek*, yeah," she said with a grin.

"Another wormhole will spawn in its place," Hirin observed. "The Corvids told us that."

"Yes, but not right away," I said. "It buys us time, and time is in short supply."

Lanar still looked a little shocked, but he managed to say, "Luta, I can't order the *Dorland* to do that. Destroy a wormhole? That's beyond my decision-making authority."

"The *Dorland* isn't going to do it," I said. "I am. If you and Commander Yu—and even Yuskeya—should leave the bridge to protect yourselves, I understand."

"We saw what happened when an energy weapon was fired into a wormhole," Hirin said reflectively. "I think the particle beam would do it."

"I can't let you do this," Lanar said, regaining some of his composure. "It's too dangerous."

"For once, I am in complete agreement with the Admiral," Sedmamin said. "Admiral Mahane, you must take control of this vessel. I know this is your sister, but she's obviously—"

"Shut up, Sedmamin," Lanar said without even looking at the ex-Chairman.

"I'm not saying yea or nay," Rei offered, "but remember that the *Dorland* is going to be behind us. We'll have to get them clear before we do it."

"We'll have to get everyone in the vicinity clear," Viss said over the ship's comm. He was always privy to the bridge conversations. "When the Corvids wrecked the other wormhole, we were tossed around pretty good, and as I recall we were all out for a minute or two. And we weren't even all that close."

But I didn't answer either of them. I took the few steps that separated me from Lanar and put my hands on his arms. "You don't have to be part of this, Lanar. But it's the only move we have in the game. You want me to lock you up in your quarters, I'll do that. But I'm not Protectorate, little brother, and," I leaned closer to put my mouth next to his ear, because this was for him alone, "*you're not the boss of me.*"

OKEJ, MAYBE TECHNICALLY he was the boss of me. The Nearspace Protectorate administered the law in Nearspace wherever there was no planetary jurisdiction.

But we weren't *in* Nearspace, were we? And by the time we were through the Split and back in that jurisdiction, things would be moving too fast to worry about it.

My brother looked down at me for a long moment. Finally, he said, "If you do this, Regina might not want you to join the Protectorate anymore."

I realized I'd been holding my breath, not entirely sure if Lanar could accept my decision. "And that's a risk *I'm* willing to take." I smiled and gave him a quick hug, then went back to the command chair. "Let's make a plan, people."

Sedmamin announced that he was going to his room. "Perhaps someone will come and tell me if we make it through this alive," he said sarcastically. I couldn't say I was sorry to see him leave, since it removed an extra distraction we didn't need.

"He'll be back before long, anyway," Baden predicted.

By the time we made contact with Commander Mattu, we'd mapped out a sequence of actions we hoped would work. We'd enter the wormhole at speed, with the *Dorland* close behind. As soon as we transitioned from the ghosted wormhole to the Split, Baden would send a message ahead of us telling the Protectorate forces to move back from the wormhole and not to fire on us when we came through. The *Dorland* would be instructed to veer off in one direction and we'd fly straight, firing the particle beam weapon from the aft cannon into the mouth of the Split. Then we'd scramble away as fast as the burst drive would take us. The bridge fairly thrummed with tension, but everyone knew their role. None of the Protectorate officers chose to leave the bridge, which made me feel strangely proud. Finally, when I thought I might not be able to stand it any longer, Baden spoke.

"They should be in range. Sending a comm to the *Dorland* and Commander Mattu now."

After only a few seconds he turned to me with a nod. "They've pinged back. Admiral, you're on."

"Commander Mattu, this is Admiral Lanar Mahane of the NPV *S. Cheswick*. Are you under attack?"

The response came back almost immediately. "Confirm that, Admiral. Hostiles in pursuit. Can you assist?"

Lanar looked at me and told the Commander as briefly as possible the plan we'd come up with. "Admiral Mauronet is incapacitated, but Commander Yu is here with me, if you'd like to speak with him," Lanar said at the end. "I understand that this situation is highly irregular, but we're trying to get everyone back to Nearspace in one piece and we think this is the best chance." We'd decided not to tell the *Dorland* crew exactly what we were planning to do to the Split—we didn't need to argue with anyone else about it. Lanar had told Mattu that getting out of the way was to allow other ships to take up positions around the wormhole mouth.

Mattu hesitated for a moment, taking it all in, I guessed. Commander Yu stepped in to reassure him. "I concur with the Admiral's assessment of the situation," he said firmly. "It's the best chance we have."

"Then we'll follow your plan," Commander Mattu said. "We're outrunning them for now, but it can't last forever. I'm glad to hear there's no-one left to retrieve from the planet."

Since Yu and Mattu had both been on the bridge when the *Dorland* followed the Chron ship through the Split and the ghosted wormhole, I told them to simply do whatever they'd done that day. It didn't seem very complicated—they'd done nothing except engage their own skip drive to enter the Split, and then simply followed the Chron ship through as closely as they could.

"I know you've been through the Split once," I finished, "but my pilot has done it several times. I'm going to get her to pass along any tips she has for a safe passage. It's going to be a trickier proposition going back the other way, transitioning between the two wormholes."

Rei threw a look over her shoulder at me that asked in no uncertain terms why I hadn't prepared her for this, but turned back to do the best she could. I knew I'd catch hell for that later.

Actually, if we pulled this off, I'd be happy to let Rei yell at me all she wanted.

The last bit of waiting for the *Dorland* to reach us was the hardest. The Chron ships kept pace but didn't gain, but even more had appeared on the long-range scan. They obviously hadn't known we'd discovered their wormhole doorway, but as they got close enough, they were finding out now. The glowing cone of plasma from the activated wormhole shone like a beacon. If we didn't manage to shut down this entry point into Delta Pavonis, they'd roll over Nearspace like a spidery black tide, and no-one would ever even know about PrimeCorp's role in our civilization's downfall.

SEVERAL OF THE lead ships surprised us with a burst of speed as the *Dorland* drew close. They'd held back, but they had burst technology, too; ours had probably been reverse-engineered from theirs. But they'd left it too late, and the *Dorland* wasn't giving up with escape from the system in sight. Whoever was piloting managed to wring a little more speed out of the drives.

"Rei, Viss, are we ready to go?" I asked.

They both answered in the affirmative just as the *Dorland's* shields flared.

"Chron pursuers have opened fire," Yuskeya reported. "*Dorland* is taking evasive action."

"That will slow them down," Jahelia said. "They should just keep coming and take the hits."

"They'll have to drop their shields to enter the wormhole," Lanar said. "They'll have to get loose to do that safely."

I stood up again, but there was nowhere to go and nothing to do. We couldn't go to their aid without risking getting too far away from the wormhole and having it close. They had to make it to us. We were the getaway car, and all we could do was sit and keep the engine running.

"We could angle a bit and give them some covering fire," Hirin suggested.

"Maybe. But I'm afraid we might hit the *Dorland*."

The shields flashed again. "Open a comm channel to them, please," Lanar said.

When Commander Mattu answered, Lanar said briefly, "We're watching. Just stay with the plan and we'll take you through."

"Thank you, Admiral," the Commander replied. Light flashed around him as the shields absorbed another impact. "I think we'll make it."

"Raise our shields," I told Hirin. "Let's not take any chances. Drop them just as we enter the wormhole."

It was a good thing we did so, since some of the oncoming Chron launched a few tentative torps in our direction as well. They were too far out, but it gave me something else to worry about—what if a rogue torpedo were pulled into the wormhole? I suspect one of the Chron commanders must have had the same notion, because after a few attempts, they stopped shooting at us.

As the *Dorland* neared, some of the pursuing Chron ships spread out as if to flank us, but they must have known we planned to escape through the wormhole. Maybe they thought it safer to attack us from the sides, but we didn't wait around to find out.

Sedmamin slipped quietly onto the bridge and went back to his chair. Baden threw me a wink.

"Baden, send the tracer ping," I said. I didn't know if we could trust the result, since the communications signal hadn't made it through, but we at least had to try to warn anyone on the other end of the wormhole that we were coming through.

"Sent."

Commander Mattu commed us, unnecessarily, to say a breathless, "We're here," as the ship bore down on the *Tane Ikai* from behind. Two Chron fighters raced in his wake.

"Ping is back," Baden said. "But the reading is strange. It might only have travelled the first wormhole and not the Split. Maybe the same thing that happened with the comm signal."

It was time to call upon whatever gods of luck might exist. "Rei, let's move. We can trust Commander Mattu to adjust his speed."

"Here we go," Rei said. The ship bucked as Rei hit the forward thrusters, and we jumped toward the wormhole, its cone of silvery-blue plasma stretching out to grasp us. It shimmered like a waterfall in front of the viewscreen, and then the plasma burst over us and we were through.

An audible sigh of relief slid around the bridge as the *Dorland* stayed with us through the wormhole entrance.

Yuskeya had split the main viewscreen so that we could see both the wormhole stretching ahead of us, and the *Dorland* following behind. The interior walls of the wormhole swirled with the usual rainbow hues, overlaid now by the blue-white plasma of the cone. In all other respects, the skip was normal . . . except for the ship following close behind us. In theory, that should not even have been possible. But here we were, doing it.

"I think at least one of the Chron has followed the *Dorland* in," Yuskeya reported. "Thought I caught a glimpse of a wing behind them."

Rei said, "Disturbance up ahead. Assuming we're about to merge into the Split."

I gripped the arm of the command chair so tightly I was sure the padding would never regain its normal form. Ahead, the silver-blue plasma from the walls of the wormhole stretched in toward the centre, as if trying to meet. It formed a thin membrane across our path. I held my breath as we spun towards it.

We burst through and the half-formed vista of the Split lay in front of us. This would be the most difficult part for Rei and the pilot of the *Dorland*, transitioning from the usual circular skip motion of the first wormhole to the necessary half-pipe pendulum motion required by the Split. It wouldn't be easy to overcome the momentum we'd built up. I glanced at Rei and read the tension in her neck and shoulders. I could see only part of her hands, but her fingers were pressed whitely on the console, trying to control the changeover.

"Rei, do you need help?"

But even as I asked, Jahelia left the secondary engineering console and lunged to the auxiliary pilot's station. She didn't say anything, just silently added her hands to the task, using her screen. Rei didn't answer me, either. We were all knocked starwise as the ship overcame the centrifugal force and swung pendulum-like in the opposite direction. Sedmamin yelped but said nothing.

I glanced at the screen and saw the *Dorland* slide up the Split's wall, swing halfway over the line demarcating the "safe" side from the dangers of the gauzy other half, and then pull back down again. I blew out a sigh, and kept my eyes on the rear-facing view. I hoped to see the Chron fighter slide off and into hazy nothingness, but that wasn't going to happen. Of all three ships, the Chron probably had the most practice making this maneuver, or at least knew the most about it.

"A few more skips," Rei said almost under her breath.

"*Dorland* is holding steady," Yuskeya said, for those of us who weren't free to watch the screen ourselves.

And then we rocketed out of the end of the Split into the wide black expanse of Delta Pavonis. The scattering of ships standing watch near the wormhole mouth had grown since we'd left, but I didn't spare them more than a glance. None were in our way, that was the main thing.

"Baden, send a general warning to raise shields," I said. "That's all there's time for. And everyone, hold on to something."

The *Dorland* came out of the wormhole and angled sharply away from it, leaving us with a clear shot into the wormhole. I squashed a pang of uncertainty and regret at what I was about to do.

"Fire," I told Hirin.

Chapter 21 — Lanar
What Happens Tomorrow

I HELD TIGHT to the arms of my locked-down skimchair as Luta gave the order and Hirin fired the *Tane Ikai*'s particle beam into the mouth of the Split. The beam energy streamed toward the wormhole, still ringed with runnels of multicoloured plasma from our recent traversal. Then the flash came, so brilliant even through the medium of the screen that I instinctively shut my eyes and turned away. The ship shuddered as if a torpedo had scored a direct hit on the hull, and the blast force spun us away.

I opened my eyes and saw the silvery bulk of a Protectorate Bahamut-class battleship looming ahead of us, but before I could do more than gasp, Rei had steadied us and pulled the *Tane Ikai* up. We shot over the top of the Protectorate behemoth with little room to spare. She banked and brought us around to see what had happened to the Split.

I was vaguely aware of Baden telling Luta about incoming messages, but I couldn't look away from the Split. Like the wormhole leading to Woodroct's Star, the Split had been transformed. The mouth burned a sullen crimson, white streaks of superheated plasma churning in a vortex at its centre. Bursts of energy spat and fractured around the edges, like lightning bolts trying to escape a thundercloud.

The Split had been destroyed. The Chron ship following the

Dorland did not emerge.

Finally, I came back to myself and looked at the viewscreen as the *Tane Ikai* slowed and moved to take up a position near the Bahamut battleship. I realized that at least twice as many ships occupied this area than had been here when we left. And some of them were not Nearspace vessels.

"Yes, he's right here, Fleet Commander," I heard Luta say. "He'll give you a full report right away. But I take full responsibility for my actions now and since we left here to enter the Split."

"Acknowledged," Regina's voice came over the ship's comm. "Admiral Mahane, please move to a secure channel and tell me what the hell just happened. And then get over here to the *Tereshkova* immediately."

I caught Luta's eye and mouthed *thanks a lot* as I left the bridge to head for the rear airlock. I thought I might pause at the galley to grab a cup of triple caff to take with me. I didn't think telling Regina Holles what had happened was going to be a quick process.

I SAT FOR a seemingly interminable time around a table in the *Tereshkova*'s substantial meeting room. I didn't know everyone—along with Regina and me there were other Protectorate officers, including a couple of the other Fleet Commanders who'd come to meet with Regina at FarView. There were two Relidae I recognized from Tabalo, with Cerevare Brindlepaw to help cross the language barrier. And there were holograms of two Corvids, beamed in from one of their ships nearby. And to my amazement, Mother was there, with Gusain Buig and a woman I recognized as the Chair of Schulyer Corporation. Mother came to the door and hugged me long and hard when I arrived, and I didn't care that anyone was watching us.

It did take me a long time to tell the story of what had happened and what we'd learned.

Regina and the other Fleet Commanders agreed that we'd dealt with Mauronet and with the wormhole correctly, and Regina dispatched a couple of officers to fetch him from the *Tane Ikai*. Quietly, I heaved a sigh of relief that Luta would not be in trouble.

There was good news on this end, too. The Corvids had determined that the Split was, in fact, a manufactured wormhole, not a naturally-occurring one. Luta had told me after her first encounter with the Corvids that this technology existed, but I wasn't sure I'd believed it. However, if it was true, it meant Luta's destruction of the Split was not just a stopgap measure. No natural wormhole would spontaneously appear to take its place. Luta had given us even more breathing room to decide what to do about the Pitromae Chron.

"I am personally going to present this body of evidence concerning PrimeCorp to the Nearspace Worlds Council," Regina said, holding up the datachip I'd given her. All the files implicating PrimeCorp were there. It was a damning collection. "I'm going to demand that all PrimeCorp holdings be moved into an administrative trust while charges against the corporation are filed, and a Board of Trustees appointed to oversee the business. I don't think anyone will be able to argue against that. We'll launch a full investigation into the PrimeCorp involvement with the Chron. The Pitromae," she clarified, nodding to the Relidae.

"I believe ex-Chairman Sedmamin would be an invaluable resource while we carry out this investigation," suggested one of the other Fleet Commanders.

"Good idea," Regina said. "Let's send a couple of officers over to the *Tane Ikai* to 'invite' ex-Chairman Sedmamin to be a guest of the Protectorate for a couple of weeks, so that he can help us out."

I'd advise Regina later that she might want to pick up Taso for questioning as well, to add another piece to the PrimeCorp puzzle. But that could wait. "Do you really think the Pitromae will break off their incursions into Nearspace if their contact with PrimeCorp is broken?" I asked. It seemed unlikely to me, after what we'd learned. "We believe their intentions probably run deeper than whatever it was they agreed to with PrimeCorp. The sheer number of ships we saw indicate they've already changed their plans."

Fleet Commander Darvi Junan sat next to Regina. His ebony hair was streaked with amber, but his pale mauve skin was surprisingly unwrinkled for his age. Junan was a quiet Vilisian with the most subtly commanding voice I'd ever heard. He shook his head. "No, Admiral, we're not counting on that. Over the past day and half, I'm pleased to say we've formed a tentative alliance among the Nearspace worlds, the Corvids, and the Relidae." The folds of skin around his eyes puckered, showing deep thought, but I caught a hint of eucalyptus scent on the air—denoting satisfaction in the Vilisian scent language. "The Corvids also have allies whom they are sure will come to the table. We will use PrimeCorp's contact network—which we intend to uncover very quickly—to reach the Pitromae Chron and present a united front to them."

"An attack force?" I thought of Regina's repeated assertions that the Protectorate couldn't undertake offensive strikes outside Nearspace without leaving the worlds sorely unprotected. Had the addition of allies made her rethink that position?

Regina shook her head. "No. A diplomatic mission. Peace talks." She looked around the table at the assemblage of Nearspace inhabitants and aliens. "But with some teeth behind the hand extending the olive branch. And your Mother has agreed to accompany us, to explain the coming advancements in bioscavenger technology, and how it will be developed to help *all* of our allies."

Mother nodded and smiled. "I've been working with Duntmindi and Schulyer Corporations to figure out how to do this. They're helping set up an independent research and development branch of the Nearspace Authority to oversee the nanobioscavenger project. All the worlds will contribute, and everyone will benefit. No one corporation or group will control them or benefit disproportionately from them."

So that's why Mother was here. She must have been working on this plan for a while, to get the corporations on board, and then presented it to the Protectorate admin when they needed an extra incentive to take to the Chron. If we were right, and it was what the Chron wanted anyway, they wouldn't want to be left out when all the other species had them.

Regina Holles looked around the table at the assemblage and nodded. "The Pitromae will, I hope, see that we make better friends than enemies."

EVENTUALLY, REGINA LET me go back to the *Tane Ikai*. Most of the force that had gathered around the Split would soon move back to FarView Station to regroup and receive new orders, so I said I'd go back with Luta. I found Yuskeya in the galley as I made my way to the bridge. She offered me a hot drink and some food, which I gratefully accepted. The ship was quiet, in that waiting-for-the-next-thing phase that happened a lot in space travel. Or in this case, recovering-from-the-last-thing. I sat at the table and rested my head in my palms, eyes closed. The quiet was blissful after the meeting on the *Tereshkova*.

After what felt like a ridiculously short time, Yuskeya set a bowl of fragrant stew and a mug of steaming caff down in front of me, and sat down across the table with her own. As I dug in, I told her what had come out of the meeting on the *Tereshkova*. In turn, she reported that the crew of the *Dorland* had been safely returned to their ship, and the rescued PrimeCorp technicians had been sent to the *Tereshkova*. "To assist with the investigation into PrimeCorp," she said. "I told the officer who took charge of them that they were essentially scientists and should be treated as non-hostile."

"Good thinking," I said. "Anti-PrimeCorp sentiment is likely to be running pretty high, but I don't think those folks were guilty of anything more than possibly bad judgement."

"And Commander Mattu has been given command of the *Dorland*, at least for the moment."

"How did Commander Yu react?" I asked around a mouthful of stew, wondering if the Commander would be disappointed that he'd been passed over.

"He seemed relieved," she said with a smile. "I don't think he had his eye on Mauronet's chair."

"Still, I'm going to put in a word for him with the administration," I said. "He knew something was wrong with Mauronet and said so to me the first opportunity he had. And he kept his head down there on the planet."

"Admiral?"

I looked up to find Yuskeya studying me thoughtfully. "What?"

"Are you planning to recall me to the *Cheswick* now?"

"Do you want me to?"

She met my eyes, her face placid and unemotional. "I'm a Protectorate officer. I go where I'm assigned. What I want doesn't really come into it."

But I didn't think she'd have asked if it didn't matter.

I smiled. "Well, I haven't had a chance to talk to Fleet Commander Holles and the others about this yet, but I had an idea while we were discussing the new alliance with the Corvids and the Relidae. And the effort to make peace with the Pitromae. I think we should actually put Protectorate officers on special assignment on any commercial Nearspace vessels who want them."

Yuskeya raised her eyebrows. "Really?"

I nodded. "For a little while, anyway. It gives us more eyes around Nearspace, to watch for trouble until the relationship with the Chron is settled. And once the news about PrimeCorp and their plans breaks—which it undoubtedly will—I think it will make people feel safer."

"So, you're just going to leave me stationed where I am?" Despite her attempts to keep her voice neutral, I could hear the note of hope.

"Yes. I'm afraid you're stuck with my sister for a little while longer." I tilted the bowl to capture the last dregs of the stew.

Yuskeya sighed happily. "Well, sir, it's a difficult job. But someone has to do it."

I left Yuskeya so she could go and find Viss, which I was sure she'd want to do immediately. I went in search of Luta, and found her on the bridge. Rei, Baden, and Maja were there, too, so I gave them a brief run-down about what had been said on the *Tereshkova*.

Luta swiped a hand across her forehead. "So, I'm really off the hook for blowing up the Split? That's good to hear." Then her face turned serious. "Do you think they'll be able to avert a war, then? Even with what we learned from the Relidae, I don't feel like we understand what motivates the Chron. I mean, if they still just hate us, how do we counter that?"

I crossed to her and gave her a hug. "We just keep trying, for as long as we can. The first step will be to find out if there's common ground. And if there is, we'll build on that. For now, we'll stay alert and hope for the best. To that end, I'm leaving Yuskeya with you. If that's all right."

Luta pretended to think it over. "Well, I guess so. She does come in handy, from time to time."

It took me a while to find Jahelia. Finally, on a tip from Luta, I took the ladder down past the engineering level and into the cargo pod directly below it. I heard her before I saw her—the slap of bare feet on the cargo pod floor, the hollow ring of a *zelendu* staff striking floor or wall.

She'd slung her jacket across a crate and ditched her boots beside it. Her caramel-coloured hair was slicked back into a ponytail, although stray tendrils had worked their way free and now curled around her face. Sweat stains darkened the green t-shirt she wore, and the legs of her pants were rolled up to her knees.

Jahelia grinned and nodded to me when she saw me drop off the bottom of the ladder, but didn't stop her workout. "Hello, Protectorate," she said, apparently not out of breath even though the form was obviously taxing. Her voice echoed hollowly in the near-empty cargo pod. "They didn't put you in detention or anything for letting your sister blow up a wormhole?"

"Nope, but I had to promise I wouldn't let her do it again."

"Rules are just no fun," she said, moving through an intricate pattern of foot and staff work.

I shucked my own jacket and boots and moved within reach of the staff, inviting her to spar with a silent hand gesture. She grinned wickedly and came at me with the staff in a flurry of feints and strikes. Fortunately, an old Vilisian bunk mate of mine had taught me something about the art, and I managed to block or duck the brunt of the initial attack.

Unfortunately, she was much better at *zelendu* than I was, which became obvious about two minutes in to our sparring.

Jahelia stopped suddenly, leaned on the staff, and regarded me. "So, did you come here to fight, or did you come here to talk?"

I shrugged. "Sometimes it's hard to tell with you."

She nodded as if I'd said something insightful. "You know, I get that." She crossed to the crate where she'd left her jacket, laid the staff on top of it, and slid down to sit, leaning back against the side. She patted the floor next to her. "Time to talk."

Honestly, I wasn't sure what I wanted to say. I just knew I didn't want her to get on a ship when we got back to FarView, and disappear into Nearspace. She was the first woman in a long time who left me feeling totally off-balance—but in a way I liked. I sat where she'd indicated and leaned back against the crate, too, staring out across the mostly-empty cargo pod because I didn't know if I could think straight if I was looking at her. "Okay. Down on that planet—"

She interrupted. "Look, Protectorate—"

"—Lanar," I corrected. Two could play that game.

Jahelia turned to look at me and I met her eyes. "All right. Lanar. I'm not very good at this. I like you. I could tell you that I kissed you for luck or on a whim or because I thought we might both be dead in the next five minutes. The truth is, I kissed you because I wanted to." She smiled, almost—shyly? "Your sister will tell you I'm sort of impulsive."

I swallowed. "Well, I'm glad you did. Because I didn't know it until it happened, but I wanted you to, too."

"I still want to," she said, but before I could say anything else, she held up a hand. "But we have a problem. You're Protectorate. Through and through. I'm—not." She laughed. "Most decidedly not."

I waited a minute. "Are you sure about that?"

Jahelia fixed me with a stare. "What do you mean?"

"You helped Sedmamin. You—"

"For a price. He said he'd pay me well."

I ignored that and went on. "You offered to help Luta when you didn't have to. Numerous times. You see a thing that needs doing, and you do it. You can't tell me you always stop to consider what's in it for you."

"I always did," she said, tucking her chin rebelliously. She was silent for a moment. "Maybe I've changed—a bit—lately."

"But?"

"But. I've got a past. I'm not sure what I want to do with the future. I don't know what happens tomorrow. It seems like it would be . . . difficult."

I reached over and put my hand over hers, where it lay in her lap. A thin white scar traced across the back. I thought I'd like to ask her how she'd gotten it. "I agree." She looked at me, almost startled. "It might be difficult. But at least neither one of us will out-age the other. That's the one 'difficult' I've never been able to get away from."

She pulled her hand away. "*That's* the only reason you like me? Because I'm not going to get old before you?"

I grinned. "No. I just figured if I could make you mad, it would be a sign that you really *do* like me."

Jahelia glared at me for the space of a few heartbeats, then grinned back. "Well, I guess that was talking. Is it time to fight again?"

"No. It's time for this." And I kissed her.

THE *TANE IKAI* slipped quietly through the wormhole into OS-G5V-03, the system we now more properly called Kelia Rrane, in translation from the Relidae language. A giant cloud of interstellar dust greeted us as we emerged into the system. Tinted scarlet by the scattering of light across its constituent particles and suspended against the black of space like an otherworldly painting, it reminded me of the entirely different circumstances under which I'd first seen it. Then I'd been ill, and we'd been lost and trying desperately to sneak back to Nearspace past hostile aliens. I would have worried then that deadly Chron ships waited in the shadows where thick pockets of dust at the cloud's core blocked the light entirely, creating smudges of dark secrecy. Now I could merely appreciate its stunning beauty. The system's star, yellow as Earth's own sun, burned steadily in the distance.

"Laying in coordinates for Tabalo," Maja said from the navigation console. Her fingers ticked over the board without hesitation and she spoke with a quiet efficiency and confidence that had grown under Yuskeya's tutelage over the past half year. Her blonde hair had been gathered into a tidy knot at the base of her neck and she wore what we jokingly called her official-unofficial ship's uniform—a transform t-shirt she'd set to match the dark blue of the *Tane Ikai*'s shipsuits, and dark bio-weave pants. She said it made her truly feel like part of the crew, which was amusing since the rest of us (apart from Viss) rarely wore shipsuits. But I thought I understood. It was an outward manifestation that she finally felt she fit in, here on the ship.

Maja and Yuskeya now shared the navigation console in easy cooperation. Yuskeya had put her newfound free time to good use, updating the *Tane Ikai*'s medical bay and carrying out the various Protectorate liaison tasks my brother set her. To say nothing of lending Viss a hand with his never-ending upgrades and overhauls. She actually seemed to enjoy it.

"Will you see Cerevare while we're on Tabalo?" Maja asked. The Lobor historian remained a happy go-between on the Relidae planet, kept busy as diplomatic and trade relations among the Nearspace denizens, the Corvids, and the Relidae Chron continued to grow in scope.

I chuckled. "Maybe, if she has time. But we won't be on Tabalo for long. We're picking up supplies to drop at their orbital and a shipment of *fryse* for FarView." I'd sampled the deep amber "wine" the Relidae produced when I'd been a guest on Tabalo, and many in Nearspace seemed to enjoy it as much as I had. It was in high demand on stations and planets all around Nearspace.

"I'm going to see her," Rei said from the pilot's board. "We set up a lunch date when I made my vacation plans."

Baden snorted. "I guess Gerazan will be glad of the break."

Rei cast a mock-affronted glance over her shoulder at him. "He's joining us, if you must know. And don't forget, this whole vacation thing was his idea."

We'd be leaving Rei on Tabalo for three weeks. Lieutenant Gerazan Soto had been assigned to a Protectorate detail stationed in the capital city to work on expanding ease of communications between ourselves and the Relidae, and had invited her to join him for a vacation. Soto had a background in xenolinguistics as well as cryptography, which made him an excellent candidate for working with our new alien allies. I knew Rei was excited at the prospect of spending some time with Soto when we weren't lost, being chased, under attack, or trying to prevent a war. We'd muddle along without her all right—plenty of us could serve on the pilot's board when necessary. But I knew I was going to miss her.

"Incoming message for you, Captain," Baden said from the communications console. He swung his head around to toss a grin at me. "It's the Admiral, calling from the *Cheswick*. They're in-system, so it's realtime. Want to take it in your quarters?"

"No, put it on here," I said, angling my screen so I could see the video feed. My brother's smiling face appeared, and I recognized the view wall of his private quarters behind him. He wore a pale blue t-shirt, so I knew he must be off-duty. "Lanar! I didn't expect to see you here."

"*Hola*, Luta. Just doing a 'diplomat swap' on Tabalo, and I have a standing order for the bridge to let me know any time you come up on the long-range. Thought we'd have time for a chat."

I had to smile. Lanar looked good. The peace talks with the Pitromae Chron, after a tense and difficult start, were now reportedly going well. As the looming spectre of war dissipated, my brother looked lighter, more relaxed. Now that the threat had lessened I realized just how heavily it had weighed on him.

"I hear the peace negotiations are still on track," I said.

Lanar nodded. "Slow but sure. I think the dangling carrot of Mother's research is working better than any stick. The Pitromae definitely do not want to be left out when the nanobioscavs go into production. Particularly if the Relidae are going to benefit from them."

"She's completely immersed in the process. I stopped off at Kiando a couple of weeks ago but she was on Damyadi Station for another meeting with Schulyer. Gusain said she'd only been home one week out of the previous four."

"The last time I saw her, I asked what kind of a timeline they were working on to get all the approvals to put the nanobioscavs into wide production. She just muttered something unrepeatable about bureaucracy and idiots and changed the subject." Although his tone was light, Lanar looked bleak for an instant.

I opened my mouth to ask what was wrong, but over the link, I heard a door open on Lanar's end. He looked up, away from the screen, and smiled, then dropped his gaze back to me. Whatever had been in his eyes was gone.

"I think she got too used to operating outside the system," I said, not knowing who'd just entered. "She has to relearn some cooperative skills for working with other people."

"Are you talking about me? I think I've become plenty cooperative." Jahelia Sord leaned over Lanar's shoulder and poked her head into the camera range. She'd dyed her hair again, and blonde curls tumbled around her face. Her grin betrayed the perennial streak of wickedness I knew she'd never lose. "You know what I was like when you met me."

"Believe me, I shudder to think about it. However, I wasn't talking about you this time, Sord," I assured her. "I know you've become the soul of cooperation."

"You should," she said, sticking out her tongue impudently at me before dropping a quick kiss on Lanar's cheek and moving out of the camera's field of view.

I stifled a smile so Lanar wouldn't catch me grinning. I knew that Jahelia Sord had done as I'd asked and allowed Mother to test and upgrade Jahelia's nanobioscavengers. Not immediately, of course—that wouldn't be Jahelia's way—but in the end, she'd agreed to the procedures. Once Mother gave her the all-clear, and the threat level in Nearspace had dropped as peace talks started in earnest, Jahelia had worked some kind of magic and convinced Lanar to take a long-overdue vacation. They'd spent an entire month cruising aimlessly around Nearspace in Jahelia's little ship, *Shadow's Eclipse*, and had failed to discover anything about each other that they couldn't live with. I was a little surprised to see Jahelia on the *Cheswick*, but I decided not to question it. They both looked happy, so that was all I needed to know.

"You're keeping busy?" Lanar asked. "And staying out of trouble?"

"Are you talking to me, or Jahelia?"

He raised an eyebrow at me. "I already know what Jahelia's doing."

"He likes to think so," Jahelia called from wherever she'd disappeared to.

"Yes, I am," I assured him. "Both. Lots of new trade opportunities, particularly for us, since we're already familiar with some of the Corvid and Relidae systems."

"And no uptick in piracy to speak of," Hirin said from behind me, making me jump. Intent on the screen, I hadn't noticed him come onto the bridge.

Lanar narrowed his eyes. "No increase, or none to speak of?"

I shook my head. "We haven't seen any," I said. "Hirin's just teasing you. I honestly can't remember when I felt so relaxed and safe, inside Nearspace or in Corvid or Relidae space."

Hirin tapped lightly on my temple. "That's largely in here," he said.

I shrugged. "Maybe. It's a long time since all we had to worry about was cargo dropdowns, fuel levels, and whether we had enough cinnamon pano and caff to last us until the next supply stop."

"Let's make a plan to get together soon," Lanar said. "Maybe sometime next month we can catch up with Mother and Gusain for dinner."

"I should see if Karro and Aliande are free," I said. "Maybe even the kids, too. I could skip out to Earth and bring them along." I half-smiled. "We'd better start messaging Mother now to have a hope of catching her, but sure. That would be great." After working so closely with Lanar in our attempts to prevent a second Chron war, I'd realized that it was worth the effort to stay in closer touch and meet up more often. Nearspace was immense, but it took only a bit of planning to get together. It seemed that he felt the same way.

"*Gis la revido*, then, little sister," he said with a grin. "Stay safe and I'll see you again soon."

"See you soon, *little* brother," I said with emphasis. "Tell Jahelia I said goodbye for now." We closed the link.

Hirin handed me a steaming mug of caff he'd brought from the galley, then pulled a skimchair over to sit next to me.

"Why are you frowning into your caff? Isn't it hot enough?"

I shook my head and smiled at him. "It's great. I just thought—maybe Lanar had something on his mind, when we were talking about Mother. But he didn't say."

Hirin sipped from his own mug. "Lanar always has something on his mind. Comes from being an Admiral in the Protectorate, you know. And now he has Jahelia there, too. It wouldn't be strange for him to be a little preoccupied." He tilted his head so that I'd be forced to meet the blue-grey eyes I knew so well. They were compassionate and honest as always, and held the ever-present hint of mischief. "Things are good, Luta.

Don't go looking for trouble."

I shook myself a little and took another sip of caff. "You're right. I'm not. It's just . . . old habits, I guess. Like I told Lanar, this is the best I've felt in a long time. Trade is good, we're all safe and happy. Things are . . . peaceful."

Hirin chuckled. "Maybe too peaceful? The old trade route grind too tame for you now? You're longing for excitement and danger?"

I punched him lightly on the arm, being very careful not to spill anything from either of our mugs. "No thanks, old man. I've got plenty of excitement just trying to keep you out of trouble."

Hirin raised his mug. "I'll drink to that. Now, where are we going to have dinner on Tabalo? The last time we were here, Den-Aldar told me about this little place on the outskirts of the city . . ."

I leaned back in my skimchair and sipped caff, letting Hirin make our dinner plans. In the distance ahead, the alien planet was merely another bright speck against the velvet of space, beckoning us forward. *Forward*, I thought. After a long time of searching for and being haunted by the past, it seemed we were all finally moving in a new direction. That had to be a good thing. I reached out and squeezed Hirin's hand.

The *Tane Ikai* sped silently toward the planet, cradling and protecting us, bringing us with her to whatever the future held.

THE END

Author Biography

Sherry D. Ramsey is a speculative fiction writer, editor, publisher, creativity addict and self-confessed Internet geek. When she's not writing, she makes jewellery, gardens, hones her creative procrastination skills on social media, and consumes far more coffee and chocolate than is likely good for her.

Her other books include two more in the Nearspace series from Tyche Books, *One's Aspect to the Sun* and *Dark Beneath the Moon*; the middle grade fantasy *The Seventh Crow*; *The Murder Prophet*; and two collections of short stories. With her partners at Third Person Press, she has co-edited six anthologies of regional short fiction and a novel. A member of the Writer's Federation of Nova Scotia Writer's Council, Sherry is also a past Vice-President and Secretary-Treasurer of SF Canada.

Sherry lives in Nova Scotia with her husband, children, and dogs. You can visit her online at www.sherrydramsey.com, find her on Facebook, and keep up with her much more pithy musings and visual life on Twitter and Instagram @sdramsey.